THE LANGUAGE OF MUSIC

THE LANGUAGE OF MUSIC

RUTH TRIPPY

Mill City Press, Inc.
2301 Lucien Way #415
Maitland, FL 32751
407.339.4217
www.millcitypress.net

1.Single women—Fiction. 2. Music—Fiction 3. Spirituality—Fiction. 4. New England—Fiction.

Publisher's Cataloging-In-Publication Data
(Prepared by The Donohue Group, Inc.)

Names: Trippy, Ruth.
Title: The language of music / Ruth Trippy.
Description: Minneapolis, MN : Mill City Press, [2015]
Identifiers: ISBN 9781634136426 | ISBN 9781634137577 (ebook)
Subjects: LCSH: Single women—Northeastern States—History—19th century—Fiction. | Women musicians—Northeastern States—History—19th century—Fiction. | Guardian and ward—Northeastern States—History—19th century—Fiction. | Spirituality—Fiction. | New England—History—19th century—Fiction. | Steinway (New York, N.Y.)—History—19th century—Fiction. | LCGFT: Historical fiction. | Romance fiction. | GSAFD: Christian fiction.
Classification: LCC PS3620.R58 L36 2015 (print) | LCC PS3620.R58 (ebook) | DDC 813/.6—dc23

ISBN-13: 978-1-63413-642-6
LCCN: 2015913241

Cover Design by Sean Allen
seanallencreative@gmail.com
Typeset by James Arneson
Printed in the United States of America

Steve Witt – Sermon, March 1, 2015.
Referencing Dr. Alister McGrath:
If I Had Lunch with C.S. Lewis.

The beaver is talking... about Aslan, who is a picture of Christ. "He's wild, you know.... He's not like a tame lion...."

So He will do some things in your life that you don't understand.... You get very discouraged because you say, "That's not the God I know." No, He's way bigger!

Acknowledgments

My agent, Natasha Kern, said this story has the feel of a saga. Certainly, its birth and development have that characteristic. Its conception started many years ago, two years after the birth of our daughter Anne when we lived in Ft. Lauderdale. My first advisor, Ava Bronson, a longtime teacher in Detroit schools and an avid reader, is no longer with us, but I am indebted to her for her interest and encouragement.

When our family moved to Asheville, Jim Hughes, Dana Custer and I formed a group that critiqued the book's early chapters. Another move to the Atlanta area found my next writing group near Stone Mountain who met in the home of Brenda Thomas, with Gloria Spencer, Rachael Boudreaux Novak, and Nola Love. We got right down to business, twenty minutes devoted to each critique, with a "spot of tea" afterward.

When our hostess moved, I needed a new writing group and God provided one when I discovered an old letter inviting me to one near my home. I promptly joined with Gloria Spencer, and a local bookstore and other venues became our various meeting places. LeAnne Benfield Martin had founded the group, joined by Laurie Fuller and Donna Lott. Later, Laura Petherbridge, Nicole Smith, and a few others waltzed in and out, and finally Bette Noble. During this time, freelance book editor, Donna Fleicher read the novel and said, "You've an engaging story; it just needs more work!" Throughout these years, at times I fought off tears, but the book was always better for the constructive criticism.

In the meantime, another novel, *The Soul of the Rose,* was published by Abingdon Press. But eventually I returned to this, my first love, aided by Readers: Dr. Terry Ensley, Gayle Corrigan Esman, Mary Hooper, Joyce Grothmann, Candy Menedis, my parents Wayne and Jereen Folkert, sister Rose Moore, and a final critique by my sister Jan Whitford. For medical advice in the story, I'm indebted to my uncle Dr. John Santinga. Prayers from my family and friends kept me going, including those of my aunt, Anita Van Wyk. Lastly, my grateful thanks to freelance editor, Gloria Spencer, who figured so largely in my critiquing life and went over the final version with a fine-toothed comb. The saying goes that it takes a village to raise a child. Certainly, it took a small community to complete this book. Thank you, each one!

My special love and thanks go to my son Matt and my daughter Anne Trippy Morgan for telling me they believed my books would someday be published. They saw the street in Asheville named "Celia" for the protagonist in *The Soul of the Rose,* which was immediately followed by the next street "Katherine," the protagonist in this book, *The Language of Music.* I am especially grateful to God for sending me my husband Ernie. Without this "wild" man in my life, this book would not have materialized, and certainly I would have never become a writer.

One of my protagonists would say: witness how the Lord used meandering, often tortuous paths to bring about this book. A saga in itself.

Chapter 1

Connecticut – 1870

Katherine hastily lowered the black-edged handkerchief from her eyes.

"My dear!" Mrs. Bronson bustled into the boarding house parlor. "It's almost time to leave." She dropped down beside Katherine on the couch.

Katherine hoped the room's dim interior hid her red eyes.

The landlady looked at her closely. "Now, don't cry or you'll get me started. Think what an adventure it'll be traveling by train all the way to Connecticut. You'll have a whole new life!"

Katherine felt for a dry spot on the handkerchief. The dark parlor in the early morning light matched only too well her frame of mind. She gazed at the landlady, gray hair pulled back into its usual tight bun. The familiarity was comforting. "But Mrs. Bronson, don't you think I could stay here and work?"

"Oh, no." The woman's voice was tender, but firm. "It's only right you go live with your mother's godfather. Remember how kind he was?"

Mr. Emery did resemble the grandfather Katherine had always wanted, but during his visits, he had talked with Mother rather than herself. She had never seen his home, and with Mother now gone, she dreaded the new and strange.

"Too bad we haven't heard from him after that telegram I sent. But I'm sure it's all right for you to go. And, of course, they should be able to afford you—the way Mr. Emery dressed."

"Yes." Katherine's voice sounded tentative, even to herself. She glanced around the parlor. "I suppose Mr. Emery does reside in a fine house, but how can it feel home like this?" She looked around at the little knick-knacks and bric-a-brac carefully placed to give the boarders a feeling of elegance. The kerosene lamp on the central oak table cast shadows that lovingly forgave the worn spots on the red velvet couch. She stroked its soft surface for comfort.

Mrs. Bronson sighed. "But we *must* look to the future."

Just then a knock sounded and the front door opened. "Cabbie here! For Miss Edmond."

"Your ride, Katherine!" The landlady bent over to grasp the carpet bag. "I'll help with this. Now, when you don't know what to do, just remember your mama. Do what she would. She was a real lady. And don't let anyone tell you different."

Katherine rose. She glanced at the old upright piano. How she would miss this place. Only last week she'd given a recital for the boarders. She'd been careful to choose a variety of music. They'd loved the fast passages of the Mozart and the languid, romantic music of Mendelssohn's boat song.

Katherine stepped into Mrs. Bronson's outstretched arms. The landlady hugged her hard, carpet bag in one hand, the other arm circling her, bringing a measure of comfort.

"Now remember, you'll want to make the Norwalk connection. That'll take you north where you need to go."

Katherine sank into the seat, glad for this last leg of her journey.

"May I sit here, miss?"

Katherine glanced up. The middle-aged man stood some feet from her and looked vaguely familiar. His eye regarded her boldly. She wanted to say no, but he was neatly dressed, so she hesitated only a moment. "It's not taken."

He stepped forward and lowering himself onto the seat, stretched his long legs to make himself comfortable. A stale tobacco smell accosted Katherine and she quickly turned to look out the window. The strong odor was reminiscent of her father. Resentment knotted her stomach.

"Looks like we're in for some bad weather," the man at her side said. "On the platform I noticed dark clouds to the north. We'll travel right into it."

Katherine knew he was just making small talk, but she turned her shoulder slightly away from him. The last warning Mrs. Bronson gave was about talking to strangers. "You're young and pretty. Best you keep to yourself."

The train rumbled, then suddenly lurched forward.

"Ah, we're leaving," the man observed. "You going far?"

"Not too far," she answered briefly. "If you'll excuse me—" She turned her shoulder a little more decidedly. Besides traveling to a strange state and to a strange house, she hardly felt like speaking to a strange man.

Her male companion apparently gave up trying to make conversation, because he opened a newspaper. But she could feel his alertness.

She was glad for a window seat the last part of her journey. As the train steamed through the Connecticut countryside, the land's gentle roll contrasted with the angled, rough landscape she knew in Maine. Would this place ever seem like home? Rain began to wash the window. Leaning forward, the brim of her black hat touched the pane.

Suddenly the train jerked. The brim of her hat hit the window so hard it knocked askew. She reached up, straightening it to rest over her braided hair. The landlady had helped her coil the braid just so around her head. "Your dark hair, 'tis a glory," Mrs. Bronson had said more than once, "especially with its red tints." She also aided Katherine in the purchase of the black hat and coat. "Thankfully, your mother had a little money set aside. Black's only fittin' under the circumstances."

Rain now pelted the train windows in earnest. The afternoon storm was catching the northbound train full force. "What we need is a steady spring shower," a male passenger across the aisle said, "not this downpour beating us senseless."

At the train platform in Norwalk, Katherine had noticed more than one lady passenger clutching an umbrella, grateful for it rather than the more fashionable, but flimsy parasol.

She remembered Mrs. Bronson saying her destination was just an hour north of Norwalk. Hopefully, her station wouldn't be too much farther.

The stale tobacco odor of the man sitting beside her assailed her afresh as he put down his paper and shifted toward her. "You know, miss, I'm pretty familiar with this part of the state. Right pleasant country. You been here before?"

Katherine didn't want to answer, but finally said, "No. But someone is to meet me. My plans after that are somewhat uncertain."

"Ah, I've been in the same situation myself—over the years. Not knowing what the next corner will bring—"

The conductor entered the coach, announcing the upcoming stop. Hers. Katherine scrutinized her coat and brushed off a few flecks of lint.

"This your station, then?" The man leaned forward confidentially. "I know some families here. The Nortons, the Albertons. Always interested in folks' comings and goings. Maybe I know who's coming for you. Which family is that?"

Katherine stiffened. The effrontery. Well, she would be leaving in a few minutes. "A family by the name of Emery. Now, if you'll excuse me—" She fumbled with her carpet bag.

The man settled back in his seat and took up his newspaper again. For the first time since she'd seen him, he seemed to relax. Was that the question he'd wanted answered all this time? She was almost sure she'd seen him somewhere before. But where?

Metal wheels screeched on metal railings. Clutching the seat, Katherine pressed her back into it as the train ground to a nerve-wrenching halt. Within minutes, passengers stood and gathered their bundles. Gazing out the window, Katherine scanned the people on the platform. Mr. Emery's tall figure should stand out. Letting the other passengers shuffle down the aisle, she kept looking out the window. After most had passed, she clutched her carpet bag and bent to reach for the wooden box at her feet.

"Let me get that for you, miss." The man nudged her aside and grasped the wooden box.

"I can manage just fine, thank you."

"Well, this here's a bit awkward. How 'bout I hand it to you on the platform?"

"All right, thank you." She preceded him down the aisle.

At the open doorway, smoke from the engine stack and chill damp air assailed her. She took in the whole rain-drenched scene at a glance. The heavy rains had stopped, but the grounds around the depot looked battered from the thunderstorm. The depot's steep roof and gingerbread-trimmed eaves still dripped water. She stepped down to the wooden platform. The man followed her.

"Here, miss." He handed her the box.

"Thank you."

"No trouble at all." He tipped his hat.

Katherine turned to the depot. Passengers were hailing family and friends, forming neat little parties, talking and laughing with each other. A couple of running boys dodged her. She looked for a well-dressed, older gentleman. No one fit Mr. Emery's description.

Had she missed him? She reached the station door and looked across the crowd, back to the spot where she had descended the train.

That man stood looking at her. In that brief instant, she suddenly knew where she'd seen him. The Maine depot. Just before stepping onto the train, she'd taken a final look at what had been her home, and she'd noticed a man standing at some distance, staring at her.

And here he was again.

Shifting her carpetbag and box to one arm, she jerked open the heavy door. As soon as the door closed, she waited and looked back down the platform. With relief saw the man ascend the train steps.

Inside, an austerely furnished waiting room offered three wooden benches. She set her belongings on one of them and strode to the ticket grate. The station agent glanced up from his paperwork. "Be with you in a minute, miss."

Standing here inside the station felt better. At least that man hadn't followed her. But who was he? The sooner the Emerys came to pick her up, the better she'd feel.

Looking around, she noticed a photograph prominently displayed. The inscription read *The 20th Maine*. "Oh!" she said involuntarily.

The station agent glanced over his spectacles. "You noticed the picture? Did you have family in my regiment?"

"Yes, my father."

"Well, well." He smiled. "The 20th Maine was a proud outfit. We fought at the battle of Gettysburg, you know. Our charge down Little Round Top helped the Union forces win Gettysburg. Turned the tide of the war."

"Yes. Did you know my father? Tom Edmond?"

"No, can't say that I did. We had a lot of men." The agent put his papers aside, looked at her with more interest. "So, miss, what can I do for you?"

"I'm waiting for Mr. George Emery."

"Well—" The agent hesitated. "That wait might be kind of long, seeing as he passed on some months ago." He scratched his chin. "Someone else should be fetching you."

"But... I don't know of anyone else." A sick feeling dropped into the pit of her stomach.

"Sorry, miss, don't know what to say. Except why not choose yourself a seat and wait awhile?" He nodded to the benches. "If no one comes, we'll see what can be done."

Katherine sat next to her belongings. She grasped the carpetbag to feel its familiar heavy texture. Mr. Emery passed on? How could that be? Her mother gone, and now Mr. Emery. Why had she left the boarding house?

The train steamed out of the depot.

The station door slammed, stragglers wandering in and out. Noises from outside filtered into the depot. A horse neighed. A man shouted unintelligible directions. Carriages departed, wheels crunching over rocks.

Finally, quiet settled in.

Katherine sighed.

A tickling sensation ran up her index finger. A black ant zigzagged across her knuckle. She flicked it onto the carpetbag and watched it run off the bag onto the surface of the bench. It stopped, perhaps, to get its bearings. With the tip of her finger, she half encouraged, half scooted it over to the edge of the bench. It scurried down the wooden leg.

She bent over and glanced around the station's bare floor. It seemed such an expanse for the little creature. Did it have a home?

Without warning, the station's street door flung open. A small wiry man in a black uniform adorned with shiny brass buttons stopped and clicked his heels together. The door slammed shut. He then marched across the room to the ticket grate. "Ah-hum."

The agent took his time looking up.

"Miss Katherine Edmond?"

Another long moment passed before the agent nodded in Katherine's direction. "Well, Higgins. She's been waiting on you. A good half hour."

The uniformed man shrugged. "That beastly storm delayed me. Had to take cover in a neighbor's barn."

"Never known you to be this late."

The uniformed man glanced over his shoulder. "So, that's her?"

"Yep."

"Ahh." He gazed at her some moments, then snapped around, his heels clicking as he crossed the wooden floor.

"She's got freight in baggage, you know."

The driver shot the stationmaster a look—"I know my job,"—then stopped in front of Katherine.

She stood, stretching to her full height.

The uniformed man's eyes assessed her. "So you've come to live with the Emerys? Pardon me, miss—but I was expecting someone older."

"I'm sixteen, sir. Or almost." She knew her small pale face made her look younger than her years. And she felt very young and inexperienced at the moment.

"You have a trunk?" His voice had an edge—as if accusing her of being some poor relation.

"A crate in baggage, sir."

The driver reached for her box. "Well then. The house isn't too many miles. Follow me to the carriage, please."

As Katherine walked to the door, she glanced back at the office window. The station agent had apparently heard the exchange, for he winked at her. She felt his encouragement and ventured a little smile.

Trying to keep up with the driver's quick stride, Katherine wanted to ask about Mr. Emery, but couldn't seem to form the question. She felt rather shy at the moment. His first impression of her obviously hadn't been a good one. But she hadn't been forgotten; that was a relief.

The driver assisted her up into a black, shiny coach with gold-embossed trim and then left in search of the crate. Katherine positioned herself carefully and smoothed her hand over the button-tufted black leather seat. Such luxury.

A few minutes later, the carriage started with only the slightest of jolts, then glided along. A coach and four couldn't have made her feel more like a princess. She wasn't wholly ignorant of horse-drawn conveyances, having ridden a buggy to the station. And Mr. Brown, their grocer, had given her a couple of lifts in his buckboard, but that jarred and shook in comparison with the silkiness of this ride.

Katherine slid nearer the window. The carriage passed the town's few shops, then rode by a row of grand homes. One rambling house had porches sweeping around both its stories. Another had two large pillars on either side of a massive front door. Farther on, low buildings gave way to open countryside.

Her eyes wandered over the landscape. Everything looked fresh and green after the rain. During the last part of the train ride it had poured so hard she hadn't been able to rightly see her new surroundings. But she'd noticed Connecticut didn't have big boulders like the fields back home. One thing was sure: it was too cold in Maine for rain to make much of an impression on the frozen ground. But with the warming spring, the rain would surely bring in the "mud season."

From time to time, the carriage swerved to avoid fallen debris. Once, the driver stopped the coach and jumped down to remove a fallen tree limb.

At one bend, Katherine spied a dirt road leading up a ridge. Evenings, Mother and she had walked up a similar hill. At its summit, they would stroll arm in arm to watch the sunset.

Oh, if only Mother were here—both of them living together in their dear old boarding house. Katherine could picture the flocked curtains in their upstairs back bedroom. And the bowl and pitcher with its pink flowers—the bowl still pretty, if chipped on the backside. Mother had stitched the coverlet on their double bed with lilies of the valley. She said lilies meant "Return of Happiness." The treasured coverlet had been carefully packed into the crate.

The carriage slowed. Katherine gazed out the window to see wrought-iron gates. Two rows of magnificent oaks stood sentinel on each side of the drive. Was this her new home? As the carriage progressed down the avenue, she heard men shouting. One man's voice stood out above the others.

The coach rode a few dozen yards farther, then stopped. She strained to see through the window what was happening. A gap yawned in the row of grand oaks, the erstwhile tree now a jagged length of trunk thrust into vacant air.

A couple of men held axes near the oak that had fallen across the drive. Others, wet and muddy, stood around a drab, muscular horse secured with chains to the thick trunk.

Into view rode a man astride a sleek mount. He towered over the scene, his horse a spirited black. Katherine had little experience with horses, yet she felt drawn to the animal's beauty. Its ebony coat gleamed.

The man jerked a signal to pull the tree trunk. The drab horse strained with the load. One of the men slipped in the mud and fell.

"Watch what you're doing, clumsy fool!" the horseman shouted. "We don't need any injuries."

Katherine cringed at the harsh words.

The worker struggled to his feet. Men and horse strained again, the huge trunk budging only a few feet.

The man on horseback shouted again. "Stop! Can't you see the chains aren't pulling evenly? You there, look to it." He cursed at the hapless man. The skittish black horse stepped about restlessly, mirroring his master's impatience.

Katherine slid back on the seat, away from the window. She didn't want to be noticed. Particularly by that foreman on horseback.

"You two, give a hand with those chains!" the now familiar voice barked.

The men hurried to obey. Straining against the dead weight of the tree, the pulling began again in earnest, starting and stopping in agonizing spurts. More grunting and groaning. After what seemed an interminable time, the huge oak was finally dragged off the drive.

"Higgins," the man on horseback commanded, "go on to the house." Then, as the carriage started, he shouted, "Wait!"

Within moments the large gleaming horse sidled up to the coach, its head at the window, snorting, fogging up the glass.

Katherine was relieved to see the window cloud over. No one could see in.

Then unexpectedly a black glove swiped it and a man's face appeared, searching the coach's dim interior. Katherine saw the grim set of a man's jaw, then from under his hat brim, dark eyes caught and held hers. She stiffened. Quickly, she averted her gaze to the tufted seat in front of her.

Leather creaked, the rider straightened in his saddle. "Ride on, Higgins."

The carriage lurched forward, and Katherine gripped the seat. Though her eyes stared ahead, her peripheral vision caught sight of the glossy black horse, hearing it snort again as the carriage passed.

Although she hadn't been touched, somehow she felt bruised. Was everyone here so coarse? So unfriendly? A violent shiver shook her.

Katherine gazed at the interior of the well-appointed coach. She believed she preferred Mr. Brown's buckboard after all.

Chapter 2

Mrs. O'Neil entered the sewing room to find one of the maids mending a rent in a black silk frock. "Whose is that?" the housekeeper asked.

"Auntie Hanover's. I was helping her put it over her head and it ripped. And, of course, nothing would do but this dress. You know how she's been looking forward to the girl's arrival."

"Well, I'm glad someone is," Mrs. O'Neil said. "None of the family met her at the train. Poor girl! I would have gone myself if I'd known. You should have seen her step out of the carriage. Eyes big as hen's eggs." She foraged through a drawer. "Oh dear, is this all the ribbon? Maybe a simple black grosgrain would be best."

"Does she seem well-mannered?"

"Fine as can be. I hope to goodness this family warms up to her. Auntie will be all right. It's the missus and Mr. Jerard I'm worried about. 'What will I do with someone else's child in my house?' I heard Missus say. 'I simply don't have the time!'" Mrs. O'Neil harrumphed. "I say, Mr. Emery would have been a mite more generous—after all, he provided for the girl's mother. This house isn't the same without him." She held up a length of ribbon. "This should do." She snipped off a yard and left the room.

ɷ

Katherine picked up the silver-laced brooch and, with care, poked it through her dress bodice so as not to split a thread. Then she reached for the mirror on the dressing table to judge the effect. She fingered the brooch's smooth surface. How well she remembered seeing it on her mother's bosom. Her eyes started to tear up.

A knock sounded at the door.

Mrs. O'Neil breezed in. "About ready? Stand up and let me see." The housekeeper cocked her head. "You look as neat as a pin, and with your dark eyes and hair, you're pretty enough. Yes, I like your hair down, flowing-like." She held out the black grosgrain. "Would you like help with this?"

"Yes, please." Katherine turned around.

"How about I sweep up the sides of your hair, and tie it up in a bow on your crown?" At Katherine's assent, Mrs. O'Neil said, "Good. Now you're ready for your first dinner with the Emerys."

ଓ

Katherine stared down the long formal staircase.

"Now, don't you worry," Mrs. O'Neil said. "I'll see you as far as the drawing room. You're a little early, which is best. Then you can get used to the place before anyone arrives."

They stepped down the stairs, the housekeeper explaining how a man all the way from Germany had carved the balusters. "Once a guest said it'd be grander if the staircase curved around instead of going straight up the wall." She shrugged with good humor. "I'd say it's fine the way it is."

When they reached the bottom, the housekeeper pointed across the marble-floored entrance hall. "That's the drawing room. If you need anything, pull the bell cord around the corner and Bates will put in an appearance. He's the butler."

She reached over and gave Katherine a little squeeze. "There, you'll do just fine."

Katherine's stomach fluttered as she watched Mrs. O'Neil walk to the back of the house, her footsteps echoing in the vaulted hall.

She crossed the marble floor to enter the drawing room, but stopped at the threshold. A massive white marble fireplace, draped in black, dominated the opposite wall. Above it hung a gilt-edged mirror, carved with intricate fruits and vegetables. Gold brocade wallpaper set off the white scrollwork moldings of the ceiling, doorframes, and windows. These last were draped in black as well, all signs of Mr. Emery's passing.

Without warning, her mother's death stabbed her. She stood motionless, then a couple of sharp quivers shook her. But oh, she could not give into weeping now. She blinked fast to dissipate the gathering tears. When she met the family tonight, she must put her best foot forward.

She stepped into the room to the edge of a large Oriental rug. Divans and chairs in green and blue brocades, their arms and legs carved in intricate designs, sat in conversational groupings. On the walls, large tapestries and paintings depicted scenes from long ago.

Everything was so grand. And beautiful.

She felt like a mouse—a little brown mouse escaped from the garret. Oh, she didn't have the heart to meet the family tonight. She must locate the bell cord, to tell Bates she felt unwell.

Turning, she noticed a dark polished grand piano at the far end of the room. Its ivory keys shimmered. She forgot her concerns and hurried across the room to the instrument. Would she be allowed to play it? Once again she heard her landlady's voice: "*When you get to the Emerys', do that pretty, runny thing you played at our last Friday get-together.*" Katherine knew her friends at the boarding house enjoyed her recitals even though the upright had a rather thin, tinny sound. But this instrument! She could imagine its rich, resonant tone. Her fingers touched the keys, caressing them silently.

Footsteps echoed in the hall. Quickly, she stepped away from the piano.

A plump elderly lady entered, dressed in black silk. Fuzzy white hair surrounded her face like an aureole. She wore round spectacles.

Katherine relaxed. Her guardian wasn't at all formal and imposing the way she'd pictured her. She stepped forward. "Good evening, ma'am."

The woman startled. "Oh, hello there! I didn't know anyone was here." Old age quivered her voice. She crooked her neck, peering through the thick lenses. "You must be the girl we're expecting."

"Yes. I'm Katherine Edmond."

"Well, well. Come here beside me so I can see you better. Yes, yes, you're a pretty little thing." She extended her hand. "I'm glad to meet you, Katherine." She motioned to a couple of chairs near the fireplace. "Why don't we sit here while we wait for the others."

The aged woman arranged, then rearranged her skirt. "There! Now, I should introduce myself. I am Mrs. Robert Hanover, but everyone calls me Aunt Elsie. My given name is Elizabeth, but that never seemed to suit. Too formal. So, I was Elsie as a girl, Elsie as a married lady, and now Aunt Elsie as a widowed aunt."

"So—you're not my guardian?"

"Oh, no!" The old lady laughed. "Emma, Mrs. Emery, is your benefactress. I'm her sister-in-law."

"Excuse me." Katherine felt her face flush.

"Oh, my dear, don't worry. Why, I make so many mistakes I've grown accustomed to them. In fact, I think a body my age is entitled to a few. My gracious, the way some folks get irritated when things don't go exactly right." The old aunt straightened her skirt again. "Now, as I was saying, I am—or was—sister to Mr. Emery, your mother's godfather. He was kindness itself and gave me a home here after my husband died. You know, he was twenty years his wife's senior, but still, his death was a shock." She pulled out a handkerchief and blew her nose. "His passing was sad. I miss him so. Just like my dear Robert."

"I'm so sorry."

"Thank you, dear. It's been ten years since Robert's passing, and some people think I shouldn't talk about him anymore." She sniffed. "They call me a sentimental old fool." She sniffed again, then gave her nose a good blow. "Now, where was I?" She carefully placed the hanky in her pocket.

"You were telling about yourself?"

"Oh yes, and the rest of the family. Actually, besides your guardian Mrs. Emery, there's just one other person. Jerard, her son. He runs the estate now his father's gone." As she spoke, raised voices resonated from the stairs.

"To top it off," a male voice said, "the men moved like thunderstruck nitwits."

"With the storm and all, you can hardly blame them."

"All they had to do was follow instructions. We barely managed to get the tree off the drive. I'll have to have it cut up and removed tomorrow. The stump as well. I'll not have *that* remain."

"Yes, son. Certainly *not* the stump, but only so much can be done in this weather." Then her voice hushed. "However, we'll discuss this later." Their footsteps echoed across the marble hall.

Katherine grasped the chair arms. That man's voice—was it the foreman's? She watched the threshold as a middle-aged, patrician woman entered with a younger man, obviously her son. Both were dressed in black, and both were impressive in stature with handsome, chiseled features. The woman's iron gray hair pulled into a tight chignon gave her a severe appearance. The man, his dark hair waved near his brow, looked at Katherine as he crossed the room—yes, those same dark eyes had drilled her this afternoon.

She rose, willing herself to stand tall.

"Katherine Edmond? I am Mrs. Emery, your guardian." The woman gestured toward the man at her side. "And this is my son, Jerard Emery."

Back ramrod straight, Katherine forced out, "I'm pleased to meet you."

The man merely inclined his head.

Mrs. Emery glanced down at the old aunt. "I see you've already made Mrs. Hanover's acquaintance. I assume she told you we call her Aunt Elsie."

Both Katherine and the aunt murmured their assent.

Mrs. Emery chose a chair at hand and nodded to the one Katherine had just vacated. "Why don't we sit until dinner." Her son turned on his heel and crossed the room, seating himself near an assortment of books and newspapers. "I hope your journey was pleasant."

"Yes, ma'am, it was."

"And our driver located you without delay?"

"Well, I did wait awhile, but he did everything he could to make me comfortable." Katherine felt far from comfortable at the moment, but her mother always encouraged her to make conversation at the boarding house dinner table. "It was my first ride in such an elegant coach."

"I thought the closed carriage best. The sky threatened, and spring can bring such severe thunderstorms. Do you find Connecticut quite different from Maine?"

"The land rolls more gently. And the temperature seems to be somewhat warmer. I did enjoy the drive to your home."

Aunt Elsie moved forward in her chair. "The ride through the oaks is so impressive."

"I've never seen so many trees lined up on both sides of a drive—they are beautiful."

"A cursed shame, that gap." Mr. Emery's harsh voice interrupted from across the room.

His mother turned in his direction. "I know. Those trees were your father's pride and joy. And now with one of them gone—"

"Gone? What do you mean?" Aunt Elsie asked.

"Lightning struck one of them," Jerard said. "Only a ragged stump left."

The old aunt took out her hanky for another good blow. "Oh dear, and those oaks over seventy—maybe eighty years old."

Jerard opened the newspaper with a forceful snap. "After we get rid of the trunk, I'll have the men look around for another oak to plant in its place."

"Son, you could never replace that tree. Too large. It was magnificent, like your father. I think it best left alone at present."

Aunt Elsie turned to Katherine. "You see, many years ago, when Jerard's grandfather acquired this property, the first thing he did was to plant those oaks, even before building this house."

"He was quite the visionary," Mrs. Emery said. "When everyone else considered cutting trees a sign of civilization, he purposely planted them. He'd seen the allées of France and wanted something to remind him of his time there."

The silence that followed seemed to signal the end of the subject. No one spoke again until Mrs. Emery cleared her throat. "Well, then. Katherine, tomorrow I'd like to examine your wardrobe to see if you have appropriate clothing." She leaned forward. "By the way, that brooch you're wearing is exceptional."

"Thank you. It was my mother's—a gift from her godfather, your late husband, that is."

"Come here, dear," Aunt Elsie said. "I'd like to see it."

Katherine rose from her chair and bent over the aunt.

"It's lovely. My brother always showed good taste. I knew he was fond of your mother, and a piece like this only goes to prove it. That, and the fact he included both you and your mother in his will."

At the mention of the will, Mr. Emery lowered his newspaper, then shook it back up.

Katherine could hear disapproval in his abrupt, punctuated movements. She glanced at her benefactress. Had her lips tightened?

Aunt Elsie patted Katherine's arm. "There, dear, you may sit down. I'm glad my brother provided for you in the event of your mother's death."

A long pause ensued.

"And accept our condolences on your mother's passing," Mrs. Emery finally said.

"Oh, my!" Aunt Elsie's hand went to her mouth. "I'm so sorry. Fancy me not saying anything to you before this. Where is my mind nowadays?"

"In any case," Mrs. Emery said, "my late husband made provision for your education until such time as you can earn your own living. I will see his wishes fulfilled."

"Thank you, Mrs. Emery."

Long moments of silence followed. Thankfully, the butler entered.

"Dinner is served."

Mrs. Emery rose. "Katherine, you may accompany me. Jerard will escort his aunt."

Crystal goblets, silverware, and hothouse flowers graced the table. Porcelain birds rested on either side of the yellow roses.

Katherine gazed at the array of forks and spoons. She would have to watch Mrs. Emery to see which was used first. People had often commented on her grace, but faced with this mass of cutlery—and luxury—she felt extremely awkward. She held her hands neatly folded to keep from fidgeting.

The first course of potato soup was unlike anything she'd eaten at the boarding house. Closing her eyes, she savored its creamy richness. Did the family always dine this way, or was the elaborate dinner in honor of her arrival?

Talk of a textile mill dominated the mealtime conversation. Katherine sat quietly, glancing at Aunt Elsie while Mrs. Emery and her son discussed business pros and cons.

"But our family's been inactive in the mill for so long," Mrs. Emery said.

"I know. But I've examined the situation for several months. I'm convinced the conversion from water to steam can be made. In fact, must be made."

Mrs. Emery shook her head. "The stockholders will be reluctant."

"That's why I want to visit the Rhode Island mill, to see if their changes would work for us."

"Son, have you considered the capital needed for such a venture?"

"Yes, and I have a plan for raising it." Jerard glanced in Katherine's direction. "But we needn't discuss that now. Later, in your room."

Katherine caught the glance and stared down at her food. Obviously, Mr. Emery didn't want to talk about finances in her presence. She hoped she wasn't considered something of a nuisance coming to live with them.

It wasn't until dessert was served that Mrs. Emery turned her way. "I want to discuss your education, Katherine. My late husband stipulated you be tutored in the regular school subjects. A friend of the family, Mr. Lanning, has agreed to take you until we find a regular teacher. He is well-educated, so I'm certain your time will be productively spent. You'll meet him tomorrow." She shifted in her chair. "Also, learning to run a household is essential for a female. Hopefully, someday you'll marry a nice young man, and we want you to be a credit to our training. Our housekeeper will see that various members of the staff teach you sewing, cooking, and the like." Taking up her fork, she added, "I believe a young lady should also have musical instruction. I don't suppose you've had any."

The question had the suggestion of a slur. Katherine pushed down a feeling of anger, or embarrassment, and quickly gathered her forces. "Mother and I sang together. She also taught me to play the piano. Our landlady had an upright in her parlor and let me practice afternoons. She said I could continue as long as no one complained."

"Did anyone complain?" Jerard asked.

"No, no one ever did."

Mrs. Emery nodded her approval. "Well then, you must have a certain amount of talent. I think it would be wise to continue with the piano and see how you progress."

"I couldn't help noticing your instrument, ma'am. It's beautiful."

"Thank you. Jerard studied some, but he proved to be the singer of the family. We really bought it for—well—to return to what I was saying earlier, I will inspect your clothes first thing tomorrow."

Dessert finished, Mrs. Emery said, "Now, Katherine, you best retire early. You've had a long day."

Katherine closed her bedroom door. The maid had turned up the lamp before leaving, but now Katherine turned it down. She felt stiff and tired, and wanted the quiet haven of darkness after the brightly lit, overly stimulating drawing and dining rooms.

The bedroom, situated at the back of the second story, looked curiously simple in contrast to the lavishly decorated main floor. A single bed with a blue coverlet, a dresser and washstand against the opposite wall, and near the window a small desk and chair. But she was glad for the simplicity. It was restful, and more what she was accustomed to. There sat her crate. She would unpack it in the morning and place her beloved coverlet over the foot of the bed.

She walked across the room and seated herself at the desk. Did the Emerys always dine with such formality? Everything was beautiful, but so precise, so perfect. Could she measure up to this family's expectations? Both Mrs. Emery and her son wore an assured manner, looked capable of handling any situation. Mr. Emery, especially, had a sharp eye that seemed to miss very little. She remembered her reaction to the disagreeable foreman, then her consternation on discovering he was the son of this household. Would she need to see him every day? A knot tightened in her stomach. She sat a minute trying to rub it away.

But Aunt Elsie. A faint smile came to Katherine's lips. Surely she could expect kindness from her. Maybe they would be friends.

She rose and stepped over to the window. The moon, nearly full, bathed the grass, trees, and outbuildings in soft light. Mother had loved moonlight. Katherine could picture her now on a summer evening enjoying the cooler air, her white muslin dress and shawl reflecting the moon's glow. The dress came from more affluent times when her mother had lived in her parents' home. Katherine could remember the scent of lily of the valley whenever she wore it. Despite their circumstances, Mother always had a refined air. Even the landlady had said, "If you have any doubts about what to do, just do what your mama would."

Without warning, a sharp stab of sorrow pierced her. How she yearned to feel Mother's arms around her.

She glanced at the crate. Had the top been pried open for her? She crossed the room. Yes, the lid lifted easily, so she reached for the coverlet on top. She wrapped it close around her shoulders, then crawled onto the bed and lay down. "Oh God, why did she have to die? Why must I live here?" She pressed her head into the pillow to stifle her sobs.

After the sharpness of the grief passed, she lowered herself off the bed and crossed the room, still grasping the coverlet around her. She stood at the window, gazing at the moonlit yard. Yes, Mother had loved moonlight. Recalling other memories, Katherine leaned her head against the cold pane until the ache in her heart eased.

Chapter 3

Heavy gray clouds hung near the horizon. Head tilted back, Jerard Emery scanned the sky outside the stables. He breathed in long and hard, tracking the weather like a hound ready for the hunt. Regardless of the coming storm, he was going riding. He needed to think.

Last night at dinner the subject of the mill had been broached. Afterward, in her rooms, he'd told Mother how he regretted Father selling most of the family shares—the mill his grandfather had founded.

"I know," his mother said, "but your father wanted the life of a gentleman farmer. He had no desire for business."

Jerard had interest in little else. Buying and selling energized his creative powers.He'd sounded confident about raising the needed capital, but could he do it? Would it be possible to offer the owners, the stockholders a price they couldn't refuse? He wanted to regain control of the mill.

But he now needed to feel his horse under him in a good run. Clean-limbed and strong, Taggart was built for speed and endurance. The black hadn't his equal in these parts.

Entering the stable, Jerard noticed the closed carriage positioned to be taken out. His bull terrier ran to greet him, and he rubbed the big dog's silky head. A moment later the Emery driver joined him. "Taking my mother for a ride, Higgins?"

"No, sir. It's the young miss. She's to go to Mr. Lanning's for tutoring."

"I'd forgotten. Will you be gone long? We could have a storm later this afternoon."

"I'm not sure, sir. I'm instructed to drive her there and wait."

"Well, have a care to the horses and don't keep them out in bad weather."

"Yes, sir." Higgins touched his hat.

The young new groom led out a horse for the carriage. "Did you want something, sir?"

"Yes. I sent word to saddle Taggart. I expected him to be ready."

"Sorry, sir. I'm behind. I was polishing the tilbury when Mrs. Emery required the carriage for the young miss and then I got the request for your horse. I was doing things in order, sir."

Jerard cleared his throat. "I'd like to leave as soon as possible. And you needn't spend much time on that tilbury. We don't use it."

"Quite the racing gig, sir. A real beauty." The groom hesitated, but couldn't seem to help asking, "You don't use it, sir?"

"No, and never will. Now, get my horse."

"Yes, sir—ah, would it be all right if I first harnessed the other horse to the carriage and then get it outside, out of your way?"

"I suppose so."

The bull terrier growled. "Quiet, Rett." Jerard stroked the dog's head again. Patience wasn't one of his virtues either.

The groom hurried from the room with Higgins at his heels. Jerard overheard Higgins. "Charlie, the tilbury's something we don't talk about. Don't let Mr. Emery see you even fussing with that gig. He doesn't like to be reminded."

"Reminded?"

"An accident!" Higgins said impatiently. "The master had an accident with it. It's not to be spoken of."

"I won't bring it up again."

"See that you don't!"

A couple minutes later, Charlie entered with the second horse, avoiding Jerard's eye. Watching the groom hitch the horse to the carriage, Jerard tried to expel the memory of the sporting gig.

The tilbury—and now this girl. After breakfast he'd apologized for not extending her a welcome the night before. Hadn't wanted to do it, had apologized enough these last years since the accident.

In some strange way the girl reminded him of... and both of them with the same hair color—

Blast! Why his father had to include her in his will he'd never know. Then to have her live here. A boarding school for girls would have been more appropriate.

He scratched at the short hair around the powerful dog's neck then rubbed down its back. Given the girl's looks, her mother must have been attractive, but looks could be deceiving. The prettier they were, the more difficult they could be, and one difficult person was enough in this household. A corner of his mouth drew up. Lord knew his mother had enough trouble raising him. Last night he'd asked his mother how long the girl would stay.

"Until she's come of age."

"That long?"

His mother assured him the girl would be farmed out to a tutor for formal education, and to the housekeeper and maids for practical training. Except for dinner he needn't see her.

He expressly asked that the girl do her piano practice when he was absent. He didn't need another reminder. His mother said the girl seemed a quiet thing, that she shouldn't be much trouble.

Much trouble? How long had he been waiting for his horse? He scratched his dog's head hard. "Charlie, I don't have all afternoon."

"Yes, sir! Just about finished, Mr. Emery."

The carriage rolled sedately along the quiet country lane. An occasional bump jostled Katherine as the vehicle trundled over a small branch or swerved around a larger one. The road still needed to be cleared of debris.

She sat dressed in the black coat, hat, and dress she'd arrived in the day before. Mrs. Emery had expressed shock that her other two dresses were calico and worn. "You'll need to wear the dress you traveled in yesterday." And within minutes Mrs. Emery instructed Mattie to take measurements for a new one.

Katherine hoped the dress would be pretty. It had been only a few months since Mr. Emery's death and she had just lost Mother, so the color would be subdued. Gray maybe? That gentle hue reminded her of a swath of distant deciduous trees in winter.

She looked out the window. What would her tutor be like? Similar to the Emerys? Instinctively she straightened her back. She was grateful for the education she would receive, but what would she do when she left the Emery household? For surely, just as soon as they felt they had done their duty by her, she would have to leave. Could she teach? Be a governess? The mill Mr. Emery mentioned last night—she hoped she wouldn't have to earn her living that way.

They turned into a lane. Through the bare tree branches she could see a rambling, dark green house. A stone porch ran its full length. On one corner rose a turret covered with a cone-like cap. A steep roof topped the rest of the two-story house. She decided the building had a cozy, whimsical appearance despite its large size.

As the carriage drew up, an attractive older lady hurried down the porch steps. She smiled at Higgins who doffed his hat and hopped down from his perch.

"Will you wait, Higgins, or return later? It'll be a couple of hours."

"If it's all the same to you, ma'am, I'll wait."

"Fine. The sky looks a little dark to the west. If it begins to storm, take the horses back to our stable."

"Thank you, ma'am." Higgins assisted Katherine down.

"I'm Mrs. Lanning." The lady held out her hand. "I'm so glad to meet you. Won't you come inside?"

As Katherine followed, she studied the woman. Despite her age she moved with grace. And Katherine loved the way her soft silvery hair coiled back into an elegant chignon.

Mrs. Lanning ushered her into a room filled with books and maps, its windows overlooking a lawn bordered with a dense wood. A white-haired gentleman rose from a desk piled neatly with sundry papers.

"Dear, this is Katherine Edmond."

The man's brilliant blue eyes crinkled in a kind smile. He took her small extended hand into both his large ones. "Hello, Miss Katherine. We've looked forward to your coming. Won't you sit here?" He indicated a chair near his desk. "And how was your travel yesterday?" The way he looked at her, Katherine could feel his sincere interest as she answered. Then he said, "We hope you will find your time here to be both profitable and enjoyable."

He looked at his wife. "Martha, I think we can begin our studies now. Come for us in an hour, if you will."

His wife smiled assent and left the room.

Mr. Lanning sat behind his desk. "Now, let's see how you fare in the basic disciplines." He handed Katherine a book. "Will you please read this selection aloud? Then, afterwards, I'll question you on the passage."

Katherine strove to read with a clear voice, looking up when struggling over the pronunciation of a word. Sensitive to Mr. Lanning's approval or correction, she answered his questions hesitantly at first, but under his quiet encouragement felt herself responding with more confidence.

"Good. Let's see how you do in other subjects." Mathematics followed, then history. Mr. Lanning was about to tackle geography when his wife appeared at the door.

"It's a little over an hour, dear."

"Thank you, Martha. Well, Katherine, geography will have to wait until tomorrow." His eyes twinkled. "I think Mrs. Lanning has a surprise for us."

"You two follow me," she said. "A storm looks about to break, so I set tea in the family sitting room. It's cozier in there."

Yellow and pink cabbage roses papered the room they entered. A low table near the fireplace was laden with a silver tea service and plates of fancifully cut sandwiches and tiny iced cakes. Katherine looked from one adult to the other. Was this all in honor of her?

Mr. Lanning clasped his big hands together. "This looks delightful, my dear."

"Well, let's sit down." Mrs. Lanning laughed pleasantly. "The food is meant to be eaten, not only admired."

The next hour, despite heavy rain and occasional cracks of thunder, for Katherine nothing could quench the warmth created by the lovely room, delicious food, and genial company.

Mrs. Lanning offered her a second cup of tea. "This house is quiet with our grandson Christopher at school." A loud clap of thunder interrupted. "My!" she laughed. "It's *usually* quiet here. What I was going to say is that the silence reminds us of how much we miss our grandson. Young people bring life to a house." She turned to her husband. "Katherine will be coming every day, won't she?"

"Monday through Friday mornings. She will be a fine student."

The words of approbation caught Katherine off-guard. But how cheered she felt.

Mrs. Lanning then asked about her life in Maine. Katherine told them of her years at the boarding house, her love for music, and then about Mother. The time to depart came all too soon.

As the three of them stepped onto the porch, Mr. Lanning said, "The sky has cleared. Your drive back to the Emery's should be enjoyable."

"You've been a delightful guest," Mrs. Lanning said. "We look forward to seeing you tomorrow."

Katherine thanked them and climbed into the carriage. She promised herself she would study diligently in the coming weeks. How she longed to become as gracious and educated as these two people. She returned their goodbye waves, hugging the thought to herself of the many pleasant hours ahead in their home. Something about Mrs. Lanning reminded her of her mother. Was it her natural grace? And how she wished her father had been kind and encouraging like Mr. Lanning.

She glanced around the interior of the luxurious coach. Life had taken on a more hopeful aspect. The carriage slowed when it approached the Emery estate.

Katherine slid to the end of the seat and, looking out the window, strained to better see the grand oaks bordering the avenue. As soon as the carriage passed the gates, it sped up. Higgins was giving the horses their head.

In another few moments she should glimpse the house. A large square portico shaded the entrance under which the coach would stop. The housekeeper had explained the massive columns at the portico corners were topped with Ionic capitals. Katherine couldn't believe she'd come to live in such a fine place.

The horses suddenly slowed.

Ahead, a voice shouted, "Move faster! We don't want this to take all afternoon!"

Mr. Emery. Katherine shrank into the corner of the coach. She could imagine him on his spirited black mount, but any desire to look at the beautiful horse couldn't tempt her to gaze out the window. She felt a flush staining her cheeks.

"Mind what you're doing!" he shouted again.

Higgins halted the carriage, to watch or to stay out of the way, Katherine didn't know which. But how she wished they would move on. Would Mr. Emery look into the window again? A loud thump sounded in front of the carriage. Another. Then another. "Make sure those logs land in the wagon!"

Men were grunting hard. They must be removing the wood and other debris from the oak.

Katherine had been basking in the Lannings' loving attention, but now found her hands gripping the seat.

After several minutes, Mr. Emery shouted, "All right, Higgins, move on!"

The carriage started with a jerk and, for a moment, the dark horse filled the window frame. Katherine's breath caught. Then the huge animal was gone.

She stared ahead. Was this Mr. Emery's habitual manner? So unpleasant? He reminded her of—Father.

Sitting very still, she wondered if her life had come full circle. Father, and now this man? When she was young, she had wanted Father to be home with Mother and herself, the three of them together as a family. But as she grew older, she had to admit that life was more difficult when Father was present. Had Mother felt that way?

She swallowed past the lump that had formed in her throat. Was this the way life was to be in the Emery household, a mixture of the lovely—and the disagreeable?

Chapter 4

"Oh, Cook, isn't it terr-rr-ible that tree's gone?" Mrs. O'Neil said, shaking her head while checking the table linens for spots. "Every time I walk down that drive this last month my heart gives a turn. Can you imagine how the missus and Mr. Jerard must feel? All these years nothing happens and now with Mr. Emery not six months in his grave, one of his cherished oaks struck by lightning. I tell you, I'm glad he never lived to see the day."

Cook sat peeling potatoes, pressing her lips together tightly.

The housekeeper went on, "The going of that tree reminds me of Mr. Emery's passing. Sudden-like, leaving a hole as big in our hearts. I don't know if things will ever be the same here."

"Uh-um!" Cook agreed.

"And then that gossipy Sylvia Pruitt comes this morning wearing a peacock blue dress." Mrs. O'Neil slapped down the damask napkins. "It just isn't fittin'. She could'a worn dark blue if she'd a mind to wear blue, but she had to wear that *peacock* blue. It's an affront to this household that still mourns its dead. 'Course a woman like that doesn't have a fine feeling in her bones, certainly never appreciated the worth of a man like Mr. Emery." She straightened a napkin. "And then I heard she's organizing a special concert to benefit the poor, wondering if Mr. Jerard would sing. 'He has such a wonderful voice,' the woman crooned. 'I know he hasn't been in church for a while, but maybe he'd do this for the needy.'" She jerked her index finger at Cook. "That woman always gets in her little barbs. You know she didn't need to go and mention Mr. Jerard's lack of church attendance. Serve her right if he turned her down."

Bates appeared at the kitchen door. "The ladies are ready for the salad course."

Cook nodded to the tray of dressed greens.

Mrs. O'Neil took a long, deep breath. "Of course, family name and money go a long way toward making someone like Sylvia Pruitt tolerable. But that woman didn't come around so much when George Emery was living."

ᘓ

Mrs. Pruitt took a quick bite of salad as Bates left the dining room, then resumed her questioning. "So you say Katherine has a father, but the authorities can't locate him?"

"Yes," Mrs. Emery said. "He left his wife and child years ago, but it's been impossible to find him. For our purposes, he's as good as dead."

"But I don't understand. Where are the child's other relatives? Her grandparents, for instance? I don't see why you should have to raise her."

"The grandparents died years ago and we don't know of any other living relatives. You know, George tried to be a good godfather to Katherine's mother," Mrs. Emery said with dignity.

"Then George knew the grandparents well?"

"Had known them for years. Happened to be with them when the young couple eloped."

"Eloped!"

"Yes." Mrs. Emery put down her fork. "George told me the family was well-situated financially, and with Katherine's mother the only child, she would have inherited it all. The difficulty lay in that her father was so suspicious of any would-be suitor, she tired of waiting and left secretly one night to marry."

"If it wasn't so disgraceful—" Sylvia coughed over her bite of salad. "I'd say—aouk!—it seems rather romantic."

"Are you all right?"

Watery-eyed, Sylvia nodded.

"As I was about to say, romance wears off when one loses one's money."

"What?"

"Yes. When the father discovered his daughter had eloped, he disinherited her."

"Disinherited his only child—aouk! But what happened to all that money?"

"Went to one charity or another. It's a pity the grandparents never knew of Katherine's existence—they died before she was born—or provision might have been made for her."

"That certainly is a shame. Money given to charity when a little charity was needed right at home."

"Yes!"

Sylvia blotted her eyes with the napkin. "I'll bet that husband sang a different tune when he got wise to his wife's penniless condition."

"Undoubtedly. George never said as much, but it certainly looked that way and, of course, the husband eventually deserted his family. George, being good-hearted, checked on Katherine and her mother from time to time." Mrs. Emery shook her head. "For years I tried to stay out of the whole business, but, of course, I can no longer do that. Despite my distaste over the affair, I'm determined to carry out my husband's will regarding the girl. No one will be able to accuse me of neglecting duty."

"All I can say is, I admire you. I wouldn't have taken the girl in." Sylvia took another bite of salad. "This is delicious, Emma. By the way, I wanted to ask about Jerard singing for the benefit. He will, of course."

"He won't be able to, Sylvia."

"My goodness, why not?"

"It's this new venture at the mill." Mrs. Emery took up her fork. "He'll be traveling to Rhode Island at that time."

"Couldn't he change his plans?"

"I'm afraid not. Besides, you know how difficult it is to change Jerard's mind on anything."

"I don't understand." Sylvia's large eyes blinked. "He has such a wonderful voice."

ꝏ

Katherine paused on the back steps, trying to decide where to picnic. Mrs. Emery had suggested the idea after learning Sylvia Pruitt would stay for lunch. Katherine had thought of the nature notebook Mr. Lanning assigned her. She could have a picnic and collect wildflowers at the same time. She dutifully greeted Mrs. Pruitt, then stopped by the kitchen for her lunch basket. Under the food she placed several well-dampened cloths between which she would arrange her flowers.

Katherine considered the woods to the side of the house. Wildflowers would surely grow there, and a field beyond the stable in back also held possibilities.

She skirted the edge of the wood, searching for the best place to enter. The gray mourning dress she'd worn for Mrs. Pruitt was her second best and she didn't want to soil it. But she dare not change it until the woman left in case she saw her again.

How Mrs. Pruitt had eyed her. Those big eyes. The errand boy at the boarding house would have called her bug-eyed. At any rate, Katherine would have thought something was wrong with her appearance if Mrs. O'Neil hadn't reassured her by saying, "Don't worry. You're pretty enough with your dark eyes and hair. Gray makes some look peaked, but you've got enough sparkle for two girls."

Holding a branch aside, Katherine picked her way into the forest. Ahead was a fallen log—a place to sit and eat. She removed the cloth covering from the basket and smiled. Cook had included a meat pie made from last night's dinner as well as a large slice of buttery pound cake.

She hoped Mrs. Pruitt wouldn't stay too long. Her piano practice started at two and Mrs. Emery was most particular that it end at three. When would she be able to spend more time on her music? That hour turned out to be one of the highlights of her day—that, and the time spent with Mr. Lanning.

Yesterday, after lessons, he had offered to accompany her home. Walking across the back lawn, he led her to a wooded path overhung with trees. Bending under a limb, he said hadn't walked the path in a long time. It connected his property with the Emerys and was still used by servants of both households. When his grandson and Jerard Emery were boys, one summer they'd made quite a project of widening it.

Katherine asked if his grandson and Mr. Emery still did things together. Mr. Lanning replied, "Not anymore. As they grew older, they gradually went their separate ways. Part of it, too," he said, smiling, "was because Jerard liked to organize and manage, and Christopher no longer wanted to be managed. Both have independent natures, though Christopher's is the more easygoing."

"Will your grandson be coming home soon?"

"In another month. He wants to roam the countryside and paint. He aspires to be an artist."

Katherine thought if the grandson were anything like his grandfather, he would certainly be enthusiastic about nature. As they passed various trees and plants, Mr. Lanning gave interesting information about their unique characteristics. She learned a white oak needed to be at least fifty years old before it produced acorns, and settlers built their homes where these trees grew because they indicated the richest soil.

At the edge of the wood they stopped to rest. A gentle breeze blew across the open field. The Emery house loomed in the distance like a large ship, the outbuildings trailing like dinghies in its wake.

"I wonder if I could walk this path to your house for lessons instead of taking the carriage."

"It's possible," Mr. Lanning said, "but Mrs. Emery will have to decide. Why don't we ask her."

As they approached the back lawn, they saw the stable door swing wide. A groom led out a black horse followed by a large dog. The animal ran circles around Mr. Emery's stallion.

At that moment, Mr. Emery exited the stable.

Mr. Lanning waved as soon as he recognized his neighbor. Mr. Emery, however, did not return the greeting. Instead, he mounted his horse and disappeared around the far side of the house.

Surely, Mr. Emery had seen them. Katherine glanced at Mr. Lanning. His cheek seemed flushed. How could Mr. Emery be so rude? But her tutor said nothing.

Even now, as Katherine sat with her lunch spread on her lap, she found it puzzling. She took another bite of the meat pie. Was there some tension between the two men? Mr. Lanning was friendly enough. Well—Mr. Emery must be at fault.

After a few more bites of pie, she put it aside. It was more than she could finish if she wanted to sample the pound cake. With care, she wrapped the remainder of the meat pie in the napkin and placed it at the side of the basket. As she nibbled the dessert, she surveyed the area. Already she spied trillium and lady slippers. They would make a nice beginning.

Brushing off the last of the crumbs, Katherine threaded her way to the flowers. She picked them carefully and placed them between the damp cloths.

The good dress was a bit of a nuisance. Staying clear of brambles, she combed that part of the forest as best she could. After an hour's careful work, she examined the flowers collected so far. One specimen in particular pleased her, a jack-in-the-pulpit.

She exited the wood near the front of the house and saw Mrs. Pruitt's carriage. Not relishing meeting the woman again, she circled back toward the stable. She set her basket under a shade tree. Maybe she could take a few extra minutes to scout the meadow.

Sun streamed down on the field of green grasses dotted with yellow and white wildflowers. It wouldn't take long to pick these for her collection. A mild breeze blew through her hair. How she would love to lie down and soak up the comforts of both wind and sun. But the gray dress precluded that idea. Instead, she raised her face to the sun, closing her eyes to soak up its warmth, delighting in the cool breeze. Sighing with contentment, she slowly opened her eyes.

Something in her peripheral vision jolted her out of her dreamy state. Mr. Emery's huge dog had appeared from nowhere and now nosed through her basket.

She ran toward him. "Get away! Get away!"

The dog looked up.

Spying a stick near the edge of the meadow, Katherine swooped it up and brandished it round and round.

The animal growled, standing his ground.

Katherine stopped, not sure what to do next, then drew herself up and jabbed the stick at the dog. "Get away from that basket! Get out of here!" His fierce bark made her jump back.

She grasped the stick tighter, held it high, but as soon as she moved, the dog growled fiercely, its muscles tense.

Eyes wide, breath now shallow, Katherine stared at the menacing animal. A tingling sensation crept up her arms. Was it true a person's hair could stand on end?

"Stay, Rett!" Mr. Emery strode from the stable, dark brows drawn together in a frown. "What the devil! Have you been swinging that stick at this dog?"

Katherine's legs buckled and she dropped to her knees. "My basket—I was trying to retrieve it."

"Threatening this dog with a stick will only provoke him." Mr. Emery stepped toward her and snatching the stick from her hand, flung it into the meadow. "Never use a stick with this animal." He stepped over to the dog, and bending down, ran his hand over its head. Then he roughed the back of his neck. The animal quieted.

Straightening, Mr. Emery looked at Katherine. "A person can't be a stranger to a dog like this. Come here."

Katherine considered the dog, then Mr. Emery. "I don't know if I could, sir."

"Nonsense!" His tone of voice brooked no argument.

She stood reluctantly.

"You must master your anxiety or this dog will sense your fear. Come here."

Katherine took a few steps. The dog stretched his neck and nudged his nose against her dress. She stumbled back.

"Don't be afraid." Mr. Emery's voice cut through her. He stripped off a riding glove. "Now hold out your hand."

Katherine held it out, willing it not to shake.

Mr. Emery seized her wrist, stretching her hand to the dog. She felt its cold nose—then wet tongue—explore her fingers. She desperately wanted to snatch her hand away, but she endured the ordeal until Mr. Emery let her go.

"Sit, Rett."

The dog lowered immediately.

"It's to your advantage to make friends with him. He could be a powerful ally if you're ever in trouble." Mr. Emery cleared his throat. "Now, what was so important about this basket that you brandished a stick?"

"Inside are flowers for my botany notebook. I hope they're all right." She looked over at the basket, yet, she hesitated to bend near the dog to recover it.

"Rett. Inside." Mr. Emery nodded to the stable. Instantly, the dog rose and ran to the open doorway.

"Thank you." Katherine felt herself relax. She moved to inspect the basket's contents. "My jack-in-the-pulpit—it's unharmed!" She looked up. "This flower is rather difficult to find, you know. Mr. Lanning told me to keep a special lookout for it. He said it was an example of the beautiful detail God puts in His creation." She bent over the bloom.

Katherine heard Mr. Emery clear his throat. "Yes, it's quite unusual. But tell me, does Mr. Lanning often talk to you about God?"

"Yes."

"But is he training you to think for yourself, or does he spoon-feed you his own ideas?"

Katherine felt surprise at the question.

Mr. Emery folded his arms across his chest. "Of course, you are still very young."Katherine felt loyalty for Mr. Lanning rise up in her. "I admire Mr. Lanning. He's learned and has traveled a great deal."

"I know. I also realize Mr. Lanning can present his beliefs convincingly. But you must know his views represent only one perspective."

"Suppose they're true?"

"Aren't you rather inexperienced to come to that conclusion?"

"Maybe so, but I can think quite clearly for myself, and I have learned one thing—to be careful whom I trust." She looked at him straight on.

"What do you mean by that?"

Katherine saw something in his eyes, a flicker of anger?

Pride? She decided to change tack. "Well, take my father, for instance. You've heard of him?"

He nodded.

"Ordinarily one can trust one's father. But I found I couldn't." Her mind ran to circumstances surrounding her father, how his drinking took money needed for food, how he'd absent himself for days and they would not know where he was—things she couldn't tell this man.

Mr. Emery stood looking at her, as if waiting for her to say more. He finally said, "I understand he left you."

"Apparently." She looked at the ground. An almost imperceptible sigh escaped her lips. "I missed him, then I remembered when he was home he was always challenging Mother, especially about her faith. They disagreed a lot about that." Katherine looked up at Mr. Emery. "That is why I like and respect Mr. Lanning so much. He believes in God the way my mother did."

Mr. Emery's eyes narrowed. "Bravo for Mr. Lanning." A slight edge crept into his voice. "Of course, you might feel the need for someone to fill your father's shoes. However, that doesn't mean you have to accept everything Mr. Lanning says. Life can be viewed in a number of different ways."

Katherine pressed her lips together.

"Clearly you don't take to my suggestion." His dark eyes narrowed to drive home his point. "You have a lot to learn, Miss Edmond. For instance, you should have known a dog would nose around a basket in which lunch had been left." Without further word, he turned and strode toward the stable.

Katherine stared after him. Gazing at the door through which he disappeared, she dropped to her knees. His abrupt departure felt like a slap. Her cheeks burned. She was sure Mother would have called him rude.

She grabbed the basket handle. Of course, she wasn't the only one to smart under his abrasive manners. Over the month she'd lived here she'd noticed his high-handed way with the servants. And the sharp tone he used with Aunt Elsie.

Thinking back on their conversation, she couldn't believe she'd brought up the subject of her father. Fingering the basket handle, she considered the similarities between Mr. Emery and her father. Both viewed life so differently from Mother and herself. Certainly, both had little to do with God.

"This whole dog business!" The words suddenly burst out. She had never liked big dogs, and this one evidently had the run of the premises. What in the world would she do now? Her mouth set in a firm line. Give him and his master a wide berth, that's what!

Clutching her basket, she rose and marched to the house.

Chapter 5

The old hickory tree marked the spot where Maggie, panting, emerged from the woods. She would be relieved to be back in her own kitchen at the Lanning's. She hardly noticed the lovely green of the newly leafed-out trees. It wasn't often she took this path from the Emery's, but today it had to be done. Mister Christopher had come home.

He surprised them last night by arriving early from school. Chocolate cake was his favorite, and with her out of cocoa, nothing was to be done but to borrow from the neighbors. She stopped a moment on the stoop to catch her breath and looked underneath the basket's red-checked napkin, making sure the cocoa was intact. Much of her windedness had to do with her girth, she knew, but my, she was excited to have Christopher home.

As soon as she yanked open the kitchen door, she spied a tall young man with wavy brown hair charge out of the pantry. "Mister Christopher! What's you doing in there?"

"Maggie!"

"Land sakes alive! Didn't you have enough for breakfast?"

"I was only scouting out what you'd cooked for later today. That food at school makes me yearn for your home cooking. You wouldn't deprive a boy of whetting his appetite, would you?"

"You ain't a boy no more. You's a young man and should know better." Maggie knew the irritation in her voice wouldn't hide her delight in Christopher being here. But she felt she had to keep him in line someway. "My gracious, can't I be gone from my kitchen more'n a minute without you scrounging around my pantry?"

"Now, Maggie, I didn't take a thing, not after your wonderful breakfast, but you *have* been gone more than a minute." Christopher wagged his finger at her. "I came in here all of ten minutes ago to ask what you planned for lunch, and finally had to satisfy my curiosity by looking myself. So there! I'm not the scrounger you make me out to be." He crossed the room to help with her shawl. "By the way, where have you been?"

"You would ask." She folded her shawl with precision. "If you must know, I was over at the Emery's. Of course, with you nosing around my kitchen there's little chance of me keeping dessert tonight a secret."

"You're making my favorite chocolate cake." He bent over to grab her shoulders in an affectionate squeeze. "I can smell that cake warm from the oven right now."

Maggie gave Christopher a good-natured scowl. "There, I told you it wouldn't be a surprise. Now off with you. I've got work to do."

"All right, but not until you've told me the latest gossip." He leaned against the counter like he had all morning. "How are things at the Emery's? Is Jerard his usual congenial self?"

"'Bout the same, I hear. He's taken off for Rhode Island or thereabouts and won't be back for a spell. Cook said he's gone to see a textile factory. Thinkin' of putting money into the old mill here. She thinks he's plum crazy." Maggie held onto the counter with one hand while she bent over to get a large crockery bowl. "But what he does is his business. Of course, I know more'n one person over there is relieved he's gone." She thumped the bowl on the counter, righting herself with a huff. "He didn't used to be so waspish. But since his father died, he's taken a decided turn for the worse."

"Oh, he was already headed in that direction. I noticed it after his brother—well, hard things in life bring out the worst in some people."

"Guess that's true." Christopher was probably right, although in Jerard's case, she thought allowances might be made. However, she wouldn't stir up *that* wasp's nest. It was too good to have her boy here. She searched for a more palatable subject. "By the way, did your grandfather mention the new girl living at the Emery's?"

"Yes, he did. What does Cook say about her?"

"That she's as good as she is pretty. She don't give no trouble and is real eager to learn."

"Pretty, eh? What does she look like?"

"Oh, she's got lots of wavy dark hair. I saw her in church. Has big eyes and dark lashes with a creamy white skin. The best part, Cook says, is that she don't know what a looker she is—is as sweet and nice as they come."

Christopher laughed. "How old is she? Has she been spoken for already?"

"Pshaw. She just had her birthday—sixteen, I think."

"Becoming a young lady, I see. We must hope Jerard doesn't wear her down. He can grate on a person."

"Then it's good he's gone a spell. Now! That's *all* the talking I'm doin' this morning." She took a large wooden spoon and swooshed it at him. "If you don't get out of my kitchen right quick, I'm going to mix you up in this batter and bake you with the cake."

"I'm going, I'm going!" Christopher laughed again. "Flying even!" Flapping his arms like a chicken, he bolted out the door.

☙

With Jerard Emery gone, life for Katherine settled into a quiet routine in the household. Aunt Elsie seemed especially cheerful to have him absent. She said at her age it was about time she had a little peace and quiet.

Katherine hadn't forgotten her confrontation with Mr. Emery and the dog. Afterward, she found herself keeping up her guard whenever the man was around—the way she had with Father. So she was relieved to see him leave as well.

However, her peace of mind didn't last long. Hearing about the arrival of the Lanning's grandson brought on a fresh bout of anxiety. She valued her special place in the Lannings' hearts and loathed giving it up, even to a grandson. Apart from her mother, the Lannings had been the only other adults who'd felt like family. Mr. Lanning, in particular, was special. She adored him as a teacher, and he was like the father she'd always wanted. Already she found herself wondering when this grandson would be returning to school.

Two days later they met. Immediately she noticed the twinkle in his eye.

His grandfather introduced them. "Not only is Katherine a good student, but she's also a fine pianist. I ran into Mr. Anson in town the other day and he's quite impressed with her."

"Impressed, eh?" Christopher grinned at her. "I struggled with lessons for years and he never showed much enthusiasm for my playing."

Katherine felt a warm glow at the compliment. "But I've heard you're a fine painter. That's as great an accomplishment."

"Well, thank you." He bowed with alacrity. "I'll tell my professors my fame has already spread outside the confines of the classroom." He then told her a couple of funny stories about school.

Katherine had never known anyone who joked as he did. And he smiled at her when he talked. Apparently he didn't see her as a rival for his grandparents' affections. He seemed pleased she was part of their lives. Without realizing it, Katherine's guard dropped, and by the end of the week she liked him almost as much as she did his grandparents.

"Miss Katherine," he asked one day, "why don't you ask permission to come along with me on one of my painting jaunts. I usually pick an interesting spot in the countryside. You could gather flower specimens for your nature notebook."

Gratified he'd asked her to tag along, Katherine wasted no time obtaining the necessary permission. Mrs. Emery had looked up and absently said yes, then returned to her work. Later, Katherine overheard one servant talking to another, wondering that the missus didn't look out more for her ward, allowing her to spend time with a young man, unescorted.

The following day, Christopher called for her in the buggy and drove to a grassy knoll overlooking a pasture. An old gray barn sat off in the distance next to a clump of trees.

"Maybe you'd like to wander around this meadow a bit and explore the woods," he said. "I'll set up my easel here. Just be certain to stay within calling range."

ଋ

Katherine wandered back across the meadow to where Christopher worked intently. She stopped behind him, surveying his work.

"What do you think?" he asked.

"I like it very much. Your painting looks like that scene, yet different. Freer somehow. I can't quite put it into words."

"You've a good eye." Christopher turned around to face her. "Not long ago one of my friends returned from Paris and demonstrated how some of the artists there are using an easy, looser style." He fastened a clean sheet of paper to the easel. "Let me show you what I mean. See that maple tree over there? Instead of drawing a meticulous copy of it, I could suggest the same thing with a few bold strokes. Like this." He dashed off a sketch.

"I see what you mean. You immediately captured the life of the tree, and so well."

"I think this evokes my joy in the object better than an exact representation."

She stepped to his side. "You love to draw and paint, don't you?"

"Yes, and I want to devote more time to it, travel to Paris someday and study the great masters in the Louvre."

"The Louvre?"

"It's a huge museum displaying centuries of artwork from all over the world." His eyes twinkled. "In fact, it's so big, *little you* would get lost in the place." Resting his hands on his knees, he became serious. "You know, Katherine, painting is a hard way to make a living. Most artists half starve. I'm fortunate. Summers I come here to pursue my art and, at the same time, learn to run Grandfather's place. Not many aspiring artists have my comfortable circumstances."

"Well, it's like that for me, too. If I didn't live with the Emerys, I wouldn't have the good teacher or time to practice piano."

"So, we're both fortunate." With a quick change of mood, Christopher struck a comical pose. "What would we do without our esteemed elders?"

They both laughed.

Christopher took out his watch and frown lines quickly furrowed his forehead. "Would you look at that, I promised you home in fifteen minutes. Quick, Katherine, or I'll be in trouble with our *esteemed* elder, Mrs. Emery."

Katherine hurried to place her basket of pressed flowers in the buggy while Christopher gathered his easel and paints.

He snapped the reins to get the horse moving. A mile or so down the road, he turned into a little-used lane. Tall weeds in its center brushed the wagon and woods lined both sides.

Katherine glanced up at him.

"A shortcut," he said, and pointed off to the right. "These woods belong to the Emerys and I would guess their house less than a mile distant."

A few hundred yards farther and the forest opened to a clearing with an old farmhouse. A few dilapidated outbuildings stood nearby. All were a cheerless, weather-beaten gray with weeds and a few scraggly wildflowers dotting the yard. "This farm belongs to a family by the name of Hodges," Christopher said. "They keep eking out a living here though other neighbors have sold their land to my grandfather or George Emery and left to try their luck out west."

As the buggy approached the house, a girl of about ten in a faded pink dress hurried out the front door, stopping at the edge of the stoop. She stared at them, her short curly blond hair glowing in the sun.

"Cassie!" a woman's voice called from inside.

On impulse, Katherine turned and waved. After a moment's hesitation, the little girl waved back. A woman stepped out the front door, gazing at the passers-by. Her homespun dress covered a lean, angular figure.

Katherine turned to Christopher. "They are very poor, aren't they?"

"Yes, but I guess they make do."

From experience Katherine knew how hard things could be. How did the family survive? She and her mother had been rescued by the kind generosity of the late Mr. Emery.

She studied her companion. He sympathized with poverty-stricken painters, but didn't seem to think much about the poor close to home. Not wanting to dampen the merry spirit of the outing, she didn't feel inclined to take him to task, and she had no idea what she could do to help, but she resolved to remember where the family lived.

Christopher directed the buggy onto the main road and within a few minutes turned into the Emery drive. After they stopped under the portico, Christopher jumped down to assist her.

"Thank you for bringing me along," she said. "I really enjoyed myself."

"We'll go again," he said with a wink.

As Katherine walked up the staircase to her room, she determined to quell the little cloud that had descended on her after noting Christopher's reaction to the Hodges. Instead, she decided to think about the good time they'd had. In the days ahead, she and Christopher would become the best of friends. She was sure of it.

Chapter 6

The next weeks passed as a lovely dream. With her son away, Mrs. Emery no longer limited Katherine's piano time, and her music flourished. Mr. Emery had told his mother he now planned to extend his travel to St. Louis to investigate possible textile markets.

The summer seemed full of promise. Christopher continued to invite Katherine along on painting outings. Sunday afternoons she liked to walk, exploring the estate. One day she decided to take a ghost of a trail that veered off from the Lanning's forest path. The trees had leafed out to a rich green, not yet dulled by the dust and heat of summer.

Clouds hovered after an earlier rain. A fresh smell lingered in the air. Katherine stopped a moment, closing her eyes, drinking in the damp, still wood. A faint odor of smoke from someone's chimney drifted in. She could picture a family gathered around the fire playing games or popping corn—a home like she wanted someday.

An image of her mother and their sweet life together came to mind. Her favorite memories were when they would cuddle under the coverlet and talk. Without warning, a terrible sense of loss gripped her as if a huge hand squeezed her heart. She stopped, half-turned to go back the way she had come. But no. She couldn't return to the house just yet. Sorrow like this came less often than before, but being alone now, she could let the tears flow. Early in their acquaintance, Mrs. Lanning said she must give expression to her sorrow, so she cried while she walked, grateful the quiet, wet forest seemed so in tune with her grief.

A quarter mile down the path the forest opened unexpectedly onto a road. On the other side sat a weather-beaten house, the same one she'd seen with the golden-haired child on its stoop. How worn and forlorn it looked. Riding in the buggy with Christopher, Katherine had determined to remember these people, to do something for them.

As she gazed at the house, the little girl stepped out the dilapidated door and crossed the yard to the barn. She wore the same pink dress, but with a dingy gray jacket. Katherine suspected it had once been white and she stood at the edge of the forest a moment longer, then turned back the way she had come.

That night at dinner she mentioned her concern about the family to Mrs. Emery.

"That's commendable, Katherine, but you should become better acquainted with them before doing too much. Maybe you could take some of the goodies you help Cook make on Saturdays. Higgins could drive you in the carriage."

"I can go on foot. It isn't more than a mile."

"That might be true, but I'd rather you take the carriage. It'll let them know your standing in the community."

Katherine determined to visit Cassie and her family within the week. The next Saturday she and Cook baked extra rolls and cookies, bundled them in a soft white cloth, and placed them in a basket.

When Katherine stepped from the carriage, Mrs. Hodges came out the door with Cassie trailing behind. Unsure how to begin, Katherine decided on a direct, friendly approach. She introduced herself and told of arriving that spring and handed over the basket. "We made cookies and rolls. I hope you enjoy them."

"I didn't expect a visit from the Emery household. You must have some of these cookies with us." Mrs. Hodges ushered Katherine into what passed for the front parlor, offering her a seat. "Cassie, why don't you stay with Miss Edmond while I get some milk."

Katherine chose a worn armchair. A lumpy brown sofa and two ladder-back chairs also circled a box draped with muslin. She glanced around. On one end of the simple fireplace mantle stood an oil lamp and on the other rested a bright blue vase with a handful of dried wheat stalks. The room lacked fine furniture and knickknacks, but nonetheless had a pleasant air. Cassie lingered behind one of the ladder-back chairs.

Katherine broke the silence. "That wheat color looks pretty with the blue vase."

"Harvest time I cut it from the field out back."

Katherine smiled her approval. Did the child have an eye for color, or did the arrangement just happen that way? Katherine decided on the former. Sitting here with Cassie, she enjoyed the sensation of being the adult. In the Emery household she was considered very young, hardly meriting consideration.

"Do you go to school?" Katherine asked.

"Yes, with my big brother—after the harvest."

"That's a bit later than the other children."

"Yes."

"Can you read?"

"A little. My older brother shows me some, but with chores and all he doesn't have much time."

"Well, maybe I could help."

Cassie's face lit up and she cautiously made her way from behind the ladder-back chair to lean on Katherine's armchair.

A tender feeling sprang up as the girl leaned so near her. As an only child, Katherine had never felt the joy of talking to or playing with a sister or brother.

"It looks like Cassie has welcomed you into the family," Mrs. Hodges said, entering with glasses of milk.

Katherine told of her offer to help. "If you like, next time I come I could bring my first reader."

"Are you sure?" Mrs. Hodges asked.

"Yes, in fact, I think we could start next week." Katherine glanced at the bright-eyed child and they smiled at each other.

ꝏ

Katherine found the Hodges' household a cheerful place to visit. Often she'd thought life with her mother and father would have been happier if there had been more money, but now she wasn't so certain. The Hodges were content despite having so little. And teaching Cassie interested Katherine. The child proved such an eager student; from the first reader, she progressed quickly to the second. Katherine began to wonder if teaching might be her chosen work when she left the Emerys. That was sure to please Mr. Lanning.

Months passed. At the dinner table Mrs. Emery, Aunt Elsie, and Katherine comprised a quiet threesome. Late that summer Mrs. Emery voiced a wish that her son were present. "Nothing like having a man around," she said. Now and then, she related news from one of his letters. He liked St. Louis, calling it quite an "up-and-coming" city. He had even ventured farther west to see more of the country. "I hope he doesn't run into any Indians!" his mother said.

Katherine glanced at Aunt Elsie and smiled. The old aunt's look said she wished he'd do just that.

The next letter from Jerard said he was on his way home, but would stop at Rhode Island one last time. Both his mother and Aunt Elsie concluded it had something to do with enlarging markets for the mill.

At last, a telegram stated he would arrive the next day. A glow suffused Mrs. Emery's features where cold formality usually reigned. Katherine wondered if the father of the prodigal son had reacted with as much eagerness. In preparing the household, Mrs. Emery did everything but kill the fatted calf.

The wanderer breezed into the house, his manner conveying his certainty of a warm welcome. He said he'd had enough of travel for a while and was ready to enjoy the comforts of home.

Conversation that evening proved pleasant. Even Katherine had to admit a man's deep voice added to the festive atmosphere. Jerard was full of his new acquaintances and experiences.

Midway through dinner he sat back in his chair. "This meal is delicious, Mother. I'd forgotten what a good table you set. You could teach a few things to the most discriminating New York restaurant."

"Thank you, son. It's so good to have you home I couldn't resist having Cook fix your favorites."

"I appreciate it." He smiled. "Now, I wonder if you'd humor me further."

Mrs. Emery's eyebrows lifted in question, but she smiled indulgently.

"Do you remember von Weber, one of the men I met in New York? Well, I've almost convinced him the renovations for the mill will be profitable. If he supports me at the next shareholders' meeting, I'm sure the vote will go my way." He leaned toward his mother. "I'd like you to help me make sure he comes through by inviting him and his family here for a weekend. Nothing like seeing this place to convince him we're from good solid stock. The von Webers have two children. One about Katherine's age. The family could take the train from the city Friday and stay through most of Sunday." He paused, waiting for his mother's assent.

"This takes me rather by surprise," she said. "We've socialized so little since your father's death. But this would get us started again." She leaned toward the table, tapping her index finger on the tablecloth as plans formulated in her mind. "We could host a Saturday evening dinner party and invite a few friends. I would need a fortnight or so to get the house in order."

"It's already in perfect order, Mother."

Mrs. Emery straightened. "Jerard, let me do things my way. The house should have an extra polish. I'd like our guests to think your business enterprise will be run with as much efficiency and style as your home." She smiled. "Besides, this will be an occasion worthy of a little effort."

☙

"Well!" Aunt Elsie said as she laboriously climbed the stairs. "We'll see how far he gets."

As a rule, Katherine and the aunt retired early, and now Katherine supported the older woman's arm up the stairs. Aunt Elsie's attitude surprised her. She'd heard occasional references to the mill but knew little about it. Auntie invited Katherine to step inside her room and was surprisingly lucid on the subject.

"You might remember Jerard's grandfather founded the mill, oh, early in the 1800s. Of course, the depression in '29 forced many mills out of business. In order to survive, he cut production. But by the autumn of 1830, conditions had so changed for the better he could no longer keep up with demand."

"I hadn't realized the mill was that important to the Emerys," Katherine said.

"It's how they made all their money. But Jerard's father, the second generation, didn't want to fool with it any longer. He loved land and animals and preferred the quiet life of a country squire. So he sold a large portion of his mill shares. He upgraded the farm then saved or invested the rest. I don't know where that money is now, but I believe Jerard plans to use it to finance his big ideas about the mill—with a *little* help from others," she added with unaccustomed sharpness.

"It doesn't sound as if you like his ideas."

"Oh, Jerard thinks he knows so much. I'd like to see him get his comeuppance. Forgive me, child, but that's the way I feel. He's stuck his oar in my boat once too often." She reached over and gave Katherine a good-night hug. "Let me give you a piece of advice. Stay out of his way or he'll end up managing you as well."

☙

At breakfast the next morning Mrs. Emery announced she required an extra week to get ready for the dinner party as each of them would need a new dress. "We are still in mourning somewhat, but that is no reason to look too somber and certainly not dowdy." She caught Katherine's questioning look and added, "Yes, Katherine, you will need to be fitted for a dress as well. The von Weber children need a companion. And besides, you need experience mixing socially."

The household was too well run to admit of much last minute preparation, yet it had been so long since a house party that excitement ran high. Though they lived in small town surroundings, they knew their home to be exceptionally elegant and wanted it to appear to best advantage before Mr. Emery's New York business associate.

The afternoon of the arrival, the family carriage, polished to a black, satiny sheen, waited at the train depot for the guests to arrive.

When the von Webers entered the house, Katherine viewed them with interest. Both husband and wife stood tall, solid in girth. Mr. von Weber had a hearty laugh and talked a great deal. The missus was quiet and carried herself daintily despite her robust build. Their son Theodore—or Teddy as his mother called him—was only two years below Katherine's age but acted much younger. He made faces at Bates behind the man's back.

Claudia, the eighteen-year-old daughter, meticulously coifed and dressed, seemed to have eyes for no one but Mr. Emery. Katherine had been aware of the interest he stirred among females, but had never witnessed quite such a display of charm for his benefit. It amused her to think what a go-around Claudia would have if she ever snared Mr. Emery. Katherine wagered her felicity wouldn't last a week.

Eighteen guests arrived for Saturday's dinner. Besides a few friends from town, the Lannings were present. Katherine felt disappointment that Christopher was off to visit one of his college friends for a fortnight. But she brightened when Mr. Lanning remarked how lovely she looked in her dove gray, and Mrs. Lanning admired its rosettes and organza overskirt.

"We all went to the dressmaker in town the day after the date of the party was set," Katherine said. "See Mrs. Emery? She decided on that lace-covered silk. And don't you think Aunt Elsie's choice of dark gray sets off her silver hair?"

"Yes, indeed," Mr. Lanning agreed. "The whole Emery household looks handsome tonight."

"And black tie and tails suit Jerard wonderfully," Mrs. Lanning said.

Claudia joined the group already assembled in the drawing room. Her low-cut purple gown displayed a bountifully endowed figure. Katherine supposed it was all part of that magic age of coming out, but still it seemed daring.

When the group walked into the dining room for dinner, Theodore was paired with Katherine. A head shorter, he tried to make up the difference by standing up shock straight.Katherine found herself seated in the middle of the long table. Mrs. Emery and her son sat at some distance from her at either end, so she relaxed and drank in the beauty of her surroundings. The crystal goblets and silverware reflected the light of the chandelier. Candles glowed on either side of a silver epergne overflowing with colorful fruit and hothouse flowers. Dinner opened with Consommé à la Victoria, then progressed to Salade d'Homard Monté. For a few moments Katherine closed her eyes, savoring the delicately seasoned lobster in the salad.

Mrs. von Weber turned to her host. "If your business is run as well as your home, it should be a grand success."

"Thank you, Mrs. von Weber. The credit for our home goes to my mother. As to a business venture, I hope to do more of that with your husband."

"It's true, I'm in charge of the house," Mrs. Emery said, "but the estate is Jerard's responsibility, and it's running so well I believe he's ready for more challenges. He has a business head like his grandfather."

"A head for business is important," Mr. von Weber said, "but if the last shareholders' meeting is any indication, it will take more than that to unite those men. Strong leadership is required." He took a large bite of salad, then added, "I think of my old country before Bismarck arrived to take charge."

"What do you mean?" Mrs. Emery asked.

Mr. von Weber addressed his answer to the entire table. "Groups in Germany warred for years. Centuries, I might say. At one time Germany was divided into more than three hundred virtually sovereign states. Even when the German Confederation formed in 1815, the structure was loosely bound, and the alliance uncomfortable."

He cleared his throat. "It took a man like Bismarck to bring about a united country. I'll grant he used 'blood and iron' tactics—like we heard about these last months in the Franco-Prussian War—but we are pleased Bismarck united Germany at last." His hand thumped the table to emphasize his point. "With your Civil War so recently ended, I'm sure you understand my sentiments."

Mr. von Weber turned to face his host. "It takes a forceful leader to unite strong factions. I believe you, Mr. Emery, demonstrate that quality. Before this visit, I was against making changes in the mill, but now I am convinced you'll make a success of the venture." He raised his glass. "I think this is an appropriate occasion to announce my backing for the mill."

Jerard rose at once. "This is indeed gratifying news. Thank you, sir! A toast everyone." He raised his glass high and the assembly followed suit.

After this, a jovial mood took hold of the gathering, each guest talking animatedly with his neighbor.

By the time dessert was served, conversation shifted to family backgrounds. Mrs. Lanning turned to the guest of honor. "Mr. von Weber, your name has interested me. You share the same surname with the great composer Carl Maria von Weber. Perchance, is he on your family tree?"

"You're not the first person to ask," he said, laughing. "No, we are not so fortunate, although my wife would love to claim the relation. All she would need is a little help from her imagination."

"Mr. von Weber! You malign my imagination so," said his wife.

"My dear, you know you've wished many a time we could boast such a blood connection."

"Of course! His operas were famous. Seeing how I love a good singing voice, I'd have had a special rapport with him."

She turned to her host. "Mr. Emery, you have an exceptional speaking voice. Do you sing as well?"

"If I answer truthfully," he said, smiling, "I might incriminate myself."

"Now, Jerard." Mrs. Lanning raised her hand, admonishing him. "We should inform Mrs. von Weber you have a wonderful voice. It's a shame you don't use it more often."

Claudia leaned forward. "Please sing for us before we leave. Could you do so after dinner?"

Jerard's eyebrow arched. "Mrs. Lanning, see what you've started?"

"We haven't heard you for so long, it would be a real pleasure."

"Oh, please could you?" Claudia pleaded.

Jerard leaned back in his chair and surveyed the assembled guests. "Well, I would need an accompanist."

After a moment's silence Mr. Lanning said, "Katherine, would you try?"

Sudden warmth rushed to Katherine's cheeks. She'd been enjoying the conversation with the detachment of a spectator. Her eyes scanned the faces of the guests on the other side of the table.

They smiled, encouraging her to accept.

"Well, Katherine?" Mr. Emery asked.

She turned to him. Did she imagine a skeptical look in his dark eyes? She well knew his demanding standards. However, she had enjoyed accompanying various students in her teacher's studio. The excitement at performing made her rise to the bait. "I'd be willing, if the music isn't too difficult."

Mr. Emery regarded her speculatively, then addressed the table. "All right then. After dinner we'll retire to the drawing room."

Chapter 7

Katherine followed the dinner party as they walked leisurely into the drawing room, yet she noticed an undercurrent of excitement running through the group. Mrs. Emery had instructed the butler to rearrange the seating so everyone could see and hear her son's performance.

Mr. Emery disengaged himself from Claudia's clinging arm and motioned Katherine to his side at the piano. "This songbook is good for my range. Do you think you can play any of these?"

She glanced through several of the numbers. "Yes, I think I can."

"Good. I'll choose two or three." He scanned the index. "I want to start with a good melody—rather slow—then finish with something rousing. Here are two good ones." He pointed to the titles he had chosen.

"I'm familiar with both." Katherine hesitated. "But I can't guarantee a perfect performance, not having practiced with you."

He smiled for the first time. "Don't be overly concerned. If you miss a few notes, just keep the rhythm going." He continued to thumb through the book. "Wait, I've an idea. Can you play this one?" At her nod, he said, "It's humorous and will get our audience in a mood to expect good plain entertainment rather than a polished performance." He handed her the songbook, then reached back to the piano for another copy. "All right then. This one first, then the other two."

Katherine slid onto the piano bench, arranged the music then looked up at Mr. Emery. Her stomach fluttered nervously, but she was determined not to embarrass him or herself.

Mr. Emery scanned the assembled group, waiting until all eyes were on him, then cleared his throat with an air of importance.

"To satisfy the demanding musical taste of our company this evening, we have imported an acclaimed soloist. He is from Germany, the homeland of our honored guests." He bowed to Mr. and Mrs. von Weber.

"May I now present Wilhelm von Schnitzenheimer." With a grand flourish, he flung his arm out to an imaginary gentleman at his side. Then he stepped to the spot he'd just indicated, adopted the stance of a great operatic singer, and continued in a German accent. "Ladies and gentlemen, I vil now zing for you some beloved zongs of my native land. First, a zelection to give a little amusement." He gave his accompanist an exaggerated nod.

The short ditty of a song lived up to its reputation for humor. Mr. Emery sang it with a lilt, exaggerating its wit. The von Webers smiled broadly while others tittered and chuckled. One of the men guffawed at the punch line, which set off a reaction of contagious laughter and enthusiastic clapping.

The soloist held up his hands. "Please, please, you do me too much honor." He swelled out his chest in a mock-dignified manner. "Next, I vil zing a love zong for zee ladies."

Katherine stared at Mr. Emery, fascinated by the chameleon-like change in his personality. She had never seen him be humorous or put himself out to be entertaining. With effort she focused her attention on the next song. The accompaniment was simple so she listened for nuances in his interpretation, trying to complement them. The slow, sonorous melody brought out the rich timbre of his voice. It was something of a shock for Katherine to hear such an expressive, resonant sound come from someone she so little admired.

Silence hung in the room after the last note. Then the company broke out in fervent applause.

Jerard bowed low. For a moment he dropped his impersonation of von Schnitzenheimer and simply said, "Thank you."

After the applause died away, he adroitly stepped back into character. "My last zelection vil be a patriotic zong vitch I dedicate to the land of my birth." He gave Katherine an emphatic nod and she followed his lead with a spirited introduction.

The song's rhythmic beat prompted smiles from the audience, several keeping time with their feet. The exuberant gusto of Mr. Emery's rendition prompted Katherine to play with an abandon she seldom exhibited. Both of them ended the song with a dramatic flourish, evoking immediate applause.

"Bravo!" cried Mr. Lanning. He stood and others followed his example.

Jerard broke into a wide smile, turned toward Katherine, and gestured her to stand. She rose, all smiles, and curtsied.

Then everyone started talking at once. Claudia and Mrs. von Weber came to congratulate Jerard while Mrs. Emery stepped up to Katherine. "My dear, you were marvelous. I am very proud of you."

Katherine felt her face flush in response to Mrs. Emery's effusiveness.

Mr. Lanning joined them and put his arm around his pupil's shoulder. "See, didn't I say you could do it?" He gave her a little squeeze. "I will admit, however, that I didn't expect such a thrilling performance. Katherine, you are a gifted accompanist."

"Thank you, both of you," she said, laughing. "I was rather surprised at the outcome myself. Fortunately, Mr. Emery chose songs that were not too difficult."

Singly or in small groups the guests came up to compliment the host and his accompanist. After the last of them drifted away, Mr. Emery turned to Katherine. "I don't know what you were afraid of. You played exceptionally well. I'd have been hard pressed to find a better accompanist."

"Thank you, sir. It was a privilege playing for you."

"Well then, we'll do it again sometime."

He turned to the group nearest him. Katherine was left staring at his back, at a loss what to do next. Then she noticed Theodore sitting alone and walked over to join him.

Mrs. Emery announced that tables would be set up for a game of contract. Katherine saw her lean down to Mrs. von Weber and ask if she didn't think it was about time their two young people retired for the night. Mrs. von Weber immediately agreed and walked over to Teddy.

"Aw, it's not late yet," he blurted.

"Teddy, keep your voice down. Tomorrow will be a full day, what with going to church, traveling home, and all. Mind me now and go up to your room." She looked at his disgruntled countenance and said, "Maybe you can read awhile to settle yourself."

"Do I have to? What about Claudia? Why does she get to stay?"

"Claudia is older, and besides, she is engaged right now." Her eyes glanced at her daughter, talking animatedly to Mr. Emery. "Yes, you must go."

"Can't I stay fifteen more minutes? Katherine just sat down to talk with me."

Mrs. von Weber sighed, glanced at Mrs. Emery then said with firmness, "Theodore, do I need to call your father?"

He looked at her, then at his father. "Oh, all right!" Slowly, he raised himself from the chair and scuffed toward the doorway.

Katherine saw Mrs. Emery motion her in the same direction and, with reluctance, she followed suit. The evening had been such an unexpected pleasure.

Teddy shuffled across the hall, mumbling to himself about being treated like a child and always missing out on the fun. Katherine couldn't help sympathizing. She didn't want the evening to end either.

They both paused at the foot of the stairs. Teddy eyed her. "You know, we should do something to finish this night off right." He looked up at the banister. "Dare me to ride down that thing?"

Katherine, sympathetic to a point, told him that was out of the question.

"Why?"

"It isn't proper."

"Who cares about being proper?"

She searched for another reason. "Well, you might fall and harm yourself."

"Say! You're talking to Teddy the Terrific. I *don't* fall."

"But if something should happen, Mrs. Emery would hold me responsible."

"So now it comes out. You're scared of the old lady. Have you forgotten I'm company? You're supposed to please your guests, remember?" His eyes narrowed with a sly look. "And don't forget, my dad is backing your—uh, Mr. Emery. You want my parents to think I didn't have a good time?"

Katherine looked around for help. The hall was empty. If only Bates would put in an appearance.

"Aw, you're a poor sport," Teddy said. "I'm doing it anyway." He ran up the stairs.

Katherine glanced in the direction of the drawing room. No one could be seen. She gazed up. The banister looked long and high. How could he think of doing such a thing? What would happen if he fell? A potted palm stood at the bottom of the banister. She stationed herself between it and the newel post. Her hands clenched the polished wood of the rail.

Teddy hopped up and swung one leg over. He positioned himself rather clumsily, with a devil-may-care swagger. Then loosening his grip, he started to slide. "Get out of my way!"

Katherine held her breath.

Halfway down, he lost his balance, one of his arms flailing out. Katherine stretched up to help, but as he toppled, he grabbed at her to break his fall.

"Ow!" she cried out, as he landed heavily against her. Simultaneously, a palm stalk stabbed her in the back.

The palm's Chinese porcelain pot teetered an instant and then, with the weight of both their bodies, fell over on the marble floor with a thump with Katherine and Teddy in a heap. He tried to scramble up, but his shoe caught on Katherine's skirt, and she heard a rip as he tripped and fell. "Drat you!" he exploded.

Katherine felt herself flush hot, so angry she couldn't find words to speak. She tried to right herself as several guests rushed into the hallway, Mr. Emery striding at the fore.

"Katherine!" His dark eyes blazed at her.

Sharp embarrassment replaced her anger.

Claudia stepped to his side, and Katherine saw disdain in her look. Glancing around, she viewed the scene through the other girl's eyes—an overturned potted palm, dirt scattered over the floor, and herself, a big puddle on the white marble floor. Her heart sank.

With a quick motion, she lifted her skirt out of the way and, rising, saw Mrs. Emery at the drawing room door, stiff and foreboding.

Bates appeared. Walking briskly to them, without delay he righted the potted palm. "There now. We'll have this cleared right away. Only an accident, I'm sure."

Mr. Emery had opened his mouth as if to say something damning, then apparently changed his mind. "Yes," he said, making an effort to regain his composure. "It looks as if the young people had a little mishap." Turning to the company with arms wide, he gestured them into the drawing room. He glanced back at the mess, then at Katherine. "We'll get to the bottom of this tomorrow."

Katherine's insides twisted. Grabbing her skirts, she ran up the stairs without a backward glance at Teddy. Not until she gained her room did she look at her dress. Dirt smeared an entire panel and the side hem was torn. Her beautiful party dress. Waves of humiliation flooded her as she removed it gingerly. And this was supposed to have been a distinguished occasion.

Mr. Emery's face had been livid.

And Mrs. Emery, what would she say tomorrow? Why, oh why, did this have to happen?

Chapter 8

Half awake, Katherine raised her head off the pillow and gazed out the window. A blue gray sky. What day was it? She rubbed her eyes.

Then the whole weekend swept over her: Saturday night's humiliation and the Sunday morning visit by Mrs. Emery. Dressing for Sunday breakfast, she had heard a knock on her door—not the quiet tap of the maid. "Come in," she said.

Mrs. Emery stepped inside. "I want to talk with you, Katherine."

Katherine quickly offered her benefactress a chair.

"I would have spoken with you last night if I hadn't had the responsibility of the guests. The incident with Theodore was most unfortunate, particularly after all we had done to make this a memorable occasion. I cannot express my mortification." Mrs. Emery cleared her throat. "However, after a night's sleep and some reflection, I decided to hear your side of the story. You've always been truthful."

With trepidation Katherine related what had occurred.

A long moment of silence hung in the air before Mrs. Emery spoke. "I see now the difficulty of the situation. It is hard to curtail a strong-willed boy, a guest who's bent on doing something irresponsible. But of course, you should not have been involved in the first place."

"I know," Katherine said. "I'm very sorry. Was—was there something I could have done differently?"

"You should have gone upstairs immediately. If Theodore had determined to behave in an uncivilized manner, you should have left him to his just desserts. By remaining, you implicated yourself in the trouble."

Katherine's insides tightened at the reprimand.

"In the future I trust you'll be a wiser girl." Mrs. Emery rose. "For now, we'll consider the matter closed. Breakfast will be served in a few minutes. Please, be on time."

Katherine had somehow made it through the morning greetings. Not as much note was taken of the previous night's mishap as she'd dreaded. In fact, Mr. Emery, engrossed in his conversation with Mr. von Weber, didn't even acknowledge her. The process of attending church, sharing a final dinner with the guests, and speeding them on their way proceeded without a hitch.

Katherine rolled over in bed and a faint smile played over her lips, remembering the departure. Claudia had waited and waited for Mr. Emery to assist her into the carriage. First the driver offered his aid. Claudia declined, saying she needed to find something in her reticule. Then her father started to help her, but Mrs. von Weber reached out an unobtrusive hand to hold his arm with a telling look in Mr. Emery's direction. Mr. von Weber muttered something about the silliness of women.

Finally, Mr. Emery noticed Claudia. When he offered his help, she took his outstretched hand, artfully lifting her skirt to step up into the carriage.

Katherine dutifully waved good-bye, but as she climbed the steps to the house, inwardly admitted relief in seeing the guests go who had earlier been so anticipated.

Now all that was behind her. It was Monday morning and a new day. She flung back the blue coverlet, sat up in bed, and stretched. Life should settle back to normal.

ꕥ

The Emery household ran on a strict schedule, especially Katherine's schooling. This she had come to appreciate, not so much because of the regularity it imposed, but she'd adopted Mr. Lanning's philosophy that regular exposure to learning enabled her to wrest from the world's fund of knowledge new discoveries which made each day interesting. A casual observer might have thought her life dull because of its predictable nature; instead each day held new vistas and insights because of the very discipline placed upon it.

Mornings with Mr. Lanning were a special joy. He appreciated all branches of learning and communicated this to Katherine. She loved sitting in his book-lined study, poring over maps of places he'd visited, asking about Germany, Italy, France, and of course, Paris and the Louvre.

The same joy extended to afternoons on the piano. This particular Monday held a special interest. Katherine hurried to the instrument with more than her usual eagerness. She hadn't touched it since Saturday's triumph and was pleased to discover Mr. Emery's songbooks just where she'd left them.

She played the accompaniments once more. A warm glow pulsed through her as she relived that evening's performance. Thinking back, she knew it wasn't only playing the piano that had thrilled her. It was accompanying a wonderful voice, the memory of it a beautiful undercurrent to her otherwise troubled thoughts of the weekend.

Here, a strange dichotomy developed. As she practiced, she began imagining that voice not as Mr. Emery's, but instead belonging to his funny German impersonation. In fact, the two men became quite separate: the charming Mr. von Schnitzenheimer, someone altogether different from the disagreeable Mr. Emery. As she played, she imagined she accompanied the humorous foreigner instead of the master of the house.

In coming days, whenever she knew she was quite alone, she amused herself staging conversations with "the Count," as she began to think of the German character. She imagined uproariously funny times as they performed together and, in her flight of fancy, the Count's peculiar mannerisms became but the outer shell for a warm, vibrant heart.

Katherine discovered that Saturday night duo had sparked—then ignited—something in both her music and her heretofore-quiet personality. She found herself displaying a growing flair for the dramatic and a budding sense of humor. Both were born—it seemed—out of nothing, but such was the offspring of that one evening's entertainment. Something in her soul had been captured, energized.

As another birthday came and went, she felt herself blossoming. Over the weeks, she tried other songs, imagining how the Count would perform them. Humming along, she accompanied herself. If the song struck her fancy but the words were in German or some other unfamiliar language, she would sing nonsense syllables. The language was of her own making, foreign to every ear including her own. But she hardly cared; she reveled in the sound of music for its own sake.

Toward the end of the summer on a weekday afternoon Katherine amused herself with just such a pastime, singing and accompanying herself in an uninhibited manner. Absorbed in her music, she was completely oblivious to her surroundings.

☙

Jerard Emery's plan to renovate the mill had taken a decided turn for the good. The stockholders voted in favor of his proposal. Subsequently, he applied to the bank for a loan. Now, entering the tree-lined avenue to the house astride Taggart, he smiled. The deal had been satisfactorily concluded and he felt both enormously stimulated and free from the mental encumbrances that usually occupied him. Mother should be the first to hear his good news.

No one appeared when he entered the back door of the house. Where was everyone? But he heard unusual sounds coming from the drawing room. A singing or warbling, he couldn't tell. He walked quietly down the hall and stopped outside the doorway. For some moments he was content to listen, unwilling to interrupt the ardent songstress, whomever it might be.

Could it be Katherine? But she was demure, almost prim. This girl's voice held the quality of a bird in flight, the high tones sweet and lyrical.

He folded his arms, listening, half amused yet strangely transfixed.

It must be Katherine. Wasn't it at the von Weber dinner party that the girl's musical gift had struck him? Since then, however, so much had vied for his attention, he had thought little about it. But now he heard a delightful sound: impulsive, ardent. He stepped around the corner, careful to remain undetected.

Just then the singing and the girl attacked the piano with a force that suddenly reminded Jerard of someone else. His brother Evan. Her white dress was the color of Evan's white shirt when he would remove his coat to play with vigor. Both had the same dark hair with a trace of auburn. For some moments, Jerard saw his brother playing. First, there had been a sharp pain of remembrance, but that eased into a recognition of someone dear, of a brother he had loved. Somehow, the picture before him comforted him. He stood listening. Then the image of his brother faded and all he saw was Katherine.

Her fervor mellowed and her slender hands and arms danced lightly over the keys. She began singing again. The skirt of her white muslin dress draped gracefully over the piano bench.

Jerard stood very still. A curious feeling welled up inside him. Filled with something he did not stop to identify, he strode into the room clapping his hands. "Bravo!"

Katherine rose with a start, one hand flying to her throat.

"What a display of talent. Bully for you!" Jerard leaned over the instrument to examine the music. "Ah, the words are German. The piece would be stronger in its original language." He smiled. "Yet, I daresay, the song has rarely been performed with more feeling than you now displayed. What were you singing? Utter nonsense?"

"Well, yes." Katherine's face reddened. "I didn't realize anyone was listening. Otherwise, I—I wouldn't have—practiced in such a manner. Usually, no one is around this time of day."

"Ah!" He was enjoying her most becoming blush, her discomfiture. He felt energized. "So, at this hour the house is yours, not to be intruded upon by another mortal?"

"Why, of course this is your home and you can return whenever you wish. I—I just wouldn't have sung—if I'd known anyone was listening. I know you like a quiet, dignified household."

"Yes, most of the time I do. And Mother certainly concurs. But on occasion I don't mind a little life." He bowed.

Katherine's blush deepened.

"Don't be embarrassed. You look as if I'd caught you doing something improper, but your singing and playing have a refreshing boldness. We have enough timid mice around this house." He hit the piano with an open hand. "I'm tired to death of everyone tiptoeing around, afraid of arousing my ire. In fact, sometimes this place is dreadfully dull."

He continued in a more business-like tone. "As I said, I liked what I heard. Your voice shows promise. You already study piano. I think you should add voice to your studies. Of course, it would be necessary for you to take up German as well. No self-respecting vocalist would sing without knowing the language. Schubert's lieder are unsurpassed."

"I already study French with Mr. Lanning."

"Well, add German to your list of accomplishments. I know singing in Italian is the vogue now; however, we never know when the von Webers will be houseguests again. It would flatter them to hear you sing in their native tongue. I'll speak to Mother tonight. She naturally has the responsibility of such matters. She can speak to Mr. Lanning, and they can decide whom to engage for you."

Katherine's hand clutched her skirt. "I have a full schedule of studies, sir. I really wonder if I could fit in German—or anything else, for that matter. My present French is only passable, and I need to devote quite a lot of effort to passing examinations."

"Nonsense. Talent such as yours is too good to waste." He wondered—. "How old are you?"

"Seventeen, sir."

"Well then, there's not much time, but still enough to do justice to what I have in mind if you work hard." His mind was already envisioning the deed *un fait accompli*. "I'll speak to Mother today."

Katherine said nothing, her back ramrod straight.

Jerard dismissed the stiff manner. "Yes, I'll take care of it right away." He touched his head in a brief salute, "Good day, Miss Edmond," then turned and strode out the drawing room.

Chapter 9

Spent from running on the forest path, Katherine dropped down on a large log. Sitting quietly, she willed herself to notice her surroundings. Afternoon sun filtered through the trees, dotting the ground with golden specks. A thrush trilled in the branch above her. Taking a deep breath, Katherine closed her eyes.

Before many moments her eyes opened again, staring, her mind attaching itself to her problem like a magnet to iron.

Who did Mr. Emery think he was anyway? He'd paid little notice of her all this time in his home, and now he suddenly felt called upon to manage her life—as if he had any idea what was best.

Her heel dug into the earth. This afternoon she'd been immersed in practicing, when all of a sudden, he'd appeared. Hadn't offered an apology when a blind man could see how upset she was. Then before she could think what to say, he'd walked out the door.

Her lips pressed together. She'd noticed it before, this way Mr. Emery had of treating others. If things didn't go his way, he'd get domineering. In her case, if she didn't comply with his wishes, a confrontation was inevitable. He'd be angry—not because he cared a twit about her, but because *his* plan had been rejected.

Her father came to mind. Now, why did he crop up at this moment? This had happened other times when Mr. Emery upset her. Katherine's eyes narrowed. Were the two men so similar?

Father had considered his own desires before his family. The way he treated them was proof. The mere memory made her feel hot all over. Wherever he now lived, she hoped he was having a hard time of it, abandoning them as he had.

For some minutes she sat, miserable.

Katherine pulled a hanky out of her pocket and pressed it to her eyes. And, she needed a good blow, as Aunt Elsie would say.

How was Mr. Emery like her father? He certainly looked out for himself. Then her mind went blank. She sighed. Oh! It was too much to figure out, particularly when she was upset. She closed her eyes a few moments, trying to think what to do.

She supposed if she felt this strongly, she shouldn't undertake the extra lessons. But a confrontation with Mr. Emery was the last thing she wanted. She stared hard at the forest path. The Lanning's home wasn't too far away. Could he help her?

She stood at once. Mr. Lanning was wisdom itself. Maybe he was home.

Relieved to have decided on a course of action, Katherine brushed any dirt from the back of her dress and now with purpose in her steps, hurried down the path.

ℜ

Christopher knelt in the backyard beside his grandfather and caught up a fistful of soil, inhaling its earthy aroma. "Even this dirt smells satisfying—rich and musky." He gazed over the yard. A mass of magenta phloxes bloomed nearby. And in the direct sunlight bunches of black-eyed Susans. "I can't tell you how restful this all looks."

Mr. Lanning leaned over and grasped Christopher's shoulder. "I'm happy the place looks that way. Your grandmother and I are glad to have you here summers, we miss you when you're at school."

"I haven't said anything till now, but I learned a lot more than art this year."

"Oh?"

Christopher sat back on his heels. "Yes. I finally learned to appreciate your wisdom. After all these years, saw it running through my life like a strong, steady river."

Mr. Lanning's eyes crinkled affectionately. "So what happened that brought about such a conclusion?"

Christopher repositioned himself, crossing his legs. He knew his smile was sheepish. "Actually, this involves a little confession on my part."

"Oh?" Mr. Lanning settled on the grass beside him.

"I've wanted to tell you this for some time." His grandfather waited while Christopher searched how to begin. "My first years at school—away from home for the first time—I didn't feel the normal constraints. Just had a good time. I drifted from one thing to another, and for a while I'm afraid I forgot why I went to school." He picked up a trowel and traced its tip through the dirt.

"Then this year an incident occurred that started me thinking. It was back in the fall. It had rained all day, so I felt I needed to get out awhile after it stopped. I left our rooming house with two of my friends. On the road in front of us was a first-year student. He had a reputation for being a real scholar and one of those sensitive types. One of my friends wanted some fun, nudged me, and on the spur of the moment hatched a plan. I didn't say too much, just went along.

"We came up from behind, walked with him a ways, and without seeming to forced him to the side of the road. Then we started shoving each other, all supposedly in good fun. You know, after a rain there's always mud. Well, it all went according to plan. We *accidentally* shoved him, and he landed in the muck.

"He looked up, didn't say a thing. But I'll never forget his eyes as we laughed. I saw hurt in them and felt mean for probably the first time in my life. We'd cooked up pranks like that countless times—a lot of tomfoolery—but this time it felt different.

"I don't know why, but a picture of you and Grandma came to mind. I saw you at the round table in the sitting room drinking tea and eating sandwiches and cake, and I remembered all the good, clean fun we had together. And saw that what I'd been doing—poking fun at that first year student—would have disappointed you. Right then, I helped the young man up and told my friends to go on without me.

"Lying in bed that night I realized how much foolishness I'd been involved in over the years. Somehow that incident made me see this. As I lay there, one of the verses you had me memorize as a boy came to mind, the one in the first chapter of Proverbs. 'The fear of the Lord is the beginning of wisdom.' You emphasized that the word *fear* meant awe or reverence. It struck me for the first time how little I reverenced God. Instead I was always thinking about myself and the next good time." Christopher paused. "Know what I mean?"

"Yes, son."

"You've give me so much, Grandpa—I felt ashamed. As a result, I began working hard at school for the first time."

Mr. Lanning reached over and shook his grandson's knee. "Christopher, thank you for telling me. You know, I've tried to obey God over the years, to share His truths with my family as each day unfolded, as Deuteronomy says, to 'talk of them when thou sittest in thine house, and when thou walkest by the way....'"

His gaze lifted to the forest, then looking back at Christopher, he added, "Since you've been away at school, I've more or less adopted Katherine as a granddaughter. And been teaching her as I did you."

Christopher sat quietly. In the peace of the backyard he heard the quiet buzz of bees. "You're very fond of her, aren't you?"

"Almost more than I can say. Since we have no blood granddaughter, Katherine's taken the place of one."

"What do the Emerys think of that?"

"They've let me do what I think best. In ordinary circumstances they might have said more, but you must remember Katherine was, in a sense, foisted upon them by George Emery's will. And while I admire much of what Mrs. Emery has done for Katherine, I don't believe she's taken the girl to her heart."

Christopher shook his head. "And with Jerard's high-handedness, she wouldn't get much kindness from that quarter."

"I believe you're right. So because the Emerys give her little affection, your grandmother and I try to fill in for her family. Not that we seek to undermine her loyalty to the Emerys, but where there's been an obvious need, we try to fill it." Mr. Lanning smiled. "I will have to say she's noticed a fundamental difference in outlook between the Emerys and ourselves."

Christopher laughed. "I'll bet! Would it be their orientation toward the material instead of the spiritual?"

"That puts it about right. While I've been careful not to attack the Emerys' philosophy of life, I have encouraged her to make a more diligent study of the Bible than they feel necessary."

"I take it she's a good student."

"She is." Mr. Lanning's smile widened. "Her mother emphasized the importance of study, and prepared her young heart for a real love and dependence on our heavenly Father. Whatever I've said has fallen on receptive ears." Mr. Lanning raised himself to his knees, then, reaching for his hoe, rose slowly. He regarded his grandson speculatively. "You know, from the beginning Katherine has been a lovable girl. Reserved, but with charming little ways. Someday she will capture the heart of some observant young man."

"She's not of age yet."

"Maybe, but she's maturing. I see her flowering out." Grandfather cupped his palms over the hoe's handle, leaning on it. "I don't know what it is—maybe she's more free in her speech or manner—but something's there."

☙

"Hello-o-o!" Katherine called as she ran out of the woods. What a relief to see the Lannings in their yard.

Christopher jumped up from his crouched position and stood beside his grandfather.

"What a surprise to see you!" Out of breath, Katherine extended her hands to Christopher. "You actually weed flowers? I thought all you did was paint them."

Christopher laughed. "I'm a man of many talents. Know me long enough and you'll be simply amazed. Say, I planned on visiting you later this evening—but it's good to see you now. That dress suits you wonderfully."

"How nice of you to say so." Katherine stepped over to slip her hand through Mr. Lanning's arm, her lips widening into a smile. "I came for only a short visit. You know, Christopher, at this hour I'm usually in the midst of *grueling* homework—" She looked up fondly at her tutor. "—not that I don't love every minute of it."

Mr. Lanning returned her look. "Glad you like your grueling studies. And it's good to see you in good spirits. If young women knew the particular charm they wield when they smile, we'd be living in a more gracious world." Mr. Lanning nodded at their weeding. "We're about finished here. Could I prevail upon you to join us for tea?"

"I'd like nothing better, but I've already promised Aunt Elsie. Tomorrow?"

"You're always welcome."

"Thank you. But, I do need to talk with you." She released his arm. "Do you have a few minutes?" He nodded and she continued, "It has to do with something that happened earlier this afternoon." Almost tripping over her words, she explained the situation with Mr. Emery. "... and he means to speak with his mother about my studies, then consult you about adding voice lessons and German." Her voice had a pleading tone. "Could you please convince her it's not in my best interest to start anything new?"

"I'm not sure I understand." Mr. Lanning rubbed his forehead. "Mr. Emery liked your singing well enough to suggest lessons?"

"I suppose you could put it that way."

"I would take that as a compliment. I don't see the problem."

"The problem is Mr. Emery dictating what he wants without considering what I think."

Christopher chuckled. "I see Jerard is up to his old tactics, although I've never seen our usually calm and composed Katherine upset by them."

"Little do you know how I really feel."

"I can guess by the way you're giving off sparks."

"Giving off sparks?" Suddenly Katherine's face scrunched up. "Am I overreacting?"

"Oh, I wouldn't worry about it." Christopher grinned. "Jerard has a way of bringing it out in people."

"What do you think, Mr. Lanning?"

"About voice and German?" He paused. "To tell the truth, I thought you'd rather fancy voice lessons."

"I don't think it's just the lessons themselves, Grandfather," Christopher said.

"I see." Mr. Lanning's eyes narrowed. "Well, Katherine, Mrs. Emery and I will weigh all the factors. We want the best for your future."

"I do appreciate that, but I also believe adding two new studies would be more than I could handle right now. Truly."

"Then I'm sure something can be worked out."

Relief flooded Katherine, and she suddenly felt the necessity to soften what she'd expressed earlier. "I hope I didn't say too much about Mr. Emery. I really am grateful for everything the Emerys do for me." She reached up and gave Mr. Lanning a quick kiss on the cheek.

"Hey! Am I next?" Christopher asked.

"That's all for today." Katherine deliberately made her tone impish. "I've just remembered Aunt Elsie is expecting me." She turned as if to leave.

Christopher reached quickly for her arm. "I'm planning another painting jaunt tomorrow. Want to come?"

"Of course—if Mrs. Emery will let me."

Chapter 10

A few days later, Mrs. Emery led the household to the back sitting room after the evening meal. Since the von Weber dinner, Katherine's status had been elevated so that she now accompanied the rest of the family to either the sitting room or, if company was present, the drawing room.

The rose-toned sitting room was cozy by contrast with the formal rooms at the front of the mansion. Chairs were large and generously stuffed; a couch upholstered in muted brown velvet dominated one end of the room. Mrs. Emery walked over to this and sat in her accustomed place. Aunt Elsie took her usual comfortable armchair at one end of the couch and Jerard took his on the opposite side. A large, low table served as hub around which sofa and chairs were grouped.

When Katherine was first allowed to join the family after dinner, she had chosen a seat opposite Mrs. Emery—to keep a little distance between herself and her benefactress—but the lady of the house had directed Katherine to sit on the couch near Aunt Elsie, provided she sat quietly. Mrs. Emery disliked reaching across the table to serve Katherine, and this way her ward could keep Aunt Elsie entertained while she herself talked with her son.

Bates entered and carefully arranged the coffee service on the table. Everyone settled back except Aunt Elsie who kept shifting in her chair.

"Katherine, help Aunt with a cushion," Mrs. Emery said.

After assisting the aunt and seating herself, Katherine caught Mr. Emery's intent gaze, his dark eyes pinning her like some insect on a mounting board. She quickly looked down at her folded hands.

"Thank you, Bates," Mrs. Emery said, reaching for the coffee service.

Jerard leaned forward in his chair. "Katherine, I did not hear the outcome of the proposal I made for your studies. What has been arranged?"

The dreaded topic hadn't been alluded to at dinner. When each subject closed, Katherine feared the introduction of the new and had felt on tenterhooks the entire meal. Now here it was. She cleared her throat. "It was decided to begin voice this fall, but to— postpone—the German."

Jerard's eyebrows lifted. "When something like *this* is postponed, it usually dies a quiet death, unless someone forcibly resurrects it." He turned to his mother. "What's this about Katherine not studying German? I thought it clear she should."

His mother handed Aunt Elsie her coffee. "Mr. Lanning and I talked at length and in the end decided to honor Katherine's desire in not taking on the extra study. After all, it does mean quite a bit more work." She turned to fill Katherine's cup.

Jerard looked at Katherine. "So you had the deciding vote. I wouldn't have thought it possible in this household." He sat back in his chair. "While Italian has been the language of choice for song, German is coming into its own. In fact, much of the great song literature is being written in the language." He paused, his tone clipped. "Studying voice without it would almost be a waste of time."

Katherine felt herself blush. "I believe I might try a good number of songs in French. Since it's the language I am studying, that would seem a logical choice. And, of course, I can always sing in English."

"Ha! It's hardly logical to omit the most pure and elevated lieder from one's musical repertoire. No one has surpassed Schubert or Schumann."

"I suppose I could learn a few songs in German."

"And not learn the language itself? Mouthing meaningless syllables or at most learning snippets of words and phrases? Is that how you intend to appreciate the great song masters?" He leaned forward. "Listen, Katherine. You are young and have spent your life in circumscribed circles. You should heed your elder's advice." His hand cut the air impatiently. "You know little of the world."

"That might be true. I'm sorry, sir, but as to following the advice of those older than myself, I am content to do what Mr. Lanning and your mother prescribe."

"I think, my dear," Aunt Elsie said, "the person Jerard is referring to as your elder is himself. He would like you to take *his* advice." She leaned toward her nephew. "The von Webers have influenced you too much. Let the child be, for goodness sakes!"

"Aunt," he said, "if, for the rest of her life, Katherine decides to live in small town surroundings like ours, she might not need the extra polish of German lieder. However, should she move to a large city such as New York, her chances of gainful employment would be enhanced if she took on the extra study. Since you never had to make your way in the world, you would know little of such things." He took a quick swallow of coffee then set down his cup. "I'm surprised, Mother, you didn't impress that point on Mr. Lanning."

Mrs. Emery put down her cup as well. "We discussed it, Jerard, but since Katherine's musical study is mainly instrumental, her preference was the deciding factor."

Jerard turned quickly to Katherine. "So it comes back to you. You'll reconsider, of course."

Katherine let her cup rest on her lap, not daring to lift it, lest her trembling hands be noticed. "Sir, I have considered the matter and see your point, but do not believe I could add

German to my present studies."

"*Could* is hardly the right choice of word. *Would not* is more accurate." Jerard's voice bore down on her. "You know I'm right, but are too stubborn to admit it."

The accusation caught Katherine off guard. In her confusion she couldn't think of a reply.

"I see your mind is made up. If you elect to remain narrow in your course of study, then I wash my hands of you and your curriculum." He gave her one last look, reached for a newspaper and snapped it open.

Every cup sat still in its saucer, the room quiet. Then, with forced cheerfulness, Mrs. Emery said, "Well, I think that's settled then." She turned slowly to her ward. "Now, Katherine, I wish to discuss an article I saw yesterday in *Lady Godey's*. It pictured an indoor garden in one of the most beautiful glass containers I've seen. Since terrariums are all the vogue, I thought you and Mr. Lanning could take a botany lesson and devise one for our center dining room window."

☙

Relieved to be retiring, Katherine climbed the stairs to her room. Halfway up, she heard Mrs. Emery call out. "Wait, Katherine."

She stopped and Mrs. Emery joined her.

"Katherine, I must tell you the reason I took your part regarding your studies. Mr. Lanning urged me to do so. Otherwise, I would have sided with my son—you know, he has a great deal of worldly wisdom in these matters."

She smiled slightly. "However, I recognize he can be harsh. It is only his way when his advice goes unheeded. You should know he discussed at some length his ideas for your curriculum. He would not have done so unless he felt it important." She continued up the stairs with Katherine and paused at the top. "So, you must not feel hurt his playing Pilate, washing his hands of you and such. He was piqued, that's all." She patted Katherine's arm. "I do not want you to feel unduly upset. Go to bed now and get a good night's rest."

A few minutes later Katherine sat at her dressing table gazing in the mirror. Except for the drooping corners of her mouth, her face reflected little of the fatigue she felt. How could she look so fresh when she felt so jaded and weary? Mr. Emery's accusation about her youth must be the explanation.

She was glad the evening had finally ended. Ever since this morning when she learned of Mr. Lanning and Mrs. Emery's decision, she'd wondered when Mr. Emery would be informed. With nothing said at dinner, she'd hoped the whole matter had been settled.

She remembered his figure behind the newspaper, stiff and disapproving. Squeezing her eyes shut, she tried to expel the picture from her mind. In the sitting room she'd had to force herself to concentrate on Mrs. Emery's wishes regarding the window garden. Finally, Mr. Emery had declared himself finished with the paper and quitted the room, much to her relief.

She put her head down on the dressing table. For a long time she remained motionless. As she relaxed, however, tears coursed down her cheeks. Her shoulders shook in soft accompaniment.

The cry finally spent itself, and at length she sat up and looked in the mirror. With a degree of perverse satisfaction she noticed the damage the tears had done. Her eyes were red, her cheeks blotchy; she looked properly woebegone. She made a face. How foolish to notice such a thing. But that tense bottled-up feeling had gone. What a relief.

Sitting back in her chair, she still winced inside—like a hurt puppy booted by its master. Mr. Emery's short-lived approval of her music had been gratifying, and judging by how she now felt, had meant more to her than she'd realized. She grimaced. Well, she would just have to live without it. Mr. Emery had never given her much encouragement anyway.

She rose and walked to the armoire. As she undid the buttons on her dress, she remembered one of Mrs. Emery's remarks, about the time and energy Mr. Emery had expended in convincing his mother of the new curriculum. It was unusual for him to exert such effort in her behalf. Outside of a purely functional greeting at dinner, he rarely spoke to her.

Katherine carefully considered the matter. The idea of a personal interest in her or her welfare was unlikely. More to the point was that he believed he'd unearthed some talent in her, had crowed over the discovery, and disliked having his *well-founded* advice rejected.

A giggle burst out of her. Of course, that was the reason he was upset. His vanity had suffered. Giggles continued to bubble up inside as she raised her dress over her head. Oh dear! How could she laugh when only minutes before she'd cried? Probably some kind of nervous reaction on her part.

She started to arrange the dress on a hanger, then stopped. Mr. Emery had advanced some good arguments for studying German. Was he right after all? Was she being stubborn?

Katherine dropped the hanger on the rod. Oh, it was too much to think about tonight. If she let herself dwell on the day's troubles, she would never sleep. She plucked her nightgown from the hook in the armoire and tossed it on the bed. Rest was what she needed. Especially after feeling she'd done battle all day.

Chapter 11

Summer passed, and with fall in the air, hints of red, yellow and orange peeked from the trees. In another few weeks the forests would display their glorious zenith of color in the Connecticut countryside.

Not only was the season changing, but the atmosphere had changed in the Emery household as well. Aunt Elsie and Mrs. Emery were their usual selves, but Mr. Emery acted distant, almost cold when he passed Katherine in the hall or out-of-doors. At dinner he rarely addressed her. She tried not to let it bother her, and his attitude was easier to endure with Christopher around. He had decided to take a break from school and spend more time with his grandparents, so painting excursions continued, providing welcome interludes for her.

This particular afternoon she had an unexpected visitor. Mr. Lanning. He'd come on an impulse, he said. Together they strolled the garden while she looked for flowers to cut for the house. At one point he stumbled and she caught his arm. He didn't exhibit his usual energetic nature. Passing up the tawny red and gold chrysanthemums, she decided instead to gather white ones.

They entered the house at the back door and she stopped in the kitchen to arrange the flowers. Afterward, they made their way to the drawing room and she set the snowy mums on a low table. *White stood for truth, for purity,* she told Mr. Lanning. She hadn't added that the message of these flowers suited him, speaking of why she honored him so.

Sitting there, he'd had a dizzy spell. She rushed to his side, about to summon a servant, but he waved away her concern. Afterward he became so much his normal self she wondered if she was becoming overanxious. Then, when Sylvia Pruitt was announced, he made his excuses and left for home.

And until Mrs. Emery appeared, Katherine would need to play hostess. She kept covertly glancing at the door, hoping for her benefactress. Within a minute of sitting down, Mrs. Pruitt launched into a favorite topic: her dog's antics. Poochy this and Poochy that. Katherine tried to make her smile seem less frozen.

No wonder Mr. Lanning left when Mrs. Pruitt was ushered into the drawing room, Katherine thought as her guest prattled on. He had politely refused Katherine's offer of a buggy, saying he would walk home through the woods. The exercise would do him good.

Katherine hoped so. However, she remembered her mother's sickness all too well. If only she could have accompanied Mr. Lanning home. She straightened the skirt of the sky blue dress she was wearing, his favorite color.

Mrs. Pruitt took a deep breath, about to recount another of her little dog's tricks, when Katherine mentioned the room seemed stuffy and excused herself to open a window. Mrs. Emery would have rung for a servant, but Katherine wanted to check the weather.

Sunshine had warmed the air earlier in the day. Now, looking down the front lawn and gardens, Katherine noticed the wind picking up. She leaned nearer the pane. Clouds scuttled across the sky. The sunny day had changed to a gray, forlorn-looking afternoon. She didn't remember Mr. Lanning having a wrap.

Turning from the window, she steeled herself for another round of minutiae when, with relief, she heard Mrs. Emery speak from the doorway. "I'm sorry to have been detained, Sylvia. I hope Katherine saw to your needs."

With Mrs. Emery's permission, Katherine excused herself. She wondered if there was time to catch Mr. Lanning. He might have stopped to talk with the help. As she hastened down the hall toward the back door, she met the housekeeper taking off her shawl.

"Brr—it's getting cold!" Mrs. O'Neil's solid frame shivered. "Be sure to wear a coat if you're going outside, dearie."

Another time Katherine would have chatted with the warm-hearted housekeeper, but instead she groped for an old cloak kept in the back closet. Feeling like an escaped prisoner, she closed the back door, quickly crossed the lawn, and reaching the outbuildings, broke into a run.

Mr. Lanning would take the path across the fields. If so, she might see him before he entered the woods. But when she turned the corner around the last building, he was nowhere in sight.

A sudden gust caught her cloak, snapping it, fanning it out behind her. For a moment she halted, the sharp wind pressing her and exposing the sky blue dress. She spotted field hands in the distance talking with a man on horseback. Mr. Emery easily sat astride his black mount. He looked in her direction.

Snatching back the cloak, she wrapped it around her, feeling her cheeks flush warm. The blowing cloak must have caught Mr. Emery's attention. Hating herself for feeling self-conscious, she nonetheless disciplined herself into a respectably brisk walk down the field path to the woods. All the long way she kept comforting herself that her concern over Mr. Lanning would prove unwarranted. On reaching the cover of trees, however, she began running again. She should see her teacher at any moment.

The thick wood increased the gloom brought on by the cloudy afternoon. The air felt chilly. The thought of Mr. Lanning being cold made her angry—angry with Mrs. Pruitt for choosing this afternoon to call, angry with Mr. Emery for being in the field, and angry with herself for being self-conscious.

Straining to look ahead, she again tightened the cloak around her shoulders and pushed to run faster. Then, around the next bend, she cried out; she almost tripped over Mr. Lanning's prostrate form.

She threw herself down beside him and put her head near his. Slight warmth emanated from his parted lips, but she winced at the pallor of his face. "Mr. Lanning," she said softly. Then more urgently. "Mr. Lanning!" She tried chafing his hands and cheek, shook his shoulder.

"Katherine. . . ." His words were just above a whisper. "I fell . . . my left side. I can't seem to move it."

She groped for his left hand. It felt soft and slack. His huge frame was too heavy for her to raise. "I'll go for help," she said urgently. "Don't worry." Her mind flashed back to Mr. Emery, and her anger of a few minutes before changed to a fervent prayer he would still be in the field.

"I'm giving you my cape." She unfastened it and draped it over Mr. Lanning, it just covered him. She embraced his inert form. Oh, God! Please help him to be all right, she prayed silently. "I'll be back in a few minutes."

She then rose and ran wildly back down the path. If only Mr. Emery were still there. Her imagination saw him gone, already back at the stables.

Emerging from the woods, her eyes sought the place she'd last seen him. Thank God, he still talked with the men. He had dismounted and was examining the soil. She shouted frantically, flailing her arms, not caring now if she looked foolish or distraught.

Mr. Emery gazed at her only a moment. In four easy strides he reached Taggart and swung himself into the saddle.

Digging his heels into the horse's flanks, he urged him into a fast start.

Katherine bridged the last few feet as Mr. Emery drew in the reins. "It's Mr. Lanning. He's fallen in the woods."

"Where is he?"

"Around the third or fourth bend. Something's wrong with his left side."

Mr. Emery twisted in the saddle, lifted his arm, signaling the workers. "Men!" he shouted. "Follow Miss Edmond. Mr. Lanning's collapsed in the woods." He bent down. "Katherine, steady yourself. Lead the men to Mr. Lanning. I'll ride to the house to send for the doctor and rig up a stretcher." His saddle creaked as he straightened. Kneeing Taggart, Mr. Emery urged him into a gallop. The horse's hooves kicked up clods of dirt.

Katherine saw the field hands lumbering across the space toward her. She couldn't wait—she turned and raced to the woods, but by the time she reached its edge, the workers caught up with her. Without comment, the three men fell into single file entering the path, jogging after her.

Finally arriving at Mr. Lanning's side, panting from the run and excitement, Katherine dropped beside him and looked for a change in his countenance. For some moments she gazed at him, then circled her arms around his inert frame. Gently, she rested her head against his shoulder.

Mr. Emery found her thus with the men standing helplessly by. Without waiting, he set up a makeshift stretcher. "I have enough blankets," he said, helping her rise. He removed the cloak draped over Mr. Lanning and placed it around her shoulders. Bending down, he motioned the men. "Help me roll him onto the stretcher."

Katherine watched every move, fearful Mr. Lanning would be unnecessarily jostled. But Mr. Emery was gentle, carefully tucking a blanket around him.

"Men, each of you take a corner; hold the stretcher taut. A wagon is waiting at the edge of the woods."

With care, the small group labored through the forest. When they reached the open field, Katherine broke away and jumped into the wagon. She backed into a corner while a couple men climbed in to receive Mr. Lanning. After he had been settled, Mr. Emery dismissed the others and jumped in himself.

"Katherine, I'll steady his body while you take his head and shoulders."

Katherine leaned over the dear figure, supporting him as best she could while the wagon bumped down the path. Once she glanced up to find Mr. Emery gazing at her. Did he find her devotion to Mr. Lanning so strange? She bent over her mentor once again, holding him closer.

When the cart reached the back of the house, Mrs. Emery stepped out the door. "Bring him into the sitting room. We can make him comfortable there."

The large tea table had been moved aside so the men carrying Mr. Lanning had a clear path to the large brown velvet couch. Katherine followed and stood near her teacher's head.

Bates quickly placed an upright chair near the patient for Mrs. Emery, then set a basin of water within arm's reach. Mrs. Emery loosened Mr. Lanning's cravat and began bathing his pale face.

"Bates, would you stoke the fire?" Mrs. Emery glanced at her ward. "Katherine, hand me that spoon and brandy." Mrs. Emery forced the liquid down Mr. Lanning's throat.

Katherine's hands pressed hard against her sides; she hoped this would help him.

Jerard said, "He's been very still since Katherine found him. Do you think he's had some kind of stroke?"

"I don't know. Katherine, during his visit this afternoon, did you notice anything unusual?"

"He did have a couple brief dizzy spells. That's the reason I followed him, to make sure he was all right."

Mrs. Emery looked down at the patient, shaking her head. "I wish the doctor would arrive. Mrs. Lanning and Christopher have been sent for and should be here shortly." She reached over to press her hand on his forehead. "Jerard, I'm going to consult Mrs. O'Neil. Please keep your eye on him for any change."

Mr. Emery motioned Katherine to the empty chair. She sat, glancing up gratefully at him, glad to be near her mentor. Mr. Lanning's arm had slipped from underneath the blanket. Reaching for it, Katherine surrounded his cold hand with her warm, slender fingers, willing her vitality to penetrate him. Oh, if only he would return to his normal self.

Moments later Jerard removed a white handkerchief from his pocket and held it out to Katherine. "Take this. You've bitten your lip."

Her tongue touched her lip and tasted blood. "Thank you," she said as she reached for the proffered cloth. After blotting her mouth, she dropped the handkerchief on her lap and turned back to her teacher.

Only an occasional rattle of shutters or a far-off sound from another part of the house broke the stillness. Jerard stepped to Katherine's side, and they both watched over the old gentleman. Suddenly, Katherine shook with silent sobs. Jerard leaned nearer, and she glimpsed his hand hovering a few inches over her shoulder, then dropping again to his side.

After a while subdued voices sounded in the hall. Katherine looked up. Bates motioned Mrs. Lanning and Christopher into the room. Mrs. Lanning looked pale, and for once, Christopher was solemn. Jerard grasped Katherine's elbow, helping her rise from the chair to give place to Mrs. Lanning, then bent to retrieve the handkerchief that fell from Katherine's lap.

She saw the blood stain. "I'm sorry," she whispered, "I'll wash and return it."

"That's not necessary, I'll attend to it." Jerard folded the handkerchief carefully and tucked it away in his coat pocket.

"When did Grandfather collapse?" Christopher asked.

Katherine looked at Mr. Emery. "Was it an hour ago that he left the house? But—had he been long in the woods before I reached him?"

"Not long, Katherine. I noticed him walking across the field, and you followed a short time later."

"Did he seem unwell during his visit?" Mrs. Lanning asked.

Katherine couldn't remember her voice sounding kinder or sadder, and briefly told what had occurred without dwelling on her own fears.

Christopher stepped nearer his grandmother and put his hand comfortingly on her shoulder. "We're grateful you found him so quickly." His gaze returned to his grandfather. The air was heavy with foreboding and unanswered questions.

Moments later Jerard bent to whisper in Katherine's ear, then addressed Mrs. Lanning and her grandson. "We'll leave you alone with Mr. Lanning until the doctor arrives."

Mrs. Lanning nodded her assent.

Jerard motioned Katherine toward the door, leaving wife and grandson to continue their vigil in private.

Chapter 12

A single lamp glowed in the darkened sitting room. Katherine sat in a straight-backed chair, keeping watch over her teacher.

Two days had passed since Mr. Lanning's collapse in the woods, and his condition remained unchanged. The doctor advised he not be moved from the house, so Mrs. Emery insisted a small bed be brought down, as it was easier to move than the massive bedsteads occupying most of the upstairs bedrooms. A hush had fallen over the entire household.

The patient stirred. Katherine leaned forward. "Mr. Lanning, Mr. Lanning," she whispered as her hands gently touched one of his.

The man slowly opened his eyes and turned his head toward her.

"Mr. Lanning, it's me, Katherine." She lifted his hand and kissed it, then held it to her cheek. "I'm so glad you're awake."

The old gentleman looked at her as if trying to focus. Tenderness welled up in his eyes. "Katherine. I'm glad you are here." After some moments, he struggled to speak again. "Tell me ... how long have I been here?"

Katherine hesitated. She didn't want to alarm him, but wanted to remain truthful. "This is the second day since your collapse."

Mr. Lanning considered that.

"Would you like me to get you something? A little water? Another blanket?"

"No."

She looked at him closely. He appeared pale and drawn, nothing like the vigorous man she had known only days ago. But she was grateful he was awake. She treasured these moments with him. People had crept in and out all through the day, but this last hour she'd been alone with him.

She thought back to the time when they'd first met, sipping tea in the yellow and pink cabbage rose room. Would such times come again? Yes, they would.

"You'll get better," she said. Oh how she wanted to sit here longer, just the two of them, but she felt her selfishness. She sighed. Everyone would want to know he was awake and talking. "Would you like me to send for your family?"

His right hand weakly squeezed hers. "Not yet. Katherine, you are dear… like my own… ." His eyes closed.

"Yes, and you are like a father to me."

The words seemed to remind him of something. He took a long, slow breath and opened his eyes. "Katherine, I need to talk with you… about something, before it's too late." He paused to catch his breath.

"You don't have to talk now."

"Dear child… I must. When I started teaching you… was glad Mrs. Emery didn't find someone else… to take over. Would not have willingly given you up."

She would not have willingly given him up either. More than a teacher, he was the father she'd always wanted. The kind of man who told her what was right and true, a man who lived what he believed. Her soul clung to him like the tendrils of a young vine attaching itself to an old oak.

"I've seen you mature these last months… blossom into womanhood. Am so proud."

A glow flamed up inside her. "Thank you, Mr. Lanning. Thank you." Her hands clasped his. "I'm so privileged to be your student, to be like your—daughter. We'll have more times together. You'll see! You will get well and strong and we'll go on as before."

"I hope so, child. But I must speak...you see, I want the best for you. But first something must be faced... dealt with."

"What is that?"

"I've sensed...how troubled you are...when speaking of your father. I know some of the wrongs... he committed against you and your mother. Why you feel the way you do. That is only natural." He paused at length, as if to emphasize what he said next. "But Katherine, Christ does not call us to follow... the natural, easy way. If a person has wronged or hurt us, Christ wants us to forgive him. It is the only way to peace within ourselves...and with God." With difficulty he moved his head to better see her face in the lamplight.

Katherine stared into his entreating eyes. "But I don't know if I can forgive my father. He hurt me so many times." She looked away from Mr. Lanning into the dark room. "Once he demanded my treasured locket, the one from my mother that her parents had given her. He wouldn't tell me why he wanted it, but later I discovered it was to pay for his drink. I never got it back. That was only one of many things." Her lips tightened. "I don't see how I can change how I feel about him."

"Such feelings are understandable." A tender smile crooked one side of Mr. Lanning's face. "However, if you were to wait for feelings to change... before forgiving your father, you would probably never do so."

Her head jerked back to look at him. "But how can I forgive a man who will likely never change, never say he's sorry?"

"Katherine, I know it's difficult. Terribly difficult. But think of it this way. God forgives us far more... than we will ever need to forgive others. When He sent His Son to earth to die, He hurt Himself...to clear the way for our forgiveness. Now, as His children, we are to extend...the same costly forgiveness to others." He rested before going on. "At times we do it...not because we want to forgive the person in question, but because we want to be obedient to our Heavenly Father. We want to honor Him." He searched her countenance. At length he asked, "What is it?"

"Oh, Mr. Lanning! It's too hard."

His breath expelled slowly, then refilled his lungs before continuing. "But Katherine, we don't want anything...to mar our fellowship with the Lord. Let the Lord deal with your father. Please...let your anger and resentment go."

Katherine fought to hold back the tears welling up.

Mr. Lanning closed his eyes, his lips moving in a silent prayer, then he finished in a whisper, "Spirit of God, please help her."

Katherine's shoulders shook as sobs escaped. Finally she said, "Oh, Mr. Lanning, I know you're right. I want to please God." She wiped her eyes. "Will you help me?"

"Of course, child. Kneel beside the bed. We'll pray together."

Katherine began, at first halting. When she stumbled, her teacher filled in. After she finished, she rested her head near his side. For a few minutes she remained close. "Thank you, Mr. Lanning. My heart is starting to feel as if a terrible burden has been lifted."

"I know, child. It's a wonderful feeling, isn't it?" He cleared his throat. "And if dark thoughts come back...which well they might...hand them over to the Lord. Trust Him to work out circumstances...for the good of both you and your father."

"I will." She lifted her face to see him better. "Mr. Lanning, you've given me so much. I know God brought you to me since my parents were gone. You must get better. Soon." She stretched up and kissed his cheek.

"Thank you, Katherine." His right hand lifted, searching for hers. "I won't go... before my time. But I do wonder... if it might be near." His hand closed over hers and he smiled tenderly. "Now maybe we should... send for Mrs. Lanning and Christopher."

Chapter 13

Katherine rushed down the front steps of the house. How she wanted to be alone. Crossing the drive to the gardens, she drew a black shawl closely around her shoulders, tying the ends securely. She stumbled into the garden, seeking a place hidden from the house, dreaded being seen by anyone who chanced to look out a window.

Misery over Mr. Lanning's death had swelled up like waves throughout the afternoon. How could he be gone? The distance between them yawned like a vast chasm. Her hand covered her mouth, stifling a cry.

Nearby, within an enclosure of trees and bushes, sat a stone bench. She gained the sheltered spot and fell to her knees, clinging to the bench's hard, angular surface. Another surge of sorrow started low in her abdomen, pushing hard into her chest, and rose to force itself out her mouth. She cried then groaned. Was this all she could do to relieve the anguish that cut through her like a sharp pain?

"Oh, God, why did You allow him to die? No man was his equal. No one!"

She crushed her forehead against the hard stone bench. He'd been more than teacher and friend. He'd been a father. Yes! A father. Not to see him this side of the grave was unthinkable. First Mother, and now him.

A dark, deep pit seemed to engulf her. "Oh God! This is so hard. Help me!" Crying brokenly, she pressed her face into her arms.

Ø

Standing at the opening to the enclosure, Jerard gazed at Katherine. On impulse, he had followed when she excused herself without warning from the sitting room. He had seen her slight figure disappear into the garden. He kept his distance and made no move to approach, but stood motionless.

Watching her grieve, his face suddenly contorted. He turned and hurried farther down the path. Some distance from the house another enclosure opened, guarded by two tall yews. He stepped inside and crossed to a wooden bench. Sitting down heavily, he braced his elbows on his knees and dropped his head into his hands.

ᘓ

Twilight fell. Katherine dabbed bleary eyes with a damp handkerchief, then raised herself off the ground to sit on the bench. Her storm had passed and she felt a measure of relief, yet a heavy ache remained in her heart. "Oh God. What will I do without him? So wise—and one who loved me so." She thought of the time at his bedside a few days ago, how he had seen her heart, how she needed to forgive. She had complained just one time about her father. Who else would have been so discerning?

The Lord is my Shepherd. He is my comfort in life and in death.... Scriptures, like welcome friends, came to soothe her. She looked up and whispered, "God, Your Word says You are the God of all comfort. I will believe that."

She sat still awhile, then rose wearily. A walk through the garden would help compose her. The path meandered away from the house, and she followed it, pausing at a group of pine trees, inhaling deeply their spicy scent. This last week distraught she'd forgotten what it was like to smell anything, forgot what it was to experience a momentary joy. A breeze picked up, fluttering the leaves of the surrounding trees.

Katherine walked on. It had been difficult for them all, Mrs. Lanning particularly. Yet that wonderful lady had taken the time to comfort and counsel others. Everyone had been kind. Even Mr. Emery had shown a consideration foreign to his nature. The day Mr. Lanning collapsed, he had responded without delay and seemed to know just what to do.

Katherine turned to look at the Emery house, now at a distance. Light emanated from several windows, but the house did not beckon her. Too many thoughts tossed about in her mind. A few yards ahead two tall yews guarded an entrance to another garden-like enclosure with a bench on which she could rest awhile. Her very bones ached.

At the opening of the yews, she stopped abruptly.

Mr. Emery.

The tall form on the bench gave vent to a deep groan, shaking his head from side to side.

Katherine bit her lip. She stared, amazed. When had Mr. Emery ever expressed such emotion? Thoughts rushed wildly through her mind. Should she stay, try to give him comfort? Or should she go? He didn't seem the type of man who would appreciate anyone around at a time such as this.

It was disconcerting to see him this way. But her heart went out to him. Just now she had experienced such terrible grieving herself. If there was anything she could do, let him know someone else understood—

Her dress rustled as she entered the space. Mr. Emery did not move as she stepped near. However, he removed a large white handkerchief from his coat pocket, wiped his lowered face, pressing the cloth to his eyes.

"Mr. Emery, can I help?" She leaned down. "I've been grieving over Mr. Lanning. Did you love him, too?"

He lifted his head for a moment looking perplexed. "Mr. Lanning?" He replaced his handkerchief in his pocket. "No. I was thinking of my father. And—"

"Your father and—" Was there something or someone else beside his father?

He looked at her as if weighing whether to say more, then rose. "Won't you sit?"

Slowly, she took his place on the bench.

He stood so she could see only his profile, then he began tentatively. "Regarding my father—I don't think you knew—his death was similar to Mr. Lanning's. Last week I relived the past events. It was strange."

He stared at an invisible scene, conflicting emotions flitting across his face. Katherine waited for him to continue.

"The day in question I had returned from a long trip. After all the travel, home felt good. My father and I were walking the fields that afternoon. I was at a distance from him, had turned to look at something—don't remember what—when he collapsed. Our foreman happened to be with us, and I straightway sent him for help. We lifted Father into a wagon, just like Mr. Lanning. The similarities—they're uncanny."

Katherine looked at him, amazed. To think he had gone through all this—like herself.

"Mother took him to the same room, placed him on the same couch. He died a short time later." He paused, then added bitterly, "He wasn't supposed to die. A loving God wouldn't have allowed that to happen."

A soft night wind picked up, rustling leaves in the treetops. A gentle, comforting sound. Yet despite it, Katherine sat with clenched hands.

Jerard turned and looked at Katherine. "And there's you. Robbed of the two people you loved, your mother and Mr. Lanning—then your father wandering around who knows where. Where's God in all that?" She felt his attitude press down on her. "Surely, you don't believe God cares. If He does, He's doing a poor job of showing it."

Katherine's breath constricted. "Please don't say that. I don't know why my life has been this way, but—but somehow there's a purpose in it." Her voice lowered, yet she said distinctly, "Before dying, my mother was bedridden, so we had a lot of time to talk. She impressed on me a number of things: how she loved me, how much she regretted leaving me at my young age. But she assured me God would take care of me, that He had given us Mr. Emery—your father—to provide for us. 'Our suffering,' she said, 'has a purpose.'"

Katherine pressed her fingers to her temples. "She repeated those words so often, they are emblazoned on my memory. I've wondered how coming here could fit in with God's design." She lowered her hands, clenching them, then consciously relaxing them. "I still feel my mother's loss, and if I had the choice, would go back to our simple life together. But I have come to accept my lot in life. I must believe it all has a design, or I could not live. It would be too painful."

She sighed. "I have to admit, however, this last week I've had the flimsiest of faiths. I miss Mr. Lanning terribly—can hardly believe he's gone. He's left such an empty place in my heart."

Moments passed. Then Mr. Emery said, "It would be difficult to take his place—almost impossible. The man who wished to do so would have the challenge of a lifetime."

She glanced up at him, trying to search out his meaning. "At times this week I've felt as if I've been walking on thin ice in the middle of a river, fearful of breaking through and drowning. Yet I keep looking to God to somehow mend the broken pieces of my life and put them back together."

Impulsively, she rose. "After I cried a while ago, a verse in Romans came to me. 'All things work together for good to them that love God.' I do believe that promise is true for me. And true for anyone who loves God."

"That certainly excludes me."

She took a step forward, near enough to see his face in the falling darkness. "But Mr. Emery, I pray someday it will be true for you." The words burst from Katherine's lips. She had never prayed for Mr. Emery's salvation, never considered doing so, but now wondered if she had committed herself to some divine task. She drew back, surveying his face to gauge his reaction, but it remained inscrutable.

After some moments he broke the silence. "I think you'd better return to the house now. No," he said, as she turned from him, "I'll escort you." He stepped near, holding out his arm. As she rested her hand on his coat sleeve, he said quietly, "I am sorry about Mr. Lanning."

"Thank you. And I'm sorry about your father. I didn't know the circumstances of his death, never realized you'd had such a grief."

He placed his hand over hers and held it close a moment, then motioned her to accompany him. He led her out of the enclosure and they started up the path to the house.

During that silent walk together, Katherine felt some type of understanding had grown between them. Something that hadn't been there before. *Sympathique,* the French called it.

Darkness had fallen, and except for a few stars, the lamps in the mansion were the only visible light. As they neared the house, Katherine gazed at it, marveling at the change in her perception. Before, it had invariably intimidated her with its pillared grandeur, but now, walking with Mr. Emery beside her, it seemed just very beautiful.

He guided her across the drive and up the front steps, stopping in front of the massive doors. "Thank you, Katherine. More than you know." Looking at her a moment longer, he added, "I need to walk awhile—there's something else I need to think about. But you should go inside." He released her hand and, leaning over, opened the door. "Good night now."

Katherine stepped across the threshold into the lighted hall. The brightness almost cut her physically. She turned to her companion, but the door was already closing. Feeling both comforted and bereft, she crossed the hall to mount the stairs.

Chapter 14

Jerard entered the house with a light step.

Bates closed the door behind him. "Good to see you return, sir. How was New York?"

"Business was good." Jerard took a deep breath. "But it was a long two weeks. I don't know when I've looked forward more to coming home."

"Glad to hear that, sir. I trust you enjoyed the autumn colors."

"Never seen them better. Surely we've had years as good as this, but apparently I've never noticed. Makes me wonder where my observational powers have been."

"Well, sir, glad to see you looking so well. I'll have your bags brought up to your room in a few minutes."

"Thank you. Where is the family?"

"Your mother is conferring with Mrs. O'Neil in the sitting room. Your aunt is resting upstairs. And Miss Katherine is on an errand of mercy—of sorts."

"Oh?"

"Yes, sir. She went to see the little blond-haired girl she's been tutoring. She should be back within an hour or so." Quick footsteps echoed from the back hall. "Ah, here's your mother."

Mrs. Emery embraced her son, then held him at arm's length. "You're looking well. New York must have agreed with you. Take tea in the sitting room and tell me about your trip."

ᘓ

Jerard entered his bedroom and ambled to a window overlooking the front grounds. The late afternoon sun brought out in blazing relief the fall colors of the garden and countryside beyond.

He noticed a buggy whirring up the drive. Curious as to the occupants, he remained at the window. Katherine with Christopher? The breeze ruffled the skirt of her dark mourning dress, her slim figure leaning toward her companion.

Jerard bent to open the window as the buggy circled the drive to stop beneath the portico. Katherine's voice drifted up. "Before you go let me show you where I want to put the memorial stone. Can you come to the garden for a few minutes?"

Jerard turned from the window and exited his room. He purposefully walked the upstairs hall to a door opening onto the roof of the portico. Quietly, he stepped outside onto the overhead porch. The main path of the garden could be seen near its railing so he edged forward until the path came into view.

"I've already talked with the head gardener," Katherine was saying. "He thought it would be fine if I placed a simple stone in one of the enclosures."

Christopher accompanied Katherine down the garden path. The two disappeared into the same enclosure in which she had grieved not long ago.

Jerard crouched on one knee, listening intently. After a few minutes he heard a distant sob. Stretching up, he saw Katherine and Christopher leave the enclosure. Her head was bent, hands covering her face. Christopher's arm encircled her, assisting her up the path.

As they neared the house, Christopher said, "It's terrible to know he's gone. I'll never be able to sit and talk with him again, to hear his words of wisdom. I well up with tears myself." The two crossed the drive. "But Grandfather is experiencing joy beyond our imaginings."

"Yes." Katherine's voice caught as they moved underneath the portico. "Except—it's still so hard."

"I understand. Go ahead and cry now. But remember what Grandmother said. 'If you can laugh, do so as well.' It's what Grandfather would want. He's in heaven and he's happy now."

"I know." Katherine's voice smiled through her tears. "It will all be so wonderful when we're together—in heaven—won't it?"

"Yes. Would you like my handkerchief? Wait, let me dry your tears." After a few moments, "There. You look quite your old self—pretty as ever. Are you ready to go inside now?"

Jerard's eyes narrowed. He heard the door below open. Abruptly he crossed the portico and entered the house.

☙

"Well, what do you think?" Mr. Emery asked. "Should we plant the back twenty in rye this winter?" He stopped his horse beneath a large over-arching elm. His foreman followed suit.

"Yep, that's what I'd do."

They had spent most of the morning inspecting the estate's farm acreage, riding in silence much of the way, but now the taciturn foreman waxed eloquent. "That back twenty's a far piece." He paused. "Ever think of selling? Or swapping for something nearer?"

"I've thought of it." Jerard looked sideways at his crusty companion. "Any possibilities?"

"That road up there leads to the Hodges'. Missus got ten acres lying fallow. Mebbe she'd sell or rent."

"It's adjacent to our property, isn't it?"

"Yep."

"I wonder if there's additional acres nearby for sale. Then we might consider selling that back twenty."

"I'll check around." The foreman nudged his horse to follow Mr. Emery's.

Moments later, he looked across Mr. Emery's mount, jutting out his chin. "Miss Katherine, sir."

Jerard turned in his saddle to look. Down the road, strolled Katherine at Christopher's side. In another minute the couple would reach them. Jerard reined in his horse. "I've business here. I'll see you back at the barn."

The foreman nodded assent and, without a backward glance, trotted his horse down the road.

When they approached, Katherine hailed, "Good day, Mr. Emery."

Jerard nodded his greeting.

Christopher halted a few feet away. "This is a surprise. On an inspection tour?"

"Yes." Jerard eyed Katherine. "What are you doing out here?"

"Visiting the Hodges. We brought them food and clothing. They always appreciate it so."

"I understood you were there only a few days ago." Jerard crossed his arms over his saddle horn. "How often do you visit?"

Katherine's expression went vacant a moment. "Ah, that was to bring Cassie a new book for her studies. You know Cassie—the youngest child?"

"I remember her." He shifted in the saddle. "But you haven't answered my question."

"How often? Usually once a week."

"Your charity's commendable, but I think it's inadvisable to walk alone. This road is usually deserted."

Katherine glanced at her companion. "But, since Christopher's been home, he often accompanies me."

"A member of the household should accompany you. Then Christopher wouldn't be inconvenienced."

"It's no trouble," Christopher said, "and I enjoy it."

Katherine smiled brightly. "Christopher and I are old friends, you know. I often accompany him on his painting jaunts around the countryside."

"Oh?" Jerard's tone invited more.

"Yes, we've been doing it ever so long, since he first arrived home from school."

"I see." He took up the reins. "Well, since I'm on my way to the house, you may now ride home with me, Katherine."

Katherine looked doubtfully at Christopher.

"I don't mind walking her home, Jerard."

"Yes," Katherine said, "and I love to walk."

"As I said, someone from the household should accompany you. I'm not going to argue the point. Come, Katherine." Jerard held out his hand. "Christopher! Help her up. She can sit side-saddle."

Katherine gave Christopher a long look as if to say she'd appreciate his not making a scene. He smiled at her, then guided her to the horse's side. Stooping, he cupped his hands to support her foot.

Jerard leaned back in the saddle and Katherine sprang up lightly in front of him. He caught her and, after she settled herself, clasped his free arm around her waist.

"Good-bye, Christopher, and thank you!" Katherine just had time to get the words out before Jerard urged his horse on.

"I'll let you know about next time," Christopher called after her.

ᘓ

The mild fall afternoon was perfect for a brisk walk. Christopher rounded the last corner on his grandmother's drive when he caught sight of the Emery carriage. The driver stood near the horses. Approaching, Christopher called out, "Hello, Higgins."

"Hello, Mr. Christopher. And how are you?"

"Fine, thank you. Which of the family are you waiting on?"

"Mrs. Emery."

"Ah! Something momentous must be afoot. The lady comes here only on important business."

That moment the front door opened. Mrs. Emery preceded Mrs. Lanning, and Christopher quickly approached to assist the ladies down the steps. "Thank you, Christopher," Mrs. Emery said. "How are you today?"

"Very well, Mrs. Emery. So how was your call this afternoon? Have you managed to solve all the world's problems?"

"Levity usually suits you, Christopher. However, this time you're off the mark. Among other things, we discussed the latest news. Chicago has had a terrible fire. Jerard came home with the story just before I left."

"When did this happen?"

"Sunday night. He said thousands of people fled before the flames, pushing belongings in buggies, wheelbarrows, baby carriages, anything with wheels."

"Then it was really serious."

"Unquestionably! Things got to such a state that officials thought the city prison was endangered, so they just up and released the convicts. Saloonkeepers gave away bottles of whiskey. Even jewelers, expecting the fires to destroy their stores, passed out gems to the general public."

"That's hard to believe."

"I know. But human nature will surprise you when faced with catastrophe." She paused a moment longer before stepping into her carriage. "Such a tragedy. Those poor souls will need help. I think we should all do our Christian duty and send items for their relief." Settled in her carriage, Mrs. Emery looked past

Christopher to his grandmother. "I suppose I'll see you both in church Sunday?" Her lips formed a smile. "Good-bye, then."

When the carriage swept away, Christopher said, "What horrendous news." He glanced down at his grandmother. Her face had a set look. "Something wrong—besides the Chicago fire?"

"Come inside, Christopher."

"I was hoping to have a cup of tea with you on the porch." Christopher reached for his grandmother's arm as she started for the door. "Let me get the tea. If Mrs. Emery had other unsettling news, it can wait."

"You're a dear. I could use something to drink." Mrs. Lanning sat down wearily in one of the wicker chairs.

Before long Christopher returned with a tray. "Here you are, Madame!" He handed her a cup with ceremony. "You must have read my thoughts, tea was already made."

"Well, I thought Emma might want some, but she declined."

"So, what was the real reason for the august lady's visit?" He helped himself to tea and sat down easily in a chair near her. "You look all in."

Mrs. Lanning laughed wryly. "Well, at times Emma has a way of taking the wind out of a person's sails. I suppose it's nothing major, really, but it does involve you."

Christopher winked at his grandmother. "Shoot your big guns, Grandma. I'm man enough."

"It has to do with Katherine. I don't relish telling you this. Mrs. Emery requested you no longer accompany her unchaperoned around the countryside."

Christopher looked at his grandmother, then shifted his gaze to the maple trees with their half-fallen leaves. He chose his words carefully. "You know, Grandma, Katherine and I have been such good friends, and we've gone around together for months. It seems strange for Mrs. Emery to dictate a change like this, so suddenly."

"I know. But I suppose it's because Katherine's getting older—I mean, she is becoming quite a young lady. Mrs. Emery feels she should no longer go out alone with young men, no matter how trusted or what the practice has been in the past." She smiled at him. "I suppose I can see her point."

"I wonder if this new dictum has anything to do with our meeting up with Jerard a few days ago."

"Oh? Did something happen?"

"Nothing, really. I was walking Katherine home after we had taken the Hodges food and other things. We met Jerard on horseback, and he insisted Katherine ride home with him." Christopher rose and stepped to the railing. "He kept asking her questions such as why she went to the Hodges and how often. He all but ignored me. Then he went on about not wanting her to walk alone. When Katherine said I often accompanied her he stated one of the Emery household should be doing that."

He turned to face his grandmother. "Katherine and I are helping people the Emerys should be assisting. Mrs. Hodges' husband used to work at the Emery mill, and if the Emerys had any real Christian charity, they'd be over there with food and clothing. You know, Mrs. Emery has plenty of sympathy for the victims of the Chicago fire. She should look a little nearer home. Does she mean to stop *our* charitable works?"

"She didn't say that. But one solution for you would be to include others so as to make it a group venture."

"Maybe." Christopher was silent, tapping the tips of his fingers on the railing. "I'll wager Jerard is at the bottom of this."

"Has Jerard shown much interest in Katherine's comings and goings? I understand he largely ignores her."

"True. But he and I have been rivals since boyhood. Maybe the fact Katherine was with me—and he considers her part of his household—was enough to make him turn dictator." He shook his head. "For once I'd like to see him get served with his own tactics."

Grandmother shook her head. "I don't want trouble with the Emerys. You know, I feel responsible to set them a loving example." She put down her teacup. "Jerard can be difficult, has been more so since his father's death. And, so much of it, I feel, came as a result of that terrible mishap with his brother." She sighed. "I don't think he knows our Lord, and we can't expect him to act like a Christian when he isn't one."

"Oh, I know Jerard has had difficulties but he's had time to get over them. I just don't feel sorry for him anymore. I'm worried about Katherine. Where does this leave her, being raised in a household that merely follows society's mores? When society says, 'Go to church,' they go, and whatever society says not to do, they don't. What kind of upbringing is that?"

"I know. But we must remember the Lord began a beautiful work in Katherine years ago at her mother's knee and He promises in His Word to complete that work."

"I'm sure you're right, Grandmother, but it still disturbs me to think of Katherine over there. You'd do a better job of raising her."

"Thank you for your vote of confidence." Mrs. Lanning smiled. "I admit at times I wonder how things will go now your grandfather's gone and Katherine doesn't have him to guide her." She grasped the teapot. "But then, I have to remember that in the providence of God, Katherine was placed in the Emery household and not ours. Sometimes life is hard to understand—like the Chicago fire." She held out her hand for Christopher's cup. "Sit down, Christopher, your tea needs warming."

After he settled himself, she continued. "You know, much of the city was reduced to ashes because the buildings were constructed of wood. Emma said three and a half square miles of city burned."

"Three and a half miles!"

"Yes, and more would have been destroyed but, thankfully, late Monday a steady rain began to fall and by Tuesday the fires were nearly extinguished. That rainfall was evidence of God's mercy." She looked pointedly at her grandson. "The same can be said for Katherine. We don't understand why in the providence of God she was sent to the Emerys, but somehow the purpose of God is being furthered by her living there. Just as the purposes of God will be furthered by that fire. When people go through difficult, even tragic times, they invariably look to the Lord for help. Many people will be drawn to Him."

"I see what you mean." Christopher took a sip of tea. "Back to Katherine, does that mean we sit here and do nothing?"

"Of course not. I see no reason why our influence should stop because your grandfather has passed away. But we must wait on the Lord to see what He would have us do."

Christopher gazed at his grandmother, so wise, yet he felt exasperation rising. "I know you're right, but I just want to charge over and rescue the fair maiden from the Emery clutches. Especially Jerard's."

"Oh, Christopher!" Grandmother laughed. "How like you. But impulsiveness won't win the day. Patience is best, particularly after Mrs. Emery's visit this afternoon. If there's one thing your grandfather was, he was politic. That's the reason he got along with so many people. He never compromised principles or convictions, but he always allowed people to grow at the rate God had in mind. We should emulate his example."

She leaned over and put her hand on Christopher's. "In the meantime, we'll pray for Katherine's well-being, both mental and spiritual. I will also ask the Lord what else can be done. That way whatever we propose for her will be exactly right. How does that sound?"

"I guess you're right, Grandma." He laughed suddenly. "So—I guess I won't charge over just yet and play Sir Galahad."

Chapter 15

"Mattie, you finished dusting?" Jerard asked as he breezed into the drawing room.

"Just the piano to do, sir."

"Very good." He smiled genially. "After you're done, please place this music on the rack. Then send Miss Katherine down. I do not want us to be disturbed, so inform Bates. I'll return in a few minutes."

Mattie stared at the master as he left the room. "My, what a good mood we're in," she said under her breath. She refolded her cloth and dusted the piano with energy.

ଓ

With tentative steps, Katherine descended the stairs. Sunlight from the dining and drawing room windows diffused into the hall giving it unusual brightness. However, her mood hardly matched the cheery aspect of the house's formal rooms. Katherine couldn't forget Mr. Emery's manner the other day, how he had *demanded* she ride home with him instead of walking with Christopher. His arm around her had been unnecessarily tight. And now he had sent for her.

Stopping a moment on the bottom step, she'd half a mind to decline, to say she was busy. After all, she had promised to help the gardener later. Then she heard his voice vocalizing in the drawing room. Was he going to sing? Curious, she entered the drawing room and saw him standing near the piano.

"Here you are." He strode across the room to meet her. "I have a favor to ask. I've been requested to sing at a party in New York. Several new business associates will be present, and I need your help to rehearse the song." His hand was already under her elbow leading her toward the piano.

Katherine halted. "I promised your mother I would help the gardener arrange plants in the conservatory this morning."

"You can do that later. I need your help now."

She hesitated, searching for some other excuse.

"What's wrong?"

Her eyes flickered down, then looked up at him. "I don't know if I should speak of this, but—what happened a few days ago is still bothering me."

"A few days ago?"

"When Christopher and I were walking home from the Hodges—the way you arranged things." She chose her words with care. "It seemed you felt you were the only one who could take me home. It was most awkward."

"Oh that. It was getting late, and someone from our own household should escort you. You are growing up, you know. I'm sure Christopher had other things to attend to." He looked at her more carefully. "Well, if I was brusque in my handling of the situation, I apologize."

A few seconds of silence passed. Katherine could hardly believe what Mr. Emery had just said.

Jerard smiled. "Now, Mademoiselle, will you deign to accompany me on the piano?" He clicked his heels together and made a grand bow. "Your virtuosity is well known in these parts. May I escort you to our fine instrument?" He held out his hand.

Not only had his apology been unexpected, now his change of mood caught Katherine off guard. He reminded her of her imaginary count with whom she had practiced after the von

Weber dinner party. A smile pulled at the corners of her mouth. She felt torn. Would it be silly and perverse to continue being upset? She looked at his outstretched hand. To see him playful rather than difficult was certainly preferable. He wasn't asking her to do anything odious—she loved to accompany. And his mood was infectious.

She curtsied and took the hand he proffered. "Thank you, sir."

Mr. Emery led her across the room with the same measured tread a couple might have danced with a century earlier. Stepping near the piano, he lifted her hand high and guided her onto the bench. Then he opened the piece of music on the rack. "This doesn't look too difficult, does it? The song should sound like this." He sang the first few bars.

Katherine felt herself rising to the challenge of the music, moving in rhythm to his beat.

"Now, do you think you could try it with me?"

"Yes, if you will give me a minute to scan it." She looked over the piece for difficult passages, which she quickly fingered. "I'm ready, I think."

"All right. Go ahead with the introduction, and don't be timid."

With that admonition she seated herself more squarely on the bench and let fly the first notes. As Mr. Emery began to sing and music filled the room, Katherine couldn't help noticing how beautifully the accompaniment had been written to complement the soloist. She concentrated on doing it justice.

When they finished the song, Mr. Emery's palm hit the top of the piano. His dark eyes gleamed. "That was good. Very good! Let's try it again."

Katherine felt a burst of pleasure. "Thank you. I'd like to, but just let me first play over a few phrases to make sure they're correct."

Performing the music a second time was even more delightful. They executed the piece with an energy that set them both smiling.

"Ah, how we make music together." Mr. Emery extended his hand. "Give me yours, Mademoiselle."

When she offered her hand, he bent and placed a light kiss on the fingertips. "That," he said with aplomb, "is a gentleman's homage to talented appendages. However, I must warn you." One of his eyebrows lifted. "The next song is more difficult."

Although surprised at Mr. Emery's bantering, Katherine had no time to dwell on it when she saw the complexity of the next piece. She looked it over closely, determined to do well. When they started, she raced to keep his tempo, playing the rapid passages as best she could. The song had a lilt that stirred the soul. With determination she ended with a flourish of chords and arpeggios. "There! That's the best I could do at first pass."

"Well done, Miss Edmond. You didn't miss a beat."

"No, only a few notes," she said, laughing.

He smiled. "You sight read extraordinarily well. We should do this more often."

"I enjoyed it. Thank you for asking me."

They looked at each other in pleased silence. Then Jerard asked, "Do you think I should prepare an encore?"

"Yes, of course. The guests will demand one."

"What do you suggest?"

"After that last rousing song, I would think something more *andante*."

"I know." He laughed. "I could sing an old-fashioned love song and have the ladies swooning at my feet."

"Then you best take smelling salts." Her voice caught on a giggle.

"But there's a problem. I'll be singing and my accompanist will be too busy playing to help the ladies. Who will administer the salts?" He snapped his fingers. "You're a capable young woman; I could take you. In fact," he said, gesturing broadly, "I have a better idea. I'll take you as my accompanist. Our hostess can administer the salts." He slapped the piano again. "A capital idea! You can come with me to New York."

"What are you talking about, Jerard?" Mrs. Emery asked as she entered from the library.

Jerard turned to address his mother. "Why not have Katherine accompany me at the New York party?"

"Son, the child is no more ready for that than the man in the moon."

"Even under my guidance?"

"Don't be silly. She needs a woman chaperone."

"How about yourself? I'm sure I could get you an invitation to Mrs. Melton's soirée."

"Jerard, I have no intention of going to New York. And, Katherine will not either." Impatience edged her voice. "We've things to attend to. In fact, I came to remind Katherine she promised to help the gardener this morning. Had you forgotten, Katherine?"

"No, ma'am, I—" Katherine looked from Mrs. Emery to her son.

"Don't blame her, Mother. I insisted she help me with this music, and she's played extremely well. So well, I considered taking for the New York event." He smiled at his mother. "You've done an exceptional job in seeing to her musical training."

"Thank you." Mrs. Emery now smiled. "That's high praise from such a critic as yourself. But we must get on with our morning."

Jerard gathered the music from the piano. "Anyway, we're finished for the present."

"Good. Then follow me, Katherine." Mrs. Emery turned to leave.

Staying Katherine with his hand, Jerard looked down at her and said in an undertone, "Thank you, Mademoiselle."

"You're welcome, Monsieur." Katherine adroitly slid from the bench to catch up with her benefactress.

Chapter 16

Katherine stood gazing out the front door. Dusk would soon settle on the peaceful winter scene. The snow of three days ago crusted lawn and bushes, adding a shimmer to the lovely landscape. This unplanned hour was a luxury. She wasn't needed at present so decided to take a walk before dark. Perhaps she would ramble through the gardens.

The head gardener had left the flower heads and clumps of bushes unpruned so the garden's form could be appreciated. Shades of brown and gray peeked from underneath snow-white caps. As Katherine walked the paths, she thought back to pastel spring shades—and bright summer colors, but these snow-covered clusters had a strange beauty all their own. The wintery grounds with their quiet adornment delighted her.

The scene's harmony and loveliness reflected the newfound peace she felt in the household. Everyone seemed amiable this winter. Even Mr. Emery. Katherine smiled. Amiable was too mild, too sweet-tempered a word to describe Jerard Emery. One had to be on one's toes with him. Still, the irascibility that had characterized him at her arrival almost two years ago had lessened and he was easier to be around.

The winter had gone well in other respects as well. Her new tutor proved to be knowledgeable and kind-hearted. Furthermore, he'd pronounced her advanced enough in her studies so that her dream of teaching seemed a veritable reality. Of course, she already taught Cassie. Besides that, Katherine had shown her how to read music so she could sing in the church choir. The child had a lovely, light-timbered voice.

So life had been good these winter months. Katherine halted a few moments to consider the thought. She knew it was God who had brought good things into her life. In spite of the sharp sorrow that had come her way, He'd sent blessings to keep up her spirits and her faith. Blessings such as Mrs. Lanning and Christopher and the Hodges, this beautiful estate to live in, and the wonderful piano she played each day. Yes, all this was more than enough. With a renewed step, she left the gardens to wander down the tree-lined drive.

Though frozen, the road was largely free of ice and snow. Strolling along the avenue, she stretched taller. The stately arches of the oaks made her feel like a queen. She stopped and threw back her head to scan the sky. Dark branches etched lacy patterns against the pearl gray heavens.

"Katherine!"

Instinctively she stepped back. The intense, low voice had come from her right. Beyond the oaks a man's lean frame appeared from behind the snow-covered bushes. She turned to flee toward the house.

"Stop, Katherine! Don't be afraid. It's me, your father."

She glanced behind her.

"Katherine, don't you recognize me?" The man drew off his hat.

In the gathering dusk she studied the man. It *was* her father. Shabbily dressed.

"I know it's been years. But please, come here." He motioned her to the roadside. "Please. A father wouldn't harm his daughter. I only want to talk a few minutes, after that I'll be on my way."

She considered his request, then, with caution, cautiously approached the tall oaks. "What—what are you doing here? How did you find me?"

"Back when your mother died—I wasn't able to come, so I sent one of my friends. When you left the boarding house, he followed you on the train."

So that's who that stranger was.

Her father remained near the cover of bushes beyond the trees. "Well, my little girl all grown up and quite the young lady now. You remind me of your mother, except for the hair. Yours is darker like mine. But you're just as pretty. Maybe more so." He smiled. "You're a daughter to be proud of."

Katherine examined her father. He looked older, harder. Yet, she could still see vestiges of the handsome man her mother had fallen in love with. Had he changed? She asked the obvious question that came to mind. "What have you been doing all this time? I thought—we thought—you had left us, disappeared for good."

"Well, that was true at first. I didn't plan on coming back. Sorry." He had the grace to look embarrassed. "But when I got into trouble and was put away, I started looking at life differently."

"Put away? What do you mean?"

"Sent to prison."

"Prison!"

"Yes. A bit of a shock, isn't it? In fact, that's where I was when I heard about your mother's death."

She tried to digest this unsettling fact. "Did Mother know? About prison?"

"No. She would've been ashamed, coming from such a fine family. Course, with her gone now it doesn't matter, except for you, that is." He fingered the brim of his hat. "You know, I've been here quite a while, trying to figure a way to see you. Had no idea this family was so rich. Are they treating you good?"

"Yes." Without warning she shivered. Apparently the cold had penetrated her outer wrappings. But the surprise, the shock of seeing her father like this, and the fact he'd been in prison ... she made a conscious effort to rally her thoughts. "Yes, they've been good to me. I'm ward to Mrs. Emery who has seen to my education, and there's an elderly aunt who is kind. And Mrs. Emery has a son, who's away a lot on business."

"He runs a business besides this place?"

"Well, he's part owner of a factory."

"How old is he? Is he married?"

"He's about ten years older than I. No, he's not married."

"Ever try setting your cap for him? You'd be set for life."

Katherine suppressed a quick retort. "That would be impossible. We're too different. Besides, as soon as I'm able to support myself, I'll be leaving. The senior Mr. Emery's will and testament provided a home and education for me until I can become independent. I'll soon turn eighteen."

"So you plan being out on your own." He nodded. "That's good. You know, I'm going to make a new start out west. Where there's lots of opportunity."

"Out west?" Indians came to mind. "How far? Any idea where you'll be going?"

"Not sure. But far enough—that's why I came to see you one last time." He looked off to the side. "So try not to hold too much against me."

"I've already forgiven you."

"Oh? Well, thanks." His fingers fidgeted with his hat brim again. "I'm sorry about your ma. Too bad, you not having any parents around, but as it is, I can't do anything for you. Best I stay out of the way." He looked down at the ground. "Well, I won't be hanging around much longer." He glanced at her, then looked off to the side again. "Any chance of you giving me some food before I leave? And a little money? I could pay you back when I get work out west."

Katherine stepped back. "I—I don't know." Her old wariness returned. "I'd have to go to my room for the money."

"That's all right. I can wait." His hands gestured nonchalantly. "I suppose I could meet you somewhere near the house?"

She tried to think of a likely place, this all seemed so strange. "Well, how about the main back door? The kitchen's right there, where I'd get the food."

"Not at the door. I'll watch for you nearby. And, uh, I wouldn't mention I'm here to anyone."

Katherine looked at him a long moment. "All right. This will take a few minutes."

After removing her carefully saved funds from her bedroom dresser, she hurried down the back stairs, trying not to make noise gathering food from the pantry, then slipped out the rear door. She scanned the yard. No one was in sight. Thank God Mr. Emery's dog was inside the house. Had she done right by not alerting anyone about her father? She disliked keeping anything from Mrs. Emery.

Then she saw him. He motioned her from bushes near the stables. She tried to walk at a normal gait across the lawn so as not to attract attention. Suddenly, she was relieved her father was leaving—and would be far, far away. She suppressed a twinge of guilt, feeling so relieved he would soon be gone. Yet, how well she remembered life being difficult when he was present.

She stepped near the snow-covered bushes. "Everything's in this sack. I wrapped the money separately."

He took the bag and glanced inside. "What's this?" He took out a book. "A Bible?"

He opened it. "Your mother's. And now your name's on the flyleaf. You'd better keep it. It'll get more use that way."

"No! Please take it. And read it. The references underneath my name are ones Mother jotted down." Her eyes begged him as he held out the Bible to her. "This is the best parting gift I could give you."

He shrugged his shoulders and stuck it back in the bag. "Okay, but I've got to travel light."

He asked a few questions about the estate, then awkwardly placed his hand on her shoulder. "Now, take care of yourself. I'll stay till you get inside. Don't look back. Like I said, it wouldn't do you any good for anyone to know I'm here."

"All right. Good-bye, then ... Father." She hesitated, then leaned forward to give him a brief hug. "God bless you."

ꟹ

Katherine walked to her bedroom window and looked over the darkened yard. Rectangular patches of light dotted the lawn from the mansion windows.

She sighed. The unexpected appearance of her father had unsettled her. After all these years. By now he should be a good mile or two away. She tried to visualize him on the dark frozen road, maybe resting on a log or rock until the moon rose.

She stood at the window thinking back over their early years as a family. Her first memories were of a little rented house out from town with three rooms: a large main area and two bedrooms. A nice fenced area in back where a garden grew with string beans and tomatoes. The owner's wife had taken a liking to Mother and, when she saw how much Mother loved flowers, had given her a few seeds and told her to plant the marigolds by the vegetables to keep away pests.

Father helped on the owner's farm during planting and harvesting. Then he would go into town to see about work, but she couldn't remember him settling into anything. He would talk how someday they'd have it nice and comfortable—when his boat came in. Had he meant Mother's inheritance?

But things changed. Was it after he discovered Mother had been cut out of her parents' will? He started drinking, would make promises, and most of the time not keep them. Money was scarce. Some days that last year they didn't have anything to eat. Mother took in laundry for extra income, but if Father could get his hands on it, he'd spend it on drink.

Now and then, the farmer's wife sent them food. But when none was in the house, Father would get angry and stay away, sometimes for days. Then one day he never came back.

After that Mother decided to go into town to find work. They moved to the boarding house and shared a room with a big double bed. Mother said not to worry because their Heavenly Father would take care of them. Katherine discovered Mother had learned early in her marriage to look to God for help.

Katherine's mind drifted back to her father. What had he been doing to end up in prison? Hearing that had been a shock. He said he'd started looking at life differently. But had he changed? Would he now try to build a better life?

She visualized again those last minutes near the stable. Would she ever see him again? Before they parted he'd asked about the hired help on the estate. He seemed interested in the stables. Had he contemplated asking for a job here instead of going out west?

Then it struck her. He had kept glancing at the stables. Was he thinking—?

She turned from the window and walked to the closet, pulled her shawl off its hook and quietly made her way down the back stairway. She couldn't think about what she might discover. But she had to confirm her suspicions.

Reaching the main stable door, she stood mute. Scuffling, scrambling noises erupted from inside.

Her father's voice!

She raised her hand to open the door when something hit violently against it. Startled, she sprang back. There was a side entrance. Finding the door ajar, she swung it open and stepped into a short hall.

Out of sight around the corner she heard grunts and heavy breathing, then more scuffling. The horses stirred restlessly in their stalls.

She hurried to the end of the hall, cautiously peering around the corner. Her eyes widened.

Mr. Emery!

He lay sprawled on the floor, his immaculate clothes disheveled, a red welt raised on one cheek.

Her father rose from his knees and limped toward the horse he'd already saddled.

Taggart!

Katherine dashed across the stable to her father. "What are you doing here? Was this your plan all along?" She grasped the horse's mane. "You can't take this horse. It's Mr. Emery's—his favorite."

Her father didn't answer, caught the reins.

"You haven't changed at all, have you?"

Just then Mr. Emery elbowed past her and grabbed her father around the middle, dragging him backward. Her father staggered and Mr. Emery swung him around, pinning him against the stable wall. Mr. Emery seized the older man's throat with his hands. "We hang horse thieves, you know."

Edmond gagged while Katherine watched in horror. She clutched Mr. Emery's arm. "Stop! He's my father."

Jerard glanced at her, his scowling face registering surprise.

At that moment Edmond punched his adversary hard, below the belt. Jerard doubled over. The older man swung at Jerard's head with all the strength he could muster and Jerard collapsed to the stable floor.

Her father scrambled over to Taggart, glancing at Katherine. "Now stay out of my way." He grabbed the horse's reins, pulled the stallion to the stable door, then flung up the latch and swung the door wide. Cold air rushed in. As he hitched himself into the saddle, he looked back at his daughter. "This is something I have to do. Now, good-bye!" He urged the horse into the wintry night.

Katherine stood stricken, her hand covering her mouth. She glanced back at Mr. Emery. He lay sprawled on his back. She hurried to his side, knelt down, uncertain what to do. Looking for signs of life, she saw his chest rise and lower. Relief flooded her.

She should go for help. Starting to rise, she saw him stir. She knelt over him once again, trying to make her voice sound firm and confident. "Mr. Emery, I'll go for help."

"Oh-h!" He winced, trying to raise himself on one elbow.

"What can I do?"

"Jus' do wha' I say." He held his head. "Go to th' bunk house. Get Smith, Higgins—and Riley—to go after that d—your father."

"I'll get you a cold compress."

"Not at th' house. From th' barn—rags near the door."

Katherine ran out the stable. By the time she returned with the compress, men were saddling horses. The groom was readying one for Mr. Emery who leaned against a stall.

"You're not going, too?" She thrust the wet cloth into his hand.

His movements were slow and deliberate. He pressed the compress under one eye. "Go directly to your room." His voice no longer slurred. "Don't say anything to anyone—especially Mother." He motioned for the horse. She saw him wince as he raised himself into the saddle. Her insides tightened. "All right, men, let's go. He's got a good head start." Without a backward glance, Mr. Emery rode out the stable doors.

Gazing after him, riding that strange horse with the small band of riders following him, Katherine shivered. She tightened the shawl around her. Her limbs felt cold and shaky—but nothing like the cold she felt inside.

Chapter 17

A knock sounded on the bedroom door. "Miss Katherine!" Another knock, then Mattie rushed in. "Sorry I'm late, miss. Everyone's in the kitchen talking." Katherine turned over in bed to see Mattie studying her. "Are you well? You look peaked."

"I didn't sleep much last night, that's all." With effort, Katherine sat up.

Mattie poured fresh water into the basin. "You won't believe what happened last night. Taggart was stolen—Mr. Jerard's prize horse! And he and some of the men rode out to catch the robber. I tell you, nothin' like this has ever happened here before."

"Did they catch the thief?" Katherine asked carefully, climbing out of bed.

"No, miss, and Mr. Jerard came home fit to be tied." In vivid terms Mattie told all the master had said and done. "At least that's what the stable boy told me. I tell you, a body doesn't feel safe." Then, with a quick change of subject, she asked, "Which dress would you like to wear, miss?"

"I'll get it, Mattie. Has breakfast been served?"

"Not yet. Sorry I was late, miss, to put you behind so."

"That's all right, I can manage. Go ahead with the rest of your work."

Fumbling with her shoe buttons, Katherine's mind raced. If the household had known her father was involved, Mattie would have said something. She closed her eyes. The maid wouldn't have been so apologetic if she'd known who the thief was. Bad enough Mr. Emery knowing—but the whole household? And Taggart. Why did her father have to steal Taggart?

At breakfast Katherine observed Mrs. Emery. After some minutes she decided the lady didn't know who stole the horse, for she acted as cordially as ever. For some reason, Mr. Emery hadn't told his mother. But Katherine wanted to avoid *him*. Mattie said he'd been in a temper after his return.

Katherine finished breakfast as soon as decorum permitted and made an excuse to go to the kitchen so she could use the back stairway. When she reached the top step, she looked up and down the hall, then hurried to her bedroom. She would not come out until lesson time.

❧

When her tutor was packing to leave, Bates walked in. Never had he entered the sitting room during lessons. "Mr. Emery would like to see you in the library, Miss Katherine."

Katherine forced herself to go through the motions of graciously seeing her tutor to the front door. After saying goodbye, she pressed her hands to her stomach. It felt queasy. She closed her eyes in a short prayer.

When she opened the library door, she saw Mr. Emery sitting at his desk, face averted. He finished reading a document and signed it. Finally, he looked up. An ugly dark bruise marked his right cheekbone. "Come in." He nodded to the wing chair near his desk.

Reluctantly, Katherine crossed the room and took a seat.

"We didn't catch the thief." His voice was clipped. "Taggart is gone."

Katherine already knew this, but to hear him speak in that tone cut her to the quick. She hadn't cried until this moment, but now tears welled up. Turning her head into the chair's wing, she tried to stifle the sobs.

"Stop sniveling."

Her sobbing increased.

Mr. Emery stared at her, then finally said, "Why didn't you tell someone your father was here? Were you aiding and abetting? That would make you accessory to the crime." He stood up. "This whole thing might have been avoided if you had let someone know."

Katherine groped for a hanky in her pocket. "I'm sorry—I'm sorry. He told me not to tell. I didn't realize he'd steal anything."

"You trusted him?"

"I thought—I could. I'm sorry."

"Regret won't retrieve my horse."

"I know, I know. It's horrible. I'll—I'll pay for Taggart. Make restitution somehow."

"With what? You have money I don't know about?"

Katherine pressed the hanky to her eyes. "I don't have any at present, but I do get a small allowance each month. I'll give that to you."

"That'd take years."

"When I start teaching—"

"A pittance. You'll be lucky to have anything left after living expenses."

She wiped her nose, sat up straighter, trying to regain her composure. "What you say might be true, but I *will* do my best to pay for—for Taggart."

"Taggart cannot be replaced. Your offer is ridiculous. Besides, do you think I'd take money from someone who's all but destitute?"

"I insist."

"You insist nothing. The matter is settled when I say I'll not take your money." He sat down and looked at her in exasperation. His fingers drummed the desktop. "However, if you want to help, you can do something."

"What is that?"

"You could aid in the apprehension of your father. A possibility exists we might even retrieve Taggart." He leaned forward. "Do you have any clue where your father might have gone?"

"He wasn't specific. Somewhere out west, he said."

Mr. Emery's hand hit the desk. "You know no more than that? This is no time to protect him."

Katherine watched him wide-eyed. "Nothing more, sir. I'm sorry."

His dark eye scrutinized her as if to ferret out anything she might be holding back. "Katherine, if you hear anything, you *will* let me know."

"Yes, sir."

She looked down in shame before his piercing gaze. More than anger shown out his eyes. They looked stricken. He *did* love that horse. She felt terrible.

"You may go now," he said.

Halfway to the door she stopped, turned, and approached the desk once more. "Sir, I want to thank you for not divulging the relationship," she whispered, "between the thief and myself. If anyone knew, I think I'd die." Her eyes lowered. "Especially your mother. I don't want to be a discredit to her."

"My mother is part of the reason I chose not to say anything." Mr. Emery's tone softened. "You may rest assured I will not reveal the relationship between the thief and yourself."

Katherine looked up, her eyes filling up once again. "Thank you, sir." She whirled around to the door as tears threatened to spill down her face.

ॐ

Cassie Hodges looked out the front window. "Mother! She's here." Cassie raced to the door, clasped her teacher's hand, and led her to the front parlor.

Katherine chose a seat in front of the window so the sun would warm their backs. The extra heat felt welcome this chilly winter afternoon. And to sit here was a relief after the recent interview in the library. She handed Cassie the book and, while the girl read, studied her.

Her student's blond hair shone in the sunlight, its color like warm honey against her faded blue dress. As she leaned over, a tress drooped across the page. She seemed oblivious to the inconvenience, so intent was she on her studies. Katherine reached over and gently placed the wayward lock behind the girl's shoulder.

Cassie looked up and smiled. "Thank you."

Katherine gently squeezed the girl. She didn't often touch someone, but at this moment it seemed the most natural thing in the world. Since beginning to teach Cassie, she'd felt an affinity with her; in fact, felt a kinship with the whole family. While she shrank from any of the Emery household ever knowing about her father's theft, she had a feeling if Mrs. Hodges ever found out, she would be as loved and accepted as ever. How glad she was to be of service to this family. They gave her confidence that in the future she could be on her own as a teacher.

And now becoming independent was more important than ever. She must pay back Mr. Emery. In a few weeks she'd be eighteen. Was there any way to earn extra money?

Her thoughts returned to Cassie. Katherine wanted to hug her once again. But Cassie would wonder if she showed such open affection a second time. Katherine sat straighter. It was just as well not to let sentimentality rule. Both Cassie and she had a lot to accomplish in the coming months.

☙

Walking home through the woods, Katherine passed the big beech tree Mr. Lanning had pointed out on their first walk together. She missed him terribly. Longed for his counsel—and love. He had encouraged her with such hope for her future.

What would he have said about her father's visit? Mr. Lanning had urged her to forgive him. She had done so to the best of her ability, but today felt strained whenever she thought of him. Would Mr. Lanning say to forgive him again? She needed more time. Her emotions were too raw.

She advanced up the back lawn to the house. As she approached the kitchen door, one of the downstairs maids stepped outside to shake a rug.

"Hello, Miss Katherine. You out here alone?" She gave the rug a snap. "Lands, that thief might still be around." She looked at the stable and shuddered.

Just then the stable doors opened. A carriage exited with Mr. Emery inside. He looked in their direction, but gave no further acknowledgment.

"Friendly soul, isn't he?" the maid said. "Never mind. I hear he's leaving on business and won't be back for a spell."

Katherine followed the maid into the house and opened the back hall closet. So Mr. Emery would be absent awhile. She took off her coat and hung it. The truth was she hated the thought of her unresolved debt, but more than that, the fact her father had taken Taggart. That horse of all horses. Just like he took her treasured locket. Grabbing her coat, she buried her face in it. A cold, outdoor smell still lingered in its folds. "Thank you, Lord, that Mr. Emery's gone," she whispered. Now she wouldn't have to dread meeting him every day—with this trouble between them.

Chapter 18

Aunt Elsie held up a hand to stop her maid. "Please leave my jewelry box here, and when you're finished clearing up, see how Katherine's coming along with her dressing." She looked in the mirror and fluffed the lace at her throat. "When she's finished, have her come here."

"Yes, ma'am." The maid quickly put away odds and ends and left the room.

Aunt Elsie picked up the portrait of her deceased husband from her dressing table. "Well, Robert, we shall see what we can do for these young people tonight. They make such a nice couple, don't you think?" She smiled at the picture, then turned from it to await her protégée.

Katherine closed the door to the aunt's room. The overskirt of her white silk dress drew up in back to form a rosette at the waist. Another silk rosette adorned the discreetly lowered neckline. *How absolutely lovely Katherine is,* Aunt Elsie thought.

"Why, Auntie, you look like the cat that swallowed the canary. What have you been doing?"

"Nothing, dear. I have something for you, though." Taking Katherine by the arm, she drew her to a nearby chair. She returned with the merest scrap of cloth, fine and delicate. "Smell this." She wafted it under Katherine's nose.

"Heavenly! What is it?"

"My own little secret which I'll divulge in time, my dear. But the scent does include lilac. We'll fasten this into the wrist of your dress. A couple stitches will hold it in place." She picked up a needle and thread. "Now, give me your right arm. That's the one you'll extend if a gentleman offers assistance."

"Aunt Elsie!" Katherine laughed. "It's only a family party for my eighteenth birthday. You know as well as I do the only gentleman around my age will be Christopher. Mr. Emery is still out of town on business."

Aunt Elsie finished her stitching. "Christopher's such a nice young man, don't you think?"

"I've thought so since I first met him."

"But I mean, he's particularly nice. The kind of man you'd like to be special for. And, of course, this is a special occasion." Aunt Elsie reached to the table and picked up a box. "And now, this is for your birthday. I want you to have it before the dinner party."

Katherine scrutinized the small square present and looked up fondly at the old aunt. "What is this?"

"Don't say anything, just open it."

Katherine's hands undid the flowered paper wrapping, then lifted the lid. Silver filigree pendant earrings rested on black velvet. "Why, Auntie, they're beautiful."

"Try them on at my dressing table."

Katherine fastened them and then gazed at her reflection in the mirror. The earrings set off her dark hair drawn into an elegant chignon. "I look—"

"You look lovely and sophisticated, my dear." The aunt stepped back and examined Katherine with satisfaction. "I can't imagine anyone prettier."

"Auntie, you're prejudiced."

"Then I've been prejudiced since you first arrived. I think it's your eyes. They're sort of shiny, not lackluster like so many. And they're kind." Aunt Elsie turned back to her jewelry box. "Now, where is that bracelet?" She fumbled around inside. "Here, take this." She pulled out a dainty silver circlet.

"Aunt Elsie, what can I say?"

"Say nothing. Just enjoy it for this evening."

Katherine looked at the insistent woman, then held out her hand to take the bangle. She looped it over her wrist and held it off for inspection. "I feel so like an adult." She paused. "I shouldn't take it." Then the corners of her mouth curved up. "But I will for this evening."

☙

Katherine was still smiling as she descended the stairs. Aunt Elsie. What a dear to understand her desire to look grownup on her eighteenth birthday.

Below, she noticed Bates walking briskly out the front door. A carriage must have arrived. The dinner guests would make a perfect eight around the table. Christopher and his grandmother. Her music teacher. And the minister and his wife.

She had almost reached the foyer when the front door swung wide. Suitcase in hand, Bates preceded the recent arrival.

Mr. Emery!

Katherine stopped.

The traveler hesitated in the doorway, gazed at her a moment, then approached the stairway.

Standing on the bottom step, Katherine's eyes were almost on a level with his. She felt herself blush.

"All dressed up, I see." His eyes left hers, glanced at the dangling earrings. He stepped back and looked at the brightly-lit drawing room and equally brilliant dining room. "Mother entertaining? What's the occasion?"

"My eighteenth birthday, sir."

"Your birthday. Well, it seems I've arrived home just in time. May I congratulate the birthday girl?" He stepped near her once again and extended his hand. When she raised hers for him to grasp, his head bent over it. The fragrance wafted through the air and his hand tightened. He lifted his head, his eyes searching hers.

Her discomfiture deepening, Katherine withdrew her hand.

Bates reappeared from the dining room.

"Will you see another place is set for dinner," Mr. Emery said. "And tell Mother not to expect me in the drawing room beforehand. When I come down, we'll dine at once. Now, Katherine, if you'll excuse me." He stepped past her to mount the stairs.

Katherine looked at his straight back as he ascended, then turned to glance at the dining room entrance. She wondered absently how his mother would react to the table's lopsided number of place settings.

ᘓ

The first guests to arrive were the minister and his wife. With a bow, Rev. Hanlin presented Katherine with a wrist corsage of white roses.

Mrs. Hanlin said, "I asked Mrs. Emery the color of your dress."

"The white rose represents spiritual purity," Mr. Hanlin said.

Mrs. Hanlin reached out and hugged her. "So appropriate for you, my dear."

That begins the evening on a high note, Katherine thought.

She smiled as she moved into the dining room to the place of honor, looking around at the assembled group. Mr. Emery entered with a quick step and began talking animatedly with the music teacher seated on his left.

Katherine had to admit the consternation she'd felt at his unexpected arrival. Now he looked as if he hadn't a care in the world. Had he forgiven her for the loss of Taggart? Katherine resolved not to let his presence or their last unpleasant confrontation spoil her birthday dinner. She turned to Christopher and endeavored to talk with him in her liveliest manner.

Mrs. Emery motioned that her ward be served first and soon Katherine was swept along in the specialness of the occasion. Cut glass and silver on the table reflected the candlelight. During the meal, she saw the guests' eyes turn to her and smile and heard them remark how charming she looked.

After dinner, everyone rose to move to the drawing room. With a glad little tug at her heart, Katherine took Christopher's arm. Over her shoulder, she noticed Mr. Emery detain his mother. He said in an undertone. "Katherine seems to have blossomed this evening."

"Yes, she's looking particularly attractive tonight. If I may say so, she's a real credit to my upbringing. I'm glad I had that white silk made up for her. It sets off her coloring."

Just inside the front hall, Christopher paused and pulled his grandmother aside to ask a question. While Katherine waited, she heard Mr. Emery and his mother continue talking just out of sight.

"I don't remember seeing those earrings before," Jerard said. "Were they your birthday present?"

"No, son. I don't know who gave them to her."

"They're not from Christopher?"

"Christopher wouldn't do such a thing. They're too personal and costly a gift."

"I was just wondering. You're right, however, about the dress."

"I'm glad you returned in time for her birthday. Let's join our guests now."

Katherine's cheeks flamed to hear herself discussed, to be eavesdropping, albeit unintentionally. Before Mr. Emery and his mother appeared in the hall, she took a step nearer

Christopher and his grandmother so as to seem part of their conversation.

After coffee, Bates rearranged the chairs with Katherine at the center for the games. Mr. Emery took a seat on the group's fringe.

She glanced at him, surprised. She knew he wasn't fond of parlor games. After his travels, everyone would have understood if he had excused himself. But he crossed his legs as if getting comfortable for the duration of the entertainment.

"For this first game—" Katherine walked amongst the group, handing out sheets of paper and pencils and explaining what each person was to do. At first, she felt self-conscious, but as she continued, her embarrassment subsided. In front of the group again, she concluded, "—that's how we will proceed."

"You explained that exceptionally well, my dear," the minister said. "No wonder I heard such glowing reports of your teaching Sunday school last month."

"Thank you, sir. Maybe that's because I love to teach. You know, I hope to make it my profession someday." She smiled. "Now then, is everyone ready?"

As the games progressed, a good bit of laughing and joking spiced the atmosphere. The guests easily dropped their formal manners. Everyone seemed to like Katherine's choices for entertainment.

"Now for the final game," she said as she stood. "It is a familiar one, but any who haven't played, I hope you will enjoy it. Pay attention, because this one will test everyone's ability at recall." She set herself to act seriously. "I have chosen a number of poetry selections, each four lines long. You must repeat word for word the four lines. If you make a mistake, you will pay the forfeit." Katherine's voice caught on a giggle. "I know each of you will enjoy the others paying their forfeits.

"Aunt Elsie has contrived the forfeits. Each has been devised to suit the person who fails." She nodded to Aunt Elsie who held up her cards. "If you cannot figure out how to fulfill the obligation of the forfeit, you may look on the back of the card where a suggestion has been provided." Katherine looked down at the page of poetry selections. "Now, I will first challenge my esteemed music teacher, Mr. Anson." She read four long lines, then looked up expectantly.

"How could anyone repeat all that?" her teacher asked.

"That's the object, Mr. Anson." She smiled. "It is my fond hope each of you will have to pay the forfeit."

The music teacher tried to repeat the lines but failed, so marched over to Aunt Elsie. With ceremony, she handed him his card. After reading it, he paused. Then he faced the group, held one hand half clenched in front of his face. Three fingers pumped up and down while he buzzed a song through stiffened lips.

"I believe our friend is favoring us with a trumpet solo," Christopher said.

Mr. Anson gave a last blast on his imaginary instrument. The little audience laughed and clapped while he bowed.

When the applause died, Katherine beckoned to Christopher. "You're next."

He too failed to repeat his four lines so he approached Aunt Elsie to receive his card. "This is impossible, Auntie," he said as he read the forfeit.

"Look on the back of your card and you'll see the hint," she said.

Christopher asked for a lighted candle. Then he walked over to Katherine. "Now, watch as I kiss my shadow." He held up the candle behind his head to cast his shadow on Katherine's face, then bent to kiss her cheek.

"Oh!" Katherine laughed.

Christopher smiled. "Thank you, Aunt Elsie, for a most pleasurable forfeit."

Katherine involuntarily glanced at Mr. Emery. Everyone was laughing but him. She beckoned to Mrs. Lanning. "Would you like to be next?"

Mrs. Lanning also failed to repeat her lines. Her eyebrows went up when she read her forfeit. "Sit upon the fire?" Then she turned over her card and smiled. She asked for a pencil, wrote "The Fire" on her card, held it up for everyone to see, then placed the paper on her chair and smugly said, "I shall now sit upon the fire." Without further ado, she seated herself. Everyone laughed.

"I think these forfeits are the best part of the game," said Rev. Hanlin.

"Then you're next," Katherine said.

He failed—as did everyone after him. Each forfeit was accompanied with laughter and jesting.

Jerard was last.

"Mr. Emery, even though I didn't anticipate your attendance, I did bring an extra selection of poetry. So, you must try one, too," Katherine said playfully. "Aunt Elsie, do you have a forfeit?"

"Oh yes, I thought up one a few minutes ago."

Katherine proceeded to read a difficult selection. After she finished, Jerard said, "I see you mean to make me fail, but I will manfully try." He manfully tried. And failed.

Sauntering over to Aunt Elsie, he said, "I guess I will have to take my medicine with good grace like the rest." He took the card from his aunt. "Hmm..." He pursed his lips. "I see Auntie has planned my soon demise. My forfeit says, 'Read your will.'"

He thought a few moments. "Very well." He struck a pose with the card, holding it so that it seemed like a long legal document. "I, Jerard Hogarth Emery, being of sound mind and body, name the following recipients of my most generous will. First and foremost, I will my hair to the esteemed, but bald, minister of our parish, the right Reverend Mr. Hanlin."

A titter of laughter followed his announcement.

Jerard then nodded to the minister's wife. "Secondly, I will my most sensitive and discerning ears to Mrs. Hanlin, to better hear her husband's sermons."

Another appreciative titter swept the group.

Jerard looked at Christopher a moment before saying, "Thirdly, I will my eyes to Christopher so he may better see his true interest in life—devoting himself to art and art alone." He bowed to his neighbor. "Next, I will my strong right arm to my mother which she will need in order to run this estate after my untimely death."

His mother feigned a muffled cry of mourning and Jerard walked over and comforted her by encircling her shoulder. Everyone smiled approval.

He stepped back and addressed the music teacher. "To Mr. Anson, I will my nimble fingers so he can better play the trumpet, or any other instrument which suits his fancy." He glanced around the group, seeing whom he might have missed. "Ah, Mrs. Lanning. To you dear lady, who have with courage sat upon the fire, I will my skin to repair any damage you have suffered."

Several of the ladies clapped their approval.

He turned to Aunt Elsie who sat apart from the rest. "Aunt Elsie, may I compliment you on your clever little forfeits. Yet, I fear I must will you my common sense," he said with a half smile.

He paused, then turned to Katherine. "Last, but not least, to our most lovely and piquant birthday young lady, for such an occasion I must will the best part of me. To you—" He paused and bowed low. "I will my heart."

Katherine inclined her head, acknowledging the bon mot.

He rose, smiling. "Now! I hope you all feel enriched by the bequests of my last will and testament."

Rev. Hanlin led a round of applause. "I, for one, would be glad to acquire some of your hair on my bald pate."

Jerard saluted the minister and turned to his mother. "Does this conclude the games for this evening?" At her nod, he said, "Well, ladies and gentlemen, this ends the evening's entertainment. But you're all invited to stay as long as you like."

Rev. Hanlin beamed. "I'm sure I speak for the missus and myself that we've both had a delightful time. However, tomorrow's work means we must rise early. I regret being the first to break up this party." He made his way to Katherine, congratulated her once again on her birthday and then turned to Mrs. Emery.

This seemed the signal for the remainder of the guests to do likewise. Mrs. Emery called for their coats and carriages and a friendly hustle and bustle ensued. Katherine stood at the front door and cordially saw them off.

Christopher approached. "The birthday girl, lovely to a fault. Let me congratulate you, again." Katherine held out her hand to say goodbye. He grasped it, squeezing it warmly. "Such a fun forfeit this evening. If I was bolder, I'd chance fulfilling that same forfeit right here and now."

"You wouldn't!" She laughed.

He laughed in turn. "Ah! The conventions of society. Someday I might throw them to the wind."

"You always joke."

"Don't be so sure, birthday girl. Don't be so sure." His eyes gleamed. "But for now, I bid you a fond farewell and will hand you over to our esteemed piano teacher."

After the last guest departed, Katherine turned and moved toward Mrs. Emery standing at the stair. "Thank you for a wonderful birthday dinner and for inviting my favorite people. I enjoyed it so much."

"You're welcome, my dear." Mrs. Emery grasped her ward's hands. "You carried out your part of the evening admirably. I am proud of you." She paused. "Why don't we join Aunt Elsie in the sitting room. I'm sure we're all too excited to go to bed just yet. I'll order warm milk with nutmeg, and we can talk over the party." As she released Katherine's hands, she asked, "Has anyone seen Jerard?"

"I think he went to the library," Aunt Elsie said.

ঞ

The next three-quarters of an hour the females of the household chatted over the details of the dinner. Katherine had never felt more a part of the family. She basked in the glow of the after-party talk.

At length Aunt Elsie yawned. "Well, my dears, I'm most gratified with the evening and my part in it, but I must retire. I will sleep well tonight."

"I'm ready as well," Mrs. Emery said. "Coming, Katherine?"

"Yes, ma'am."

As the three exited the sitting room and started down the hall, the library door opened. Jerard's frame filled the doorway. "You ladies retiring?" he asked. "I'll say good night then." He appeared about to turn back inside when he added, "Oh, Katherine, could I see you a few minutes?"

Mrs. Emery looked at her ward, then her son, "Well, only a minute because it's late, Jerard. Come, Auntie."

Katherine said good night to the two ladies. Mr. Emery motioned her inside, and she walked uncertainly into the room.

"I have something for your birthday," he said. "Why don't you sit near the fire?" One of the dark red damask chairs had been drawn up near its warmth.

Katherine tried to hide the surprise she felt and sat as directed.

Jerard walked to his desk and picked up a wrapped box, then stepped over to Katherine and handed it to her. He rested one hand on the chair's high back.

Katherine turned the package in her hands. "The wrapping is exquisite."

"Open it."

Under his intent gaze, she fumbled with the paper. Finally, she succeeded in undoing it and opened the box's cover. A pair of silver combs nestled on a bed of white satin. Her breath caught. "They're beautiful." She glanced up at Mr. Emery, then back to the hair ornaments. She thought back to his arrival that evening—remembered him being surprised it was her birthday. How could he now give her a present?

"The gift is—" She looked up at him again, weighing what to say next. What had she overheard his mother and him talking about just after dinner? "They *are* beautiful. But I'm afraid it would be improper to accept them."

"Improper?"

"They might be considered—too expensive, too—" She couldn't say the word *personal.*

"You are part of the Emery household. That makes it right and proper." He motioned carelessly toward her earrings. "Now, if you received those from a man outside the family, that would have been improper." He paused. "You know, I've never noticed those earrings on you before tonight." His expectant look encouraged an explanation.

"These?" Her hand went up to one ear. "Aunt Elsie gave them to me this evening for my birthday." She stretched out her arm. "And she lent me this bracelet to complete the effect."

Jerard's jaw relaxed. "And a very nice effect, I must say."

"Thank you." She lowered her arm.

He nodded toward the combs. "So, we'll have no more nonsense about accepting my gift."

She looked at him, taking the measure of his resolution. His dark eyes regarded her steadily. Hers dropped. "If you think so. Thank you." Quickly she added, "Now I must go upstairs. It's late."

"Yes, you are still young." He held out his hand.

She handed him the box. Then she realized it was her hand he'd offered to take. She covered her embarrassment by straightening her skirt as she rose.

He continued to study her.

She reached for the box, felt her cheeks glow. "Good night, sir. Thank you again, ever so much."

"I'll see you to the door." He slipped his hand under her elbow.

She walked as sedately as she could. When they reached the doorway, she murmured, "Good night."

"Good night, Katherine."

Like quicksilver, she slipped away from his supporting hand. She glanced up at him and, much to her chagrin, caught an amused gleam in his eye.

Chapter 19

Jerard stepped briskly out the back door of the house, his steps crunching on gravel. When he entered the stables, Higgins looked up in surprise. "Hello, Mr. Jerard. You look right hearty this Sunday morning. It seems spring weather is putting a bounce in your step. What can we do for you?"

"I'd like the buggy hitched up for church instead of the usual carriage."

"Is someone staying home?"

"Yes, Mother has a bad cold, and Aunt Elsie is indisposed as well. I will be taking Miss Katherine to service, so a smaller conveyance will do. You won't need to drive this morning."

"Right, sir. The buggy will be ready at the usual hour."

ᘓ

Katherine seated herself in the drawing room to wait for the carriage. She straightened the skirt of her emerald green suit and adjusted the white lace jabot at her neck. She had taken special care with her dressing this morning. With her hair done up and the little green hat perched jauntily on her head, she felt quite ready to represent the Emery household in their assigned pew. She pictured herself explaining to various members of the congregation how the family fared.

Occasionally, either Mrs. Emery or Aunt Elsie was absent, but never both. She looked forward to attending service alone. It was only a matter of time before she would be on her own, so this provided a small opportunity to feel what it would be like. But then, she reflected, she would truly be by herself, not sallying forth with the Emery equipage at her disposal.

Bates stepped into the drawing room. "Your ride is ready, Miss Katherine."

"Thank you, Bates."

He opened the front door for her, but when she stepped outside, she halted.

Mr. Emery tipped his hat as he ascended the steps. "Katherine, I'm escorting you to church, and it's such a beautiful day I saw no reason why we shouldn't take the buggy."

Minutes later, that same buggy made its way through the avenue of trees. The day was glorious, Katherine had to admit, with its blue sky and invigorating air. But to find Mr. Emery sitting next to her larger than life, when she'd expected to be alone, was disconcerting. She kept looking out her side of the buggy, averting her face.

"Well, Miss Edmond," Jerard said, "aren't you the magpie this morning."

"I'm enjoying the beautiful day—or trying to."

"Trying to? Why should today be an exception? Many's the time I've seen you run for joy on a day such as this."

The thought of him watching her run brought her face sharply around. She caught the amused look in his eye. "Well, I didn't think you'd be going to church."

"I understand your surprise, but I would think you'd be delighted to see the lost sheep making his way back to the fold."

"Yes, of course!"

"Now Miss Edmond, don't sound too enthusiastic, or I shall doubt your sincerity," Jerard teased. He gestured at the passing scenery. "Look here, why don't you relax and enjoy the ride? I promise to be a model driver so that you arrive at church in as fine a feather as when you left the house." He glanced appreciatively at her attire.

He was right. She should be enjoying the ride, and thankful he was going to church. After all, she'd been praying for him almost daily. She put aside the discomfiture of having him at her side.

A bright yellow bank of daffodils greeted them on the slope up to the church. Katherine turned to look as they drove past. Jerard followed her gaze. "They are beautiful," he said, "and a fitting end to our ride. Now, I'll assist you off in front of church and park the buggy."

After disposing of their conveyance, he joined her and extended his arm. "Will you accept my escort? I believe you're old enough."

For a moment Katherine hesitated, then placed her hand on his arm and together they walked up the steps to the front door. Entering the vestibule, several people turned to look. Katherine saw one woman whisper behind her glove.

Jerard paused. Two men approached, welcoming them to the service. One of them gestured toward the doorway so they could be escorted to the family pew. When they were seated, Katherine bowed her head to offer her accustomed prayer. How she wanted the quiet and beauty of the stained glass sanctuary to still her soul. That whispering woman in the vestibule had unsettled her.

The opening hymn was announced, and Katherine reached for the hymnal, but realized Mr. Emery had already grasped it. Surprised, she withdrew her hand. She usually aided Aunt Elsie in these matters and was not accustomed to being helped herself. Mr. Emery was playing the perfect gentleman.

As soon as the congregation started singing, she heard his wonderful voice.

What a contrast to Aunt Elsie's. Dear Auntie sang with such devotion, but her wide vibrato could drive a person to distraction. Most of the time Katherine found herself mentally blocking it out. Mr. Emery sang harmony to her melody, then melody when she changed to alto. To hear his baritone voice blend with hers thrilled something deep within her. She couldn't help glancing up at him. He was enjoying it, too. Then, on the last verse, when he sang melody, she sang an obligato. What had he said when she last accompanied him? "How we make music together." Yes, they did, even with their singing. Thereupon, she realized she'd forgotten to pay attention to the hymn's words. She mentally chastised herself.

When the minister announced the Scripture reading, Katherine opened her Bible to the familiar passage, the Old Testament story of Elisha and the leprous Naaman.

Mr. Emery offered to hold her Bible. As he grasped it, she noticed his hands. They were strong and well-shaped, arresting set against his starched white shirt cuffs and black onyx links. Funny, she had never noticed them until this moment. She glanced up at him again. He stood tall and straight in his black broadcloth suit. A little thrill of pride shot through her. He was doubtless the most handsome and distinguished man in the congregation.

At that she brought herself up short. If this was how she worshipped, she might as well have stayed at home. The minister was already well into the Scripture reading. Her hands clenched, she resolved from here on to keep her mind on the service.

With the last hymn and the benediction pronounced, Katherine rose with the rest of the congregation to greet friends and neighbors. This one and that asked about Mrs. Emery and Aunt Elsie. Throughout, Mr. Emery stood courteously at her side.

As they made their way up the aisle, Katherine caught Mrs. Pruitt's eye in the group ahead. She hoped to bypass the woman without speaking so made herself keep moving. But

Mr. Emery turned to speak to a business associate, and Mrs. Pruitt sidled up to her.

"My dear Katherine," she said, "how nice to see you. Whatever has happened to my dear Emma?"

As Katherine explained her benefactress's indisposition, Mrs. Pruitt was all sympathy.

"That's too bad. You must tell her we missed her." Then she added in an undertone, "But look how you have fared. How did you get him to come to service? I know the other girls are green with envy, as green as your fetching little suit." She poked Katherine's sleeve. "I noticed, too, how attentive he's been. You'll be the talk of our small town."

Mrs. Pruitt's honey-toned voice was all smiles, but Katherine drew away from the woman as if she were a snake. Until Mrs. Pruitt's insinuations, Katherine had been warming herself in the glow of Mr. Emery's attentiveness. Indeed, she had been feeling like one of the family. But a few sly comments from Sylvia Pruitt, and she suddenly felt an interloper. Was it wrong to enjoy the status of being the only Emery female present? And to enjoy Jerard Emery's company?

He turned to her and asked if she was ready to go. She managed to respond with a sedate, "Yes." Lifting her chin ever so slightly and smiling, she willed herself to walk seemingly unperturbed at his side.

Seated in the buggy, Mr. Emery looked at her. "Now to home." He slapped the horse with the reins and started down the church drive with the pleased assurance of a man in control of the day. But instead of making the accustomed turn to the left, he turned right.

She glanced at him. "Is this—"

"I thought we'd take a more picturesque route. You liked the daffodils so well I thought of another place to show you." After traveling a mile or so he directed the horse into a shady lane. "Just beyond that curve, we should see a meadow."

As they rounded the bend they came upon two people with the same idea. Christopher was helping his grandmother descend from their buggy.

Katherine waved her hand in relief. "Hello!" In her joy at seeing her friends, she said, "Isn't it good to see Christopher and his grandmother? I didn't have an opportunity to greet them in church. Could we stop?"

Christopher and Mrs. Lanning returned the wave and waited as Jerard and Katherine approached. But Jerard merely paused beside his neighbors and responded to their invitation to join them by saying, "No, I believe Katherine and I will drive over yonder. There's another view I have in mind." He jerked the reins, urging the horse forward.

Katherine was quiet as Mr. Emery slowed the buggy and then stopped. She craned her neck around. Christopher and Mrs. Lanning were nowhere to be seen.

"This is a better vantage point," he said. The large expanse of meadow stretched before them. In another few weeks it would be lush with newly grown grass. "There's something special at the top of that knoll. Let me help you down."

"Do we have time?" Katherine asked. "Cook will have lunch waiting."

"This will take only a few minutes."

She dutifully walked beside him to the top of the knoll. She appreciated the trouble he was taking to show her this meadow, but walking alone with him seemed strange, awkward somehow.

When they reached the top, Jerard pointed to an area on the other side. Hundreds of deep purple violets dotted the incline. "How lovely," Katherine exclaimed. God's creation was so rich. She wondered if Mr. Emery had any inclination to recognize it as such. Near her feet grew bunches of flowers, and she stooped to pick a few. "I'm going to bring these to your mother and Aunt Elsie." She was thinking how Christopher and his grandmother would enjoy them as well, but decided against suggesting the idea.

They stood in silence, then she asked, "Did you enjoy the service this morning?"

"I found it enlightening."

"In what way?"

He laughed. "You'd find my answer irreverent. I'd best keep it to myself."

"Oh." She felt at a loss to continue, then lit on what she considered a reasonable enough question. "What did you think of Rev. Hanlin's sermon?"

"His discourse on Naaman the leper?"

"Yes."

"Well, as usual, Mr. Hanlin did a fair job of telling a story. As I understood it, Naaman, the captain of the Syrian army went to the prophet Elisha for healing and when he was told to wash seven times in the dirty Jordan River, didn't want to. But, of course, at length he complied and his leprosy disappeared. That an accurate summary?" He smiled, but a challenge glinted in his eyes.

"A succinct summary," she said, "but what did you think of the main point of his discourse?"

"The main point? You mean about Naaman's pride?" He cleared his throat. "I'll have to confess my mind wandered at times—more interesting things were at hand." He glanced at the emerald green hat perched on her coifed hair, then looked off to the meadow. "But I think one could say the moral of the story is never be too proud to do anything."

She couldn't help smiling. "I suppose, if one wants to make the sermon sound like an Aesop fable, it might be put that way."

He looked at her quickly.

She noted the look, but pressed on. "Remember Naaman's words after he was healed? 'There is no God in all the earth, but in Israel.' I thought the point of the story was that God showed Himself to be truly God."

"Yes." Mr. Emery's voice took on a condescending air. "That conclusion is all very well if a person believes the story ever happened. But I think it best to take such stories with a grain of salt." His hand flung out impatiently. "As for God, from what's going on, I think it's plain that He has little to do with this world—or anyone in it."

Katherine's eyes widened.

"Take myself, for example. Look what I've accomplished. I acquired a good education. Improved the estate to run more efficiently than ever. Refinanced and expanded the mill so that in a few years it should be the finest of its kind in the region. When it comes down to it, I haven't needed God."

Katherine's chest rose. She fought down feelings of exasperation. "But who gave you the intelligence to do well in your pursuits? Who placed you into the Emery family so you had advantages in life? Who gave you life itself—the strength to breathe?" She looked at him pointedly. "God did. And His gifts go on and on."

"That's debatable." Mr. Emery's jaw took on a firmer line. "God cannot be seen, so how do we know He does anything for humanity or, in fact, exists? But I *can* see what I've accomplished, what I've gained through hard work and ingenuity."

"But if you're not even sure of the existence of God, why did you bother going to church this morning?"

A moment of silence followed, then with an edge to his voice, Mr. Emery said, "I'm beginning to wonder that myself."

Katherine stared up at him.

Mr. Emery's brows drew together in a frown. "This outing, which promised to be pleasurable, is turning out to be less so."

What had been niggling at the back of her mind suddenly burst out. "Well, you can take part of the blame for that."

"What?"

"I'm referring to how you treated Mrs. Lanning and Christopher. It was rude to drive on as you did, almost without stopping."

The lines of Mr. Emery's mouth tightened. "Listen, Miss Edmond, I don't know why you put such stock in the Lannings. This was my outing, and I believe I can conduct it as I please."

"Oh, by all means let us please ourselves."

The sudden angry look in his eyes warned Katherine she'd gone too far. "You don't seem to have enjoyed the view as much as I expected," he said. "We might as well leave." He grasped her arm and hurried her down to the horse and buggy. Without further word, he assisted her up. His firm grip hurt, but she dared not say anything for fear of upsetting him even more.

He started the buggy with a jerk, quickly passing the spot where the Lannings' conveyance was parked. He didn't seem to care if they bounced over ruts or not. Just as they were to enter the main road, the horse lost her gait and stumbled. Mr. Emery abruptly pulled to a stop. He climbed down and walked over to examine the mare. He inspected the right front foot and swore under his breath.

At first Katherine sat motionless, not daring to speak. Finally she asked, "What is it?"

"A piece of glass caught in her hoof. The soft underside is cut. It'll take some doctoring." He looked at the foot again. "Blast!"

Katherine debated whether to say anything, but when Mr. Emery stood without speaking, at length she said, "Maybe we could ask the Lannings for help."

Mr. Emery glanced at her sharply. Katherine's stomach tightened. He looked as if he was about to say something, but instead walked back down the lane. At that moment the Lanning buggy rounded the bend. He hesitated, then held up his hand. When the Lannings drew beside him, Katherine heard part of his explanation.

"Your groom could doctor it, couldn't he?" Mrs. Lanning asked. "We could send him as soon as possible, and take Katherine with us in the meantime."

Mr. Emery walked back to his buggy. "All right, Katherine, you'll return with the Lannings." He assisted her down and escorted her to their buggy. But when Christopher jumped down to help her, Jerard held firmly onto her arm.

Christopher watched Jerard settle Katherine, then nimbly jumped up to sit beside her. He smiled down at her. "Are you comfortable?"

"Christopher, I'd appreciate it if you'd hurry," Jerard said. He then wheeled around to attend his own horse and buggy.

Chapter 20

Sylvia Pruitt sipped her tea and put her cup down with precision. "Emma, if you could have seen the way he looked at Katherine, offered to hold the hymnal for her, then her Bible—"

"My son has done the same for me whenever he's gone to church."

"It was the way he did it, Emma. The way he leaned toward her. Believe me, I wouldn't come to you if I weren't concerned." Sylvia looked at her friend with a knowing look, then lowered her voice. "You wouldn't want either of them hurt, would you?"

"Sylvia! What you're saying is preposterous. Both Jerard and Katherine have too much sense to even contemplate an alliance. Think of their differences in—social position, age, temperament. Why, it'd be a complete mismatch. And, Katherine said the other day how she's looking forward to teaching. She's not ready yet—"

"Oh, I wouldn't wait too long," Sylvia said. "I'm still convinced your son is showing special interest in her. It's none of my business, of course, but if I were you I'd start looking for that teaching position right now. Out of sight, out of mind—"

Mrs. Emery put her teacup down with as much force as the delicate china would tolerate. "I appreciate your concern, Sylvia. And will keep your suggestion in mind. But I think you're reading far too much into Jerard's common courtesy."

A quarter of an hour later, Emma Emery showed her friend to the door. As the carriage drove off, she turned back inside and held her fingers to her temples.

Bates entered the hall. "Anything wrong, madam?"

"Just a headache; it started coming on a short time ago. I think I'll lie down awhile." She reached for the handrail. "I tell you, Bates, that woman can be such a gossip."

ᘓ

Evening wore away as Katherine sat staring at the French essay she was translating. After she finished the homework, it would be time to retire.

Her mind drifted to the conversation she'd had that afternoon with Mrs. Hodges, how Cassie would work in the textile mill as soon as possible. Sweat shop, some called it. Katherine would hate seeing her go there. Did Mr. Emery ever think about how hard people labored in his mill? Little doubt he would be a difficult man to work for. Her lips twisted into a wry smile. She had only to remember their ride home from church last Sunday.

Katherine put the unpleasant thought out of her mind, returning instead to Cassie. She enjoyed teaching her. The girl had a fine mind. The last book Katherine loaned her from the Emery library was probably finished by now. Mrs. Emery had finally agreed to regular lending, and both Katherine and Cassie made sure each volume was returned in good condition. Katherine was glad to see the meticulous manner with which Cassie took care of things. That was another reason she disliked seeing her start at the mill. So much fineness wasted in such repetitious, tiring work. Maybe Cassie could read at night, if only for a few minutes, something to continue developing her mind.

Katherine brought her thoughts back to the translation. As a reward for finishing early, she would pay the Emery library a visit and look for Cassie's next book. She smiled. A volume for herself might be in order as well.

Approaching the library, she noticed a soft light coming from the half-open doorway. Someone was presumably inside—Mrs. Emery or her son—neither of whom she wished to disturb or engage in lengthy conversation. She determined to find her books as quickly as possible and leave.

Entering, she saw Mr. Emery seated in a large armchair facing the fire, staring at the burning logs. Strange to see him so quiet and pensive. It was as though she'd entered a private world, uninvited. Almost she wished she hadn't come.

He turned to see who entered.

"I'll be only a minute, sir." She walked to the far end of the room where the fiction was shelved. A volume for Cassie presented itself, but she couldn't readily find one for herself. She'd return on the morrow. Tiptoeing across the floor, book pressed against her light blue dress, she debated whether or not to bid a quiet good night.

"Katherine, why don't you sit awhile by the fire?"

She stopped, turned, but paused before answering. "Thank you, sir, but I plan to retire."

"Please." He motioned to the chair near his. "Tomorrow I leave on extended business."

Feeling it would be awkward not to comply, Katherine seated herself and placed the book on her lap. An embarrassing silence ensued while she waited for him to say something.

"You may read if you wish."

Surprised, she looked at him to judge his sincerity, but then opened the book she had chosen for Cassie. *Pride and Prejudice* was a favorite of hers. At the opening paragraph, a ghost of a smile pulled at the corners of her mouth. She had forgotten it began in just this way. *It is a universal fact that a young unattached man of goodly income must be in want of a wife....* Present company excepted, of course. She glanced at that present company and surprised a steady gaze directed at herself. Her eyes dropped and she felt the warm rush of blood to her cheeks. She hoped the light in the room was not sufficient for Mr. Emery to see the blush. She read on, determined to keep her eyes from glancing up again.

After some minutes, Mr. Emery cleared his throat. "Your story is engrossing?"

She looked up. "Very. But of course, I enjoy reading."

"You know, my father would have been pleased with you, would have considered you a good return on his investment."

The unexpected compliment drew a spontaneous smile from her. She relaxed back in the chair and looked into the fire. Its crackling warmth felt good.

"By the way, have you ever heard from your father?" Mr. Emery held up his hand. "I don't mean to pry. I'm merely interested."

"No, I haven't. And truthfully, I don't expect to." Her eyes closed a moment. "Mr. Emery, I want to tell you again how sorry I am that incident ever happened. I haven't forgotten about paying for the horse. In fact, I already have a small amount of money set aside."

"I told you not to worry about that." He straightened in his chair, looking directly at her. "I don't want to argue, so let the matter rest." He paused. "However, I do have one bone to pick with you."

Her eyebrows raised.

"You call me Mr. Emery. From now on I prefer that you use my given name. We've known each other long enough. Besides, you're—almost family."

"That is kind of you to say so, sir."

"And no more 'sir' business, either."

"Mr. Em—" Her hands fidgeted with the book in her lap. "I don't think I could become accustomed to calling you anything else."

"I believe you can. It'll only take some practice. Why don't you begin right now?"

She hesitated.

"Try it. Let me hear you say my given name."

Katherine shifted in her seat. But he kept encouraging her with a smile. Finally, she murmured, "Jerard."

"Ah! Never knew my name could sound so good." He leaned forward. "Say it again." When she acquiesced, he said, "Now say it in a sentence."

"A sentence?"

"Yes, something like, 'It's a lovely evening, Jerard.'"

Embarrassed, but determined to keep him in good humor, she repeated his words.

"That's better. There's no reason why we shouldn't use each other's given names. When I think of when you first arrived—was it a little over two years ago?—it's hard to believe how you've changed." His steady gaze appraised her. "You've become quite the young lady."

She felt inordinately pleased. "That's one of the nicest compliments I've ever received. Thank you."

"Well, the best has been spent on you, to use investment terms again, and you've turned out very well." He smiled and held out his hand. "May I offer my congratulations, Mademoiselle?" When she extended her hand, he grasped it gently and pulled it to his lips.

Once again, she could feel warmth stealing up her throat to her cheeks.

"Excuse me." Mrs. Emery sailed past Katherine to the shelves across the room.

Katherine slipped her hand from Mr. Emery's.

"What a busy day it's been," Mrs. Emery said. "I felt I needed some distraction before I retired for the night."

Jerard rose from his chair and sauntered over to his mother. "How about this red leather volume, Scott's *Ivanhoe*? That should take your mind off your concerns."

"You don't know anything about my concerns, but I'll take your recommendation anyway." She reached for the book, then turned toward Katherine. "It's getting late. You coming?"

"Yes, ma'am."

"Good. We can go upstairs together." She strode to the girl's chair and motioned her ahead. Katherine rose quickly, with as much grace as she could muster.

"Good night, Mother," Jerard said, his tone amused. "Good night, Katherine."

Katherine let a ghost of a smile escape her.

"Good night, Jerard," Mrs. Emery said, then with a firm step followed Katherine out of the room.

ଓ

Earlier that afternoon, sunshine had streamed into the sewing room window. Now a large dark cloud blocked the sun's cheering rays.

Mrs. Emery held up the makings of a black wool skirt. "Do you think you could have this outfit finished by the end of the week, and the others in another two weeks?"

"I don't know, ma'am," Mattie said. "That's a lot of sewing. Of course, I'm happy for Miss Katherine to have new clothes, but do they have to be done so soon?"

"Yes, it's imperative they be finished by the end of the month. If you can't, I'll have the dressmaker in town to help."

"Oh, I like sewing for Miss Katherine. I'll have to set my mind to it, that's all."

"All right. I'll leave you to your work."

ଓ

Mattie held up the black skirt she'd finished hemming. She glanced at the pile of material stacked nearby and, pressing her lips together, shook her head.

The door opened and the housekeeper walked in.

"Mrs. O'Neil, I sure am glad you're here. Could you keep me company awhile?"

"Of course." Mrs. O'Neil looked at the pile of cloth near Mattie. "What's all this?"

"It's for Miss Katherine. I've been wondering—is anything going on?"

"What do you mean?"

Mattie held up the heavy black skirt. "Look. Miss Katherine's not going to need this anymore this season. It'd be better for that cold, cold weather we had this winter. And look, a jacket to match. A regular grown-up outfit." She placed it on the table in front of her. "What I'd like to know is why I have to finish this right now when she won't need it until next year? It doesn't make sense." Her eyes widened, then ventured, "You don't think Miss Katherine's leaving us do you?"

"Leaving?"

"Well, she's always talking about teaching, about finding a position someday."

"Nothing's been said that I know. Besides, I thought it was understood she wouldn't go for a good while yet."

"But all these clothes made up all of a sudden. And Mrs. Emery insists they have to be done by the end of April."

The housekeeper scratched her head, then said with sudden certainty, "You might have put your finger on something."

"Oh, Mrs. O'Neil. Do you think so?" Mattie's face reflected her disappointment. "I hope I'm wrong. But why is everything so secretive?"

"I don't know. Something must have stirred the nest."

"I thought things was going well."

The housekeeper blurted out, "Oh, you know the missus. One can never tell with her, she gets her ideas."

"Don't I know it."

"I remember when I first saw Miss Katherine. You recollect she'd just lost her mama. She stepped out that coach with big dark eyes all worried. Why, I wanted to take her in my arms right there, poor thing." The housekeeper pressed her lips together. "This whole time she's tried to make them like her. Always does her best whatever she puts her hand to." She shook her head. "I'll bet there *is* something going on we don't know about."

Mattie nodded her head in agreement, then sighed.

Mrs. O'Neil lifted the hem of the black skirt. "Here, I'll have the skirt pressed for you. Then I'm going to see if anyone knows more about this business with Miss Katherine."

Chapter 21

The Emery carriage arrived home from the party earlier than expected. Its unanticipated arrival and ensuing upset had Bates scurrying around. The normally unflappable butler snapped his fingers, calling other servants for help. As soon as things quieted down, he hurried up the wide staircase to Katherine's room and rapped briskly.

Katherine opened the door an inch. "Excuse me, Bates." In her dressing gown, she half-hid behind it. "I was retiring. Is something wrong?"

"Well, Mr. Emery's come home earlier than anticipated and has asked to see you. Immediately. He's in the library."

"My hair is down and everything." Her eyes fell to her dressing gown. "Could it wait until morning?"

"I'm afraid not, miss. To tell you the truth, Master's in a dither. Best get something on right away and come down."

"Of course. I'll dress as quickly as possible."

"I'll send up one of the maids to help you."

Not a minute later, Mattie knocked and entered. "Which dress would you like Miss Katherine?"

Fumbling with the last nightgown button, Katherine said, "The light rose wool. That's the easiest to slip on." As the maid hurried to the closet, Katherine said, "I thought Mr. Emery was at the Sefton's party with his mother. I wonder why he came home so early."

"I don't know, miss, but I hear he's in one of his moods."

"Oh, dear. Do I have time to put up my hair?"

"I wouldn't, miss. He all but shouted at Bates a few minutes ago. Besides, your hair's beautiful down. I'd get right on down to the library."

"Mattie, you're making me nervous."

"Just tellin' you like it is, miss. Here, put on these slippers. You don't have time to button no shoes."

Katherine straightened. "Do I look presentable?"

"Not exactly fit to go calling, but you'll do for this. Anyway, you look pretty."

Katherine gave Mattie a forced smile before racing to the stairs. She tripped down the first step, caught herself with the banister, then forced herself to slow her descent. As she hurried down the hall, her stomach felt queasy. What would she find in the library? She stopped outside and drew in a deep breath.

Opening the door, she saw Mr. Emery pacing in front of the fireplace. He stopped and stared at her when she entered. Though the light was dim, the stark white of his shirtfront stood out in sharp contrast to his black formal coat. "Close the door and come here," he said.

She promptly obeyed. A bright fire crackled in the grate and a settee was drawn up near it, but the scene looked anything but welcoming. The elegance of Mr. Emery's evening dress did little to soften the angry line of his jaw. Katherine stopped on the far side of the settee near a wing chair and fastened her gaze on his white shirtfront.

Mr. Emery stood so quietly, after some moments she felt compelled to look up. A hard bright light shone from his eyes. "You're leaving. Within the week."

"Y—yes." His challenge caught her off guard. She hadn't expected him to hear about her departure just yet. She sought to soothe the troubled waters. "It is rather sudden, I know, but I've been preparing to support myself since I first arrived. And when this opportunity for employment presented itself, it seemed too good to ignore." Her hand nervously fingered the pearl button at her throat.

"When was I to be informed?"

"I don't know. I supposed your mother would tell you."

"Obviously she didn't. The secrecy—was this her plan?"

Katherine's eyes dropped. She had felt awkward about Mrs. Emery's decision to keep her plan from him, but she didn't feel free to say as much. She cleared her throat. "Your mother and I were uncertain of my being hired, so thought it best not to tell anyone—for a while."

Jerard turned to grasp the marble mantle and stared down into the fire. "I understand you are to be a governess. To a family by the name of Kemble."

"Yes, they have two children. So, I hope the position will be quite manageable."

"I also understand the family resides in New York." His voice was now taking a more even tone.

"Yes," Katherine answered with forced cheerfulness. "And the good part is I'll be able to continue my piano study. Your mother arranged that."

"I'm surprised my mother allowed you to take a position in a city I frequent," he muttered. Abruptly he turned from the fire and stepped near.

She involuntarily stepped back.

He gestured to the settee. "Sit here. Please."

She sat, her back straight. Turning to the fireplace, he seized a piece of wood and crouched to drop it on the fire. Sparks flew as the log hit the glowing embers.

Katherine watched him as he tended the blaze. His coat tightened over his broad shoulders as he repositioned the wood with a poker. Why was he asking her all these questions? And why had he come home early from the party? As one of the most sought-after bachelors in the area, he was sure to be missed. In fact, how many women her age and older wouldn't thrill to be alone with him right now? Her eyes closed a moment. But those women didn't know him, really. How she wished she could trade places with any of them right now.

Jerard rose and replaced the poker. With deliberation, he sat next to her on the settee. "Katherine." He stopped, willing her to look at him before continuing. "You've no idea what a turn it gave me tonight to hear of your—proposed departure. It slipped out while Mother was explaining to Reverend Hanlin why you couldn't sing at next week's service." His mouth tightened. "To say I was upset—is an understatement. I couldn't believe something of this nature had been kept from me. I left the party immediately, leaving word I would send the carriage later for Mother. On the ride home I was furious with everyone who must have known about this affair and said nothing to me. I was even angry with you." He slipped his arm over the back of the settee. "Katherine, you must not leave. There's no need for you to earn your own living. Certainly not as a governess."

"It's all been arranged," she answered softly, not wanting to seem contradictory. "It seems an ideal situation."

"I realize that. But you don't want to leave, do you? Haven't you been happy here—enjoying every advantage and opportunity we've given you?"

"Oh yes. More couldn't have been done for me. I've come to love it here."

"Well then, I don't see why you should leave." He paused as if considering how to proceed, then added gently, "That should settle it. You belong here."

Katherine saw the same deep understanding in his eyes she had seen so many months ago in the garden after Mr. Lanning's death. Her heart warmed as she remembered that time. Each had sympathized with the other over a dear one's death. Her back relaxed from its ramrod position.

Mr. Emery moved nearer. His arm slipped from the back of the settee to gently encircle her shoulders. It was as though a brother, a friend, touched her. She felt a sudden, strange sweetness. "Katherine, you belong here." His gentleness wrapped around her like a warm cocoon, making her feel loved and protected. It was curious how quickly and easily came this sudden change of posture when moments before she'd felt so wary.

"I would miss your gentle self." He spoke earnestly. "You do not know what a balm your presence has been to me. My work is interesting and stimulating, but I need times to come away. To rest." He cleared his throat. "Katherine, you must remain here."

She listened, hardly believing his change of manner. It was so unlike his often irate, domineering self. She drank in the gentleness, so different from the treatment she had expected when entering the room a few minutes ago. The fragrance of musk on his dinner jacket encircled her, soothed her. Did he need her help? Her heart began to turn from her own plans. She fastened her eyes on his black silk tie. It was difficult to think clearly.

He reached up to touch her hair. "Beautiful," he murmured. Then smoothed it from her forehead. "Katherine, you've brought beauty into this family. And kindness." He smiled. "But you've brought fire and sparkle, too. How could we live without that?"

Katherine felt herself surrounded by his tenderness. She looked up. "I hardly know what to say. The Kembles are counting on my services. All the arrangements have been made." When she said that, the solidity of her commitment bore down on her. She drew away a little. "I appreciate your kindness, more than I can say."

Jerard looked at her a tense moment. "Katherine, I'm not talking about kindness. I—I've taken an uncustomarily long time to say what's on my mind—what's in my heart." His arm tightened around her shoulder. "I'm not talking only about how much this household, this family needs you. I'm talking about how much I need you and how much I want you to stay." He drew her close to him and softly kissed her forehead.

Her eyes closed, her lashes pressed against her cheeks, she breathed in the unexpectedness, the sweetness of the moment.

"Katherine, I love you," he whispered.

She started trembling. Her hands moved to press his coat front, whether for support or to act as a restraint she didn't know.

He lifted her face and kissed her.

Not knowing what to say—stunned—she rested limply against him. His lips moved over her hair, then her cheek. She felt mesmerized, like a small dove encircled by the warm hands of a benevolent captor. "Please don't," she said softly.

"I've wanted to hold you like this for so long, to tell you I love you." His arms tightened around her. "I've waited so long, too long. Don't deny me." His lips sought hers again, this time his kiss long and possessive.

She drew her head back suddenly, looking into eyes gazing into hers with an intensity that frightened her. With a vigorous twist she freed herself and stood to her feet, trembling. "No, don't!" She had almost shouted the words as he tried to grasp her hands. Afraid he would pull her to him again, she stepped to the end of the settee. Grasping one of its arms for support, she hid the other trembling hand behind her skirt.

Jerard stood quickly. "Don't be afraid, Katherine. I know this has come as a surprise. Maybe I was too sudden, too precipitate. But you must know I was half out of my mind when I discovered you were to leave. This nonsense must be stopped."

Katherine's trembling increased. She struggled to maintain her composure. "And if it isn't—nonsense?"

"Of course it is. Katherine, don't you understand? I'm asking you to marry me, to become mistress of my home."

Katherine gasped at the enormity of the proposal. To be mistress here, of this beautiful place—to have a home of her own—? Her resolve faltered for a moment, then veered back to reality. "But I cannot marry you."

"Why ever not?"

"We are too different. Our families are different; we've different backgrounds. I haven't a penny to my name. Socially, I'd be a pariah. Think what your mother's friends would say."

"Hang those infernal gossips."

"But it's more than that." Tears started to well in her eyes. "We're different in important areas of life."

"What areas?"

"Our ages, our temperaments. Our beliefs. Especially our beliefs." She looked at him, sorrow rising in her. "I cannot marry you."

"Katherine!"

She forced herself to continue. "Please try to understand."

"Blast! I don't." He stepped across the space separating them and grasped her shoulders. "All I understand is I'm giving you a bona fide offer of marriage—to become my wife." He looked at her closely. "Think of all you'd be giving up if you say no. And for what? To be a governess? That's little more than a hireling."

"I'm not denying most women would gladly accept your proposal. A dozen would wish to be in my shoes." Katherine felt his fingers dig into her arm. Her heart sank at the change in him, but then as the pain sharpened, anger started to rise. "But the most important reason is that I don't love you. And furthermore, because we're so different, I doubt I ever could."

His hold on her tightened, his eyes hard and bright.

"You're hurting me. Take your hands off!"

"You giving me orders?" His color deepened. "You seem confused as to who's in charge here, Miss Edmond." He then forced her against him, holding her so that she could barely breathe. This time his kiss was hard, punishing.

She jerked her head back.

"Katherine!"

Her lips felt bruised. *She* felt bruised. "You had no right to do that." She saw his eyes blazing with something she didn't understand, didn't want to understand. "You don't love me!"

He released her so suddenly, she had to catch her balance. "Leave then. Go!"

She righted herself and stepped back, making sure she was out of reach. But instead of leaving, words tumbled out of her. "More than differences separate us. It's you. Who you *are*. Oh, you are rich and handsome. And you can be charming when you choose. But if things don't go your way, you become hard and selfish." Her hands clenched into two fists at her side. "Some consider you strong and decisive, but they've never felt the lash of your temper. And that is something, Mr. Emery, I choose to live without."

He stepped toward her.

She moved away. "I cannot marry you. I will not marry you. I'd be dishonoring the whole institution of marriage!" Her eyes met his squarely for a few seconds, challenging the flint in his. *Good night* sounded hypocritical, so she decided to say nothing. She whirled and crossed the library with as much dignity as flowing hair and slippers would permit. Without a backward glance she flung open the library door and marched out.

Chapter 22

Mattie peeked inside the spacious linen closet. "Oh, Mrs. O'Neil, I'm so glad I found you, I'm not sure what to do. I just opened Miss Katherine's door and she's dead to the world. Didn't even stir at my knock. Should I call her for breakfast?"

"She's probably sleeping off last night's upset. Bates said Mr. Jerard was terribly disturbed."

"Well, I happened to be downstairs when he arrived home from the party, and I can tell you, he was in some kind of mood. Wanted Miss Katherine right away. I even had to help her get dressed to hurry her."

"My! And do you know what happened?"

"Hardly. I did get a peek of Miss Katherine marching out the library afterwards. Flushed pink as her dress, and in no mood to talk. I skedaddled, believe you me. Didn't want to see the likes of Mr. Emery coming out that room."

Mrs. O'Neil pressed her hand over the pillowcases, flattening them. "A body wonders what went on in there. This morning Mr. Emery told Bates he was leaving for the mill, not to have lunch for him, he was going straight to the afternoon train."

"Mr. Emery leaving? I'll bet Miss Katherine will be relieved. The lion's den couldn't have been worse than going into that library last night."

"Then let the poor lamb sleep," Mrs. O'Neil advised. "Just bring up her breakfast before her tutor comes. Mrs. Emery won't know the difference. After the party she's sleeping late herself."

❧

After dressing, Katherine closed the door to her bedroom, ready to attack the day with a vengeance. She had been right last night, she knew she was. Still, she was glad when Mattie informed her that Mr. Emery had left. Now she wouldn't have to wonder when he'd appear around the next corner.

That evening after dinner Katherine excused herself early, pleading an unfinished writing assignment and a French review. How she was going to finish her studies before leaving for New York, she didn't know.

But it was good to be busy. It helped keep her mind from troubling thoughts of last night. All day they'd threatened to jump out and assault her like unwelcome intruders.

Those same intruders were kept at a distance until she began getting ready for bed. As she unfastened her dress, the memory of unbuttoning her nightgown the night before came back in a rush. In quick succession various scenes of the evening came to mind: that first moment seeing Mr. Emery pace the room, him throwing a log on the fire, then sitting next to her and slipping his hand around her shoulder. She stopped there.

She hung up her dress, turned away from the closet, and at the dressing table, took down her hair. It was a relief to do so. She had not yet gotten used to pinning it up like a grown woman. She shook it out, smoothed it back from her face. But as soon as her hand stroked her hair, she remembered Mr. Emery's touch.

She turned from the dressing table, resolved to avoid dwelling on that. She would get in bed as soon as possible. Read awhile and pray.

Methodically going through her bedtime ritual, she felt more in control of her fickle mind. She finally got into bed and leaned over to turn down the lamp. But the room had not been dark long when the one thought she'd been trying to keep at bay all day leapt out at her. He'd said he loved her.

But how could that be? She was a nobody. Just a girl who'd come here to learn how to earn her own living. She lay on her back, trying to relax, then restlessly turned onto her stomach, raising her hands to rest under her cheek. Lying in the dark, impressions, thoughts, one after another scurried about her in crazy, helter-skelter fashion.

When she had first entered the library how angry he'd been. Then just minutes later he was considerate and tender, like a brother. She had not thought he could be so caring.

But then—he'd held her in his arms and kissed her.

She buried her head into the pillow and groaned. Could she ever feel like her old self again?

After his declaration of love and his kisses she had torn herself away, trembling. How upset he had become, gripping her shoulders, and that final hard kiss ripping away her self-control. She shuddered.

Had she gone too far in saying the things she did? She raised herself up on her elbows. It had been a relief to give voice to those words. She was sure he had never heard the truth about his pride and anger, his misuse of people and things. Every word she'd said was true.

But how confused she felt. Could anger and tenderness be mixed up in a few short minutes? She stared at the headboard of her bed. In another week, in less than a week, she was supposed to leave for the Kembles to teach. Everything had been arranged. When all was said, what was to be done? Was there any way she could stay here and—?

Impossible. For so many reasons. He hadn't changed.

She must go to the Kembles. All this soul-searching was useless. This must be put behind her. She turned from her stomach onto her side and drew up her knees. Feeling more comfortable, she made every effort to empty her mind. Yes, everything had already been decided. She *must* get some sleep.

ଔ

The week passed and Katherine tried to put the library incident out of her thoughts. It helped that Mr. Emery was not present.

The last few days were a time of good-byes. Friends at church gave her small remembrances. One girl handed her a fancy paper cutout declaring undying friendship, another a handkerchief with their initials intertwined in a corner.

And there was Cassie. Katherine hated the thought of leaving her. She made a point of visiting her student one last time. Mrs. Hodges set out a special little tea.

Katherine noticed every bit of tender preparation. As the three of them sat around the makeshift tea table, Katherine didn't know when she'd enjoyed seed cakes more. At the last, tears stung everyone's eyes and Cassie hugged her, not wanting to let her go. "You will come back and visit us, won't you, Miss Katherine?"

Katherine promised she would, if possible.

When Higgins drove her away, she looked out the carriage window, waving to mother and daughter. Even the old weather-beaten house looked dear. What sweet memories she had of her many visits there. Finally the buggy turned the corner, the forest blocking the Hodges from view.

ଔ

The day before leaving, Katherine woke with a strange feeling in the pit of her stomach. Mr. Emery had been gone the entire week. He should return today or at the very latest tomorrow morning. Surely she would see him before she left.

Katherine dreaded meeting him, but knew she had to. As the week wound to a close, she began to see the night in the library through different eyes. One thought disturbed her.

Mr. Emery had approached her in good faith with his marriage proposal, had been tender and gentle. But what had she done? Rejected him flatly, angrily. Thinking back on it, she asked herself if she could have done it more kindly, with greater equanimity. Did she have to make such a scene and attack his character as she did?

What she had said was true, but *how* she said it was another matter. She blushed even now to remember her words spilling out in anger. Such uncontrolled anger. The very thing of which she had accused him, she was guilty of herself. Apologizing wouldn't be easy, but she must do it. He knew she claimed to be a Christian—but how drawn would he be to a Christ whose follower lashed out in anger? The more she thought about it, the more she wondered if she had betrayed her Lord.

By afternoon she gathered the courage to ask Mrs. O'Neil when Mr. Emery would return. Surely the housekeeper would know; his room would need to be readied for his arrival. But the housekeeper shook her head. "No, Miss Katherine, he never said when he'd be back."

With Mrs. O'Neil's words rankling in her mind, the first real doubt formed as to whether Mr. Emery would come home before she left. It was a hard, hurtful thought. Standing in the front hall, digesting what the housekeeper said, Katherine suddenly felt the need to get out of the house. She turned down the hallway and grabbed her cloak from the closet.

Where would she go? She stood on the kitchen stoop, looking at the outbuildings and then to the newly furrowed fields and forest beyond. She would head in that direction.

On reaching the last outbuilding, the wind caught her cloak and fanned it out behind her. With a rush, the memory of that autumn day came back when she had run after her sick teacher. Mr. Emery must have seen her when he'd been in the field with the workers. Her heart warmed at the memory of how gently he'd handled Mr. Lanning. That was the first time she'd seen any real consideration, any tenderness in him.

She left the field's hard path to enter the forest, saw again the spot where Mr. Lanning had fallen. Then passed his favorite beech tree. What would he have thought of Mr. Emery's proposal? Would it have surprised him?

Well, he would never know. And no one else must know either. She would not tell even dear Mrs. Lanning. Suddenly, she decided to talk with her old friend.

When Katherine reached the house, Mrs. Lanning quickly pulled her inside. "Katherine, what a treat. And the day before your departure, too." She led the way to the back sitting room. The yellow and pink flowered wallpaper bid Katherine as cheery a welcome as it had on her first visit.

They talked about good times—and Mr. Lanning. After a second cup of tea, Mrs. Lanning said, "After we returned home from that trip, my husband picked me up like a sack of potatoes, threw me over his shoulder, and carried me over the threshold. He said, 'That's how you get carried in after your second honeymoon, Mrs. Lanning.'"

Katherine laughed. "You must have had great fun together."

"Yes, we had a wonderful life. I've no regrets. With my husband's sudden passing, I've always been thankful no angry words were spoken that last day."

Katherine smiled in sympathy.

"Of course, I was blessed with a man whose interests and temperament were much like my own. I didn't realize when I was younger how unusual that was. Many people marry others quite different from themselves."

Katherine was silent a long moment. "Could I ask you a question?"

Mrs. Lanning nodded. "Of course, dear."

"I thought certain differences between a man and woman made it wrong for them to marry. Like differences in belief. And other crucial areas: differences in temperament, upbringing, and social standing."

A loving light shone from Mrs. Lanning's eyes. "Well, you're certainly right in the matter of belief. The Bible tells us a believer must not marry an unbeliever. And it's prudent to consider the other areas you mentioned. I would have to say from my own observation the differences you pointed out can make for a difficult marriage.

"But that's where we need God's guidance." She paused, considering her words. "If two people marry with profound differences, the way becomes well nigh impossible if God isn't in it. On the other hand, if He has called them to this union, these differences can bring Him great glory, and work toward their own greater good than if they had remained single."

Katherine silently gazed into her tea cup, considering her friend's words.

Mrs. Lanning smiled. "This is serious talk on a subject that seems moonlight and roses to most girls." She leaned over to grasp Katherine's hand. "But I'm glad we're able to speak about deeper things from time to time. I've missed having a daughter, and you've been like my own flesh and blood." Her brow furrowed. "And now you're leaving."

"I know." On impulse, Katherine embraced the older woman. "I'm going to miss you so. You and your family have been such an example to me. And comfort." Katherine hugged her again. "My mother would have thanked God if she could have seen you in my life."

Mrs. Lanning's eyes started tearing up. "Katherine, your going will leave a void here. I know Mrs. Emery wants this opportunity for you in New York, but I'd hoped we'd have you for another year."

"Leaving this soon was unexpected, but I know it's for the best." Katherine dabbled her own eyes with her handkerchief. "Now I must go. They'll be wondering about me at the house."

Mrs. Lanning sighed. "I hate to see you leave, but I'll ring for your cloak. Would you like to take our carriage home?"

"Thank you, but I want to walk through the woods one last time."

"I understand." At the back door, Mrs. Lanning said, "Now, this isn't good-bye yet. Tomorrow Christopher and I will see you at the train station."

"I'm glad for that."

Katherine reached the edge of the woods and turned to see Mrs. Lanning blow her a kiss. Her heart warmed at the impromptu gesture. Such a love of a lady. Almost she ran back to hug her. But no, she would see her tomorrow.

Chapter 23

Katherine held up the earrings Aunt Elsie had given her. This evening was her last with the family. Surely Mr. Emery would be present. Would the earrings be too elaborate? Probably. With resolve, she put them away and unpacked her mother's brooch.

The family was ushered into dinner, entering without Mr. Emery, and then Katherine noticed the table was set for only three.

Conversation was subdued. From time to time Mrs. Emery spoke of trivial matters. Aunt Elsie all but ignored her sister-in-law and focused her attention on Katherine. She had made it plain many times how she felt about Katherine's leaving. Dessert was being served when Mrs. Emery quietly said, "I'm afraid my son won't arrive home before you leave, Katherine. But I know he wishes you well in your new life."

The pronouncement came like a thunderbolt. Katherine sat very still, then forced a smile. "I'm sure it couldn't be helped. Thank you for telling me." Conscious of Mrs. Emery's eyes on her, she took a bite of dessert then choked. When her coughing died down, Aunt Elsie advised she sip some water. Katherine tried to make light conversation while forcing down the remainder of the dessert. But after dinner when Mrs. Emery asked if she would go to the family sitting room, she declined, saying she still had a few things to attend to.

Excusing herself, she bent over Aunt Elsie to kiss her lightly on the cheek. "See you tomorrow, Auntie."

"Wait, Katherine. I'll accompany you upstairs."

Katherine turned to Mrs. Emery, gave her a light kiss as well, then took Aunt Elsie's arm and assisted her up the stairs. As soon as they reached the aunt's doorway, she said, "Come into my room, child, for just a few minutes."

The frizzled-haired woman sat in her armchair and motioned Katherine to the footstool near her feet. "Something's been on my mind since dinner. At first I wasn't going to say anything, didn't want to excuse any part of Jerard's rude behavior. But child, I saw your face when Emma told you he wouldn't be returning before your departure. What I say now is for your sake, not his, to lessen your—well, to help you understand."

Katherine had situated herself as comfortably as she could on the stool, and now looked up attentively.

"Your moving to New York—and Jerard not hearing about it until the last minute—upset him. You know he is accustomed to being in control, and this sprang up already decided, without him having any say in the matter. More than that, I know he began to think of you—like a sister, I believe—and he cannot afford to lose another member of the family. As you know, his father died. But there was someone else." Aunt Elsie paused. "His younger brother."

She paused, drawing her thoughts together. "Actually, this happened a good number of years ago. Jerard was about fourteen, just when boys are reckless and think they know it all. His brother was ten. Their father had bought a new sporting carriage, a tilbury. Tilburys can go fast and are not as stable as a buggy or most carriages. Anyway, Jerard begged to take his younger brother for a ride.

"I didn't see it happen, but was told Jerard started the horse at a spanking trot. Then, upon returning home, his brother asked to drive, and Jerard let him. Once, again, the tilbury was going fast and when it tried to take a corner, it overturned. Jerard survived with minor scratches, but his brother was flung wide and hit his head on a tree stump and died. The family was devastated.

"Jerard changed. I saw it in the way he reacted to things that troubled him. He would become angry, unreasonably so. And it seemed he was angry more often than not."

Aunt Elsie sighed deeply. "There. I wanted you to know it isn't only your leaving so suddenly that's causing Jerard to act so unreasonably. This goes back years. Like I said, he's never been the same."

"Oh, Aunt Elsie!" Katherine dropped on her knees to embrace the aunt. A few minutes later, Katherine closed the bedroom door, and leaning against it, stared down the darkened hallway.

How confusing. Discovering Jerard had a younger brother, that he'd died, and Jerard's part in the tragedy—it overset all her ideas of him.

She walked to her own bedroom and shut the door, glad of the dark. She stood for some minutes, feeling stricken. Her legs began to quiver. Fumbling her way toward the bed in the semi-darkness, she eased herself up onto it.

She lay without moving. Some minutes passed before the tears came, and when the crying started in earnest, she smothered her sobs into the pillow.

ଔ

After the weeping finally spent itself, Katherine lowered herself off the bed and walked to the window. The moon cast an eerie light on the lawn outside.

Her heart went out to Jerard. How terrible to feel he played such a part in his brother's death. It was beyond her comprehension.

But it had happened so long ago. Could something like that have such a long-term effect?

No one had mentioned this brother to her before. Not even Jerard in the garden that night when he'd revealed how his father's death had affected him. Had remembering his father brought up the old wound of his brother's death?

She looked over the darkened lawn, memories of her time in the Emery household following one another, especially Jerard's temper, his irascibility. She was now seeing it differently.

This matter about his brother, however, she couldn't help him with it; she didn't know how. All she knew to do was to pray. She covered her face with her hands, and eyes tightly closed, prayed fervently. Some minutes later, after feeling an easing of the shock, she lowered her hands, and stood silently by the window.

Her mind slowly turned to the problem at hand. This coming separation from the Emerys—and the fact that Jerard would not come to say goodbye. She had reacted to the news with such emotion. Why?

It was evident she felt hurt Jerard couldn't come to see her off. Her lips tightened. *Wouldn't* would be more accurate. Was it her rejection of his offer of marriage that had made him leave? Or was it her attack on his character? Either might have set him off, but something else troubled her she couldn't put into words.

She fell to her knees and rested her arms on the windowsill. "Oh God, I feel I am missing something. Please show me."

Where had all this upset begun? She pictured Jerard at the party, talking with his mother and Rev. Hanlin; tried to imagine how he must have felt when he found out she was leaving. And not having been informed of it. At that her heart smote her.

She pressed her eyes. Something was wrong in her not telling him about her departure. Friends didn't treat each other that way. Were they friends? No... but some frail bond existed between them, something with sweetness to it. Had she showed how little she valued this—this *something* they had by agreeing to a secret departure? Had he felt...she searched for the right word...betrayed?

Her chest tightened.

In all fairness, Mrs. Emery had insisted upon the secrecy. Katherine had felt guilty about it, but had put her feelings aside due to her benefactress' wishes.

Why *had* Mrs. Emery urged the secrecy? Did she guess her son's feelings and sought to cut them off by insisting her ward leave? She remembered that night in the library when Jerard had kissed her hand and Mrs. Emery entered without warning.

Of course! Mrs. Emery would be mortified if her only son married a penniless girl with no social standing, the very girl she'd been kind enough to take into her house and educate.

But what of Jerard? Her thoughts went back to the night of the party when he'd come home early. He'd been upset, but had mastered his anger and treated her with tenderness. The memory of that had been a recurring thought all week. And then she had crushed his gentle overtures with wild accusations. That thought was becoming increasingly painful.

She rose from the floor, lit the lamp at her desk, and sat down.

Could she do anything to mend this rift between them? Bridge this gulf brought on by her hasty words and actions? She didn't want to be the cause of yet another barrier between him and God.

She looked down at the paper on her desk. Maybe she could write a note and make sure he received it on his return. Taking up a pen, she closed her eyes. "Dear God, please give me the words." She paused, thinking. She would only deal with the coming separation, not mention her knowledge of his brother's death.

Later, she read what she'd written:

I write this on the eve of my departure. I am very conscious of the present breach between us and it pains me. I know this is due in large part to my angry outburst that night in the library. And to my thoughtlessness in not telling you I would be leaving. Can you forgive me?

I want us to remember the happy times we've had, especially our mutual interest in music. It is memories like these I treasure, and hope you do the same.

You and your mother have done much in giving me a home and providing a wonderful education. I will never forget this.

Since it does not appear I will see you before I leave, I wish you well in the coming years, and prayerfully commit you to God who loves and cares for you.

Sincerely,
Katherine

She put down the note. It sounded stilted. And as she was writing, she felt herself soften toward him. But no, she must remember the real issue. Despite the new information she now knew about him, he was an unbeliever. And as self-centered a person she'd ever met.

Shaking her head to banish unbidden thoughts, she disciplined herself to end the task. She placed the note in an envelope and sealed it, addressing it to Mr. Emery. Now, how could she make certain he received it? She dreaded a third party examining it, wondering what was inside.

With sudden decision, she rose from her chair, crossed the room, and opened the door. Listening for anyone in the hall and hearing no one, she stepped outside. How dark it was. Had everyone gone to bed? She reentered her room to get a lamp.

When she reached Mr. Emery's room, she hesitated. To slide the note under the door could be accomplished in a moment. But now that she was here with no one around, she was curious. It was the one place in the house she'd never been. Before letting herself consider further, she let herself in, easing the door closed so as not to make a sound.

In the lamplight she could make out the majestic proportions of the room. A magnificently carved Gothic bed dominated one end of the chamber. Deep red wallpaper with a muted gold stripe covered the walls. Long crimson moiré drapes hung from mahogany Gothic valances. With care, she walked across the rug, an intricate French needlepoint, the only concession to anything delicate in this massive, rich, masculine apartment.

The room suited him.

Suddenly, she longed to see the room's master. The thought surprised her.

Beside a huge rosewood armoire stood a sturdy valet. On it hung a gray monogrammed dressing gown. She walked over to examine it more closely. Standing over it, lamp held high, she touched its rich, soft fabric. She noticed in the breast pocket a white handkerchief. But something was amiss. She moved the lamp closer. A red mark showed on the handkerchief just where the line of the pocket touched it. She lightly pressed back the cloth, to see it better.

A dark stain blotched it. Curious. She couldn't imagine the fastidious Mr. Emery keeping such an article. Moreover, the stain looked like blood.

A strange feeling welled up in her. Her mind went back to the afternoon of Mr. Lanning's collapse. She had blotted her bleeding lip on just such a handkerchief. She tried to think back to that day. She remembered offering to wash it, but then Mr.

Emery assured her he would take care of it.

And why was this in his breast pocket? For some moments her womanly intuition and imagination took flight. Was this stain her blood, and had he kept it because it meant something to him?

Her eyes widened. If he had begun to care for her then, how patient he'd been. Never, never had she associated the word *patient* with him. But that night in the library, when he had been so angry before proposing to her, he had yet controlled himself. Was that a sign of patience or something akin to it?

She saw him, again, leading her to the settee. Saw him throw a log on the fire, then kneel to tend it. He looked the epitome of a masterful, successful man. How his evening clothes had set off his dark good looks, his smooth hair waving near the brow. The memory stirred something—his virility, his manliness struck her... his tallness and strength. A thrill ran through her.

Sitting together on the settee, he'd spoken to her with such tenderness. Like a brother or father, he kissed her forehead.

Her hand went up to touch her lips. But *that* kiss had not been that of a brother or father. She felt herself blush in the dark. Even though she had no experience of such things she knew that kiss was different. The kiss of a lover. She had never felt a man's lips on hers before. Thinking back on it now, it seemed fearfully sweet.

Light flashed at the windows. Lightning! Moments later, thunder rumbled in the distance. The imminence of a storm brought her back to reality. She must quit this apartment before any more wayward thoughts took hold. And before someone like Bates discovered her as he checked the house before the storm. Hurrying, she crossed the room, knelt down, and placed her note on the floor just inside the door.

Back in her room, she undressed. Rain pelted her bedroom window. The harder it fell, the more its noise punctuated her confusion.

Having hastily drawn her nightgown over her head, she knelt at her bedside. "Dear Lord, this has all been so painful, so strange." She looked up with a catch in her throat. "Father, keep me strong for I feel weak and perplexed. Help me do everything according to Your will." She paused. "Please, Father, bring Mr. Emery—Jerard—to yourself. Not for my sake, but for his. And if I never see or talk to him again in this life, please let me see him in heaven. I pray this in the precious, holy name of our Savior. Amen."

☙

The next morning the air was still damp from the night's downpour. The carriage left the house in plenty of time to meet the train. Mrs. Emery saw to that.

The station bustled with passengers and well-wishers. "You're not your usual joking self, Christopher," Aunt Elsie said as he helped her down from the carriage. The aunt squeezed his hand, sympathetically, then added, "I know."

Christopher held out his hand to assist Katherine. "Why don't I escort you ladies inside the station? Then I'll see to Katherine's trunk." He left the threesome alone until a few minutes before the train was due, then walked up and asked, "Is everyone doing all right?" They assured him they were.

Mrs. Emery said, "Why don't we go outside now; the train should be here any minute."

"And when it arrives, I'll take Katherine aboard and see her settled," Christopher said.

Mrs. Emery nodded. "That sounds like a good arrangement." She rose to her feet and led the little party out of the station.

The sun had driven away the last of the mist. In the distance the train whistled. Mrs. Emery hugged Katherine briefly. "We'll be interested to hear how you're getting along. I know you'll be a credit to our upbringing."

"Mrs. Emery, I can't thank you enough for all you've done."

Next Aunt Elsie claimed her. She held Katherine long. "I'll miss you so much, my dear. Please come soon for a visit. I know you must get settled in with your work and all, but don't forget us."

"I won't." Tears swam in Katherine's eyes. She squeezed Auntie tightly.

The four watched as the train rounded the bend and screeched into the station, billowing steam.

"Here, Katherine!" Christopher shouted as he held out his arm. He led her to the train steps, then stopped as she looked back and waved good-bye. Mrs. Emery waved in kind while Aunt Elsie fluttered her white hanky up and down.

Inside, Christopher found Katherine an empty seat, then crouched by her side. "Grandmother was sorry to be taken ill. You know how she wanted to see you one last time. But she'll be praying for you."

"I treasure her prayers. Now I'm especially glad that I visited her yesterday. Please assure her of my deep affection and tell her I'll let her know how things are going once I get settled."

"Now for myself." Christopher reached for her hands and held them warmly. "I'm glad I could see you off today. Katherine, I had no idea how hard this saying good-bye would be. We all expected you to be here a good while longer, and here you are leaving so suddenly." He looked down at her hands before continuing. "I'm going to give you time to see the world, grow up a little, and then I'm going to come visiting." He looked up, light shining from his eyes.

"Oh, I would love that, Christopher."

"I'm serious. Take advantage of everything New York has to

offer, then maybe we'll take that trip to Europe someday." He winked at her.

"All aboard!" the conductor called.

"Don't forget." Christopher raised her hands to his lips and pressed them tenderly. "The Lord be with you. Be sure to let us know if there's anything you need or if any difficulty arises. I'll be praying, too."

"Thank you, Christopher; thank you ever so much." A tear spilled from one of her brimming eyes.

"Good-bye, then." He gave her hands a final squeeze and turned to make his way down the aisle.

Katherine fumbled in her purse for a handkerchief. She wiped her eyes and cheeks, then stood at the window to wave. The train started with a jerk and rumbling beneath her, gained speed and left the station behind. The last thing she saw was Aunt Elsie's white hanky waving frantically.

Chapter 24

Katherine looked around in amazement at New York's Grand Central Depot. The ornate train station was huge. The driver from the Kemble household who collected her proudly informed her that Cornelius Vanderbilt had completed it the year before.

"It was inspired by a station in Paris. Let's see,"—he searched for the words—"it's some Empire-style or other. You think this is large? You should see the train shed. The entire railroad complex covers thirty-seven acres."

He assisted her into the open landau and seated atop his perch, proceeded to thread his way through New York's busy streets. The city teemed with coaches, buggies and commercial wagons of every description. Throngs of people walked in both directions, some crossing the street at a half run to avoid getting struck by conveyances. Voices shouted, bells rang, whistles blew. Horses snorted and whinnied. The din of the city hit Katherine forcibly.

And such smells. At the station there'd been the heady perfume of a smartly suited dowager. Now the odor of animals and their droppings assailed her. While the carriage passed restaurants, aromas of onions, garlic and all sorts of food escaped open windows. One establishment reeked of smoking grease.

Store fronts with brightly painted signs passed in dizzying succession. Katherine turned this way and that, taking in the motley yet fascinating mixture of sights, sounds, and smells.

The country quiet she'd known only yesterday now seemed a distant world.

The carriage turned, leaving the busy business district and its noise. Stately townhouses rose on either side of the street. Katherine's conveyance stopped in front of a dignified brownstone embellished by a wrought-iron fence.

The driver assisted her out and, opening the gate, preceded her up the short walk. Katherine glanced to the left. Spacious bay windows gave hint of a large front parlor. Stone steps led to a covered entry with a massive oak door.

The driver knocked and when the door opened, motioned her to precede him inside. The butler greeted her. "My name is Framton, miss. I trust your journey was a pleasant one."

"It was, thank you." She cast a fleeting glance at the dark wood staircase spiraling to the floors above as he ushered her through an archway to the left.

"This is the front parlor. Mrs. Kemble will be with you in a few minutes." Katherine walked across a thick Brussels carpet. The butler gestured to an armchair near the window. She sank into deep crimson cushions, a high back and curved arms encircling her. Katherine felt small and slight in the large, luxurious chair. She glanced out the window to see a couple of men unloading her trunk. Little else moved on the quiet street.

Turning to examine the room, she noticed a large rosewood piano. She smiled in relief. One condition for her acceptance of this position was that she have time to practice—at Mrs. Kemble's convenience, of course—and that she give each child music lessons. She couldn't wait to play the instrument. Chopin would be her first choice. His repertoire would test the piano's degree of fineness.

Beyond the grand piano, massive mahogany folding doors opened to a second parlor. Richly paneled walls set off the jewel-toned upholstery of the furniture. Large, comfortable chairs and couches in gold damask and sapphire-colored silk sat in conversational groupings around the rooms. Additional doors at the far end of the second parlor opened to the dining room at the back of the house. What a graceful area for entertaining the three combined rooms created.

At that moment a lady entered through the archway. *Mrs. Kemble.* Katherine rose.

The woman's thick blonde hair gleamed with reddish tints. Her robust, matronly figure wore the latest fashion, a cream-colored silk afternoon dress showing off her figure and complexion to advantage. "We're so glad you've come," Mrs. Kemble said. "Please be seated." She took the crimson chair opposite and proceeded to ask about Katherine's trip, expounding on the advantages of train travel then deftly shifting the conversation to Katherine's work.

"I do hope you'll enjoy it here. The children need a good education. I'll depend a great deal on your judgment, my being so busy with my charitable work and social responsibilities."

Katherine sat smiling through the monologue, trying not to feel overwhelmed.

"I must say you are prettier than I expected. One thinks of governesses as rather plain. The children will be pleased. They'll parade you around indefatigably—to the park, the museum, an occasional matinee. I hope you're prepared for all the activity." She caught her breath and continued. "And I want to convey how much I count on you for discipline. You need to be rather more strict than their last governess. The children ended up getting the upper hand. I confess they've gotten a bit beyond me, I just don't have the time or energy to deal with them."

A bell rang in the entryway. Before the butler could answer, a voice called out, "It's me, Framton. Don't bother coming to the door." Into the parlor strode a statuesque young woman with blond hair a shade darker than Mrs. Kemble's. "There you are, Auntie. Oh, I'm sorry. Am I interrupting?"

"I'll be with you in a few minutes, Estelle. I'm interviewing our new governess. Why don't you wait for me in the morning room?"

"All right." Estelle awarded the newcomer a disinterested glance before turning to leave the parlor.

"My niece, Miss Neville. She's in and out as suits her fancy, so you'll be seeing her often. Now, where was I? Oh yes, we were talking about the children's discipline. It'll be up to you, I'm afraid. I'm very busy, and with Mr. Kemble gone so much, he cannot be depended upon. His firm hand has been sorely missed in the children's lives. I told him he'll regret it someday when they turn out to be wild Indians, but he tells me he needs to relax at his club after a hard day's work. So, Miss Edmond—" Her hands waved away the problem in a sort of breezy despair. "—you can see I will rely on you quite a lot in that regard."

She shifted in her chair. "Now, I hope I haven't frightened you. The children can be charming. It only takes a strong, steady hand and an ingenious mind to keep them out of mischief. You look as if you have both, and, of course, I have confidence in the glowing recommendation from Mrs. Emery. I've heard she runs a well-appointed household, so I believe you will work out well." She smiled approval. "I think it will be best if you meet the children in the playroom for their dinner hour at six o'clock. You will eat with them. My husband and I are dining out tonight, but he has promised to go upstairs to introduce himself."

"That sounds fine," Katherine said.

"Now, unless there are questions, I'll ring to have you taken to your room. It's on the third floor next to the playroom. I think you'll find it quite comfortable."

Katherine changed to a dark blue dress with starched white collar and cuffs. She wanted to look the proper governess when she met the children and their father.

Ten minutes before six she opened the door to the playroom. Cupboards lined one wall with toys and school supplies stored inside. Against the opposite wall stood an oblong table and school bench. The room appeared to be a combination school and playroom. On its other end, a round table was set with three places for dinner.

Wondering what view the rear of the house afforded, Katherine walked to the windows beyond the table and pulled back the draperies.

Early evening light revealed an enclosed garden. Vines climbed the walls and a path meandered near its circumference. Dwarf trees, some fruit varieties, stood in the middle.

A soft scuffle at the doorway arrested Katherine's attention, and she turned to see two children escorted by a maid. The girl and her younger brother, both dressed in navy and white looked as if they had stepped out of a fashion magazine for the latest school wear. They stopped a few feet from Katherine, bowed and curtsied, then turned to the table.

"What's to eat?" the sandy-haired, freckled boy asked.

"Mind your manners." The maid took hold his arm, scolding in an undertone. "Be introduced to your new governess."

"Aw, I didn't mean anything," the boy said in a loud whisper.

Katherine smiled and nodded, first to the girl. "I'm glad to meet you. My name is Miss Edmond and I believe your name is Margaret. Meg for short, isn't it?" The girl with long dark hair seemed a slip of a thing for ten years, but also looked very wise and knowing. "And you are Felix. That is a fine name. Reminds me of Felix Mendelssohn, the famous composer." A sturdy lad of seven stared at her. "I've been admiring the view out your window."

"Not much there," Felix said. "Only trees and bushes."

"Well, I think your garden quite interesting. Tomorrow, if the weather is good, you can give me a tour. Maybe you'll tell me the names of some of the trees. And perhaps your mother will even let us have a small patch in which to grow a few plants."

Felix brightened. "I'd like to grow some corn. I saw pictures of corn stalks in one of my books. Besides, it tastes good."

"Do you have a vegetable garden?" Katherine asked with quickened interest. "There's nothing like fresh vegetables from one's own backyard. We had a large garden where I lived and I had my own plot to plant and weed." She looked at the girl expectantly.

"Cook grows a few things near the kitchen door. Her herbs, she calls them."

"Yeah, she's always telling me to keep out of them," Felix said.

"Well, of course, you always make a mess of things," his sister said in a superior tone. "And your idea of corn is ridiculous. Can you imagine corn stalks in our yard? Mother wouldn't hear of it."

"Dinner is served," Framton announced. While they were talking, he had entered and discreetly placed covered dishes on the table.

The children scrambled to their seats. Halfway through the meal a tap sounded on the door and a dark-haired man entered dressed in evening clothes. A bushy mustache dominated his face. "Father!" both children cried out.

Katherine rose.

"My wife is detained or she would introduce us, Miss Edmond. But I guess the children have identified me. Arthur Kemble." He nodded a brief salute. "I'm pleased to meet you."

Katherine extended her hand.

He asked about her trip from Connecticut and her first

impressions of the city. While she answered she had the distinct impression he was taking her measure.

Just then Mrs. Kemble breezed into the room, dressed in a luxurious sapphire blue silk. "Well, I see you've introduced yourselves. Excellent. Please excuse my tardiness." She walked to the table. "Oh, you have a nice supper tonight. I almost wish we were staying home. The social round can be very tiring, Miss Edmond. But, one must keep up with responsibilities." She glanced back at her husband. "So, Arthur, are you pleased with my choice of governess?"

"Quite, my dear."

"I knew you would be. See how lovely everything is already going?"

The Kembles made a few more remarks, then bade Katherine and the children good night and said they wouldn't be home until late.

After the children had been put to bed, Katherine sat at her dressing table. Her breath came out in a sigh of relief. She had played referee most of the evening, endeavoring to interest her new charges in a board game. Not until she read them a bedtime story did they quiet down, sitting on either side of her.

Feeling pensive, she reached out to open a hand-painted box in front of the dressing table mirror. For her birthday, Mrs. Lanning and Christopher had given her this beautiful jewelry box. To one side lay her mother's brooch, in the middle the earrings from Aunt Elsie. On the other side Jerard's silver combs. She reached for one of the hair ornaments, holding it up to the lamp, admiring its silky, lustrous sheen. For a few moments she fingered its smooth surface. The evening of her eighteenth birthday came back to her. When presented with the combs, she'd been seated in a crimson chair in her white silk dress. Now she'd left all that. A melancholy chord struck deep within her.

She returned the comb to the box, and closing it, placed it in its spot on the dressing table. Tomorrow promised to be a busy day. Good. The children would keep her mind occupied.

ꕥ

A week passed. Katherine closed the door to her bedroom and walked the few steps to the playroom, or rather classroom, as she now called it. These two rooms on the third floor commandeered much of her time. The one regular exception was the hour she took the children outside each day for fresh air and exercise.

A favorite excursion was to explore the garden. The children would take her through the French doors off the dining room onto the terrace then down the steps into the enclosed sanctuary. A few of the miniature trees in the center had started to sprout tiny buds of fruit. The path around the edge of the enclosure made a delightful walk. In one of the far corners, a fountain spurted water from a jar in the hands of a stone maiden. In the other, an arbor with a stone bench offered a private spot in which to sit. Vines covering the arbor's latticework would make a cool haven during hot summer months. From the arbor the walk serpentined its way back to the house where open space to one side served as the cook's herb garden.

Katherine paused in front of the classroom door. The thought of the enclosed garden with its wandering walkway brought a smile to her face. The Emery grounds it was not, but it would be a place she would often enjoy.

She opened the door to the classroom and its quietness struck her. Often Meg and Felix would be talking or arguing about something. Katherine glanced around. The children weren't even here. Studies were supposed to start at 8:30, and it was that time now. She wondered if their tardiness was accidental or deliberate. A number of times the previous week the children had challenged her authority or played mischievous pranks on each other to delay their lessons.

Taking a seat on the school bench, she considered what punishment she should impose for their tardiness. Would writing lines be best? Or maybe they should miss part of their lunch hour. Unconsciously, she began tapping her index finger on the table.

"Boo!" two voices yelled in unison from the doorway.

Katherine jumped, clutching her chest. Then she shot to her feet, the schoolmarm in her surfaced with a vengeance. "Both of you sit down at once." She pointed to the school bench. "What you did was rude and unsettling. It shows a lack of respect I will not tolerate. Don't ever do such a thing again."

Both children sat in a hurry, but their sparkling eyes and quivering lips showed they were suppressing laughter.

Hot anger rose in Katherine. Oh, she could strike them. Then a quick picture of being dismissed by Mr. and Mrs. Kemble flashed through her mind. What would Mrs. Emery say? She stiffened, almost in panic.

Clearing her throat in an effort to gain time, she stood and stared hard at the children. Then in a deliberate voice, she said, "Both of you will take out pencil and paper and write, 'I will never be rude to Miss Edmond again.' Meg, you will do so one hundred times. Felix, fifty." At Meg's remonstrance, she quickly said, "No complaining!" After the children began writing, Katherine stood with crossed arms looking out the window, glancing now and then in their direction. Her racing mind began to quiet as the minutes passed.

Later that afternoon, after the children were excused to their rooms, Katherine stood in the classroom, taking a few moments to rub her neck and shoulders. It had been a trying day and she was tired. She admitted there was nothing like having one's dignity shattered to make one feel like the rug had been pulled from underneath. She smiled grimly. It had helped to see the children laboring over the lines she'd assigned.

She thought back to Cassie. Working with her had been such a joy. Cassie had been so cooperative, had loved learning.

Katherine gathered up the last of the materials on the table and walked to the cupboard. These children required so much more than academics. They needed love and patience and training in many areas of life. Living with them all day made her feel like their mother. Did she have the mental, emotional, and physical stamina to do this job?

Katherine sighed, closing the cupboard door. Tomorrow, thankfully, was her afternoon off. Studying piano in this city had been one of her dreams. Even though she felt apprehensive about going to the business district on her own, she couldn't feel much worse doing that than she felt at the moment.

☙

The next afternoon, Katherine approached Steinway Hall. The elegant four story building had been constructed only a few years prior. Katherine cautiously opened one of the two doors and stepped inside. The large airy room was a showcase of pianos. Three long rows of instruments stretched its length to the tall windows at the far end of the room. The sheer number of instruments amazed her. To her left she noticed a well-appointed reception desk with an office behind it.

The showroom had such a dignified air. Katherine felt its aura of beauty and refinement. After her long walk, she chose to sit in one of the chairs against the wall near a wide staircase. She had just settled herself when the front door opened and a couple of music students entered with portfolios under their arms. They walked up the stairs to the higher regions of the building. Then a dark-suited man who looked to be a professor nodded to her as he strode past. A mother entered with a young girl bouncing at her side. The girl must be precocious, indeed, to study in a place such as this. Katherine could see this establishment had a standard of excellence, designed for those serious about learning. It was also a place of innate courtesy, so different from her third-floor classroom. She breathed in the fresh, rarefied air.

Just then a middle-aged, well-endowed lady descended the staircase. Something familiar about the woman brought Katherine to her feet. She stepped to intercept the lady before she could exit.

"Mrs. von Weber? I don't know if you recognize me, but I'm Mrs. George Emery's ward, Katherine Edmond. You visited the Emery home just over a year ago, and I accompanied Jerard Emery on the piano."

"Katherine Edmond? My!" Recognition dawned on the woman's face. "Why, my dear, how you've changed. I wouldn't have recognized you if you hadn't introduced yourself. What a lovely young woman you've grown to be. So what are you doing in New York? Is Mrs. Emery with you?"

"No, I'm on my own now, working as a governess for a family by the name of Kemble. I arrived last week."

"A governess. Well, well. That's a nice, responsible occupation. And you have only another month of school before summer."

"Yes, after that I'll accompany the family to the shore to help with the children."

"Teaching and working with children. Well, well. So, what are you doing here?"

"Continuing my musical studies, though I haven't started yet. I hope to find more information today."

"Let me give you some advice. I've heard some very good things about a Mr. William Mason. He is a pianist, but is also known as an excellent teacher—a master teacher, in fact. Maybe you could study with him."

"That would be wonderful. I'll be sure to ask. Thank you ever so much."

"I'm glad to pass on a little information. You played exceptionally well the night of the party and the Emerys were so kind. You know, occasionally we have Mr. Emery over for dinner when he's in the city. He's quite the businessman. My husband and he have done very well." She leaned closer. "And I'm sure you know, Mr. Emery is such a gentleman. Our Claudia dotes on him. One wonders why he hasn't married yet." Mrs. von Weber looked at Katherine as if she could supply her with a clue to the enigma. "Will you see him, here in the city?"

"Oh, I don't think so. New York is so large and now that I'm working, we move in different circles."

"Of course. Isn't that the way of the world. But I know you enjoyed the time you spent in the Emery household."

"Oh yes. And I can't help but think it will always feel a little like home. The Emerys, and their neighbors, the Lannings, were wonderful to me."

"I'm happy to hear that. Well," Mrs. von Weber said in a tone of voice that said she must be off, "it's been nice talking with you."

"Thank you, Mrs. von Weber. It's been lovely to see a familiar face in New York. The city now seems a little less strange and intimidating."

"Good." Impulsively the lady reached for Katherine's arm. "I wish you the best in your teaching as well as your music study in Steinway Hall. Good-bye then."

Katherine's gaze followed Mrs. von Weber as she disappeared out the front doors. She felt as if she'd seen an old friend. Fancy meeting someone she knew in a city this large. In the space of a few short minutes, her confidence had developed wings and she felt herself soaring. But how unusual to see Mrs. von Weber in Steinway Hall, of all places. Would she mention their meeting to Jerard? She would like him to think her nicely settled.

Chapter 25

The Kembles had taken a roomy clapboard house at the Jersey seashore for the summer. Katherine heard Mrs. Kemble say she didn't want it to be too large. She didn't feel obliged to give house parties. This was her one opportunity to get away from social pressures and she meant to enjoy it.

She took a cook, a housekeeper, one maid, and the governess for the children. When Mr. Kemble came to the shore weekends, they socialized a little; otherwise, she read, walked along the shore, shopped now and then, and sat and gossiped with her neighbors over morning coffee or afternoon tea. Thus she refreshed herself before taking on the rigors of the winter social season.

Katherine was glad life was less formal at the shore. Even dress standards relaxed. She had a couple of simple cotton dresses she wore on the beach and loved taking off her shoes to run and play in the sand with the children.

This particular afternoon a slight breeze wafted the air. Meg and Felix were finishing a giant sandcastle, pushing sticks into the sand to represent the king, queen, and their many subjects.

Katherine unbuttoned the neck of her blue-flowered dress and stuffed her socks in her shoes. Standards dictated that only a woman's face and arms be exposed, but the breeze felt so good she decided to be a little daring since no one was nearby.

She marveled at the beauty and simplicity of her surroundings—the blue gray sea, the buff-colored sand and the endless sky. Meg and Felix loved to frisk in the water, splashing each other and sometimes Katherine as well. In the city she wouldn't have allowed such liberties, but here she was a little more lenient. She didn't think it necessary to keep the rigid schedule and conduct they kept in New York. Mrs. Kemble ordered that only meals and bedtimes be strictly adhered to.

Katherine closed her eyes, throwing back her head. She dug her feet into the warm sand. The wind cooled her face, throat, and arms. Ebbing back and forth, the ocean, with its occasional gusty roar and splash, exhilarated something deep within her. And the huge blazing ball of sun toasted everything. Here on the beach it had an omnipresent quality, like God.

"Miss Katherine, look at our castle," Meg said. "We've added a moat. Isn't it grand?"

"I didn't notice you digging it, I've been daydreaming so." Katherine got on her hands and knees to inspect. "The moat adds the finishing touch. You'll have to show your mother. Why don't you tell her now? Anyway, we'd better go inside soon. Otherwise, we'll get burned."

"Aw, do we have to?" Felix asked.

"Yes," she said, and laughingly added, "the last one back to the house is a rotten egg." She grabbed her shoes and rose without warning. The children bounded up, and with shouts of one-up-man-ship, the three raced over the sand to the house.

Mrs. Kemble sat with guests on the porch sipping lemonade. "Oh, look! Don't the children seem as carefree as birds taking wing? What a picture those three make." She turned to the tall gentleman at her side. "You'll be glad to see Katherine again." Then she turned to her niece. "You know, Estelle, our governess grew up in the Emery household. Nothing but the best for my children."

The trio scurried over the last length of sand and up the front porch steps. "I almost beat you both," Felix cried out, breathing hard.

"Well, you didn't," Meg sputtered. All three were panting.

The sun had been shining directly into Katherine's face. She hadn't noticed the guests on the porch until the last moment. But as her foot hit the top step her eyes lighted on Jerard. Her heart dropped with the suddenness of a heavy stone plunging into a pool. The visitors were immaculately dressed in town clothes and sat in a civilized manner sipping lemonade. Blood rushed to her face as she became conscious of her loosened attire and shoeless feet.

"Katherine," Mrs. Kemble said, "I have a surprise for you. My niece dropped by and brought a new friend of hers—someone from your old home. I know you'll want to hear the latest news."

Jerard rose.

"Mr. Emery!" Katherine said, trying to catch her breath. She forced herself to step forward as she held out her hand to forestall—she didn't know what—the expected embrace from a former family member? She hoped her outstretched hand gave the impression of warmth onlookers would expect without seeming too forward. She took care to withdraw her hand without lingering.

Miss Neville rose and stood beside Jerard.

Katherine acknowledged her at once. "I'm pleased to see you again, Miss Neville. How nice you could visit the shore. It's beautiful here."

"So Aunt Julia told us. In fact, on the strength of her recommendation, my parents decided to rent a house nearby for the coming month." She looked up at Jerard. "And we hope Mr. Emery will be able to pull himself away from his work to visit us often."

"That will be a pleasure," he said, smiling down at her.

Katherine glanced about for the children and saw they had already disappeared inside. They should have waited to be introduced. Embarrassed, she looked at Jerard. "How are your mother and Aunt Elsie?"

"They're both doing fine, although Aunt Elsie says the house isn't the same without you."

"How kind of her. Will you please give her my warmest regards? And your mother, too?" She smiled apologetically. "I don't know what happened to the children." Eager for a reason to make her exit, she added, "Now, if you'll excuse me, I should attend to them. It's been a pleasure seeing you again." She slipped through the screen door with the quickness of a sea creature darting through water.

Katherine heard her employer say, "Well, that was sudden. You must forgive Katherine, Mr. Emery, but she is so devoted to my children. Would you like more lemonade?" The chairs creaked as everyone sat again.

As in a trance, Katherine moved in the direction of the stairs, softly dropping her shoes on a step. Her hands trembled as she fastened the buttons at her neck. She took several long deep breaths to calm herself. Gathering up her skirt, she sat on a step and covered her face with her hands.

To see Jerard again, under such circumstances. Her throat felt hot from its unseemly exposure. Why had she unbuttoned her dress? How could he be here? And to see him with a woman—Miss Kemble's niece, of all people.

Felix's voice rose, querulous, from the kitchen. She looked up. Mrs. Kemble would be embarrassed if the children were loud enough to be heard on the porch. Could she keep them happily engaged at the back of the house? Cook might allow them to bake something. It would have to be something that occupied the rest of the afternoon. She would not take the chance of appearing before those guests again.

A cry pierced the atmosphere. It sounded like Meg. Another wave of embarrassment flooded Katherine. She grabbed her shoes and hurried down the hall. To get the children out of the house would be best. They could take that excursion up the hill she'd been promising, and they would leave by the kitchen door. She'd have them put on their shoes right away and then she'd collect her parasol.

❧

"Katherine, would you come here a minute?" Mrs. Kemble sat at the dining room table poring over a book of cookery. She looked weary and indecisive. "I need your help. I borrowed this from cook, wanting to choose something special for Saturday's dinner, but now I'm all confused. Sit here, please." She indicated a chair next to hers.

"The dinner is for Estelle and her parents—and Jerard Emery. So there will be six." Mrs. Kemble placed her elbows on the table, folding her hands underneath her chin. "My niece is interested in Mr. Emery and I want to help things along, if you know what I mean. We must have just the right meal. Sitting here I was getting more frustrated by the moment, then you passed and it occurred to me, I have a decided advantage. You can tell me Mr. Emery's favorite foods." Mrs. Kemble looked eagerly at her.

"Well—" Katherine thought of Jerard coming again to the house, of Miss Neville's interest in him and his possible interest in her, and of her part in the whole affair. She could hardly think.

"Do you have any ideas?"

"I—I don't know. I would need some time to come up with a list."

"Yes, a list of possibilities, and then I could make a menu from that. Do you think you could have it completed tonight?"

"I could try."

"Good. What a relief." Mrs. Kemble shook her head. "I don't know why I'm making such a fuss over this, but I do want to do right by my niece. And, of course, Mr. Emery comes from such wealth and position I want everything to be perfect." She leaned closer to Katherine. "I can see why Estelle or any young lady would be taken with him. He's such a presence, so tall and fine looking. How old is he, do you know?"

Katherine could see her employer was in the mood for a good gossip. She shifted uncomfortably in her chair. "He's twenty-eight, I believe."

"Well," Mrs. Kemble said, "then it's time he thought about marrying. I suppose he's been busy with his work and such."

Katherine wasn't sure where the conversation was leading, but was determined to keep secret anything that had passed between Jerard and herself. However, with his present attentions to Estelle, that seemed very much in the past. She answered carefully. "While I lived at the estate, he traveled a great deal to New York and other cities. He was extremely occupied with business."

"Tell me, did he have any special lady friends?"

Katherine considered how to answer truthfully. "He had a number of friends, both male and female. I understand he was very popular at parties and such, but I was too young for those affairs."

"Did he ever single out any young lady for special attention?"

Katherine's hands clutched together underneath the table. "Well, as I said before, I knew little about his social life. He was always so occupied with the estate and developing his new business that he—" She was at a loss for words.

"Why, Katherine, you're blushing. Have I made you uncomfortable?"

"I'm quite all right. It is probably from too much sun." Katherine's hands pressed hard on her lap. "I never gave Mr. Emery's romantic interests much attention."

"Well, I'd like to see if we can spark a romantic interest in him regarding my niece. Anything you can think of to make the evening a success, I'd appreciate your telling me." She smiled a conspirator's smile. "You will help me, won't you?"

Katherine made herself return the smile. "I always want to be of service to you, Mrs. Kemble."

Chapter 26

Katherine walked the half-mile to the seaside town. Mrs. Kemble had asked her to run errands this afternoon. The business district was two blocks long and quiet, a small town with old, well-established shops—refreshing after the busyness of New York.

She decided to go first to the milliner's shop for Meg's hair ribbons. As she approached it, she noticed Estelle Neville in a doorway across the street, several stores down. A tall, familiar form accompanied her.

Embarrassment seized Katherine. She didn't want them to see her. Quickly, she stepped inside the nearest shop. She didn't think Jerard had noticed. At least, she hoped not. But curiosity kept her near the store's display window. To those inside the store, she would seem to be examining the merchandise while still keeping an eye on the couple. Glancing down at the wares, her embarrassment deepened. She had stepped inside a men's clothing store. But she couldn't leave now. Jerard and Miss Neville stood just a short distance away, discussing something. She would have to wait until they moved on.

Gazing at them, Mrs. Kemble's words came back about Jerard being tall and fine looking. Her heart swelled with—what was it—pride? That man standing there had proposed marriage to her. But then she reminded herself he was with another woman, and seemed quite interested in her.

Miss Neville gestured toward a store next to where Katherine hid, and even now Jerard assisted her across the street, his hand underneath her elbow. She watched as Miss Neville leaned more closely to Jerard than was strictly necessary. A hot little flame leapt up in Katherine's breast.

Jerard escorted Miss Neville to the store's entrance. They exchanged a few words, then Jerard turned in the direction of the men's store.

Katherine's breath caught. Surely he wouldn't come here. If she remained at the window, he would see her. She turned, her eyes searching the rear of the store for a place to hide. Several tall racks of clothing stood near the back. She headed toward them.

"May I help you, miss?" the clerk asked.

She stopped for the briefest moment. "I want to look over there," she said. "I don't need any help, thank you." The clerk's face registered surprise as she hurried on. Katherine stepped behind a rack, but on discovering it wasn't tall enough to conceal her, she knelt.

The shop door opened. Not sure who had entered, she hardly breathed.

"May I help you, sir?"

"I'm just looking, thank you," Jerard replied.

Katherine's chest constricted. She heard footsteps go first to one side of the store, pause a few moments, then to the other.

Jerard seemed to be examining merchandise, slowly making his way toward the rear of the establishment. Katherine forced herself to take long slow breaths. She didn't want to faint.

On the rack in front of her hung men's coats. She grabbed a sleeve as if inspecting the lining. If Jerard happened this far, she must be doing something logical. Her heart felt in her throat.

Just then his figure loomed over her. "Katherine! Fancy meeting you here." He looked at the garments. "You buying a man's coat?"

Katherine felt her face flush. "I was only looking."

Jerard put out his hand to assist her up. "Maybe I can be of help. For whom were you looking?"

"Oh, no one in particular."

"Well, I trust Mrs. Kemble doesn't require you to shop for her husband. That would be asking too much of a governess."

"Yes—no—I mean, she would never ask me to do such a thing. But as a matter of fact," she hastened to change the subject, "she did ask me to stop at the milliner's."

"The milliner's?"

"For some ribbon. The shop is one or two down the street."

"But you stopped here first—to look at men's coats?"

"Yes," she whispered, her eyes lowered.

Jerard was so quiet Katherine glanced up. A smile twitched at the corners of his mouth, and suddenly she knew he had known she'd stepped into this store to avoid him—and meant her to feel discomfited, just as she now felt.

Determined to regain her self-possession she said, "One doesn't expect to see a businessman—like yourself—here on a weekday. It would seem your work in the city would prevent you from leaving until the weekend."

"I made arrangements to come early. Miss Neville invited me and I couldn't resist." His smile implied Miss Neville's charms were strong indeed.

Katherine felt herself stiffen, but she replied with calmness. "Then I hope you enjoy your time here at the shore."

"Oh, I can assure you, I shall."

"Good." She clutched her purse. "Well, Mrs. Kemble will be wanting her ribbon. If you'll excuse me." She started around the opposite side of the rack.

"Oh, I forgot to ask you something the other day," Jerard said, stepping in front of her. "Aunt Elsie wanted to know when you'd be paying a visit."

Katherine looked up at him. "The Kembles keep me busy with the children. In all likelihood, I won't be able to come for some time."

"Maybe I could say a word on your behalf, so you could have a few days off."

With longing, her mind darted to the grand old mansion, her quiet bedroom, the forest path she'd walked so many times, but she quickly said, "No—I'm sure when Mrs. Kemble can spare me she will be more than happy to let me go. But, thank you, just the same."

How she would love to visit Aunt Elsie and everyone else, but she couldn't let Jerard see how much she wanted to. Better she stay away, particularly if he happened to be present. Besides, all of a sudden she felt foolish, and without warning, teary. She cleared her throat. "Please tell Aunt Elsie thank you. The invitation is very kind, but I can't go at present. Now, please excuse me." Her gaze dropped as she stepped around him. Walking back through the store, she forced a stiff little smile at the clerk who had doubtless overheard the whole of their strange conversation.

☙

Having arrived for the weekend, Mr. Kemble tiptoed around the side of the house, and headed for the porch facing the ocean. He removed his hat and slumped into a wicker chair. A refreshing breeze wafted over his face, lifting a few stray hairs. Head against the headrest, he closed his eyes, letting the rhythmic sound of the waves soothe him.

The porch door creaked. Opening one eye a fraction, Mr. Kemble saw his wife hesitate, her lips pressed together, then slip through the door, closing it with care. She selected a chair near his.

Divining her intention, he pretended not to notice her. He could hear her moving restlessly.

When she could apparently abide the silence no longer, she broke into his quiet. "Isn't it peaceful out here?"

"Yes, dear." His eyes remained shut.

He heard her hands fidget on her lap. "Arthur, you should see the children sit reading with Miss Edmond. It's a picture, I tell you. Come inside and see."

"Let me rest awhile, please. I'm tired."

"This is the most relaxing summer I've had in years. That governess is a jewel. We're most fortunate to have her. And it's certainly an advantage to have someone so refined. I believe the children are showing the effects of it." She turned to plump the cushion behind her. "By the way, did I tell you we're having Jerard Emery come for dinner this weekend? You know Estelle is quite taken with him. It's not surprising. He's so distinguished and charming, and with his wealth and position, he'd be quite the catch." Mrs. Kemble leaned toward her husband. "Arthur, are you listening?"

"Of course, dear."

"Well, it's terribly frustrating to talk with you when you look as if you're asleep. Please, at least try to appear to be listening."

"If I had a few minutes peace and quiet, maybe I'd be in a more receptive mood."

"You're alone in New York all week. Besides, I sat here for quite some time, not saying a word. You must know, we are having an important guest for dinner tomorrow night and you treat it as nothing."

"I didn't realize this dinner was such a momentous event."

"Well, maybe not for us. But for Estelle, it is. I've tried to plan all Mr. Emery's favorite foods and amusements. One never knows, tomorrow evening might be the very time his thoughts turn to love."

"Julia, you're an incorrigible matchmaker." Mr. Kemble slumped further in his chair. "But now that I've heard about the social event of the summer, please leave me in peace. Keep the children occupied for the next half-hour. I want to sit here by myself and enjoy the ocean."

"Mr. Kemble, you're impossible. Ignoring me when you haven't seen me all week and then not wanting to see your own children."

"You'll survive. Now, go. Please." He covered his eyes with his hat."

He heard the porch door close with a bang.

ଓ

Katherine paused at the upstairs banister and decided to sit on the topmost step. She'd sent the children to get ready for bed and now had a few minutes to herself. Down below in the dining room, the occasional silverware striking against china could be heard as well as the murmur of conversation. Earlier Mrs. Kemble mentioned she had considered including her in with the dinner party, seeing she had been close to the Emery family. "But it'd be like having a fifth wheel, wouldn't it? Seven at table wouldn't do. I'm sure you understand."

Mrs. Kemble had strategically placed pink carnations on the table, meaning, *Woman's Love.* Would Jerard have an inkling of the flowers' meaning?

The company below laughed. Miss Neville was speaking. Katherine could picture her leaning across the table in that low-cut silk dress, gazing at Jerard with an adoring look. The image sickened her. Almost she regretted the list of Jerard's favorite foods she'd given Mrs. Kemble.

The afternoon Mrs. Kemble had asked her to draw up the list, she'd headed for her room, plopped down at her desk, and begun the list with the most distasteful things she could think of—Brussels sprouts and tongue. Then she'd put an asterisk beside them to indicate they were Jerard's special favorites. Looking at the page, she'd gloated, her imagination picturing the dinner as it would unfold.

Then she'd thrown down her pen. This whole business was unsettling. She hadn't expected Jerard to show interest in another woman so soon, and right in front of her.

The thought of him romantically linked with Miss Neville—or any other woman—dismayed her. She had to admit her conquest of him, albeit unintentional, was a prize not easily surrendered.

What did she want? Jerard pining away, vowing never to show interest in another woman as long as he lived? Then it began to dawn on her: she was no better than a jealous schemer. And a goose to boot. She looked down at the list. What would Jesus have written? That didn't take much reflection. He would have sought to make the loveliest dinner possible, taking no thought of Himself.

Suddenly, she was appalled. "Forgive me, Lord," she whispered. A tear rolled past her long lashes. She let it course down her cheek and onto the collar of her dress, wanting to feel the full measure of her distress. Especially, she wanted to remember this moment when her old self had threatened to rear up like some wild thing.

At that moment, Jerard's voice brought her back to the dinner party below. His words were not clear, but the sound of his voice—oh, how she would love to—to talk with him again. He didn't seem angry any longer, not after the way he'd teased her in the men's clothing store. She must have been forgiven—easier no doubt now that he had Miss Neville as his new interest.

Felix poked his head out of his room. "Weren't you going to read us a story?"

Katherine turned to look at the boy. For a fleeting moment she considered staying to listen to the dinner party, then thought better of it. No, the children would provide a distraction from her present thoughts. And seeing Felix in his nightwear inspired her to change into her nightgown as well.

ꝏ

As Katherine snuggled under the covers, she realized that retiring early had been both a good and a bad idea. While she tried to relax, she heard Miss Neville playing a Chopin waltz. How stilted it sounded. A Chopin waltz should be played airily, each turn and trill a bright ornament, something to catch one's spirit and make it dance. How she would love to show her how the waltz should be played. No... she would choose a little enchanting "night music," a nocturne. Yes, Chopin's beloved Nocturne in E Flat with its beautiful, captivating melody.

She thought of the pink carnations and the message they were meant to send. Yet music had its language as well, beguiling its way into a listener's heart.

When the piano stopped, she heard gentle laughter, Mr. Kemble's above the rest. That was a relief, because he had been in anything but good spirits before the guests' arrival. In fact, he'd threatened to boycott the entire evening. Mrs. Kemble had been aghast and gave her husband to understand in no uncertain terms he had better attend the dinner. Katherine heard more family rows here in the summerhouse than in the city. Probably because of the thin walls. She didn't like hearing the Kembles argue. The iciness that followed was unbearable. Would that have been the outcome if she'd married Jerard? Both of them holding out, like the Kembles, for his or her way to the detriment of the marriage?

A soft tap at her bedroom door startled her. Through half-closed eyes Katherine saw a shaft of light shine on her coverlet as the door opened. The maid paused, saw the bed's occupant asleep and closed the door.

Katherine had pretended slumber, she didn't know why. But not long afterward, she learned why the maid had come. She could hear Jerard's wonderful baritone floating up to her room. Unaccompanied.

A happy thought cupped its warm fingers around her heart. Jerard had wanted her to accompany him. He might have stopped caring for her, but he still valued her music. Preferred her playing to Miss Neville's. Chiding her weak little heart for taking satisfaction in the thought, she couldn't condemn herself too severely. She slipped out of bed and stood by the open door, remembering how the two of them had made music together—music that delighted the very soul.

Chapter 27

At the end of August, Katherine helped the Kembles pack their belongings to return to New York. Mrs. Kemble once again took on the rigors of her social obligations and Katherine resumed studies with the children. For Katherine, life would have returned to the former routine—except for the dinner given at the shore in Mr. Emery's honor.

Mrs. Kemble had told Katherine that Mr. Emery had asked about her. At first it seemed a general interest question, but as he warmed to his topic, he expressed his views quite decidedly.

"Initially, he asked if we found you satisfactory. Naturally, I told him a resounding yes!"

Mrs. Kemble had a proud little quirk to her mouth. "Then he said his mother would want to know because she had taken great care in your training and education. And he considered you a bright and talented young lady. I told him we couldn't be more in agreement.

"Mr. Emery went on to say that when all was said and done, he had expected you to remain with them, to live out your life as a member of the family. When my husband wondered why indeed you had given up such a comfortable existence, Mr. Emery replied that because of your confounded independence you insisted on supporting yourself. 'Maybe,' he added, 'she'll come to her senses someday, realize what she's given up and return home.'

"What he said made quite an impression on us, Katherine, because after a lengthy discussion, my husband and I have decided to make your situation more congenial for a gentlewoman. After all, you were, in effect, a member of the Emery household and should be treated with more consideration than the rest of our help."

Mrs. Kemble now smiled kindly. "As a result, Katherine, you will not always eat with the children as formerly, but now and then will dine with us. In addition, I would like you to fill in for the occasional absent dinner guest."

Katherine had felt herself startle on hearing Jerard inquire about her, then her heart had warmed on hearing he thought her bright and talented, but when he mentioned her "confounded independence," she truly didn't know what to think. And she was amazed that at just a few words from him, her status changed so remarkably.

Mrs. Kemble began introducing Katherine as Mrs. George Emery's ward—the Emerys of Connecticut—whom they were most fortunate to have living with them and helping with the children's education.

"A letter for you, Miss Edmond." Elise, the maid, brought Katherine's mail to the classroom.

Katherine glanced at the handwriting. Christopher! Since the children were completing a writing assignment, she opened the envelope and perused it quickly, then returned it to the envelope. She sneezed, took a handkerchief out of her pocket to blow her nose and put the letter in its place.

Christopher was coming to New York. How absolutely delightful. She wondered how long he would stay. He'd mentioned his intention of studying in the City. Maybe she would be able to see him on a regular basis.

That would help relegate another person to the periphery of her thinking. Katherine chided herself that on two previous occasions when Jerard had accompanied Miss Neville to the house, she had avoided meeting him, but still had strained to hear his voice in the foyer below.

Katherine glanced at the children sitting at their worktable, for once doing their studies as told. They'd been restless this last week. She blew her nose again. This cold had been such a drain. When she returned the handkerchief to her pocket she felt the letter once again. She looked forward to enjoying it more thoroughly later.

Most of the morning Felix teased his sister, seeing how far he could go before getting into trouble. So far, Meg had been dealing with her brother quietly in her own way, but Katherine wondered when she would explode.

She held her breath as another sneeze threatened to erupt. It suspended for a few moments, then burst violently. She used the last available spot of her handkerchief. Maybe she should have asked for the day off, but Mrs. Kemble had left the house early, so Katherine had determined to carry on. But oh, how she wished she were in bed.

Looking at the children doing their sums and multiplication tables, she felt she wouldn't mind being a young girl for a day. She remembered with fondness how Mrs. O'Neil would have Cook bring her hot chicken soup when she had a cold. Then, when she started feeling better, Cook would make her a special pudding.

Another sneeze was coming on. Her handkerchief was all but soaked. Getting up with haste to get a replacement from her room, she said, "I'll be gone only a minute, children." She must return as soon as possible, otherwise mischief was bound to erupt. Something needed to be done with the children. Felix, of late, had been harder to deal with. How often she felt on the edge of losing control. She snatched a handkerchief from her top drawer.

She was about to reenter the classroom when she heard a loud bang, then a cry. Hurrying in, she caught Felix taking a swing at Meg with his slate. As soon as Meg saw Katherine she squealed, "Felix is hitting me."

"She called me names."

"Children! Sit down."

Meg scooted to her chair. Felix slumped down, his lower lip sticking out.

Katherine crossed her arms, trying to look severe. Both were at fault she felt sure, but right at the moment she couldn't think of a suitable response. She glanced covertly at the clock on the mantle. Lunch wasn't for another hour. Felix was pouting; she ought to make him take that scowl off his face, but she didn't welcome another confrontation.

Her head felt so foggy she could hardly think clearly. At length she said tersely, "Felix, sit at the opposite end of the table from Meg. Both of you will go to your rooms right after lunch."

She sighed. "Don't you children think of anyone but yourselves? I'm feeling terrible today, and it makes me think you have no consideration for me, or others." She walked to the window and looked over the garden. A few trees showed specks of yellow and burnt orange, but most leaves had already fallen. Yet clusters of brave chrysanthemums still bloomed deep red near the arbor.

Why did she have to teach these children everything? Not only school subjects, but how to comport themselves, taking them outside to exercise as well as to cultural events— the list went on and on. Shouldn't their parents be doing some of this? Felix, especially, needed a father, someone to roughhouse and tumble with, someone to take him fishing—or something.

Dare she share her mind with Mr. Kemble? She dabbed her watery eyes with her hanky. If she did talk with him, she'd have to feel far better than she did at present.

ಌ

Katherine was about to retire for the night when she heard a faint knock at her bedroom. The door opened slowly and in peeked a tousled head.

"Felix!" Katherine crossed the room. "Is anything the matter?"

"I couldn't sleep."

She knelt in front of him. It was unusual for Felix to come to her room. Something must be on his mind. "Did you want to tell me something?"

He looked off to the side, not meeting her concerned gaze. From behind him, he brought a fistful of red chrysanthemums. "I—I want to say I'm sorry for being so much trouble today." His lower jaw went slack and trembled slightly.

All Katherine's resentment at having to teach the boy dissolved. She reached for the flowers. "I'm glad you came and apologized, Felix." She leaned forward and hugged him. After giving an extra squeeze, she held him off. "That felt good. And you know what? I think my cold even feels better." She placed the flowers on her dressing table. "I'll put these in water in a few minutes."

His face brightened.

She returned the smile. "Are you ready to go back to bed now?"

On his nod, she took his hand and together they tiptoed past Meg's bedroom, the floor creaking despite their care. After tucking Felix in, Katherine made her way back down the hall.

Meg's dark head peeked out of her doorway. "Miss Edmond?" Another sad face. "Could I talk with you a minute?"

Katherine nodded.

Meg climbed up on the high bed and invited Katherine to do the same. "I've been thinking about today. We caused you—I caused you—a lot of trouble, especially when you weren't feeling well." Katherine could barely make out the outline of Meg's features in the moonlight, but clearly heard the words, "I'm sorry." She hesitated only a moment, then put her arm around the girl.

Later, she lay on her bed looking up at the ceiling. In the quietness—in her mind's eye—she could see God sitting on His throne. She saw herself prostrated before Him, thanking Him for the children, thanking Him for her job.

She saw Him leaning down to her. "Well done, Katherine, good and faithful servant." A warm glow enveloped her. She rolled over and snuggled into her pillow. She'd been given a responsibility with these children, and she must look to it.

☙

A few evenings later Katherine needed to collect a songbook for the children out of the piano bench. As she approached the parlor she noticed a light shining from the library. Often, when coming downstairs on an errand, she would glance with longing at the library door. The dark-paneled refuge had enough books to while away many an hour, if she'd had the leisure. A place like that promised new places to visit, new people to become acquainted with, new ideas to ponder.

Tonight the door was ajar. Maybe she could quickly choose a book to take to her room. She tapped on the doorpost. When Mr. Kemble answered, she entered and saw him seated in comfort near the fire. He turned his head and smiled pleasantly. Suddenly, she felt emboldened to talk with him about the subject that had been on her mind. "Good evening, sir. Do you have a few minutes?" On his nod she said, "I'd like to speak to you about Felix."

"Felix?" His tone implied a distant knowledge of the subject.

"Yes." She sat in the chair he indicated, giving him time to adjust to the topic.

"Is there a problem?"

"Not really." She hesitated. "But something needs to be addressed. I hope I can explain it properly. You see, Felix is all boy. He's intelligent and fun-loving, but he can also be rough and boisterous. And sort of messy, like boys will be." Her eyebrows drew together. "What I'm trying to say is sometimes he needs a man to help direct all that energy. As a woman, I don't have experience in certain areas."

She had been glancing off into the fire, trying to explain. Now, however, she forced herself to look directly at Mr. Kemble. "What I'm asking—could you spend a little time with him? A few hours on a Saturday afternoon perhaps, doing things a father and son would do?" She looked at him, hopefully.

He eyed her. "What do you have in mind?"

"Oh, playing ball, fishing, or maybe just going for a walk together and talking."

"I'm quite busy, you know."

"I realize that, sir, but I'm thinking of your son's welfare. And I believe you'd enjoy the time, too."

Mr. Kemble cleared his throat. "Well, I will consider it."

"Thank you, sir. As I said, I think you'd appreciate the time as well." Katherine rose. "If you'll excuse me I'd like to borrow a book, if I may."

Mr. Kemble stood. "I'm glad to see you availing yourself of the reading material here. Please don't hesitate to use this room. Take it as a gesture of my esteem." He bowed in a courtly manner.

She smiled her thanks and crossed the room to the bookshelves.

Chapter 28

Katherine knocked briskly on the doors of Felix's room, then Meg's. "Children, we need to leave in a few minutes."

Felix scurried out. "I'll go see if the carriage is here."

"Thank you, Felix."

Meg opened her door. "Miss Edmond, would you help me with my hair ribbon? Elise left me ten minutes ago and hasn't come back."

Katherine tied the ribbon, smiling. Nothing could dampen her spirits this afternoon. She'd been looking forward to this concert for weeks; in fact, she felt fortunate to have acquired matinee tickets. The day she'd purchased them she heard the evening performances had already sold out. She hoped the children would enjoy the symphony. She had tried to prepare them, explaining the various instruments and picturing the performance hall. Hopefully, everything would go smoothly.

When they arrived at Steinway Hall, it was already half-filled. Their seats were on the main floor, and Katherine noticed, for the moment, no one sat in front of them. She hoped the children wouldn't have anyone large to peer around.

Felix craned his neck to take in the concert hall.

"Felix, don't look around so. It isn't polite," Katherine said.

"I want to see the people in the balconies. It's sort of a horseshoe around the sides, just like you said."

"It's beautiful, Miss Edmond," Meg said. "I feel so elegant. You must feel so, too, in your cranberry dress. Look at that huge chandelier and those statues in the wall behind the orchestra."

Katherine smiled. "It is very beautiful and we're going to hear a lot of beautiful music as well. But now I'd like you to sit still and notice what's happening on the stage."

Several people filed in the row in front of them and sat in the empty seats. Katherine noted with dismay a corpulent man right in front of Felix and a woman almost as large in front of Meg. Katherine herself had the best view. If Felix couldn't see the stage, he wouldn't last the concert no matter how eager he had been to come. She leaned over. "I'll change seats with you, Felix."

As she stood, she felt conscious of people's eyes on her. Her hand went instinctively to the silver combs setting off the chignon at the nape of her neck. Sitting down, she looked at Felix and Meg. She should have brought cushions for them, but it was too late for that. Felix and Meg could change places during intermission.

A few minutes later, members of the orchestra filed in. Conversation in the audience died away. The orchestra seated, the concertmaster stood and motioned the oboe to play the tuning note. Felix grasped Katherine's arm, beaming. Both children sat up straight to better see. With each section of instruments tuned, a cacophony of scales, arpeggios, and musical phrases filled the auditorium.

After a minute, the orchestra quieted. The audience waited with hushed anticipation. When the conductor threaded his way through the orchestra, Katherine's little party of three applauded enthusiastically with everyone else.

Haydn's *Surprise Symphony* opened the program. The music swept around Katherine, lifting her. Her soul soared, singing with the melody.

At the end of the Haydn she remembered to look at the children. Thankfully, they were sitting without a lot of fidgeting. She smiled at them.

Mozart was next. This music bubbled like a fresh spring gurgling out of the ground. Its lively allegro was followed by a warm, expressive andante. Katherine's eyes closed, her head leaning back to drink in the beautiful music. Happy memories danced through her thoughts.

Intermission was still a few minutes away when Katherine noticed whispering. She opened her eyes and turned to Meg and Felix. How long had this been going on? They were loud enough to disturb anyone trying to listen intently. She reached over and touched each child on the shoulder, shaking her head no.

The children stilled, but in a few minutes their occasional movement to get comfortable turned into wiggling. She shook her head again, this time more emphatically.

Intermission arrived and the people began leaving their seats. Felix asked, "I want to stretch my legs. Can we go somewhere?"

Katherine looked down at him. "Yes, we'll walk to the foyer. Be sure to take your purse, Meg. And let's keep together. We don't want anyone getting lost."

They managed to squeeze past the two people who remained seated in their row when, in haste, an usher approached them. "Excuse me, miss, but I have a message for you from a gentleman in the balcony." He handed her a white card with a brief note:

Katherine, I noticed the children had trouble seeing the stage. Why don't you join us.

Jerard

"The gentleman is right above us, miss." The usher lifted his hand toward the balcony. "I'm to escort you, if you wish."

Katherine and the children looked up and saw Mr. Emery standing above, not far away. Miss Neville was seated near him.

As soon as he saw them looking, he leaned toward the railing and beckoned them to come.

"I'm not sure..." Katherine slowly shook her head.

"Oh please, please!" both children entreated. Felix added, "I'll never say another mean thing about Meg's nose again."

Katherine checked the smile threatening to cross her face. "All right then." At the children's ecstatic outcry she said, "But you must be quiet and on your very best behavior."

As they made their way up the aisle Katherine wouldn't permit herself to look up to see Jerard's reaction. His offer came as a surprise. He wasn't the type to consider a child's welfare. And what about Miss Neville? Katherine couldn't picture her being happy about the children sharing seats near her. Well, the die was cast, the offer made and accepted. Katherine hoped she wouldn't live to regret it.

As soon as the usher opened the door to the balcony and led them down the aisle, Katherine saw the advantage of the seats. Because they were on the front row, the children would be able to see the orchestra much better.

Jerard stepped forward. "I'm glad you decided to join us. Our seat mates excused themselves at intermission, saying they would not be returning. I'm not sure the reason, but I thought to take advantage of it."

"Your offer is very kind." Katherine placed a hand on each child's shoulder. "Children, you remember Mr. Emery." She looked at Jerard and smiled. "Meg and Felix, my two charges."

"I'm glad to see you again." Jerard nodded at Meg and held out his hand to Felix.

Both children responded with a proper, "How do you do."

"I'll arrange our seating."

Katherine watched Jerard place the children in two of the empty seats with herself next to them. He whispered a question to Estelle and she stood to move to the next seat. Katherine deduced the question and its answer. This would place Estelle a little farther from her niece and nephew. Jerard left a seat between himself and Katherine. As everyone arranged themselves, Jerard asked, "Estelle, do you need anything?"

"Could you help with my shawl, please?"

Stepping next to Katherine, he placed his hand on the back of her seat and leaned near. "Are you comfortable?"

She turned to answer and found his face inches from hers. He didn't move, but looked earnestly at her. His nearness brought back the memory of the night when they had been so close. "I'm fine, thank you."

Meg and Felix peered down at the activity in the orchestra below. Felix turned around. "Miss Edmond, do you hear the orchestra tuning again? I like that." He looked at her quizzically. "Is something wrong?"

"Oh, no, Felix. Everything's fine."

"You're all pink."

Katherine felt her blush deepen. She cleared her throat. "Sit back, Felix. The orchestra is about to begin." She shifted in her seat. That child! What would he say next? She needed to settle herself. It wasn't everyday she heard music like this. Besides, Jerard was Miss Neville's escort. She needed to keep her eyes on the stage, averted from the couple at her side.

For some minutes she struggled to concentrate, then the beauty of the music caught her. She sat forward, listening with rapt attention. At one point a violin solo played with such brilliance, such strength, she turned to share her delight with someone and found Jerard's eyes on her. His eyes mirrored her enjoyment.

For a moment, she basked in his smile, then looked away. Staring at the orchestra below, she felt him keenly on her side—too keenly. Now she would have to struggle with her thoughts in the middle of this wonderful concert. Determined to think only of the music, she turned her head an inch or two to block Jerard from her peripheral vision.

She was beginning to concentrate on the closing allegretto when Meg squealed. At once Katherine leaned over.

"Felix pinched me."

"Felix!" Katherine's reprimand was low but intense.

"Well, I'm bored." His voice was loud enough for their near neighbors to hear.

Katherine felt her face glow with embarrassment. Jerard had been so generous to offer these seats. What would he think of the lack of discipline, the poor manners of these children? She was responsible for them.

In the middle of these frantic thoughts, Jerard leaned over and touched her arm. "Let me take the boy out for a few minutes. This movement is just about finished."

"Oh, I could do that."

Jerard's hand tightened on her arm, holding her in place. "No, I insist you stay. You are my guest here and I want you to enjoy the remainder of the concert. Besides, I feel the need for fresh air myself." He turned to Estelle and explained. As everyone broke into applause, he took hold of Felix by the shoulder and guided the boy to the exit doors.

Jerard hadn't asked her permission; he'd insisted. Katherine sat some moments feeling both chagrined and grateful. A gentle sigh of relief escaped her. He wanted her to enjoy the symphony, so she would endeavor to do just that. She glanced at Meg sitting quietly. Bless her.

Jerard was quite capable of managing Felix; he managed people, animals, the estate, even a business. Felix would be no problem for him. Katherine sat back, letting the music surround her. She felt a wonderful sense of well-being. Next on the program was a short, but delightful piece. She was sorry Jerard had to miss it.

By the time the two returned, Beethoven's *Symphony No. 7* was about to begin. Felix quietly took his place.

Jerard once again took his own seat. Katherine turned to him, her lips forming a silent, "Thank you."

Jerard smiled and mouthed a noiseless, "My pleasure."

Just as Katherine turned from Jerard, she wondered, was it her imagination or had she seen Estelle stiffen? But she couldn't let that keep her from enjoying the last part of the program.

When the orchestra began the final movement, it commenced with an excited rush of melody. It swept on and on, working its way to a dramatic ending. Hardly breathing, Katherine waited for the pulsing rhythm to resolve itself. At last, the surging music ended in three grand chords. The orchestra members held their bows suspended, the auditorium echoing gloriously.

A moment of silence followed, then the audience broke into thunderous applause. Shouts of "Bravo!" filled the hall. Many stood, clapping enthusiastically. Katherine and Jerard rose, each turning to the other. Her eyes sought his. He looked down at her, deep enjoyment reflected in his eyes. She felt a moment of utter, deep pleasure. Something had passed between them, something sharp and sweet.

Never would she forget experiencing this music together—especially that climactic ending to the symphony. She stood looking at the excited audience below.

"There now," Jerard said, after the audience stopped clapping and the hubbub of movement began. "That movement was a fitting climax to the afternoon." He turned to Miss Neville. "I hope you enjoyed the concert."

"A remarkable performance. However, I was sorry you had to miss part of it." She smiled, clutching her reticule. Katherine thought her smile seemed forced.

"Under the circumstances, it couldn't be helped." Jerard turned to Katherine. "Now, is the Kemble carriage coming for you?"

"Yes, we are to wait near the Fourteenth Street entrance."

"We'll walk down with you. Is everyone ready?"

Stepping into the aisle, Miss Neville jerked her skirt around. She looked none too happy her little party of two had become an expanded party of five. Katherine saw the angry gesture, but didn't know how to extricate herself and the children without making a fuss. It would be best to follow Jerard's lead, for the quicker they located their carriage, the sooner they would be out of the way.

Coats collected, they made their way through the crowd out the entrance door. Jerard hailed a hansom cab and assisted Miss Neville inside, instructing the driver to wait. He returned to the place where Katherine and the children stood.

Katherine said, "Please, don't stay on our account. We'll be fine."

"It'll only be another minute I'm sure." He then asked about her favorite parts of the concert and seemed gratified at her fervent replies. She thanked him again for the invitation to the balcony and for helping with Felix.

As she spoke, she occasionally averted her eyes from his, looking for the Kemble carriage. In reality, she was afraid he would see how pleased she felt with his courtesy. Of course, she assured herself, he was only being watchful for her because of their past familial association. Another woman now interested him.

"Ah, there's your carriage," Jerard said.

Thank goodness. His continued presence at her side had begun to feel uncomfortable.

He took her elbow and assisted her through the crowd to the carriage. At its window, Katherine caught sight of a familiar face. "Christopher!" she cried out.

He alighted from the carriage, hesitated a moment on seeing Jerard, then reached for Katherine's outstretched hands. Holding them, he drew her close and kissed her cheek. "So good to see you."

"What a surprise," she managed to say.

"Quite a surprise," Jerard said. Both men greeted each other briefly.

"I went to the Kembles on my arrival," Christopher said. "As soon as Mrs. Kemble knew my identity, she suggested I come with the carriage to meet you. I must tell her about the look on your face when you saw me."

"Well," Katherine said, laughing, "I'll have to thank her for such a delightful surprise. And this on top of a perfect afternoon, for which I have Jerard to thank." She turned to him. "I appreciate your waiting with us. I hope we haven't intruded too much on your time with Miss Neville."

"Not at all. Glad to be of assistance. Christopher, I'll hand Katherine over to you."

After Jerard turned away, Katherine helped the children up into the carriage, then let Christopher assist her. She couldn't help thinking what a nice—and welcome—foursome they made. If only Miss Neville could have seen their party it would surely have relieved her mind that she now had Jerard all to herself.

Chapter 29

"You should have seen her acting so quiet and demure," Estelle said, pacing in front of her aunt in the morning room. "Every once in a while she'd turn and look at him with those big dark eyes. Of course, Jerard invited their group to share those seats only to be kind to your children. They couldn't see well from where they sat, craning their necks and all. I'm sure his concern was commendable, but as far as your paragon of a governess is concerned, I could have done without her." She flounced her skirt around. "And then if that wasn't enough—"

The naturally talkative Mrs. Kemble sat at her desk, held in abeyance by Estelle's angry account of Saturday's performance. Her niece continued to pace, gesturing forcefully. At last, reaching the end of her excited narrative, she dropped into the nearest chair in a huff.

"I'm so sorry, dear. It seems you did have a time of it," her aunt said. "It was most unfortunate the children sat behind such large people, and that our dear Mr. Emery felt he had to be considerate of their little party."

Mr. Kemble poked his head in the doorway.

"I thought you were in the library with your books," his wife said.

"I was, but I could hear the fuss all the way down the hall. What's the matter?"

"Oh, the Saturday matinee. Jerard Emery invited our children and Katherine up to the balcony where he sat with

Estelle, and of course, Estelle would have preferred having him all to herself."

"I see." Mr. Kemble smiled.

"You must know how things are." Mrs. Kemble gave her husband a pointed look, then an idea occurred to her. "Arthur, we already know Mr. Emery is from a fine family. But I wonder... in view of his growing association with Estelle... if we shouldn't know more about—his financial situation, for instance? You run into him in business, don't you?"

"As a matter of fact, I see him on the exchange."

"Well, what do you think?"

"Jerard Emery's in the market to make money. He's hardly conservative. I don't necessarily agree with his trading philosophy, but then, to each his own." Mr. Kemble shrugged his shoulders. "But if that's all the trouble here, I'm back to my library." Looking at his niece, he added, "I wouldn't worry too much, Estelle. Seeing Mr. Emery likes money, your having it should weigh in your favor."

As his footsteps echoed down the hallway, Estelle leaned over to her aunt. "It's all very well and good for him to say not to worry, but he wasn't at the matinee. The way your governess acted I feel quite sure she'd like to be a permanent member of the Emery family. And not as Jerard's sister, either."

"Estelle, of all the things to say," Mrs. Kemble protested, but her eyes narrowed.

"Auntie, what shall I do?"

"Well, nothing drastic. Be your usual charming self with Mr. Emery. For my part, I will assure him we make Katherine a good situation here, so he doesn't have to concern himself about her welfare. Then I'll do all I can to keep her out of the way when he comes."

"I suppose that would be the wisest course for the present."

"Of course it is, dear. Now, don't worry." Mrs. Kemble leaned over and lowered her voice confidentially. "If your heart is set on Mr. Emery, we'll do whatever is necessary to get him for you."

ଓ

Her piano lesson finished, Katherine sat near the entry in Steinway Hall. Christopher said he would be late, so she relaxed a few minutes, leaning her head against the wall.

How grateful she was for her friend's presence in New York, even if she saw him only a few hours a week. With his coming, she'd discovered how hungry she'd been for companionship—real companionship.

No one she'd met so far shared her particular upbringing, her love of the arts, her faith in God. She closed her eyes for a minute and smiled, her imagination conjuring up the walks they would take, the art exhibitions and music recitals they would attend, and the good talks they would have.

She appreciated his presence for another reason as well. He would help banish another figure from her mind. Since Saturday's performance, when Jerard had been so kind and considerate of the children and herself, she had found it harder and harder to keep him out of her thoughts.

The days following the concert, one moment she thought of him standing near the edge of the balcony, beckoning her and the children to come. Another moment she remembered him arranging their seating, and most tantalizing of all, his face bent close to hers when he asked if she was comfortable. She chided herself for allowing such musings to get a foothold. But the next hour, as she engaged in some quiet task, Jerard's handsome face would smile, sharing with her the pleasure of the music once again.

"Katherine!" Christopher stood beside her. "You startle and then blush. Do your thoughts betray you, my sweet?"

Katherine laughed, wishing she didn't color so easily. "I appreciate your meeting me after my lesson."

"This seems to be one of the few times I can see you without the children. What do you think I came to New York for? Only to study?" He grinned. "Here, take my arm and let's sail forth. I'm ready for adventure." On the entrance steps, he took a deep breath. "What are you in the mood for? An art museum? Some window shopping? A walk?"

"Let's walk and then decide." Katherine looked up at him. "Oh, Christopher, you're like a long cool drink after a scorching day in the sun."

"Ah, thank you. But the day isn't exactly a scorcher. Rather cool and gray. But I'm grateful to be what you need."

"You're just what I need."

"Exactly what I want to hear. Let's be off, then. Which way, to the right or the left?"

"To the right. I seldom walk in that direction."

They reached the corner and Christopher said, "Why, who's this?"

"Katherine." Jerard bowed, tipping his hat. "Christopher." He glanced back at the Hall. "I see you've discovered one of Katherine's favorite haunts."

"Every Thursday, I understand. And I'm taking advantage of it."

Katherine looked up at Christopher, his smile decidedly in place. He placed his free hand firmly over hers resting on his arm.

"So, how long do you plan to stay in New York?" Jerard asked.

"Oh, a number of months. It's rather open-ended. I'm studying, you know."

"Studying? So you haven't settled down to real work yet?"

"Art is work. Although I'll have to admit it doesn't pay well."

Christopher's hand tightened over Katherine's. "You keeping an eye on business in New York?"

"Among other things."

Katherine felt the tension in the air. She caught Jerard's eye. "The children and I were grateful you noticed our plight at the matinee. I want to thank you again for your kindness."

"My pleasure. Glad to have made the concert more enjoyable for you." He nodded to the Hall. "By the way, how is your music progressing?"

"Very well. I'm indebted to Mrs. von Weber's recommendation of Mr. Mason."

"Good. You remember we talked about doing music together. I have a piece in mind, an accompaniment for one of my solos."

"Thank you. I'd enjoy that."

He tipped his hat. "Well, I'll be off, then. Take good care of her, Christopher. Good accompanists are hard to find."

Christopher nodded and let his former neighbor pass to continue down the street. After a few moments he said, "Strange running into Jerard in a city this size. Do you see him often?"

"No, and never around here. I only see him when he escorts Miss Neville, my employer's niece."

"Not a romantic interest?"

"Oh, I think so."

"Well, then, if they're interested in each other, that's all to the good. Now, what say you to an art museum?"

☙

Weeks passed with shorter days and freezing air bringing snow flurries. Nothing, however, deterred Christopher and Katherine from their Thursday afternoon outings. They would begin with an invigorating walk, relate everything that happened during the week, then visit one of the many attractions New York had to offer. Katherine wondered what she had done before Christopher's arrival.

She heard via the grapevine, meaning Mrs. Kemble, that Jerard had left the city suddenly. Estelle was devastated. No one could give particulars as to his reason for departure or date of return. Katherine was relieved to have him gone. She had begun to wonder at every knock resounding through the house if Miss Neville had arrived with "her" Mr. Emery.

Toward the holidays Katherine again approached Mr. Kemble about spending time with Felix. He answered that he was particularly busy at this time and unable to do anything with his son. Her heart sank. She asked Christopher if he would mind taking Felix and his sister Christmas shopping on one of their Thursday outings. "Only this once," he said. She agreed. They shouldn't include the children every week. That would have been unfair to Christopher and to herself.

Christmas morning, the Kembles lavished their children with gifts. Katherine wished they spent as much time with their son and daughter as they spent shopping for presents.

As they sat around the elaborate tree, Katherine thought back to Christmases with her mother. How she remembered that first tree, skinny and spare of branches, hung with a few homemade ornaments. She had cut out a paper star, like the star of Bethlehem that hung over the place where the Christ child lay. She colored it a sunny yellow, oh so carefully. Then Mother and she garlanded the branches with strings of popcorn and cranberries. Later sitting on her mother's lap, she listened as Mother read her the Christmas story from the Gospel of Luke. As she became older, she would read to Mother. For a moment, she could feel her mother close once again. And imagine the sweet fragrance that belonged only to her.

Felix bumped against her. "Miss Katherine, you daydreaming?"

"Yes, a little."

"Look what I got, a big red scarf. It's huge. But I don't get that cold."

"Oh, scarves come in handy." She remembered the warm, luxurious one she'd been given her last Christmas with the Emerys. A present from Jerard and, when she unwrapped it, she discovered the ends embroidered with tiny bluebells. Aunt Elsie had exclaimed that bluebells meant "constancy," that Robert had given her those flowers on numerous occasions. Had Jerard known? He never referred to the meaning of flowers, so probably not.

But Katherine would treasure the thought of the bluebells to remind her of Mother's constancy. Her mother had shown her husband love even when he didn't deserve it, had stayed faithful to her marriage vows even when the way became difficult. And what had been her reward? Certainly not a changed husband. Katherine cringed to think of the shame Mother would have felt to know her husband was in prison. Thankfully, she never learned of it before her death.

But a child had come out of that difficult union, a child she had been proud of. That had been her reward. And Katherine would show the world her mother had done the right thing all those hard years, that good fruit would come from such constancy.

Chapter 30

Mrs. Kemble stood looking out the morning room window at the garden. A slight smile played over her mouth. She glanced up as Framton ushered Estelle into the room.

"What are you smiling about, Auntie?"

"Oh, just noticing our fruit trees. They're showing green leaves in amongst the pink and white blossoms. I think spring is here to stay."

"I hope so. I'm sick and tired of picking my way around dirty slush on the streets."

"Dear, as if you do much of that. You go from house to carriage, from carriage to store. You walk very little in the elements."

"Well, even so, I don't think there's a more welcome season than spring."

"I'll have to agree with you on that. In fact, I have an idea. Sit down and hear my latest plan for a party—a garden party." Mrs. Kemble took her usual overstuffed flowered armchair near the fire and motioned Estelle to an identical one nearby. "I thought a buffet in the dining room would be lovely. With the French doors open to the terrace, guests could stroll out to the garden. For the evening's entertainment I want a rather formal concert, everyone seated so they can listen to the music. And with Mr. Emery's return to the City I shall ask him to sing."

"Aunt, he would be the finishing touch to the program. Did I tell you he's meeting me here this afternoon? You and I will be finished by five, won't we?"

"Yes, that will also be an opportunity to see if he'll honor us by singing a selection or two." Mrs. Kemble looked at her niece more closely. "How has he been since he's come back? Has he been attentive?"

"I think so. At least I was flattered he called on me so soon after his return. I'd begun to wonder about him since he wrote so seldom. When I alluded to the scarcity of his letters—delicately, of course—he said he seldom wrote missives of a personal nature. So there you are."

"Did he say why he left?"

"Something to do with business."

"You're still enamored of him?"

"Yes. Things weren't the same after he left. Even though I was quite piqued at his lack of correspondence, all was forgiven as soon as I saw him." With the telling, Estelle's face began to glow.

"Good. Then we can get on with our party plans. We have a good two hours before he arrives."

Shortly before the clock chimed five o'clock, a knock sounded at the morning room door. Katherine entered. "Excuse me, Mrs. Kemble, but you said you wanted to see these new materials for the children."

"Ah yes, I'd forgotten." Mrs. Kemble reached for the books while Estelle turned and occupied herself with the guest list.

At that moment, the doorknocker sounded in the distance. A minute later, the butler entered. "Mr. Jerard Emery, ma'am."

"Show him in here, Framton. Wait a minute." Mrs. Kemble glanced at Katherine, then at her niece. "Miss Edmond, I'll look at these later. Would you be so kind as to bring them up to my room? Then I can decide tonight."

"Certainly, Mrs. Kemble." After Katherine gathered the books and made her way out, Mrs. Kemble gave a knowing glance at her niece. "Now I think we can see Mr. Emery, Framton."

Sunday in New York dawned mild and sunny, promising the loveliest of spring days. After church the Kembles took the children visiting. With the house quiet, Katherine sat in her room writing a letter to Aunt Elsie.

She glanced up, pen in hand. Dear old Auntie. Katherine could picture the aureole of white hair surrounding her sweet face. When would she see her again? How she missed Auntie's fidgety, but caring ways.

A discreet knock sounded at her door. Katherine startled. The house had been so still, she hadn't expected anyone. With the family gone, who would need her? Maybe one of the servants asking her to go for a stroll? She opened the door.

"Someone to see you, Miss Edmond." The young man who filled in on Framton's day off gave a perfunctory nod. "Mr. Jerard Emery."

Katherine's hand tightened on the doorknob. "Thank you, John. Tell Mr. Emery I'll be down in a minute." She headed for the mirror on her dressing table and looked at herself with a critical eye. Thankfully, she'd done up her hair in an attractive French twist for church. She looked down in dismay at her old navy wool dress. She'd chosen it this afternoon for comfort rather than looks. But there was no time to change. With haste, she opened her top dresser drawer.

Her eyes fell on a white collar with lace edging. She hadn't thought to wear it with this dress, but now she plucked it up. The white lace would draw the eye away from the dress and frame her face. In all likelihood, Jerard probably wouldn't notice her attire anyway. With that hopeful thought she fastened the collar and headed out the door down the stairs.

What could he want? She hadn't seen Jerard since the day Christopher picked her up that first time at Steinway Hall. That was months ago.

When she reached the archway to the front parlor she saw him standing tall and erect, looking out the window. The next moment he turned. "Katherine!" His dark eyes met hers. He crossed the room to meet her. She held out her hand and he grasped it for a long moment. Then he motioned her to one of the deep crimson armchairs near the bay window. After she sat, he asked how her life fared.

"It's going well, and the children are progressing nicely in their studies." She asked about his mother and Aunt Elsie.

After exchanging a few other pleasantries, Jerard said, "As you must have heard, Mrs. Kemble is giving a party, and she's asked me to sing as part of the evening's entertainment. I knew I didn't need to look far for a good accompanist. Would you do the honors?"

Katherine had heard about the party, but knew none of the details. His request caught her by surprise. "I'm greatly flattered, but I'm not sure what Mrs. Kemble plans for me that evening."

"I won't have anyone else accompany me. So, you can plan on being at the party."

"I see." She smiled. "Then I'd best accept."

"Good. Now, could we arrange to practice later this week? Say, Thursday at eight?"

He was moving fast. "I think that would be fine."

Jerard sat up in his chair, and she thought him about to leave. Her heart sank. "I have something else," he said, reaching into his breast pocket. "For you. Earlier this week a letter arrived for me with a bank draft, for a substantial sum of money. Can you guess who sent it?"

She shook her head.

He smiled and held out an envelope. "Here. This is the money you've been sending for my horse."

Her hands held stubbornly to her lap. "But that is yours. I told you I would compensate you."

"Then it will be paid twice over, because your father has now paid me in full."

"My father?"

"Yes, along with the draft he enclosed a short letter." He took a folded sheet from his pocket. "Would you like to read it?"

"Yes."

He handed her the single sheet of paper. Eagerly she read the scrawled words:

Mr. Emery:

I believe this amount should cover the cost of the horse I took from your stables. I am sorry I could not return the horse, but had to sell it to buy my train ticket west. I'm sorry for the inconvenience to yourself.

Will you give Katherine my love if she is still with you? Please tell her I have been thinking about what she said that day. Her mother would have been proud of her.

Sincerely,

Tom Edmond

Katherine's hands trembled, holding the letter. She looked up. "He didn't say where he lives."

"The letter is postmarked St. Louis."

"I see." She closed her eyes a moment. "I'm glad, grateful really, he paid you back. To tell the truth, I didn't expect it. But I'm sorry—still sorry about Taggart."

"Well, that's all in the past." Jerard held out the envelope again. "So will you take this? It is yours."

"Thank you." She looked up and his eyes smiled into hers.

At that moment the front doorknocker sounded. When the butler answered the door, a familiar voice said, "Is my aunt home?"

"No, Miss Neville, but would you like to come in?"

"For a moment, thank you. I'd like to leave a message."

Katherine's stomach tightened.

"Oh, Jerard!" Estelle said from the parlor archway. "Fancy seeing you here." She sailed into the room, a vision in lilac. "And Miss Edmond." Her eyes stopped at Katherine's dark blue dress. The look made Katherine feel exceedingly shabby. "I'm not interrupting anything, am I?"

"No," Jerard said. "In fact, we had concluded our business."

"Well then, if you were about to leave, I'd be glad to give you a ride. It's such a beautiful spring day and I'm free as a bird this afternoon."

"That would be good of you." Jerard glanced at Katherine, then back at Estelle. "And since you're free we might extend our time to include a ride in the park."

"How delightful."

Katherine hoped the smile she forced didn't look as frozen as it felt. "Would you like me to convey a message to your aunt?"

"Yes. Tell her I'll be here tomorrow for lunch. Well then—" She looked at the two of them.

"I think we can go." Jerard gestured to Miss Neville to precede him. As she turned away, he said in an undertone to Katherine, "I'll get the music to you as soon as possible."

"Thank you," she whispered. She followed them out the room, but the fill-in butler appeared in the hall to see them to the door, so she stepped back to the stair railing.

☙

That same railing guided her as she walked down the stair later that week. Framton had announced Mr. Emery in the parlor. She'd chosen a simple light blue dress with her mother's brooch centered at her throat, acting as a shield as it were.

Sunday she had cried over her father's letter, relieved over his honorable payment of the debt. Throughout the week she had been in a quandary over the coming practice session, not knowing if she anticipated or dreaded it. Today, all day, she'd felt on edge.

As she took the last stair, she hung onto the railing. Her knees felt weak; she almost wished for the privacy of her room.

Jerard rose from a chair as she approached, waiting for her to hold out her hand in greeting, then crossed the parlor with her to the piano. He asked if she approved of his choice of music.

She'd noticed the libretto was in German.

"I consider Schubert the king of song," he said. "You never learned German, did you?"

Was he needling her with that disagreement they'd had so long ago? "No, but I thought the accompaniment lovely."

"I'm glad you like the music. Of course, if we had the English translation, it would be quite instructive."

She said nothing to this.

"Well, let's begin. Will you play a C?" He vocalized a few moments. Signaling her to start the introduction, he breathed in deeply.

As he sang, the melody touched a chord deep within her. And the words—she wondered what they signified. He sang them with such expression. They were beautiful, no doubt, yet her pride would not allow her to ask the translation. And this distance she now felt between them, was her pride causing that as well?

After the practice she accompanied Jerard outside to the covered entrance. In the deep shadow, he looked at her closely, then turned to leave. She watched his tall figure down the short sidewalk and into the waiting carriage.

She closed the door on that last brief scene and hurried up the stairs. After reaching her bedroom, she paced the room. Finally, she sat down at the dressing table.

Instead of seeing the toilette articles clustered in front of her, her mind's eye recalled pictures from the last hour. When Jerard sang, he had stood very near, at times inadvertently touching her right shoulder as he moved with the movement of the song. She'd felt his warmth.

His voice filled the room. At the beginning the phrases were soft and beguiling. As the song progressed, a sharp note of pain deepened the tone of his voice. Then at the end, the song finished with a whispered pleading. The words seemed to communicate something significant. Something dear and important to him.

She turned abruptly from the dressing table, and still seated, faced the single window that looked down on the street. He had walked that sidewalk a short time ago. Where was he now? What was he thinking?

And what was this disquiet, this yearning she felt within herself? She tried to put words to the real, palpable emotion coursing through her.

She closed her eyes, thinking back, seeing her hands on the piano, her fingers pressing into the keys, feeling the music, bringing out its emotion. Even though she didn't know the song's message, she felt its specialness. Why was she feeling so emotional about this?

Thinking back on the rehearsal, she again heard the timbre of his voice. Felt the rise and ebb of emotion in him. Slowly a realization began to dawn...she wanted the emotion he evinced to include her. Wanted him to feel the specialness of the moment that she felt. Realize the uniqueness of what they did so well together—making music. The preciousness and glory of being with....

She turned back to the mirror, looking at her reflection. Her eyes grew wide. "Oh, no!" The enormity of her desire, the impossibility of it took her breath away. Did she... want some assurance he still loved her? That he cared for her as she was discovering she now cared for him? She buried her face in her hands.

Sitting very still, she forced herself to look hard at these last months. Had she been fooling herself all this time? When she glowed at his nearness in the matinee months ago, hadn't she explained to herself he was acting like an older brother looking out for his sister? Every time her heart squeezed with anxiety over seeing him with Miss Neville, hadn't she told herself she was a silly schoolgirl, that of course, he had a right to seek feminine attention elsewhere? In fact, hadn't she tried to see the suitability of the match: the beautiful, self-centered Estelle Neville an appropriate mate for the handsome, willful Jerard Emery?

But how can they marry? What chance of real happiness did they have with each other? Did they have any common ground other than social position and money?

Her hands clenched as she looked up. "No!"

Jerard would be throwing away his life. Married to Estelle, he would be embroiled in self-centeredness. He needed to be freed from himself, to acknowledge a calling beyond himself.

She sat still a full minute, then groaned. Something in the way he sang that song tonight had torn through the web of delusion she'd spun. She saw it all too clearly.

Her fingers closed on her skirt, clutching the soft fabric. And what about him, how did he feel? When she had looked at him tonight after the song, he'd acted as businesslike as she'd ever known him to behave. At the door, then those moments on the landing, he'd said nothing. Oh, how his feelings for her must have changed.

She gazed at the beautiful combs he'd given her, placed with such precision among her toiletries, laid out "in state," as it were, a little monument to the regard in which he'd once held her. Looking at their silver sheen, fierce pride wrapped its hand around her heart. Yes, he had cared once. She reached for the combs and held them close.

Chapter 31

Katherine fastened a delicate silver necklace. She straightened and scrutinized her image in the dressing table mirror. Hopefully, she would do.

She stepped away from the bench, puffing out the skirt of her dress. The light cotton batiste floated from her coaxing fingers, its pale rose a perfect foil for her dark hair. The dress was a bit of an extravagance, bought from the money Jerard had returned for the horse. A swath of delicate fabric encircled her shoulders, leaving her neck and throat to showcase the necklace. The dress fit at the waist, then billowed out in yards of material for the skirt and bustle.

She was pleased with the femininity of her toilette. In her womanly pride, she wanted her appearance to suit the occasion exactly. She didn't want Miss Neville, or anyone else, to find fault with Jerard's choice of accompanist.

A nervous flutter danced in her stomach at the thought of Jerard. She would not let her mind dwell on what her heart now knew. She had decided, beyond a shadow of doubt, he must not discover how she felt. In his eyes she wanted to appear happy and content in her life teaching the Kemble children.

"There, enough of that," she said. "It's time to go downstairs."

A knock sounded at the door. The maid held a large, white box. "A messenger brought this for you, Miss Edmond."

"Thank you, Elise."

Box in hand she crossed the room and placed it on the dressing table. Removing the cover, her breath caught as she saw the lavish spray of flowers. She plucked out the card tucked in among the blossoms.

"For my accompanist."

How lovely! How absolutely lovely. Snowdrops, jonquils, and, tucked in the middle of the arrangement, a single multi-petaled pink rose she'd seen depicted in paintings by the Dutch masters, the cabbage rose meaning "Ambassador of Love." She bent her head to drink in their fragrance. Snowdrops… jonquils… the rose… Katherine blushed. What did this mean? But Jerard wouldn't have used the flowers to send an unspoken message. He was enamored of Miss Neville.

The flowers would need to be put in water. She looked with longing at the rose. It would be perfection with her dress, but she would choose the snowdrops. They would take only a minute to fasten on her bodice.

The parlors and dining room had been transformed for the gala. Large bouquets of mixed flowers brought the garden indoors. The garden itself, Mrs. Kemble had insisted, was the real "object d'art" for the spring party. Tables and chairs had been placed on the terrace and lawn where guests could feast on its beauty.

Katherine approached the dining room table repositioned at the side of the room so guests could walk without hindrance out the French doors. The cook and her helper were placing food on the table: turkey, ham, and pressed meats. Chicken and lobster salads soon followed. Framton directed each placement to best advantage. Next came cole slaw, French pickles, various rolls and jellies.

Mr. Kemble approached the table. "A wonderful assortment of food, isn't it, Miss Edmond? My mouth is watering already." He looked at her appreciatively. "Your dress is exquisite. I venture to say you will be a delicate flower amid all the elaborate dresses and jewels we'll see this evening."

"Thank you, sir." Katherine felt herself glow.

At that moment the cook entered the dining room with a pyramid of assorted miniature cakes. Her helper followed with arrangements of fruits and nuts.

"Framton, everything looks very good," Mr. Kemble said. "Now, I believe I'll join the missus. Katherine, if you'll excuse me." With that he ambled through the French doors onto the terrace.

"I'll bring out the charlotte russe and ices as soon as the guests start arriving," Cook said.

"Fine," Framton replied.

Katherine could see everything was running smoothly. She walked to the piano to check on her music. Out of the corner of her eye she saw Framton approach the front door. Were guests arriving already?

Beyond the parlor doorway, Jerard appeared. Katherine's hand gripped the music. It had been a long time since she'd seen him in evening dress. Miss Neville stepped to his side and looked up at him, smiling. He motioned her to precede him into the front parlor.

At that moment Mrs. Kemble entered the dining room from the terrace. On seeing her niece and Mr. Emery, she crossed the parlors to meet them.

Katherine quickly turned to her music, ostensibly to look it over.

Mrs. Kemble hugged her niece and asked Jerard if he was ready to sing.

"Oh, yes," he said. "Which reminds me, I need to speak with my accompanist."

Katherine made herself turn casually to greet him. She saw him glance at the snowdrops fastened to her dress.

"How are you?" he asked.

"Very well. I want to thank you for the beautiful flowers."

"I'm glad you're wearing some of them. Let's see, snowdrops are ambassadors of hope, are they not?"

"I believe so."

He smiled. "I wanted to make sure the language of flowers was not all Greek to my accompanist. I'm looking forward to performing with you this evening." With that he bowed his head and turned to rejoin Estelle and her aunt.

Katherine hoped she looked calm and self-possessed. What did he mean by alluding to the flower code? She thought of the rose.

She glanced at Jerard. Miss Neville had claimed his arm and was leading him to the terrace. In all likelihood, they would walk around the garden. A jealous pang shot through Katherine. Yet if there was the merest possibility he still cared for her, how could she ever return his love? He hadn't changed. The two of them were as different as they'd always been—in all the important areas of life.

She couldn't see a way out of the dilemma.

When all was said and done, Jerard was none of her business; her business was with the children. Katherine resolutely turned to mount the stairs. She would check on them. They were being allowed to attend the party for the first part of the evening.

Descending from the second floor with her charges, Katherine saw guests arriving in a steady stream and the rooms resonated with animated conversation. Mr. Kemble had been right. Elaborate dresses and jewels adorned all the ladies. The guests had dressed with as much elegance and care as if attending the opera. The brilliant blues, reds, golds, and purples of their gowns made a shimmering contrast to the black dinner apparel of the gentlemen.

The first part of the evening, Katherine kept an eye on the children. Without hovering over them, she nonetheless knew where they were at all times. She supervised their selection of food at the buffet and the three of them found a table on the fringe of the gathering.

An hour later she walked them around the garden one last time. Mrs. Kemble had instructed they be whisked upstairs afterward. "I want your mind on the music, Katherine," she said with good humor, "and not on whether my children are behaving themselves."

During the course of the evening, Katherine couldn't help being aware of Jerard. At one point she entered the front parlor, not expecting him, but spotted him instantly. He sat with Miss Neville, his arm draped casually around the back of the settee, almost touching her shoulder. He looked up, smiling.

She walked on as if seeing them so closely together were of little consequence.

As dusk began to settle, and everyone had eaten their fill and conversed at length, Framton encouraged the guests to go inside where chairs had been placed for the program.

Katherine found a seat near the piano. She was glad the children were upstairs; at the last they had been rambunctious. Taking several deep breaths, she closed her eyes and thought about the music, immersing herself into its mood. She anticipated its rises and falls, wanting the accompaniment to complement Jerard's solo to perfection.

He was the last to perform. "The best should be saved till last," Mrs. Kemble had said when planning the program. "He will be the climax."

When Jerard's selection was announced, Katherine rose and made her way to the piano. Jerard took his place near the instrument, resting one hand on it. He turned and nodded for her to begin.

She played the introduction, carefully setting the tone for his entrance.

Ich traumte von bunten Blumen.

As he sang, his rich baritone and regal bearing captured the attention of everyone in the room. Katherine paced her crescendos and diminuendos to compliment the pathos of the music. Deep inside, the melody touched her. She felt strange and sweet. When his song died away, a moment of silence hung in the air before the audience broke into enthusiastic applause.

Someone shouted, "Encore, encore!" More guests joined in.

Jerard raised his hand and the audience quieted. "Thank you for your kind response. The song has become quite a favorite of mine. With your permission, I'd like to do something special for an encore. Since many gathered here don't understand German, I'd like to sing the song's English translation."

"How delightful," Mrs. Kemble volunteered. The audience smiled its approval.

Jerard stepped near Katherine and bent down as if giving instruction. He whispered, "Listen attentively, my dear."

Katherine's breath caught. As she started playing, she was aware of the first few measures of the score, but once Jerard began singing, she played without consciously looking at the music. Instead, her ear strained to hear every word of the song.

I dreamed of the sunny meadows
Where delicate breezes play,
The voice of the stream in April,
The song of the thrush in May,
The song of the thrush in May.
And then the cock with his crowing
The stillness suddenly broke;
In the icy chill of the morning
I shivered and turned and awoke, In the icy chill of the morning I shivered and turned and awoke.
But who had painted the garden That bloomed on the window pane? And left me dreaming and hoping That summer had come again,

That summer had come again?
I dreamed that I loved a maiden,
I dreamed that the maid loved me; And oh! to hear the laughter, And oh! her smile to see,
And oh! her smile to see.
And then with the cock's shrill crowing My heart awoke in pain,
And now in my lonely corner
I dream it all over again,
And now in my lonely corner
I dream it all over again.
I close my eyes and wonder,
If dreams can still come true, If flowers can bloom in the window, And the maid of my dreams be you, And the maid of my dreams be you.

When he finished, Katherine sat very still, her heart beating hard while her mind tried to grasp what he had sung. He had been singing of love. His love?

And for her? But if so, how could he still hope for her love after she so completely rejected him?

The audience rose to its feet, clapping with enthusiasm.

Jerard reached out a hand to draw Katherine from behind the piano. His eyes caught and held hers, then he lifted her hand to his lips. He turned to the audience to bow again, holding her fingers tightly.

For a moment, she clung to his hand, then glancing over the audience, saw Estelle's hard stare. When the applause died away, with as much grace as possible, she slipped her hand from his grasp. Several guests rushed forward to express their appreciation. While Jerard greeted them, Katherine edged her way around the back of the piano, hoping to avoid the crowd of well-wishers. However, one of the women guests caught her arm. "That was lovely, my dear."

"Thank you," Katherine murmured. An elderly gentleman smiled at her and bowed.

At last, she was able to exit the room through the French doors and step out onto the terrace. She breathed in the cool night air. A quiet, secluded spot was what she needed. With no one around to detain her, she picked up her skirt and ran down the flagstone steps into the garden.

Chapter 32

A nearly full moon lit the garden path. Azaleas and the formal boxwood stood out in sharp relief. Katherine headed for the arbor at the far corner. Vines luxuriated over it, giving the impression of a small room. From somewhere exuded a subtle, yet beguiling perfume. She dropped down on the bench in the enclosure. Covering her face with her hands, she prayed. "Oh, God, please help me. I don't know what to think."

Her heart ached over the impossible situation. The song had awakened the possibility Jerard still cared for her. But what of their very real differences? And Miss Neville?

She decided to stay hidden in the arbor until she regained her composure. Her absence shouldn't be noticed at the party. All that Mrs. Kemble required of her had been fulfilled. But she had been sitting only a few minutes when the sound of someone coming down the garden path brought her head up. The subject of her troubled thoughts stepped bodily into the bower.

She stood to leave.

"Please stay." Jerard clasped her arm. "We've not had a good talk since my return." He bent to look into her eyes.

Tears filled them. One tear, then another slipped down her cheeks. She tried brushing them away.

"Here." Jerard took a large cambric handkerchief from his pocket. Accepting it, she pressed it to her face. "You're distressed about something. Can I do anything to help?"

"I—" She shut her eyes and a mutinous sob escaped.

Jerard placed his hands on her shoulders. "There now, just let it all out." He drew her to him.

She pressed her face against his coat breast, and her dammed up emotions broke free. He bent his head and pressed his lips to her head. As she huddled like a hurt bird against him, he let his lips wander over her hair. After a while her sobbing became a mere tremble.

"Katherine." His arms held her like some delicate, precious gift. Lifting her face, he kissed her forehead, gently closing her eyelids with his lips. He hesitated only a moment before finding her mouth.

Hardly thinking, her lips responded.

His embrace tightened. "You care, Katherine. You do care for me, don't you?"

"Oh, Jerard." She couldn't say more. How safe and comforted she felt in his arms. She struggled to come back to reality. How had she so let herself go?

She feared she had let out her secret and now the damage must be undone. She tried to straighten herself. "I don't know how I could have lost control that way. Crying like a child." She pressed his handkerchief to her face once again. Trying to step away, she realized the enclosure didn't afford the room needed. "Thank you for comforting me. I'm quite all right now."

He looked at her a bit puzzled, but refused to take his arms from her completely, instead dropping his hands to clasp her waist. "Katherine, listen. Don't you know I sang that song to you just now? That I still love you? Love you, in truth, more than I could have thought possible a year ago?

"True, I was angry when you refused my offer of marriage, but I couldn't forget you. So many places on the estate brought back memories; after seeing you for so long at my table, I couldn't block you from my mind. The house and grounds contain a picture gallery of a past I want to reclaim."

His hands tightened around her waist. "And here in New York, my love for you only intensified. Oh, at first, I had decided to leave you to your just desserts, to the life of a governess. I went to the shore, Mrs. Kemble's niece in tow, merely to satisfy myself how you were doing. But I'll never forget you running on the beach with the children, so carefree and happy. You rushed back into my heart and life that day as hard and fast as you ran across that sand."

His arms slipped up to her shoulders. "Oh, Katherine. I didn't know how to reach you, didn't know how to kindle love in you." He drew her close again. "I kept hoping something would happen to change things between us. The first time I proposed I'd been so certain of myself, aggressive, assuming you would, of course, become my wife. Then you turned me down, forcefully. I couldn't let that happen again."

Katherine stood very still in his arms. He'd loved her all this time?

"When asked to sing at this party, it gave me an opportunity to be alone with you. While we practiced together that evening, I hoped for some indication your heart had changed. At first, you were so self-controlled, so distant, I couldn't bridge the gap."

His hand gently lifted her chin, brought her face close to his, looking into her eyes. "But your manner as I walked out the door after our rehearsal, gave me hope you were not as indifferent as you seemed. So, I determined to send that particular bouquet of flowers tonight. When I saw you'd chosen to wear some of the blooms, I felt emboldened to bring out the English translation of the text."

His fingers stroked her face near her lips. "And now you responded to my kiss. You do love me, don't you? Look at me and tell me so."

Her eyes fastened on his silk tie.

"You would rather stare at my cravat than admit you love me? Are you so proud? Do I need to kiss you again—to wrest from you your guarded secret?"

She shook her head.

"No? Then tell me the truth."

The longer Jerard held her the more difficult it became to hold out against him. She felt his intense gaze and wanted more than ever to curl her arms around his neck, draw his head down to hers, and seal with assurance the hope her first kiss awakened. Yet she steeled herself to press her hands against him. "Please let me go."

"Let you go without admitting the truth? I will not."

"Jerard, please."

"Katherine, you were always one to tell the truth."

She stood still, struggling within herself. "Very well, but only after you release me. And we must leave this enclosure."

He let his arms slip from her, then secured her hand and led her down the path toward a bench.

She sat gratefully. Her legs felt strangely weak. She looked at Jerard sitting beside her, wondering if she could be spared the telling, but the expectant look on his face told her otherwise. Her eyes dropped. "The truth ... the truth is—I *do* love you."

She said it with such despair that Jerard reached to grasp her hands. "But Katherine, I don't understand. Why are you distressed? We love each other. What is to keep us from enjoying that love?" He lifted her hands and kissed each palm.

When he looked up, his dark eyes were bright. "Our engagement should be announced as soon as possible. I can send Mother to help you shop for a trousseau—" his words continued in a rush— "and in the meantime, we will give your employer notice. When you've completed your time, I will take you home. Rev. Hanlin will be more than pleased to conduct the ceremony. The servants can have everything ready—a large or small wedding, whatever you wish. And then we'll tour Europe for our honeymoon. Paris will serve as our center. If you want, we can remain for some time and you can study music with one of the masters. I could arrange business here before I leave. Everything is running so well, they would hardly miss me. There, have I omitted anything?"

She looked up and, for a moment, enjoyed his boyish enthusiasm, enjoyed the eager proposals made on her behalf. But, resolutely, she brought the conversation back to what needed to be addressed. "You talk of all these plans for me, for us, but you've forgotten someone else."

"Whom?"

"Miss Neville."

"What of her?"

"You've paid attentions to her."

"She doesn't mean anything to me."

"But she has expectations. You can't just desert her."

"Why not?"

"Jerard, that's—you've been using her."

"Yes, I used her to get to you."

"But that's wrong."

"All's fair in love and war." His smile was broad. "Did my little friendship with Estelle pique you?"

"I don't think Miss Neville considers your attentions a 'little friendship.'" As Katherine said the words, she couldn't help feeling a womanly pride in the strength of devotion she had aroused in him, the lengths he had taken to awaken her love.

"I see that gleam of satisfaction in your eyes," Jerard said, laughing. "You are pleased with your conquest. And you should be. I would not have endured from another woman's hands what I've endured from yours."

She wanted to smile, but held it back. "Jerard, I am flattered." Her voice was earnest. "But—but nothing has changed. I cannot marry you."

"What do you mean? You said you loved me."

"I do. But you have not changed."

"There you are wrong, my dear. Ask anyone who's been around me this last year. You would discover I've been a paragon among men. Now, I'll have to admit, at times it took an iron control to keep my temper, but I've done it. And you, Katherine, have been the reason. I swore I never wanted to see that scorn in your eyes again when you spoke of my conduct. Darling, I see no obstacle to our union."

Katherine felt the warmth of his hands as they clasped hers and, for a few moments, basked in the wonderful security they offered. It was hard to persevere in doing what was right. But she needed to withdraw her hands as she needed to withdraw the love that had escaped its hiding place, love that even now wanted to encircle its tendrils around his hands and hers, binding them securely together.

She forced herself to speak. "Jerard, you must try to understand. As much as I am gladdened and humbled by your efforts at self-mastery, I also perceive that deep down no real change has taken place. Look, you were willing to use Miss Neville for your own purposes without thinking of her feelings in the matter. Do you see how wrong that was?"

His eyes held hers, but he did not speak.

"Do you remember that day after church when you showed me the beautiful meadow, the masses of lovely violets? On that day you pointed to all you had accomplished. You had improved the estate, refinanced and expanded the mill. All, you said, without God's help. Do you still maintain that conviction?"

"Yes. I have not changed in that."

She looked at him, a hopelessness growing in her soul. How could she reach him? He was so strong in his autonomy, in his conviction he could accomplish whatever he wanted. He was a self-made man and gloried in it. Had he no soft, no vulnerable spot?

Then she remembered what Aunt Elsie had said about his brother. Was that the key to reach him?

"Jerard—" how she hated saying this, but forced herself to continue, "—I know about your brother's death." Katherine felt him startle. "And I suspect how much it affected you. That day in the meadow you said it was plain that God had little to do with this world. In fact, you questioned His very existence. Has your suffering over your brother separated you from God, kept you from Him?"

"Who told you about my brother? It was not to be spoken of."

"Aunt Elsie."

"What did she tell you?"

"That his death was accidental, but that you felt a degree of responsibility. And afterward, you changed. She said little else."

"I loved my brother. Idolized him!" Jerard's hands gripped hers. "It was nobody's fault, yet everybody's fault. It was the hardest, most frustrating—over and over I've thought, *what if....*"

His eyes burned into hers. "*What if* Father hadn't bought the tilbury; it was known as a sporting vehicle that could be dangerous. *What if* my brother hadn't asked to take the reins? *What if* I hadn't given in to him? I knew he liked to drive fast but had no experience with the vehicle.

"*What if* the stone hadn't been there to turn the wheel so abruptly? *What if* Evan hadn't been flung out and the stump hadn't been there for his head to hit, killing him?"

His rush of words stopped, then he added, his voice hard, "A lot of things worked tragically together. You say God's in charge, that He's sovereign—then God could have stopped it at any point. So, why did He let this terrible thing happen?"

"Does all this anger, the bitterness I've seen in you, go back to this? You're angry at God."

"And what of my father's early, unexpected death? God certainly could have prevented that."

"Jerard, my mother died an early death. I know—I know how hard such things are to accept."

Jerard's voice softened. "Yes, Katherine, I've thought of that many times. A degree of sympathy, an understanding exists between us that I've felt with none other."

She looked full in his face. "And I know your brother's death was hard, very hard."

"Katherine! Even you don't know what it was like."

"Maybe not. But I know something else: the pain, the difficulty of having a father I couldn't trust. One that hurt me unbearably. Whose treatment of me and my mother shook the foundations of my soul, just as your brother's death did yours. Our circumstances were different, yet both have a common strain. Both were difficult, unbearably so.

"Look," she said. "God could have given me a different father, but He didn't. I could be bitter against Him as you are. But remember what I told you in the garden after Mr. Lanning's death? Mother taught me that God has a purpose in everything, even in our suffering. That helped me to trust God. Cannot you do the same?"

"I don't see it that way."

Katherine clung to Jerard's hands to emphasize her words. "God cares for you. Yes, your brother died. But think. God's Son also died—a painful, shameful death. God understands your pain, more than you realize. Moreover, He could have stopped His Son's death, but He didn't. He chose not to—so that by this same Son, the gulf of sin separating us from Himself could be bridged."

Katherine drew back from Jerard, trying to gauge his response. "God wants to bridge this gulf between us and Himself. It is sinful in us to hold onto our anger and bitterness, to maintain our independence from God." A new thought occurred to her and she blurted it out. "I believe God wants to use this tragedy to capture your attention, to draw you to Himself."

He stared at her. She saw the shock in his eyes. Had she been too abrupt? She tried to soften what she'd just said.

"God loves us. The Bible says, 'He does not afflict willingly nor grieve the children of men.' There is always purpose in our suffering. Talk to God. Tell Him what's in your heart. Just say a simple, heartfelt prayer."

His eyes had a faraway look, as if he was considering. "Katherine, I don't know." He was quiet a long time. "No, Katherine, I cannot do that. Not yet." He stood, drawing her up with him. "Here, let us walk awhile." He settled her hand on his arm but after a few steps he clasped his other hand over hers, drawing her close to his side.

Oh, how she longed to walk thus with him always. Even as she felt the distance in their thinking, their convictions, she felt a closeness, a bond with him. She allowed him to draw her along for a ways, then stopped and looked up at him.

She said the next words as gently as possible. "Then Jerard, you maintain your independence from God?"

"I—I'd like to gratify you, but I cannot...I would be untrue to myself."

Her voice was low, but she sought to make it clear. "Oh, Jerard—do you see how this affects you and me? The Bible tells a believer not to be unequally yoked with an unbeliever. That means a believer must not marry an unbeliever. I could not disobey God—"

"Katherine, you're carrying this too far! Don't you see? A loving God wouldn't keep apart two people who love as we do."

Far above in the night sky, a high air current scuttled a cloud across the face of the moon. The garden suddenly darkened.

"Jerard ..." She searched for the right words. "I can't explain the whys of everything. Why there is all this suffering. Yet, I must make this clear: if you don't feel the need for God—then, I can't marry you. I can't!" She tried to pull away.

He held her fast and, in his frustration, pulled her to him. "Katherine! Don't say that." Putting his lips to her ear, he said, "I need you, Katherine. Don't say you won't marry me." He held her in such a grip she could barely move.

She struggled not to give in to his pleading. And to the desire of her heart. Bracing herself against him, she whispered, "Please, Jerard. No!"

He buried his face in her neck for a long moment. Then he raised his head, his look desperate. "Your answer is unequivocally no? You won't relent?"

She whispered, "I can't. I'm sorry."

She felt his body stiffen. Long moments followed, then he said through gritted teeth, "Then live the miserable life of a governess. Go your own way." He withdrew his arms from around her, but held her tightly by the shoulders.

She felt the shock of his sudden change in demeanor. Her eyes clung to his, beseeching. To depart in anger—she dreaded that.

"Don't look at me like that, Katherine. I don't believe this loving God you believe in would keep us apart." His eyes burned with an intense light. "It isn't right. It isn't natural."

She stood, saying nothing for some moments, then said, "Jerard, I must obey God."

His hands dropped from her shoulders. "If that's your decision, you'd better go. While you can." His breath expelled hard. "I will not escort you to the house."

Her tear-filled eyes sought his one last time. But now he would not look at her. He motioned her to leave.

Slowly she turned. She could not bear to see him hurt so, but didn't know what else to do. Walking the interminable yards to the house, she imagined his stiffened figure watching her walk away from him. She felt like Lot's wife, wanting desperately to look back. But if she did, she knew it would be her undoing.

She stumbled up the last step to the terrace. As she reached the landing, one of the guests, seated by a table, said, "Katherine, are you all right?"

"Oh, Mrs. Templer. I'm not feeling well, that's all." Katherine's trembling hand touched her forehead. "When you're able, would you be so good as to tell Mrs. Kemble I had to go to my room? In fact, now I think of it, it'd be best if I entered by the kitchen entrance."

"Why, of course, Katherine. I hope you feel better."

Katherine retraced her steps, keeping her eyes from searching out the tall figure in the garden. Gaining the door to the kitchen, she wrenched it open and ran up the back stairs to her room.

Chapter 33

Katherine unpinned the drooping snowdrops from her bodice. Her hands shook as she put them into a basin of water. Unfastening the back of her dress, she lifted the filmy batiste in jerks over her head and draped its voluminous billow over the back of the dressing table chair. Then she flung herself onto the bed coverlet and sobbed into the pillow.

When the worst of her tears were spent, she raised herself off the pillow, and looked up. "Lord, I did my best. I tried to honor You." She felt like a wounded animal.

⁂

Throughout the evening, guests told Mrs. Kemble how much they enjoyed themselves. Her party had been a grand success. The time spent beautifying the house and garden had been worth it and, of course, the evening's entertainment was the crowning touch.

She slept well that night. So it was with real surprise a week later she learned Mr. Emery was planning a trip west. To expand his business, her husband said.

"But doesn't that sound like a rather large undertaking?" she asked. "Won't he be gone a terribly long time? For, of course, I'm thinking of Estelle. What will she say?"

Mr. Kemble shrugged his shoulders. "I'm sure you'll hear from her soon enough. As to expanding his business, I don't know if it's a good idea. Financial matters abroad seem shaky.

The Vienna stock exchange just declared financial collapse. What affects the European market will affect ours in due time. In fact, if I were Mr. Emery, I'd assess my present portfolio—all my financial concerns—and make them as safe as possible."

Mrs. Kemble hardly paid attention to what her husband said; her mind was on her niece. "The last time Mr. Emery absented himself, Estelle didn't bear it well, despite protests to the contrary." Her eye caught her husband's to better drive home her point. "Mr. Emery and Estelle got on so well at the party, they looked the perfect couple. But maybe Estelle knows something I don't."

Mr. Kemble hid behind the newspaper.

"Do you suppose there's a possibility they might become engaged before he leaves? While he's gone, I could help Estelle plan the wedding, her trousseau, and the bridal parties. Actually, it wouldn't hurt if he were gone for some time. So much will need to be done." The future looked rosier the more she thought about it.

She broached the subject to Estelle the next time her niece visited.

One of the first times in Mrs. Kemble's memory, Estelle blushed and acted as if she didn't want to discuss Mr. Emery. "Really, Aunt, I haven't heard anything about this trip out west, so I don't see how you can talk about weddings and such."

"He hasn't told you?"

Estelle's face froze, her fingers twitched in her lap.

Mrs. Kemble quickly adjusted her approach. "Your uncle found out quite by accident. I'm sure Mr. Emery will tell you soon. And maybe, just maybe he'll surprise you with a proposal before he leaves."

"Aunt! I've spoken less than two sentences with him since the party. Last time he left New York he didn't inform me. It makes me wonder if this time will be any different."

"But—" Mrs. Kemble struggled to understand the situation. "Mr. Emery seemed so attentive at the party."

"Well, he was. Until he sang, then afterward he wasn't the same. He seemed distant and... almost cold." Estelle's voice lowered as she reviewed the events. "He excused himself to go into the garden, I thought for a breath of fresh air. But when he returned and when I went up to him and placed my hand on his arm, I swear it irritated him. Oh, he didn't say anything, but he turned without warning and I was forced to withdraw my hand.

"We talked with a few people after that, or rather I did. He was unusually quiet. Then he said he needed to go, that if I would like to stay, he would arrange one of our friends to take me home. But, of course, I wouldn't leave with anyone else if I had come with him."

"But, of course." Mrs. Kemble sat back in her chair, silent a moment. "I must say, my dear, the state of affairs between you and Mr. Emery is quite different from what I'd been imagining. So, you say he was attentive up to the time he sang?"

"Yes."

"Something must have happened when he went outside. Did he talk with anyone, have a confrontation with one of the guests? That seems unlikely, though. I suppose a number of people went to the garden. I even noticed Katherine slip out."

"You did?"

"Why yes. I thought she looked rather... disconcerted. Mr. Emery did make quite a to-do over her when he sang, and I supposed her not playing often at parties was enough to give any girl the vapors."

Estelle sat very still. "I noticed something of the sort myself. In fact, I wasn't at all happy with the way he fussed over her during the performance."

"I'm sorry, my dear. But I could do nothing about her accompanying him, you know. He insisted on her, said she was the best."

"Have you told her about Mr. Emery's departure?"

"No, I've been busy, and whenever I've seen her it's been in passing. And besides, you were my main concern, Estelle. Gracious, I was already making wedding plans."

"Aunt, I need to talk with your governess."

"Would you like me to call her now? I'd be glad to leave the two of you alone."

"Not today." Estelle's fingertips twitched in her lap. "I need to think this through. Tomorrow you'll be out visiting?"

"In the afternoon."

"I'll come then."

ଓ

The following afternoon Katherine tried to hide the surprise she felt on learning her visitor's identity. When she entered the parlor, Miss Neville was seated in one of the deep crimson armchairs near the windows, faultlessly dressed in a royal blue afternoon suit.

Katherine seated herself opposite her guest. "What can I do for you?"

"I wondered if you could help me solve a little mystery."

"Mystery?"

"Yes. Something involving Jerard Emery."

Katherine felt herself stiffen. She hoped her face did not betray the apprehension she felt.

Estelle hesitated a moment, then proceeded in a calm but clear voice. "The night of the party, something happened to Mr. Emery. After he sang, I believe. He went outside, I presume to get a breath of fresh air. When he came inside later, his disposition had changed. Did you happen to see him in the garden?"

Katherine felt the intensity of Estelle's gaze. "Why—why, yes."

"Did you speak with him?"

She touched her throat. "Yes."

"Do you know of any reason for his change in demeanor?"

"I don't know if I could say." Katherine felt like an insect pinned to a display board, but she was determined, at all costs, to maintain a calm manner. "In any event, the nature of our conversation is private."

Estelle's posture stiffened. One hand gripped the chair's armrest. "You mean you will not say. It sounds to me that Mr. Emery was indeed upset after his conversation with you. In fact, it might have even provoked his imminent departure."

Katherine stared at her guest.

"Do you know he's leaving for the west?"

"No."

"Well! That's something." One of Estelle's eyebrows lifted in satisfaction. "But as I said, he seemed upset and now he's going away. Probably for a long time, because I understand he's decided to expand the business."

Jerard leaving? Katherine continued to watch her guest guardedly.

"As I said, something must have happened in the garden—considering his sudden change of behavior at the party and then this decision to go west." As Estelle spoke, she rose. "You know, since Mr. Emery has been calling on me, people have begun to couple our names. Miss Edmond, I feel I have a right to know the true nature of the relationship between Mr. Emery and yourself."

Katherine swallowed. A long moment passed before she answered. "I imagine that would be something Mr. Emery could tell you."

"Well, you're sitting here with me now. I'd like your answer." Estelle's color had risen. She took a step toward Katherine, leaning over her, a hawk about to seize its prey. "Don't trifle with me, Miss Edmond. This involves my future."

Katherine's thoughts raced. To tell what transpired in the garden, to admit the feelings Jerard and she had for one another before this—this woman—would be a desecration. And if it became public knowledge Jerard's offer of marriage had been spurned, she could only imagine the wound to his pride. She had already hurt him enough.

Katherine felt the heat rise in her cheeks, but tried to answer with equanimity. "I'm sorry, Miss Neville, I cannot help you. Again, I think Mr. Emery could better answer your questions. And now, if you'll excuse me, I must go. The children are waiting for their instruction." She rose from her chair. "I'll see Framton escorts you to the door." She stepped around the guest.

Katherine heard the woman's quick intake of breath, felt her stare, but would not stop. Instead, she sailed out of the room.

☙

The next day, as Katherine passed the dining room on her way to the kitchen, she heard Mrs. Kemble tell her husband that Mr. Emery would leave for the west the following day. She stopped beyond the doorway, hoping to hear more, but Framton walked out the kitchen so she was forced to continue walking. Afterward, she told herself it served her right, she shouldn't have been eavesdropping.

Jerard had not contacted her. As the day progressed, Katherine hoped to hear details about his departure: when he would leave and, most of all, his destination. But it seemed Mrs. Kemble was not about to volunteer information to her governess, and Katherine would not inquire.

When she retired for the night, she despaired of hearing anything. She drank some water to ease the lump in her throat, but could only manage a few swallows.

She busied herself straightening the handkerchiefs, collars and other small items in her top drawer, then stepped to her desk. She rearranged her Bible and writing paper. Everything was already in order, but she moved them slightly to the left.

Taking up her pen, she suddenly slammed it down in the same spot.

Oh! To part thus, without one word. Could he not relent, just a little? Enough to ease the pain in both their hearts? The night of the party, he had sent her to the house alone. And now this silence.

How angry he must be. She dropped down on the desk chair. An important principle was at stake: could he not treat her kindly, forgive her, even if she seemed fanatical, hard-headed?

Was there anything she could do to mend things between them?

She didn't know.

Maybe a relationship such as theirs wasn't supposed to be mended—she a Christian and he an unbeliever. She raised her hands to cradle her face, resting her elbows on the desk. "Please, God, help me."

Her gaze fell on her Bible. The Psalms often comforted her. She reached over and opened the book at random.

Psalm 138.

After reading a portion, she looked up. It all seemed to apply to her. Particularly the last verse: "The Lord will perfect that which concerneth me."

She reread the sentence. What did concern her? Jerard's anger and the resulting pain of their separation. What else? Jerard's salvation, and ... the frustration over their love for each other. It seemed without purpose. Why had she ever been sent to his home in the first place?

She rose from her chair and paced the room.

Tears blurred her vision. She knelt by the bed, wanting to pray. But she couldn't. Sobs started, quietly at first, then the dam broke. She grabbed the coverlet and buried her face in it. "Oh, God, I love him. I can't stand the thought of this anger, this separation. God, help me!" Hard weeping shook her frame.

At last, after gaining a measure of self-mastery, she whispered, "Lord, I don't know what to do. Can You somehow straighten this out? Perfect that which—"

God said He would do so in this Psalm. She wanted to believe it.

Sighing, she pushed herself to her feet and made her way to the armoire, her muscles stiff and tired. *"God is a very present help in time of trouble."* The oft-quoted verse came to mind. She *had* to believe. She must trust God with Jerard and all her questions.

Unbuttoning her clothes, she hung everything in the armoire, then reached for her nightgown. The cotton felt cool against her hot skin. She sat down on her bed. "Please, take it, Lord. Take it all. Take Jerard and do what is best for us both." Then she lay down. Minute followed minute and, in spite of the pain, her soul began to calm.

ꕥ

The grandfather clock in the library chimed five. Scant light from the late afternoon sun filtered through lace curtains. Katherine looked up, staring at the hands of the clock.

He must be gone by now. What was she waiting for? Some word?

She rose from the chair and walked across to the bookcases, hoping to fix her mind on something other than Jerard. The maid had taken charge of the children until suppertime.

After choosing a book at random, she sat in one of the leather easy chairs, forcing herself to read. She was dimly aware of a knock at the front door, the butler answering it. Some minutes later, Framton entered the library with an envelope. "Sorry to disturb you, Miss Edmond, but this came for you."

One glance at the penmanship and her heart constricted. Only one man of her acquaintance gave the "K" in her name that particular flourish. "Thank you, Framton."

She waited for the butler to leave, then moved to a more secluded chair in analcove.

Staring at the envelope a moment before opening it, she finally drew out a single sheet of paper.

Katherine,

Undoubtedly, you have heard about my decision to go west. St. Louis, I believe, offers one of the best opportunities to expand my business, having visited there before. After our last interview I decided a change of scene was in order.

I debated sending this communiqué; you know my proud nature. But I wanted to inform you of a sum of money I have deposited in your name at the bank noted at the bottom of this letter. It is intended for your use, if you should ever need additional funds.

I have no plans to return east in the foreseeable future, so you need not fear running into me at some inopportune moment. Therefore, we can go our separate ways with a measure of peace.

Wishing you the best the future can offer—

Jerard

ꝏ

Katherine looked up. How aloof and formal the letter sounded. But knowing him, she understood the effort it cost him to write even this much. Indeed, wasn't this an answer to her prayer?

While her heart ached at the coldness of the letter's tone, she was touched by his reference to the bank account. It betokened a genuine concern for her future.

One thing was certain. She could think of no eventuality that would cause her to touch that money. Despite what he said, she would return it. Maybe not right away; she'd simply leave it alone. But when she had saved adequate funds, she would see it was transferred back to his account.

She closed her eyes and lifted the letter to her lips. He had let her know he was going and where. And his hand had touched this paper a short time ago.

Bless him.

Chapter 34

Hills and valleys swept past Jerard's train window, everything verdant green, a refreshing change from New York. His head rested in comfort against the cushioned back of his seat.

He'd kept busy on the trip west—reading, talking to other passengers, refining his business strategy for St. Louis. He disciplined himself not to think of New York and memories of home. To dwell on his club and the company back east, that was permissible, but not advisable to let his thoughts stray much further.

Along the way he made himself interested in the small towns the train steamed into. Its arrival invariably drew a small crowd. He gazed at the buildings of the towns, kept the details alive so he would have something to review in his memory.

Buildings and trees looked different here. Good. Everything new was to be applauded.

He would put the past behind him. All that mattered now was the future.

ଓଃ

Jerard walked the remaining steps to his hotel. Three months had passed since he'd left New York. Summer had been busy and hot, but his work was beginning to pay off. The business meeting this afternoon had gone well. Emery Textiles would soon be ready to distribute in this part of the country.

St. Louis bustled. New buildings rivaled structures in New York. People from all over passed through this city, both those with a degree of sophistication and simple country folk. Some came to make a place for themselves in this growing city and others intended to move farther west.

As he walked up the hotel steps, he greeted the doorman. This was beginning to feel like home. In the future, someone would need to oversee company operations in St. Louis. Maybe he would do so. He liked the town and his work rather well.

He asked the desk clerk for his mail.

"Nothing for you, sir."

He ignored the disappointment and turned, glancing around the lobby. His mother would write soon.

Across the room a woman with dark hair spoke with an older man. The woman's back was to him, but her figure was familiar. Achingly familiar. He stared for some moments. If the woman would turn, he could see her profile.

He started to cross the room to make certain. Then the woman turned, and he saw a small pug nose—not the well-formed straight one he sought.

Attempting to calm his racing heart, he abruptly turned to mount the stairs to his room. Of course, the woman would be a stranger.

After getting ready to retire, Jerard dropped onto the bed, lying on his back. What would he have done if that woman had turned out to be Katherine? He didn't know. But his throbbing pulse left no doubt of his feelings. After all the effort of trying to block her out of his life. He rolled to his side and punched the pillow, trying to get comfortable. Giving up, he rose to extinguish the lamp.

It was useless to dwell on what had happened in the lobby. Tomorrow would be business as usual. Better to think about that. He pulled down the bed covers and slid under them. Yes, tomorrow would be busy, so a good night's sleep was in order.

ᘓ

Jerard awoke with a start. He sat up, staring into the darkness.

Katherine had been right here. He still sensed the warmth of her in his arms, his hand smoothing her silken hair. He had kissed her face as it tilted up toward his.

He lay back, willing himself to fall asleep again, to pick up the dream where it left off. As a boy, nightmares would come back full force, why not this?

But after a few minutes he knew it wouldn't work. He lay in bed and groaned.

He had tried to forget Katherine by keeping busy and disciplining his mind with such severity he thought he had succeeded. Until he saw that woman in the lobby last night.

Katherine! How he wanted her.

He grabbed the pillow from underneath his head and held it as in a vise, then buried his face in it. For some moments, he ground his teeth.

He released the pillow, rose and paced the floor.

Why couldn't he have her? He stopped and looked up at the dark ceiling. God! That's who stood between Katherine and him. His fist clenched.

But did God exist?

Katherine believed so. Believed it enough to turn him down twice—and he knew she loved him. Turn down everything for a belief? Only fanatics did that.

But she wasn't some wild-eyed fanatic. She was sensible and sweet. Did she know something about God that he didn't? Was it possible he'd been blind all these years?

He stood in the middle of the room, staring at the dim light shining through the crack between the drapes. When young, he'd stood beside his father in church. His father had faith. Funny, he hadn't thought about that in years. He'd been angry, bitter, after his brother's death. Then without warning, his father died. That had been the final blow.

His jaw clenched. Looking up once again, he said in a low, intense voice, "God, if you're real—if you're out there—show me. Do something. Something big so I'll know it's you—that you exist."

He exhaled, long and fierce. And he knew what he wanted God to do.

Katherine.

He felt foolish, asking something of someone he wasn't sure existed, but he shoved the feeling aside. "God, I'm asking you to bring Katherine and me together. Somehow!" He looked up hard into the darkness. "I leave it to you."

ꟹ

Days later, Jerard sat down to breakfast in the hotel dining room. On the table his usual folded newspaper waited to be read until after he ordered. Unfastening one of the buttons of his suit, he took up the paper and leisurely looked it over. By the time his food arrived, he'd finished the front page and was on to local news.

About to put the paper down, an article caught his eye. A hanging. The article described the two-hundred-pound weight used to test the gallows. Fascinated, he read on. An execution was to take place the following week. He caught the names of the three men to be executed. His breathing stopped.

No, too much of a coincidence.

He laid the paper aside, ate his breakfast, but tasted little of it. That hanging business—strange. And that one familiar name.

By the time he finished eating, he had made up his mind. He would find out if this Tom Edmond was Katherine's father. He'd noticed the new criminal justice building during his first tour of the city, a magnificent three-story structure with renaissance-style architecture. The city prison was at its rear.

ଊ

"We're proud of our jail, sir," the warden said. "Last year we had a very important visitor. The Russian Czar's chief prison official, no less. He declared he'd never seen its equal. Requested plans and ordered photographs."

Jerard looked around at the semi-circle of cells built like an amphitheater. Their grated doors fronted the center of the jail. He could hear mumbled undertones and loud talking. Then a shouted curse.

"The cells are made of wrought-boiler iron. Both walls and floor. Now, sir, if you're ready, I'll hand you over to one of our guards and he'll take you to the prisoner in question."

A guard stepped forward. "This way, sir."

Jerard followed him past the row of cells, now and then glancing inside. In one, a listless white-haired man sat. A young man in his twenties stared at him from another.

Toward the middle of the semi-circle, the guard stopped and turned. "After I unlock the door and you say it's the man you're looking for, you have ten minutes." He inserted the key and swung the grated door open. "Edmond, someone to see you."

Jerard stepped past the guard. The inmate sat with legs crossed, Indian style on the iron floor. His head jerked up toward his visitor. He was bearded and clothed in baggy pants and shirt.

Jerard wasn't sure he recognized the man. "Are you Katherine's father?"

"Katherine! You know Katherine?"

Jerard turned to the guard. "This is the man. I'll be ready in ten minutes."

With difficulty, the prisoner got to his knees, then rose to a standing position. "Sorry I can't offer you a place to sit." The cell was void of furniture. "You say you know Katherine?"

"Yes. In fact, you visited my home. Stole my prize horse."

"You!" The prisoner looked closely at Jerard. "I thought you looked familiar. But I've seen so many faces these last years." He leaned against the cell wall as if light-headed, looked down a few moments at the iron floor, then up again. "Did you get the money I sent?"

"I did."

"Good. I never knew for sure. Of course, I didn't give a return address so you had no way of contacting me. I was on the run. And I didn't want my little girl bearing the shame of my wrongdoing."

"Katherine insisted on repaying the debt herself, and was putting aside a small amount out of her meager salary as governess."

"Just like her mother. If I'd realized back then—but I was a fool, more interested in quick money than my family." He stopped, looked at his visitor. "What did you say your name was?"

"Emery. Jerard Emery."

"Well, Mr. Emery, I was all kinds of a fool. But I've changed. I see the light now." The man's face broke into a smile. "You tell my little girl I've been reading her mother's Bible. It's one of the few things the guards allow in my cell." His head nodded toward the rear of the cell. "A corridor runs between these cells and the outside wall. Still, I get enough light to read."

He coughed. "Tell Katherine. Please! It'll mean more to her than anything. I—" his voice broke "—I know now how much it must have cost her to give me her mama's Bible. To me, her no-good father." He shook his head. "But tell her it was worth it. If I could describe the peace in me—you know, when I first got here I was frantic, locked up in this iron cell knowing I was about to die."

He stooped to reach for the Bible. "But it's all here in this book. Look here, see what my wife did." He opened the Bible and held it toward Jerard. "She underlined the verses important to her. Verses about salvation she starred. I couldn't miss them. Once I started reading, I couldn't put the book down. My wife! A blessing to me all these years after her death. You'll tell Katherine, won't you?" He began to voice how much his little girl meant to him, those early years he'd known her.

The cell door swung open. "Ten minutes is up, sir."

Both men glanced at the guard.

"I haven't had a chance to find out about my daughter yet," Edmond said. "Could he stay a few more minutes?"

"Time is up."

"What Edmond says is true," Jerard confirmed. "It would be helpful if I could stay a while longer."

"Prison regulations. You understand, sir."

Jerard's mouth tightened.

Edmond's eyes watered, sought Jerard's, his voice pleading. "Can you come back? One more time. I need to know about my girl."

Jerard looked at the man, then glanced around the spare, hard cell. The place pressed in on him. "I'll see."

"I'd be grateful, more than grateful. Thank you for coming today. I can't say how much I appreciate it."

Jerard nodded, then turned to leave.

He stepped outside the prison, his eyes squinting in the late morning sun. The fresh air felt good. Free! He walked away with a quick step.

The hotel didn't beckon and he certainly wasn't inclined to talk with anyone. He needed time to think.

He ambled down one street, then another. He didn't want to return to the jail. The building was new and attractive from the outside. But it had been constructed deliberately as a hell for its inmates.

Jerard stopped and looked up at the sky. Clouds hung suspended in the still atmosphere. He was a busy man. Why this aimless wandering, where was it getting him? He had other affairs to attend to now. His curiosity had been satisfied. The man was Katherine's father.

He winced. That was the trouble.

Katherine knowing he had met her father would mean a great deal to her. What would that bring him in terms of her regard? Gratitude, yes. Deeper love and respect? Maybe. But would it change her decision? He set his jaw and turned the corner into the next street. He knew the answer to that.

Unexpectedly, he realized he'd been heading in the direction of his hotel. It stood a few blocks ahead of him. Well, he'd walked enough. He would go to his room and clean up. Then maybe call on that Randolph fellow.

He proceeded up the same stone steps he'd climbed countless times, strode through the ornate glass door to the lobby. The desk clerk greeted him. Without meaning to, he glanced at the spot where the dark-haired woman had stood a few nights before and remembered those seconds he'd waited to see if it was Katherine.

All of a sudden he wanted to do something for her. No matter how unpleasant the task, how meager the reward. For once he would do something because it was right and kind. A father sat in prison, to hang within the week, hungering to hear about his daughter. And Jerard was the only person in all St. Louis, in the whole region, in fact, who could satisfy that hunger.

As he climbed the staircase, he was suddenly appalled. He'd been unwilling to do a simple, kind act. What Katherine had said was true. He was selfish. And, in all likelihood, he was seeing only the tip of the iceberg. What else was true about himself?

ᘓ

That night Jerard sat against the headboard of his bed, legs stretched out. What would he tell Edmond about Katherine? It dawned on him the man in prison knew almost nothing of her growing up years. In fact, Jerard knew more about her than her own father. The thought pleased him. A sweet sense of intimacy took hold of him. He possessed something of Katherine few others did.

When had she first excited his interest? He'd never felt neutral about her, that was certain. Right off, she reminded him of his brother—the same hair color, a similar height—it was painful. That angered him. Her arrival also reminded him of his father, his kindness in providing for her in his will. He loved his father, but he didn't want daily reminders of his benevolence. He had an estate to run, money to make; he couldn't be doing favors for everyone along the way.

But then things began to change. He smiled to himself. That first time Katherine accompanied him on the piano, for instance. How surprised he'd been at her sensitivity, her ability to listen and follow him. He knew few would appreciate her ear for music as he did. From then on, he had felt a new respect for the intruder.

He laced his fingers behind his head.

That one afternoon he had come home unannounced and surprised her singing. And her playing the piano with such force that reminded him of his brother. Yes, that had caught his attention. He relived hearing her lilting voice, seeing her expressive body responding to the music. Was that when he'd felt his first quickening of love?

One incident after another came to mind. The time she'd come running down the tree-lined avenue. He happened to be looking out his bedroom window. She was unaware of anyone watching her, or she wouldn't have run with arms outstretched, a look of utter freedom and enjoyment on her face. When she arrived at the drive in front of the house, she dropped her arms to her sides and slowed to a more dignified walk. His smile widened. How we learn to pace ourselves according to convention.

But that was one of the reasons he loved her, the surprises beneath her calm demeanor. The tenderness, the passion, the high thoughts that lived beneath her surface.

And when had all this dawned on him? Gradually. He remembered how Mr. Lanning's collapse in the wood had triggered deeper feelings. When she first called him for help. Everything happened so fast, requiring such quick work, he didn't have time to think. But later in the darkened room, he remembered his own father's collapse in the field which had brought him to that same sitting room. Seeing Katherine stand so still beside her unconscious teacher, he wanted to protect her from the anguish and uncertainty he knew would follow.

Christopher had hovered near his grandmother. They had each other. But Katherine stood by herself, loving that old man. Mr. Lanning had been more than a teacher to her. He'd been a mentor, a father. She had defended him vehemently when she first arrived. As she stood by Mr. Lanning's bedside, Jerard felt himself instinctively move to assist her. She would need help in the coming dark days. After all, wasn't she a part of his household?

But then the tables had somehow turned in the garden. That evening she, sorrowing and needing solace, had instead comforted him. With gentleness, she reached out to him. Something in him broke, and he grieved.

With another female he would have been angry, afraid she would expose his weakness or use it somehow to her advantage. The next morning at breakfast, he had been distant, afraid she would say or do something to embarrass him, but she was clear-eyed and natural. It was apparent she would preserve their heretofore-dignified relations.

She preserved their reserved relationship all too well. He discovered he didn't want to maintain such distance, realized it when he overheard her talking with Christopher about the white memorial stone. How free and easy she was with Christopher, showing her delightful self in all too unfettered a manner.

Christopher.

Jerard's hand clenched. Christopher, in New York, was probably making his bid for Katherine's hand.

How far away she seemed. What he wouldn't give for news of her. Just thinking about her brought a warm glow, and accompanying pain.

"I'll talk to her father tomorrow," he said under his breath. Yes, tell him about her growing years. Give him something to hold onto before...it'll do us both good to talk of her.

Chapter 35

Christopher bounded up the Kemble steps. Whistling softly, he knocked on the front door.

When Katherine entered the front parlor, he extended his hands, grasping hers with warmth. "Thought I'd surprise you. It's such a beautiful day, I wondered if you'd like to take a walk in Central Park."

Her face lit with pleasure. "That is just what I need."

"Good," he said, leading her to the foyer. "I'll wait here until you get your wrap." He watched her run up the stairs, anticipation in his every fiber.

Autumn was coming; the day was warm, yet refreshing. Christopher stopped at the edge of the park. "Let's take the path to the left. It leads to a place I have in mind."

They walked in companionable silence. "The spot is beyond those bushes." He steered Katherine to a rustic bench overlooking a small field of grasses and wild flowers. "How's this?"

"Perfect, although on a day like this I could walk forever. You always seem to sense what I would like." Katherine laughed as she sat. "Some peace-loving cow would love this spot."

"I don't consider you a cow, my dear, although you are as contented. In fact, you top my list of people who are easy to please." He sat close to her.

"My! A compliment along with a lovely view."

"Certainly a lovely view." At the intensity in his voice, Katherine glanced up. Well, he might as well go forward. "I discovered this spot during one of my painting forays. But I had something in mind today besides enjoying the park."

"Oh?"

He took a deep breath. "We've been friends a long time, haven't we?"

"Yes."

"Remember that first time you accompanied me on a painting jaunt, when I sketched that old barn in the meadow? You showed remarkable artistic perception for a girl your age. And you always encouraged my work. I knew you were unusual."

He glanced ahead a moment. "When you left for New York I knew I'd miss you, although I didn't realize quite how much. I wanted to give you time to grow up, to stretch beyond the boundaries of our little world in western Connecticut. Of course, I couldn't leave you in New York forever, so I made plans to study here and give our friendship time to ripen." He reached for her hand and held it in his two large warm ones.

"Soon I'll be setting sail for Europe. I want to visit so many places I've heard about." He paused. "Remember our conversation back then? You to study music—and I art?"

Katherine nodded.

"What I'm trying to say is ... Katherine, I'd like you to come with me when I leave for Europe in a few weeks. As my wife."

Katherine's eyelashes flickered.

His words tumbled out. "I've come to love and admire you as no other woman of my acquaintance. I would be honored to have you spend your life with me. And I promise, I would love and cherish you until I die. I would protect you from the hard places of life and its disappointments." He gripped her hand.

Katherine gazed at him. Her lips parted, but she said nothing.

"You can take your time, Katherine." His words came out in a whisper.

She glanced at the hands holding hers. "Christopher, you are such a wonderful friend. But I—I'm confused. I didn't expect this." For a moment her hand clung to his, then she withdrew it. "I need time to think."

"Of course." He looked at her, checking his eagerness to know her answer, his desire to hold more than her hand. "I'm always joking around, never showing you how I really feel. I'm sorry if this came as a surprise." He cleared his throat. "Should I take you back to the Kembles?"

"Considerate as ever," Katherine murmured. "Maybe we could walk for a while. Then yes, Christopher, I'd like to go back."

ര

Katherine stood at the open window of her bedroom, looking over the darkened sky. Street gaslights flickered against the night. Over the many buildings, a suffused glow of light reached toward the heavens.

She leaned over the sill and wrapped her arms around herself. The night air felt cool and crisp. She took a deep breath, hoping it would enable her to think with more clarity. In all this vast city, she had one sure friend. She did not want to give him up. And now he wanted more.

Christopher eagerly awaited an answer. What would she tell him?

They had been having such a good time in New York. The possibility of his growing feelings should have occurred to her. In fact, it sounded as if his compelling reason for coming to New York was to be with her—and she thought it had been to study. How little she'd guessed his true motives.

And Jerard. She thought he'd been courting Miss Neville. But all the time he had been using the niece to gain access to the Kemble household, to make her jealous. Did people always have reasons other than the obvious for doing what they did?

She began to see the dilemma of being open and above-board when something important was at stake. Then thought of herself these last weeks and months, how difficult it had been to be candid with oneself when confused.

She stood at the sill, her eyes half closed. She cared for Christopher, truly she did. He would make a wonderful husband. They had so much in common. And the trip to Europe tantalized her.

A capricious wind scattered leaves on the street below. Tendrils of hair blew across her face. The gust made the air seem colder and she hugged herself more tightly. An inexpressible longing gripped her. Whose arms did she yearn to surround her? The picture of a tall man with a wave in his dark hair leapt to mind. She swayed, a sweet malady sweeping through her. A few seconds longer she indulged in the delicious elixir, then forced it from her. If only she could long for Christopher's arms to hold her, life would be sweet. But life was not so simple.

She shivered. She'd said no to marriage with Jerard. But more often than she wanted to admit, her mind's eye pictured lingering with him in different places, fantasizing about the life they could have had together. It seemed she had to constantly cut off these beckoning dreams, to remind herself he was not hers.

Was marrying Christopher the answer? Would it prove to God and herself she had indeed given up the object of her longing? Was it possible she could change her mind about loving Jerard? Would new places and people help her forget, or at least make him a dim memory?

Possibly.

But how could she marry one man when she longed for another? Wouldn't it be unfair to Christopher? She feared the results of such a decision would come to torment her.

For Christopher's sake, if she released him, gave him no hope of their ever being more than friends, might he see other women in a new light?

Katherine closed the window. She would dither no longer. She would tell Christopher tomorrow. She would pray for him, pray the Lord would help him accept her decision, and make a clean break. And she would pray the Lord would bring some other woman into his life, someone wonderful who would be best suited to him.

She walked to the dresser and bent to get her shawl from the bottom drawer. As for herself, she would keep teaching the Kemble children. And studying piano. The Lord had given her this life and she would honor Him by living it the best she could with His help.

And Jerard? She winced, then mentally set her face like flint. She would continue to give Jerard to the Lord, and pray for his salvation.

ᘓ

Mr. Kemble entered his wife's dressing room, untying his black silk tie. "A successful party, my dear. And our niece looked most attractive tonight. It seems she's recovered from Mr. Emery's desertion."

Mrs. Kemble unfastened her pearls, then turned from her dressing table. "You treat the situation too lightly, Arthur. Estelle isn't quite so much 'over him' as she appears. But she is a good little actress, my brave darling. Her feminine pride has come to her aid." She placed the pearls in their box. "You know, in all the time he's been gone, he's sent only one brief note, and that was right at the beginning. She's lost hope, I'm afraid."

"Well, maybe it's just as well. I always thought him too big a fish for her anyway." "What? Too big a fish for our Estelle? Then what about our governess?"

"Katherine? You mean she's interested in Mr. Emery, too?" Mr. Kemble laughed.

"Well, something was going on between them at my garden party. And in all likelihood, beforehand." She turned back to the mirror to take off her earrings. "Why, when I think of that girl's temerity—interested in Mr. Emery when they're from such different social levels—it's disgraceful. It must have been all her doing, because I don't see how he could be interested in a governess when someone like Estelle is available." She turned from the mirror to look at her husband. "Don't you agree, Arthur?"

Mr. Kemble rubbed his chin. "I wouldn't be so sure it was all on Katherine's side. She is an attractive, interesting girl. In point of fact, Estelle isn't in the same class."

"Arthur! You can't mean that."

Her husband leaned against the doorpost. "Well, Katherine has a serene womanliness—I think it comes from her goodness—that Estelle doesn't begin to exhibit. It's the kind of thing that makes a man put a woman on a pedestal. And even though Katherine is quiet, her eyes sparkle with life. It makes one wonder what goes on in that mind of hers." He straightened. "She's quite a delightful piece of womanhood. It wouldn't surprise me in the least if Mr. Emery were interested in her."

"Well! I don't believe I've ever heard you go on so." Mrs. Kemble's nails tapped a quick staccato on her dressing table. "It sounds as if more than Mr. Emery is taken with our governess."

"Dear, I was only explaining qualities which your usually

observant eyes seem to have missed. By the way, I didn't see Katherine tonight. Doesn't she usually attend this sort of thing?"

"Because of this contretemps over Mr. Emery, I decided not to invite her. Especially with Estelle present."

"Well, my dear, I leave it to you to handle the situation. But I think it's unfair to change Katherine's status too much without warning." He looked pointedly at his wife.

Mrs. Kemble looked long at her husband's retreating figure, then firmly closed her lips.

ʚ

Katherine gazed at the vast spray of red carnations Christopher sent the evening before his voyage. The language of flowers couldn't have been clearer: "Alas for my poor heart." Last night she had wept for her dear friend. If only things could have been different. She prayed God would give him a true heart's companion, someone who would love him better than she could.

ʚ

Mrs. Kemble had begun to visit the classroom at odd hours. At first Katherine thought she was merely interested in the children's program of study. But once she glanced up to find the lady in question staring at her, the hardness of her gaze disconcerting. During the children's music lessons, Mrs. Kemble sat in a chair near the piano doing needlework. She glanced up now and then, a frown on her lips.

Then all of a sudden her visits ceased. The family began planning an extended trip to the mountains. Katherine had never been to the mountains and started organizing special botany lessons for the children. She imagined the fall colors would be beautiful. It would remind her of her walks through the woods with Mr. Lanning.

ঙ

One day after breakfast Mrs. Kemble sent for her. Katherine entered the morning room and found her employer seated at her desk balancing household accounts. Mrs. Kemble glanced up from her ledger. Her cheeks were flushed. "I'll be with you in a moment."

Katherine glanced at the chair at the side of the desk. She had not been invited to sit. After a full minute, Mrs. Kemble looked up. The smile on her face looked set, confirming warmth from her eyes absent.

"There!" The lady of the house put down her pencil. "So many things to do before leaving for the mountains, which brings me to the reason I sent for you. You know, the children are getting older, and I feel a change is needed. With this trip two weeks away, it gives me an opportunity to do just that." Her voice sounded clipped. "Katherine, I have decided we won't be requiring your services any longer."

Looking at her employer, Katherine tried to understand the full import of what had been said. "You no longer need me to teach the children?"

"That's what I mean."

Katherine gripped her hands behind her back. The unexpectedness of the announcement threw her into confusion. Her mind raced. Clutching at something to say, she asked, "Was something wrong with my work, madam? If so, I'm sure I could rectify it."

"No, your work was quite acceptable. A change is needed, that's all. Now, if you should require a reference for other employment, I will give you one. But, of course, you have your place in Connecticut you can return to." She closed the ledger book. "Now that's settled, let me say that you can stay until we leave for the mountains. I will tell the children myself the night before we leave that you won't be accompanying us." She widened her set smile. "We'll keep everything as normal as possible until our departure. No need to disrupt the household unduly."

"Yes, Mrs. Kemble," Katherine said, subdued. She couldn't think of anything else to say. She left the room and without conscious decision, made her way up the stairs to her quarters. Her mind stuck on one fact. She would no longer live in this house. Where would she go? What would she do?

A knot rose in her throat. Was this typical of the way a governess was discharged? She felt cut to the quick. The children had been grasping their studies well. Their behavior had been so much improved. Couldn't Mrs. Kemble see that? What would the children think? Would they be distressed about her leaving without a word of explanation? But even if she said something to them, she knew she couldn't tell them how she felt.

Mrs. Kemble took for granted she could return to the Emerys.

The Emerys.

The elder Mr. Emery's will specified she be trained to make her way in the world. His widow had carried out his wishes to the letter. Now Katherine was expected to do just that.

And besides, Jerard presented a problem. Twice he had offered her his home and twice she'd refused. So now, when the way became hard, would she plead to come back, use his roof, his money, his protection, without giving him what he wanted most—herself? No! That would be wrong and cruel.

Also, she could not return for her own sake. Too well she knew her weakness. Around the places and things so poignantly reminding her of him, might she not weaken and compromise her convictions? She feared she would. No, the Emery home was out of the question.

Where to go then? Her mind struck a blank. She opened the door to her bedroom. She had just two weeks to find some type of employment. And another place to live.

Chapter 36

Jerard had promised himself he would be there for Katherine's father at the end. This morning the promise stuck in his throat. The hanging would take place at nine, only three hours away.

Sitting on the edge of the bed, he willed himself to stand. He'd slept in fits and starts during the night. He dressed mechanically, then walked downstairs to get a bite to eat in the hotel restaurant.

Since he was as close to family as Edmond had, the warden said he would be allowed to visit the prisoner before execution. But Jerard knew it wasn't only his slight connection to Edmond that afforded him the privilege. A familiar feeling growled deep in his gut about human nature: it hadn't escaped the warden's notice that the prisoner's daily visitor was a wealthy businessman.

☙

The door to the cell scraped open. Jerard stepped inside.

"Good of you to come, son."

Jerard acknowledged the greeting, then shook his head, minimizing the favor.

"I'm glad you're here because I want to give you this." Edmond stooped to reach for the Bible. "This has been my source of comfort and truth. I'm giving it to you for safekeeping. Will you bring it to Katherine?"

Jerard hesitated. He had no plans for returning to New York. "I'll see she gets it." Caldwell could take it. The young man would be accompanying a shipment back east.

"I have a request, something that would mean a great deal to me."

"What is it?"

"That you read some verses in that Bible. There's a list in the front."

Jerard considered before answering. "I think I could do that."

"Thank you, son." Edmond reached inside the Bible. "And here's a letter for Katherine. It's important she get it." He paused. "And you will give her the Bible, won't you, lad?"

"She'll get it one way or another."

The old man ran his hand over his chin, shifted on his feet. "I want to thank you for what you've told me about Katherine this week, how she grew up in your household and her doing so well in New York and all. It gave me a lot to be thankful for."

"Good. I'll let Katherine know you had peace at the end."

"I have—that I have. Of course, hanging isn't a pretty end. I don't know too many men whooping and hollering thinking of the gallows. But I know where I'm going. When that noose is round my neck—" He pointed up. "—that's what I'm going to concentrate on. You going to be there this morning?"

"Yes."

"You don't have to."

"I promised myself I would."

"Appreciate that, more than you know." Edmond's eyebrows contracted. "Something else. I know you're not much of a praying man, but I'd be grateful if you'd pray for me while I'm up on the scaffold, that I stay strong and concentrate on my heavenly home."

Jerard looked long at Katherine's father. "I'll do my best."

"Thank you." The father's face brightened. "Just think. I'll be seeing the Lord Jesus soon. That's almost more than a person can take in."

The cell door opened. The guard nodded to the visitor. "Time's up, sir."

Jerard extended his hand. Edmond took it in both of his. "God bless you. When you read that Bible, I hope it'll bless you like it did me. You're a good man, son."

ᘓ

Clouds had massed over the jail, gray and sullen. A dusty smell pervaded the yard. Jerard stood near the prison officials. A couple of them talked affably with each other. Jerard's stomach tightened in anger. Didn't they realize a man was going to die? He took a few steps away.

Yesterday, he had asked if the hanging would take long.

"No," the warden said. "We use good strong hemp that'll give a decisive snap to the neck. You can go out and look at the gallows. They've been tested. It should go just fine."

The door to the jail opened. The prisoner appeared, accompanied by a guard. Jerard could see Edmond's walk had as firm a step as any man could want. Still, Jerard felt his stomach turn.

The steps creaked as Edmond ascended the gallows. He stumbled once. The misstep reminded Jerard of his promise to pray. He didn't close his eyes, but shot a silent cry heavenward. "Help him, God. Help him!"

On the scaffold, Edmond halted beside the noose and looked at the men gathered below. He spotted Jerard and gave a nod.

Jerard nodded back.

Someone, presumably a preacher, stepped forward and read a few verses from the Bible. That finished, the hangman reached for a black cloth and pulled it over the prisoner's head, then tightened the rope around his neck.

Jerard's knees locked.

The warden gave a signal. A prison guard stepped forward and jerked out a black iron ring.

The trap door clapped down. Edmond dropped.

Jerard stared stonily at the swinging body. After a minute, he turned to the warden.

The man returned his gaze with a grim smile. The neck had snapped just fine.

☙

Jerard lay stretched on his back in bed, hands across his chest. Scenes from the hanging refused to be dismissed. The first hour afterward he'd wandered around the city. Exhausted, he returned to his room. Questions drilled through his mind like rows of soldiers marching to war.

Where was Edmond? Was he nothing now? Or was he still a somebody—in heaven as he believed?

If heaven was real, what about hell? And—what about God?

He inhaled, then deliberately let out his breath. That was the crux of the matter—did God exist and, if so, what kind of God was he?

Jerard stretched his fingers, then dropped them back into a folded position. If a person returned to nothing after he died, this whole question was moot. But if a heaven and a hell really did exist, as well as a God who decided one's fate, then....

In his eight and twenty years, he hadn't thought much about an afterlife. Even after the deaths in his family—he had been too guilty, too angry—he'd shoved the questions from his mind. And recently, he'd been busy planning and building up the estate, and then the textile business. But after witnessing

Edmond's hanging—*Katherine's* father—he couldn't *not* think about it. He turned on his side, propped up his head with his hand. His eyes glanced around the room, then rested on Edmond's Bible. The Bible Katherine had held and read.

He rose from the bed and walked to the desk, sat in the chair and opened the black leather volume. On the flyleaf, he found the list of verses Edmond had mentioned. Hebrews 9:27. In the table of contents, he found Hebrews quickly enough.

... it is appointed unto men once to die, but after this the judgment. A judgment after death?

Jerard turned back to the front for the next verse on the list. Revelation 21:8. *But the fearful, and unbelieving and the abominable, and murderers, and whoremongers, and sorcerers, and idolaters, and all liars, shall have their part in the lake which burneth with fire and brimstone: which is the second death.*

A lake of fire and brimstone. Did he fit anywhere in that category of people? He scanned the list again. *Unbelieving.* He stared at the word a long moment. Then turned to the next verse.

Hebrews 10:31. *It is a fearful thing to fall into the hands of the living God.* He shifted in his chair, felt something pressing on him.

He had largely ignored God, spending time and energy on his own affairs. But he had to attend to the estate. Who else would have done it? His hand grasped the book and closed it. He'd read enough. Besides, he was tired. He would lie down awhile.

About to doze off, he heard someone knock. He managed to rise from the bed and stumble to the door.

"Western Union, sir." The bellboy looked closely at him. "Sorry to disturb you, sir."

Jerard brought the telegram to the window, thrust the curtain aside to better read it.

Jay Cooke and Company bankrupt. Advise on mill stock.

Jerard stared at the paper, his stomach taking a nasty turn. Jay Cooke's Philadelphia banking house bankrupt? Cooke was supposed to be raising money for the second transcontinental railroad, a major undertaking. What happened? If this financier had gone under, who in America would be safe? He turned from the window. Something had gone terribly wrong. He would have to find out more details. And discover what was happening to his own stock.

He sat on the bed and reached for his shoes. Randolph should be seen. He'd been around for a while, knew the history of things.

Jerard crossed the room to get his coat. Yes, he needed to talk with Randolph. Then he would figure out what instructions to wire New York.

ന്ദ

Late that afternoon he dragged himself up the hotel stairs to his room. The conversation with Randolph had been bleak. Terrible news had been wired from New York: *Wall Street panic. Exchange closed.* He was shocked to learn America's finances were so shaken. Randolph had reminded him how last year the *New York Sun* had exposed embezzlement in Credit Mobilier. Government officials had collected nearly $20,000,000 more than was needed to build the first transcontinental railroad, secretly pocketing the surplus. Public confidence was at an all-time low.

Randolph had looked him straight in the eye. "Who knows what other shenanigans are going on in Grant's administration?" He'd gone on to say Jay Cooke's banking house failure was triggering a chain of events that might spell financial disaster for the country.

Jerard took off his coat, his body felt like lead. How much would he lose? The mill would probably go under. Would that affect the estate as well? He slumped into a chair and dropped his head into his hands.

"God!"

Everything he'd hoped and dreamed for—worked for—was slipping away. He'd been here, out west in St. Louis, unaware of how things were heating up back east. His leadership that he'd put so much faith in, his quick decisiveness, now seemed sheer impetuosity. Little, if any, financial backup existed. He'd risked it all. Those investors he'd convinced to put money into his enterprise, what were they now thinking? The Emery name—his good name—he'd disgraced it.

The hanging this morning. And now this.

He walked to the bed.

What should he do? He didn't know, he couldn't think straight anymore.

ꕥ

When he woke, the room was dark. He was lying on the bed in his clothes. Why? Then he remembered. He'd taken risks and the whole thing was going broke. A black wave rolled over him. He felt cold and dark inside.

He'd been so sure of himself. But he'd been headstrong, acting the fool. Bad enough to risk his own money, but to risk other people's as well?

The raw truth stared him in the face. He'd been calculating how *other* people's money could build *his* fortune, with scant thought of them or their lives. The bald fact hit him. He'd been playing with people's *lives.*

He felt a deep, dark hole engulfing him. Two hours passed. Three. How long had he remained there? He didn't know. All he knew was he felt chained in that pit.

He ground his teeth. Finally, with superhuman effort, he leaned over to light a lamp. Slowly, he rose from the bed. He stumbled across the room toward the door, then turned back to the bed. He paced back and forth like a trapped animal. What should he do?

Why was he even alive?

He felt angry, sick. Sick of himself. Losing all those people's money!

Suddenly, he dropped to his knees beside the bed and fumbled underneath for the leather case. Grasping it, he slid it toward him and opened the lid. The weapon gleamed in the lamplight. He lifted the heavy gun, cradling it a few moments.

Then he lifted it to his temple, and felt the cold metal press his skin.

"God!" he swore. In a flash he visualized the ball piercing his head, shattering bone and flesh. He saw himself sprawled on the floor, a gaping wound streaming blood, splattered flesh—soiling, staining the carpet.

Abruptly he lowered the gun. He grasped its handle with one hand, the barrel with the other.

Dazed, he ran his thumb along its barrel. In his mind he saw a maid working on the carpet, desperately trying to get out the stain—scrubbing, scrubbing, scrubbing, cleaning up his unholy—

No!

Something gripped him. Stopped him. Someone would have to clean up his mess—the unholy, foul mess he made. No! He set down the gun. He was already responsible for one unmitigated disaster.

Bleary eyed, he scanned the room. Then what could he do?

On the desk he saw the Bible Katherine had given her father.

Katherine.

In all this he'd forgotten her. Her lovely self.

She had known *something*—so sure of it she'd *twice* turned down his offer of marriage. He knew that last time had cut her to the quick. He knew that she loved him! She wouldn't have made that decision unless this God idea were *real* to her.

Something awoke in him. Was it hope?

He walked to the desk and picked up the Bible. He sat down and turned to the list he'd found earlier.

Katherine's mother had marked the verses like a trail. He would follow that trail and see where it led.

How foolish and shortsighted of him to have ignored God. If heaven and hell existed, he knew he was heading straight for hell. And deserved it.

The next verse was John 8:12. *Then spake Jesus again unto them, saying, I am the light of the world: he that followeth me shall not walk in darkness, but shall have the light of life.*

Light for a person's life. How he needed that. And Jesus... Jesus was central here. He'd known that, too.

He turned back to the flyleaf. Listed were Chapters 26, 27, and 28 of Matthew. Surely, this would be about Jesus. He settled himself into a more comfortable position. As he read, he recognized parts of the story, but now he paid attention to every detail.

The plot to betray Jesus. His sentencing to death, even though innocent. The brutal beating. Jesus carrying his cross to the place of execution.

Jerard winced inwardly as he visualized the Roman guards positioning the nails in Jesus' flesh. Then he saw Jesus lifted up on a cross, impaled on a beam, hanging from those nails.

He looked away from the Bible. This was nasty stuff.

But he had to keep reading.

People stood nearby, mocking Jesus. "If Thou be the Son of God, come down from the cross."

Hours passed on that hill outside Jerusalem. Finally, Jesus cried out with a loud voice, gave up His spirit, and died.

From top to bottom, the veil in the temple ripped in two. An earthquake erupted and graves opened with dead saints returning to life.

Strange. He didn't remember any of this.

Now when the centurion, and they that were with him, watching Jesus, saw the earthquake, and those things that were done, they feared greatly, saying, "Truly this was the Son of God."

Jerard stared at the words. He drew in a ragged breath and let it out slowly.

God dying.

The implication was staggering. All of this—he was seeing with new eyes.

The account went on. Jesus' corpse was placed in a tomb, and that night another great earthquake shook the ground. An angel appeared and rolled back the stone covering the grave.

The following morning women visited the sepulcher and saw an angel who told them Jesus had risen from the dead.

Jerard looked up from the Bible.

Jesus had risen from the dead. Jerard's soul stirred as it had never done in all the times he'd attended church.

Eagerly, he looked up the last verse on the list. John 6:47; Jesus' words: *Verily, Verily, I say unto you, he that believeth on Me hath everlasting life.*

A pent-up sigh burst from him. He stared ahead. Jesus had done all this for him and he'd disregarded it. All these years. How had he been so blind?

He lowered himself off the chair, dropped to his knees, and slid down onto the floor, burying his head beneath his arms. "Lord, I've been wrong. Wrong! Ignoring You all this time. I've been rebellious, bitter about my brother's death. And my father's."

And unbelieving!

"Lord, I belong in that lake of fire like all those other sinners." He groaned, remaining prone.

Quiet reined in the room. He groped to remember Katherine's words the night she refused him in the garden. She had held out hope.

He would pray. He pressed his forehead hard against the floor. "Would You ... would You forgive me, Lord?"

Long moments passed. He started weeping. He wept as he'd never done before in his life.

Finally, feeling spent, he shuddered. Looking up, he decided to read that last verse again and reached for the Bible. *He that believeth on Me hath everlasting life.*

He wanted to believe. Wanted everlasting life.

He thought again of Katherine's words. She had said all he had to do was to mean it. He whispered, "I believe you, Jesus. I believe all you've done for me."

He let that settle in. Thinking back on the last week, he remembered how this had all started with seeing that woman in the hotel lobby, then the dream with Katherine in his arms and asking God to bring her to him, somehow, some way.

He looked up. Hadn't God been answering that prayer? Hadn't He been showing Himself to be real? Surely God would forgive him and answer this prayer for everlasting life as well.

He closed his eyes, believing.

Then he smiled. *This means I'll be in heaven someday, like Edmond. Both of us, with everlasting life.*

Sitting up, he stretched his arms above his head, feeling new energy course through him. He had to do something and checked the time. Rising from the floor, he reached for his coat. He remembered a small restaurant situated a few blocks from the hotel.

Out on the sidewalk, he walked briskly. Buildings, trees, and the occasional plot of flowers—even in the dim light of early morning—seemed sharper, clearer. He stopped. He'd walked this street any number of times, but things seemed different now. Was *he* that different? He wanted to talk this over with someone. But whom?

Katherine.

She had said they were different, and he saw how right she was. But now he had something of what she talked about, he was sure of it. The implication dawned on him. Not only was he assured of going to heaven after he died but, maybe, just maybe, he could have a bit of heaven here on earth. He *was* a different man. He knew it. "Lord!" He looked up to heaven. "Thank you. Thank you!"

He retraced his steps to the hotel. It would be quicker to get a bite there. He would travel back east as soon as possible and do what he could to salvage the mill and the estate. And then, most importantly, he would see about transacting some business with a little lady in New York.

Chapter 37

Jerard rapped the large brass knocker a second time. One would think the Kemble's butler would answer more promptly.

He'd dropped off his suitcases at the club and put in a hasty hour on Wall Street before coming here. Everyone at the Exchange seemed worried. Last week the market opened after a ten-day closure. It was a worrisome situation. But he'd done all he could for the present. Now he was determined to see Katherine. He'd given her no notice of his coming, wanting to see the surprise, the confusion, the delight in her eyes.

He glanced down at the box of flowers he held. They were to remind her of their last night together, when she accompanied him on the piano. That seemed long ago. Jerard reached to rap a third time when the door abruptly opened. He didn't recognize the young maid. "Hello, I've come to see Katherine Edmond."

The girl paused. "I'm sorry, sir. She's no longer here."

"What do you mean?"

"The family left for the mountains. A few hours after they departed, she packed her belongings and left. She didn't go with them."

"Do you know where she went?"

"I'm afraid not, sir. Everyone was in a hurry, and I never asked."

"Where is Framton? I want to speak with him."

"He's off today, sir. He won't be back till after supper. Would you like to return then?"

Jerard took out his pocket watch. He still had a good part of the day left. "Thank you. I'll first see what I can learn on my own." He descended the steps as the door closed, swearing under his breath. Why hadn't the family taken Katherine with them? Had she been let go? Inconceivable.

He stepped up into the hansom cab and tossed the box of flowers on the seat. Was Katherine still in New York? Or would she have gone back to Connecticut? No. He knew her proud heart. If she wouldn't accept his home as his wife, she wouldn't return if life had become difficult.

But was it difficult? Could she be without work, holed up in some cheap boarding house? The fondly imagined picture of her in the Kemble parlor clasped in his arms, had been wrenched away. His hands clenched.

Where was she?

Then he remembered the money, the funds he'd put for her in the bank. Had she withdrawn any? He gave the driver the bank address.

He alighted from the cab. "Wait for me, cabby. This might take a few minutes."

Inside, bank personnel bustled here and there. Was it his imagination or did everyone seem tense? Had the Cooke bankruptcy affected this institution as well? He spotted the president's secretary. The president himself had assisted in setting up the account and might be able to help.

A minute later, the man greeted him. "Mr. Emery, this is a pleasant surprise. I well remember the last occasion we met. How is St. Louis?"

"Fine, at least for now." Jerard followed the man into his office. "We had matters pretty well set up to do business when I received a telegram about the Cooke financial crisis. So I came home." The president offered Jerard a chair. "So what is your assessment of New York's situation? I understand a number of banks and brokerage houses have closed."

"That's correct. Too many unsound investment schemes. And then the exposure of the Credit Mobilier scandal last year."

"I'm glad to see you're still in business."

"Yes, we've remained open. Haven't speculated in shaky ventures like some."

Jerard leaned forward, clasping his hands in front of him. "My main concern in coming today, however, is not the present crisis. It's in reference to a young lady, a friend of mine. Some months ago I set up an account for Katherine Edmond and now I'm trying to locate her. Could you tell me if she's drawn from the account?"

The president looked at Jerard, smiled then called his secretary. When she returned, he glanced at the paper she handed him. "One withdrawal," he said succinctly. "Made yesterday."

Jerard gripped the arm of the chair. "Thank you." He rose and extended his hand. "I appreciate your help."

"Any time, Mr. Emery. I hope you find the young lady."

Out on the walk, Jerard stopped in front of the hansom. People streamed past him, all bent on getting somewhere.

He was now sure Katherine was in New York, and probably without work if she needed to withdraw funds. But where to start looking?

A deep-toned bell signaled the noon hour. A church bell. It reminded him of his newfound faith. In the excitement and disappointment of his morning's hunt he'd forgotten. Was he so faithless already? Would this little fledging belief of his be sufficient for Katherine to consider him a changed man? For the first time a seed of doubt took root in his soul. When he found her, would she now accept him? Consider him worthy?

But one way or another, he had to find her. He wouldn't quit searching. In St. Louis he had prayed something would happen to bring Katherine and him together. If God had answered that prayer, surely He would help now. Jerard looked skyward, winging up a quick, silent petition.

"Where next, sir?" the cabby asked.

Jerard looked at the man. "Steinway Hall."

The place had suddenly come to mind. He wasn't sure how answers to prayer came. But he would act on the thought.

ℭ

Katherine sank down onto the iron bench. This park had been a favorite and she was relieved to find a vacant spot. She looked to it now to provide rest and the momentary refuge she so desperately needed. Being turned down after that last interview was especially discouraging.

Smoothing the skirt of her suit, she recalled the assessment that emerald green was unsuitable for a governess. Did her ensemble's style appear too fashionable? She had chosen it this morning hoping its jeweled color and stylish cut would lift her sagging spirits. As she sat on the bench a sharp, sweet memory sprang up: the time she'd worn this very suit to church with Jerard escorting her. Singing with him in harmony. The differences in their voices—his deep and confident and hers high and clear—complemented each other to make such beautiful music.

She wondered if their voices were an indication—a picture—of how their differences in age, temperament and social position might somehow make a richer marriage, than if they had been so very similar to one another. Yet the Person who could make their sharp dissimilarities blend was absent from Jerard's life.

No, she thought, their union was impossible unless Jerard somehow saw the Light. Besides, seeing the contentious marriages of her parents and the Kembles had only strengthened her convictions.

Katherine sighed. She opened her purse to find the next address and her fingers brushed a piece of fine cambric. Before Mrs. Lanning had left for Europe, she'd pressed this handkerchief into Katherine's hand. They'd been sitting in the Kembles' front parlor. "Katherine, how I wish you were going with us. I will treasure this voyage with my grandson, yet I know it won't be the same for him without you."

"You know I didn't want to disappoint Christopher. I was honored by his proposal."

Mrs. Lanning had taken Katherine's hands in her own. "Yes, dear, I know. But I believe you've made the right decision." She gave Katherine's hands an extra squeeze then spoke gently about something else on her heart: Jerard. She finished with, "Now my dear, I commend you to God. Ask for His guidance with a sincere heart and He will never fail you."

Katherine sat for some moments remembering the graciousness of the lady—and her insight. Mrs. Lanning had brought such a sense of warmth and love to her lonely heart.

A few days after that Mrs. Kemble had dismissed her. Once again she had lost her home. Katherine felt so alone among all the busy people passing the park bench. How she needed to hold to Mrs. Lanning's words now.

A knot formed in her throat.

But it was time to get back to business. She made herself search her purse for the next address. Locating a piece of paper, she turned it over in dismay. Blank. Had she left the address in her room?

No help for it; she would have to return to the Hall. Mr. Mason had been kind enough to give her an upstairs room, a temporary place to stay. She was half ashamed to return, having told him she would be gone the day, looking for a position. Maybe if she used the back entrance she wouldn't see anyone.

Approaching her door on the fourth floor, she surprised Sophie, one of the maids, coming out of her room.

"Miss Edmond! I just placed a box from a gentleman on the table. He was insistent it be delivered immediately. I told him I was quite sure you weren't here. And he gave me a letter. I put it on top."

"Thank you, Sophie."

Katherine saw the white pasteboard box with the white envelope. She dropped her gloves and purse on a chair.

As soon as she opened the letter, her breath caught.

> *St. Louis, September 1873*
>
> *Dear Katherine,*
>
> *I have asked Jerard Emery to deliver this letter. He showed me great kindness while I was in prison, visiting me daily, this last week before my execution. He also shared details of your life in his home and your many accomplishments.*
>
> *Best of all, I came to know the Lord through the Bible you gave me. It must have been heartrending for you to give me such a precious possession of your mother's, but I thank you from the bottom of my heart. I praise God for you, for my wife, and for Mr. Emery.*
>
> *Respectfully and lovingly,*
>
> *Your father,*
>
> *Thomas Edmond*

Katherine sat some moments, tears in her eyes.

Turning to the box, she lifted its lid. The delicate fragrance of roses greeted her, a sheaf of white roses and nestled in the center, a pink rose—like the one she'd been given months earlier when she accompanied Jerard. And *white* roses? Could this mean...?

She ran out of the room. The maid had stopped a few doors down. "Sophie! Is the gentleman still here?"

"I don't know, miss. Like I said, I told him I didn't think you were in."

"Oh, Sophie!" Katherine ran down the hall past the maid. Three flights of stairs had to be descended before she reached the ground floor showroom. One hand hitched up her skirt while the other grasped the banister. When she reached the top of the last flight, her eyes searched the room below. A tall figure stood by the reception desk, indecision in his bearing. She stopped abruptly, now feeling uncertain. "Mr. Emery?" Her breathless voice carried down the stairs.

Jerard looked up. Light dawned in his eyes, and he started toward her.

Katherine skimmed down the steps.

Jerard took the steps two at a time, met her halfway, and caught her in his arms. "Katherine!"

She pulled back a little and gazed up at him, eyes bright with tears.

His dark eyes moistened in response. He glanced around. "Is there a private place?"

"Upstairs, perhaps, in one of the studios."

He drew her arm through his and let her lead up the stairs past the second story showroom to an empty studio. A tufted settee sat against one wall. He seated her there and took his place beside her. "The roses—you understood my message?"

"White, for spiritual love and purity? Does that mean what I hope?"

"Yes! Katherine, I know now what you meant about our spiritual differences. It all became clear in St. Louis." He went on to relate his time out west, the unusual way he discovered her father, and how her mother's Bible had brought them both to belief in Christ.

"Oh, Jerard." Tears trailed down Katherine's cheeks. At the end of the narrative she buried her face in her hands.

"Katherine." He reached and gathered her to him and held her while she wept.

After the tears passed, she said quietly, her face hidden against his coat, "I'm so relieved about everything. Your coming to the Lord, and all you did for my father." She snuggled closer. "After forgiving him, I found I had a new concern for him. I could remember the loving things he did for me and Mother, not just the selfish ones."

"You dear." Jerard raised her face. "I am relieved, too. Terribly relieved. I can hardly believe I'm here." He paused, then said, "Katherine, I love you." He gazed at her a moment longer, then lowered his lips to hers. When he lifted his head, he held her tightly. For some moments they clung to each other.

She saw a smile break over his face.

"Has anyone ever told you that you kiss divinely, Miss Edmond?"

"No one that I can remember."

"Not even Christopher?"

Her lips hinted a smile as she drew away from him.

"Katherine!"

"I never did kiss Christopher."

"But I'll wager he asked you to marry him."

Katherine hesitated a moment before answering. It rather pleased her to detect his jealousy. "Yes, he did."

"I thought so. But you had the good sense to turn him down. You never did seriously consider him?"

"Well," she said, with perfect sincerity, hoping her eyes wouldn't give her away, "we have so much in common, and to have Mrs. Lanning as family was a strong enticement."

"But you decided against him, even while you considered me a hopeless heathen?"

Katherine smiled demurely. "I suppose you could say that."

He looked at her a long moment. "Katherine! I see that twinkle in your eye. Now to atone, you must give me complete assurance I was and am your only love." He stood unexpectedly. "Stand up, Miss Edmond. You must prove your undying devotion." He took hold of her two wrists. "Here, like so." Winding her arms around his neck, he then wrapped his securely around her. "Now," he added, "I seek proof."

She hadn't expected her bit of trifling would elicit this demand. She felt herself blush, but readily lifted her face. Inexperienced as she was, she would do her best. When she took her lips from his, she hid her cheek against his chest.

He was silent, then said with emotion, "Ample proof, my darling."

He held her tightly some moments longer, then held her off. "Now, Miss Edmond, a most important question must be considered, and I'm going to do this in the official manner." He lowered himself to one knee and reached for her hand. "Katherine Elizabeth Edmond, will you do me the honor of consenting to become my wife?"

She smiled, delight accenting every word. "Jerard Hogarth Emery, I gladly accept your proposal of marriage."

"Ah—exactly what I traveled all the way from St. Louis to hear." He rose, caught her up and swung her round. Then laughing, swung her around again. Setting her down, he said, "This calls for a celebration. Are you hungry? I thought so. We can still make lunch at Delmonico's and talk over wedding plans while we eat."

"Oh, Jerard!" She didn't know when she had felt more lighthearted. Happiness coursed through her. "Let me go upstairs to collect my hat and gloves." She took a step toward the door then paused. "Oh, your flowers in my room, they need to be put in water."

"Here, I'll accompany you to the stair. You may take care of the flowers, my dear, but don't do any fancy arranging. I've waited a long time for you. I've been patient—a paragon among men, in fact—but I can be patient no longer."

He grasped her hand and led her out of the room. "Hurry, darling!"

Chapter 38

"Hurry!" Jerard had said.

More appropriate words were never spoken, Katherine decided, seated at an elegantly appointed table behind an arching palm. Jerard had handled everything with dispatch, finding a secluded corner at Delmonico's. Katherine sat quietly as he ordered.

After the waiter left, Jerard said, "You look lovely with my roses."

She bent her head to the three blooms she had pinned to her dress. "How could I resist wearing them? When I opened the box, I thought at once of the flowers you sent before the garden party."

"I hoped you'd remember. That was a heady night for me."

"Heady?"

"Yes... when you unwittingly revealed you loved me. Until then I wasn't sure—and that was a most uncomfortable state. It's called unrequited love, dearest. And why do you think I hesitated to press my suit, waited all those months while you worked as a governess? I was that unsure of myself. And I had to see the effect of my attentions to Miss Neville." He paused, a twinkle in his eye. "So, my ploy with Miss Neville was successful?"

Katherine laughed. "Your little game was successful, mainly because I didn't realize it was a game."

She took a sip from her water glass and as she lowered the goblet, Jerard asked, "By the way, what happened at the

Kembles? I went to find you this morning and you weren't there."

"I was dismissed."

"But why? How dare they?"

"I'm not sure. Mrs. Kemble said they needed a change. But after considering it, I think the real reason had something to do with Estelle."

"Oh?"

"I think Estelle felt deserted. By you."

Jerard looked at her a long moment. "So you had to pay the piper for my—I'm sorry, darling. That was ... selfish of me, wasn't it?"

Katherine said nothing, but knew her eyes showed she both agreed with him and forgave him.

"How can I make it up to you?" He smiled suddenly. "I know! There's something I want to give you, later, when we go to Central Park."

"Central Park?" A short while ago she had been in another park, distraught. How life had changed. Could she ask for anything better than to be with him? Her womanly self basked in his loving attentiveness.

Just then the waiter arrived. He set a rimmed soup bowl in front of her. "Consommé à la Royale," he said.

Katherine smiled up at him. "It looks and smells wonderful."

"Thank you, Mademoiselle."

"Tell her what's in it."

"Very good, sir. It consists of bits of precisely cut chicken, mushrooms, and truffles sandwiched in a molded egg and cream mixture. Then flavored with nutmeg and served with chicken consommé."

Katherine gazed at the waiter, then at Jerard. How could one feel both delighted and overwhelmed?

Jerard lifted his spoon in a small salute. "To celebrate our engagement, darling."

Halfway through the dish, Katherine paused and clasped her hands tightly in her lap. "This is so delicious I hesitate bringing up a worrisome thought, but I'm wondering how your mother will take the news of our engagement. You're not marrying into wealth or station, you know."

"She will be delighted, because by my marrying you, she will now see more of me." Jerard leaned forward. "You see, ever since you left for New York, I've been absent a great deal. Whenever I did visit home, I felt a hole in my heart as big as that gaping one in the oaks on our avenue. The place simply held too many memories. Besides, once I reined in my pride and decided to go after my prize, I pretty much made New York my home." He winked at her. "Had to keep an eye on you, you know.

"Later when Mother brought up the subject of my absences, I told her outright why I spent so much time here. We also cleared the air on something that had puzzled me—how the matter of your leaving came up in the first place. I promise you, the likes of Mrs. Pruitt won't be free about the place again. So don't worry about Mother. She'll be glad to have you back."

"Oh, Jerard," was all Katherine could say.

"And think how glad Aunt Elsie will be. Even though she had you earmarked for Christopher—didn't think I was good enough for you—she will take her defeat gracefully." He grinned. "Of course, all the servants will be delighted."

It surprised her that Jerard had noticed how well she'd gotten on with the servants, even though they themselves had been so often at odds. Truly, he had been more observant of her—and her doings—than she had realized.

"Oh, and about that gaping hole in our avenue," he continued, "Mother came up with a solution. She wanted a memorial for Father, but didn't want to plant another tree in its place. It would be too small in comparison with the others. Instead, she's erected an obelisk, a monument to stand with the tall oaks."

Jerard smiled. "I must say that couldn't have pleased me more. Father stood straight and tall among men. That monument will be a worthy reminder of him. And we will see it the first time when we travel together to Connecticut."

Katherine pressed her lips with her napkin. A question had just occurred to her. She wondered if she dared voice it. "Jerard," she began tentatively, "may I ask something of a sensitive nature?" On his nod, she continued. "How do you now feel about your brother's death? And your father's? That is, in relation to your thinking about God?"

He glanced down at the table, then up at her. "On the train ride home, I had a lot of time to think about that. I remembered how you said it was sin to be angry and bitter against God. I also recalled how you trusted God with what you couldn't understand and how you said He had a purpose in our suffering." He stopped, seemingly unable to continue.

"Does this mean ..." She let the sentence dwindle, wanting him to finish.

"I don't understand it all, but somehow I now see those events as all working ... to bring me to God. Yes, that long trip back was good. I no longer wanted to hold anything against Him—when I thought of all He'd done for me."

Jerard reached for Katherine's hand. "Then I thought of how God brought you to me. First, physically to our home. Then mentally and emotionally as a bond formed between us. And now spiritually."

"Yes," she whispered. "Joy came out of sorrow."

"Yes." He held her hand some moments longer, regarding her intently.

During the remainder of the luncheon, they talked about all that had happened during their absence from each other.

Katherine noticed how Jerard had changed. He asked questions about God. Before, he would not have tolerated, let alone welcomed, such conversation.

Finished with the meal, Katherine looked around the dining room. A shiver ran through her.

"Are you all right?" he asked.

"Oh yes! It's just that this is all too wonderful. I can hardly believe I'm sitting in this beautiful room, with such marvelous food, and best of all, you so near."

"I know." He sat motionless a few moments, then reaching for her hand again, brought it to his lips. "To sit with you, near your beauty and freshness, to know you are mine, is something I'd despaired of experiencing. It is truly humbling."

Moments later, he rose from his chair. "Now, darling, if you are ready, we'll visit the park."

Jerard directed the hansom cab to first stop at his club. In a few minutes he emerged with a parcel. He put it carefully on the seat beside him, then told the driver to continue on. He drew Katherine close and a sweet silence fell between them as they rode up Fifth Avenue, past businesses, tall-spired churches, and homes of the rich. When the park appeared, Jerard directed the cab some blocks farther, nearer its center.

Jerard helped Katherine alight, then reached for the parcel. The afternoon sun warmed the grass a bright green. A light breeze stirred the balmy air.

They walked for some minutes in silence. Jerard's mind seemed far away. Katherine wondered if she should try to draw him out of his preoccupation but decided to say nothing.

He finally pointed to a bench ahead of them.

After they sat, he turned toward her. "Katherine, there's something I need to tell you." He drew in a deep breath, looking down. "This is not easy. I learned something very troubling while in St. Louis. An important banking house in Philadelphia has failed and it's affecting New York banks, even Wall Street. My financial situation now looks precarious."

He stopped, his lips pressed together. "In all probability we will lose the mill. It will need to be sold to pay off creditors. The estate might even be in trouble, though not so much in and of itself. My father planned that it would be independent of the factory. But a lien might be placed against it. I might be required to sell a portion—I don't know. The future is uncertain and whatever affects me will touch your life as well."

He reached for her hand and held it firmly, as if concerned it might slip away. "Can you live with me under such circumstances? Times might very well be lean."

Katherine looked at him, her eyes welling with tears. "Jerard ... Mrs. Lanning visited me here in New York, just before she and Christopher left for Europe. She emphasized to me the hard way is sometimes the very path a person needs to walk, and that I must not shy away from it just because it looks difficult. " Her eyes held Jerard's. "She said that if the Lord ever changed your heart toward Him, and if we felt drawn to marry, then despite our differences, our marriage could be happy if we looked to each other's welfare."

She now grasped his hand tightly. "Financial concerns never were the deciding factor whether or not I married you. It was our spiritual differences that concerned me." As she sat gazing at him, the verse from Psalms came to her. *The Lord will perfect that which concerneth me.* Someday she would share with Jerard that struggle in her bedroom at the Kembles, and how the Lord had fulfilled the promise in that verse. Just now, her heart was too full.

Jerard helped her rise from the bench. "Let's walk to the lake." He took her arm firmly through his and led her through overarching elms to the shore. A light breeze rippled the water. He halted only a minute to view the scene, then drew her along the water's edge. "It's beautiful, isn't it?" he asked.

"Yes," Katherine answered. Her eyes scanned the lake and trees before them. "To think we have such a sylvan retreat in this busy city! The park's design gives it the appearance of a country estate."

He stopped and put down his parcel. "Katherine!" She turned, and Jerard caught her in his arms. He quickly bent his head and kissed her, and drawing her more closely, kissed her again and again.

Afterward, he said, "You know, that fulfilled a dream of mine."

She looked into his eyes. She could not speak.

"Remember the Jersey shore? When you ran back into my life? Well, later that night when I was in bed, I pictured you again, running across the sand. But this time I joined you. I imagined the two of us walking by the water's edge in perfect harmony as we did a minute ago. And I kissed you. As I did just now."

His eyes held hers. "Katherine, I don't want to wait long to marry. You do remember, don't you, I'm not a patient man?"

He clasped her a little longer, then released her. "I want you to open the package I brought." Stooping for the parcel, he directed her to another bench, then sitting, settled her within the curve of his arm.

She undid the string and paper around the parcel. "Oh—" She was silent some moments. "—my mother's Bible." When she looked up, his eyes smiled, close to hers. Her heart warmed at his protecting nearness. "Did Father give you this?"

"Yes, and I think it is much the same except for the addition of a few inscriptions."

She opened the cover. Underneath Mother's name and brief sentence of presentation to herself, a scrawling hand had written another message:

I thank the Lord for my daughter Katherine. Jeremiah 32:27 is my blessing to her. "Behold, I am the LORD, the God of all flesh: is there anything too hard for me?"

Thomas Edmond

Underneath, another inscription in a fine, bold hand:

I thank my God on every remembrance of you, for your beauty and purity of soul, for your prayers and for the wondrous way this book fell into my hands which effected my salvation. To my darling, from a devoted and loving heart. Yours until the day I die.

Jerard Hogarth Emery

Katherine pressed the Bible to her breast.

Jerard's arms encircled her, tightly holding both her and the Bible. "From this day forward I take this verse bequeathed to you by your father as *our* verse. When I think of the meandering, often tortuous paths our lives have taken, and how the Lord has worked them all to bring us together, it is nothing short of miraculous."

Hearing these words, Katherine felt hope rise in her for their future, and she smiled. Seeing a certain intention in Jerard's eyes, she willingly raised her face. Eagerly, his lips met hers.

A delightful, invigorating breeze swept from the lake.

Jerard lifted his head. "That, my darling, is a seal on God's promise to us." Then he smiled widely. "A seal I will fix again and again."

Discussion Questions

1. Why do you think the author chose the title *The Language of Music*? Where do you see evidences of music in the story, and how do these bring the protagonists together?
2. Did you suspect any of the twists in the plot? Which ones? What about the first marriage proposal?
3. What does Mr. Lanning emphasize about forgiveness in Chapter 12?
4. How does attending the symphony concert in New York show a different side to Jerard, particularly to Katherine?
5. What historical events firmly set the story in the time period between 1870 and 1873?
6. How did Katherine's father remind Katherine of Jerard, so much so that she wanted to avoid Jerard?
7. Mrs. Lanning offers advice on marriage to Katherine two different times. What did she counsel?
8. What did Katherine see in Callie's home that she found attractive? What did she find in the Kembles' home that she found disturbing?
9. At one point Mrs. Lanning characterized Mr. Lanning to Christopher: "He never compromised principles or convictions, but he always allowed people to grow at the rate God had in mind." Discuss the meaning of this statement.
10. What terrible incidents brought Jerard "to the end of himself?" Discuss the idea of autonomy and how Jerard exemplifies this attitude toward life.

11. The main characters experienced the painful, unexpected loss of mother, teacher, father, and brother. Many people can't understand why God allows suffering in this world. The story sheds what light on this question? (Note chapters 13, 23, 32, & 38) Would you say anything in addition?
12. What scene was a favorite of yours? Why?

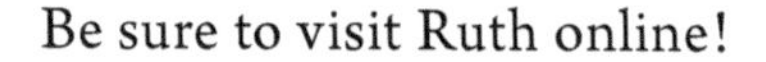

www.RuthTrippy.com

CPSIA information can be obtained
at www.ICGtesting.com
Printed in the USA
BVHW03s2021160918
527534BV00032B/106/P